Obsession FALLS

A SMALL-TOWN ROMANCE

CLAIRE KINGSLEY

Always Have LLC

Published by Always Have, LLC

Edited by Eliza Ames

Cover Design: Lori Jackson

ISBN: 9798870634470

www.clairekingsleybooks.com

❊ Created with Vellum

To the real-life Max, who is the goodest good boy.

And to everyone who doubted I could make you love the Haven brothers. Hold my beer.

About this book

He'll risk it all to protect her.

Someone is stalking Audrey Young. And she has no idea why.

It's bad enough that she's back in Tilikum. But Audrey's good at making the best of things and her new job at the small-town newspaper is just a way to get back on her feet.

Complicating matters is her landlord and new neighbor, Josiah Haven.

She doesn't usually go for the big, surly lumberjack type. But there's something about that broody man. He intimidates her a little, but she kind of likes it.

She could totally handle the mess that is her life, except the strange feeling of being watched is just the beginning. Next thing Audrey knows, she's a target, and she doesn't know who's behind it, or why.

For Josiah Haven, none of that makes her his problem.

She's just the girl next door. Fine, the frustratingly hot girl next door. But Audrey is all sunshine and her goofy dog isn't any better. Josiah is too stoic. Too solitary. Too guarded. He doesn't need a woman in his life, especially one who threatens to crack his heart wide open.

But Josiah is a protector and he can't let Audrey's troubles go unanswered, even if he has to risk everything—his life and his heart—to keep her safe.

Author's note: a grumpy loner meets his match in a sunshiney dog lover who's a little down on her luck. And once he falls, he falls HARD. It's small-town romantic suspense with CK's signature humor, endearing characters, and heartwarming happily ever after.

Obsession Falls can be read as a stand-alone.

CHAPTER 1

Josiah

FIVE YEARS AGO

THE RING in my pocket felt like it weighed a million pounds.

I had no idea what a guy like me was doing in this position. I was basically the least romantic man ever. But there I was, at Salt and Iron, one of the nicest restaurants in Tilikum, sitting across from my girlfriend of two years with a ring in my pocket.

The ambiance was right. Crisp white tablecloths, candlelight, wine. A menu sat next to my place setting; I'd already decided on a steak. I unfolded the cloth napkin and laid it in my lap while Cassandra put her menu aside.

She seemed distracted. She'd checked her phone half a dozen times since we'd taken our seats, which wasn't totally unusual for her, but it did make me wonder what was going on. Probably something with work. She was an ad account manager for a large social media company and although she usually worked remotely, she'd been stuck going to corporate several times in the last few months.

She frowned at her phone. Maybe now wasn't the time. I slipped my hand in my pocket and fingered the diamond and smooth gold band. I'd kind of thought if I ever proposed to a woman, she'd be in a better mood when I did it.

"Is everything okay?" I asked.

"What?" She glanced up as if she were surprised to see me sitting across from her. "Sorry. I'm fine. Just work."

But she didn't put her phone away. She set it on the table next to her and brushed her blond hair over her shoulder.

"Do you need to go?" I asked. We'd only ordered drinks. "We can grab takeout somewhere if that's easier. Take it to your place."

"No, this is fine." She shifted and adjusted her black dress.

Something was off. She didn't usually fidget so much.

And then it hit me. She knew.

The corners of my mouth turned up ever so slightly. She was onto me. I wondered how she'd figured it out. I hadn't mentioned anything that should have tipped her off. No slip ups. And I'd only picked up the ring that morning. There was no way she'd seen it. I'd even taken it out of the box, leaving it loose in my pocket, so she wouldn't suspect anything.

Maybe she simply knew me too well. I couldn't keep a secret this big.

That meant it was time. I put my hand in my pocket and for half a second, I wondered if she'd want me to do the whole get down on one knee thing, or if I could just put the ring on her finger without making a big scene. I hesitated and the server came back to our table. I took my hand out of my pocket, careful to make sure the ring stayed inside.

"Can I get an appetizer started for you?"

"I'd like the calamari," Cassandra said. "Do you want anything?"

"No thanks."

"Perfect," the server said with a smile. He was a slim guy with dark hair, probably a college student. "Do you want to order dinner as well, or do you need a little more time?"

"I need more time," she said. "Thanks."

The server left. I put my hand back in my pocket to take out the ring but Cassandra picked up her phone again.

This was proving to be more complicated than I'd thought. I'd figured all I had to do was get a ring, take her to dinner, and give it to her. But now that we were here, everything seemed slightly off.

She set her phone down and took a drink of her wine. I decided it was go time, but instead of worrying about the ring, I just opened my mouth to get her attention before she could get distracted by work again.

But right as I started to say her name, she spoke.

"Josiah, I think we should talk."

I was not known for being in touch with my feelings—or having feelings—but that was a phrase that could make any man's stomach clench with an icy spasm of dread.

"About what?"

She took a deep breath. "I got a job offer. It's a promotion. A big one."

"That's great." It was good news. So why did I still feel so tense?

"Thanks." She smiled. "I didn't even tell you I was applying because I assumed I didn't have a chance."

"Why would you assume that? You're amazing."

"I don't know. It just seemed like such a long shot. There had to have been so many applicants."

I reached across the table and took her hand. "Then they made the right choice."

Her smile grew but just as quickly, it faded. She pulled her hand away. "The thing is, it's outside San Francisco."

It took a second for the implications to register. "So it's not remote? You have to move?"

She nodded.

My problem-solving brain kicked in, a list of options with pros and cons already forming. "Okay. When?"

"They want me there as soon as possible. I'll stay in corporate housing until I find a place. So, next week."

I leaned back. "That fast?"

She nodded again.

"Okay." I tapped a finger on the table. The server came back but I gave him a hard glare and he backed away. "San Francisco isn't Mars. We can make it work."

"Oh, Josiah."

"What? It's not ideal but we can figure it out."

She pressed her lips together but didn't say anything.

The icy dread settled over me, like a chill freezing me from the inside. "You don't want to figure it out, do you?"

"I just don't see how. Your whole life is here. Your work and your family. Could you really see yourself relocating to a different state?"

"Were you going to give me the chance to answer that question for myself?"

"I know you. You wouldn't be happy in San Francisco."

I stared at her for a moment. "So you didn't think we should talk about it? You already accepted the position."

"Of course I did. I couldn't pass this up."

I nodded slowly. I supported her career—always had. It made her happy and that was great.

But I'd kind of thought I made her happy, too.

My hand skimmed over the outside of my pants pocket, the outline of the ring indistinct through the fabric. Maybe I shouldn't have thought she'd choose me over a promotion. But I realized as I looked at her that I had. I'd thought we would be in this together.

Apparently I'd been wrong.

The hollow ache in my chest made it hard to breathe. Cassandra hadn't put the ache there—she hadn't given me that wound. But she was sure as hell ripping it wide open again.

"I knew you wouldn't understand." Her tone took on a

hint of defensiveness. "You grew up here so this is just normal life to you. But this town is too small for me. I can't stay here for the rest of my life."

"No, I get it." I turned my gaze toward the front door; I couldn't look her in the eyes anymore. "You need to do what's best for you. And what's best for you isn't me."

"Don't make this about you. This is about my career, my dreams. I'm finally getting somewhere."

For a moment, I thought about taking the ring out and setting it on the table, so she'd know. So she'd see what she was giving up.

But I didn't. It wouldn't matter. She didn't want that life, and more importantly, she didn't want me.

I got up and tossed some money on the table to cover what we'd ordered. She started to protest, telling me to sit down. I ignored her. I was done. Without a word, I walked out and didn't look back.

She was wrong about one thing. I did understand. She wasn't the first woman to make that choice where I was concerned.

But she was sure as hell going to be the last. I wouldn't give someone else that chance again.

CHAPTER 2

Audrey

ONE GLANCE at the half-circle driveway and I couldn't help but think this was all a huge mistake.

"What do you think, Max?"

His bushy tail thumped against the passenger seat as he looked out the window.

"Of course you're excited. You're a dog. Everything is fun."

He kept wagging his tail while his tongue lolled out of his mouth.

My childhood home looked oddly cold in the June sun. It was stately and imposing, with a stone façade and tall double doors. The landscaping added to the look of formality— precisely trimmed shrubs lined the driveway and the lawn could have doubled as a golf course.

It had always been important to my parents that everything be just so. Especially on the outside.

"Here goes nothing."

I turned onto the driveway and parked, trying to ignore how this felt like failure.

Almost every inch of my little Honda Civic was packed

with stuff. Spatial abilities weren't exactly my thing, so I was impressed that I'd fit as much as I had.

It was weird to realize all my belongings fit in this car. My last roommate had owned most of the furniture we'd used. As for the rest, I'd decided to purge rather than move everything again. I'd start over once I found a more permanent place to live.

Soon. I'd find my own place soon.

For now, I'd make the best of it.

Max put his front paws on the dash, his body practically vibrating with excitement. I had no idea what kind of dog he was—the rescue group in Boise hadn't either—other than forty-five pounds of brown and white derpy joy. He wasn't exactly the smartest, and if someone ever tried to rob me, he'd probably roll on his back and ask for belly rubs rather than protect me. But he never failed to make me smile.

I got out and Max followed, running a quick lap around my legs before darting to the front door. I ducked back into the car to fish around for a leash. My mom wasn't a dog person and she'd freak out if I let him run free on the first day.

"I know you want to run amok in there, but we can't have that." I clipped the leash to his collar. "Grandma won't like it."

She also didn't like me referring to her as Grandma to a dog. But it wasn't my fault I was an only child and all her grandmother hopes had been pinned on me. That was a lot of pressure.

Especially considering I was still single.

Sigh.

My heartbeat quickened as I reached for the doorknob. Moving back to Pinecrest, the small town in the Cascade mountains where I'd grown up, had never been the plan. Like, never ever. But there I was with a car packed full of stuff, about to attempt a temporary roommate situation with my mother so I could start a new job.

Maybe it was a huge mistake. Taking the job. Moving back. It felt like coming home with my tail between my legs. Such a failure.

This was what happened when you got laid off and couldn't find another job for months on end. Your savings dwindled and you jumped at the chance to work at a small-town newspaper, even when it was in Tilikum, one town away from where you'd grown up.

"Come on." I wasn't sure if I was talking to myself or to Max. Didn't really matter. They were basically the same thing. "This is going to be fine."

I opened the door and the scent of my childhood greeted me. The house always smelled like Downy dryer sheets with an undertone of Clorox. The inside was just as stately and formal as the front. Marble floors, stylish furniture, expensive art. It was quite lovely, although I always felt under-dressed when I visited, as if the atmosphere required a dress and heels, rather than my tank top, shorts, and sandals.

I kept an eye out for Mom's cat, Duchess. Hopefully she'd smelled Max and was staying upstairs. Max wouldn't hurt a fly, but his version of play was probably not what my mom's cat would consider fun.

In the formal living room, off to the right, a family portrait hung on the wall above the gas fireplace. The three of us were dressed to the nines, Dad in a full suit and me and Mom in black evening dresses. I'd always thought it looked stuffy, but Mom called it elegant.

It was weird to see my Dad smiling down at me, knowing he wasn't going to waltz through the door after work, his big voice booming. It had been over two years since he'd passed, but it was easy to forget he was gone.

"Mom?" I called, keeping Max next to me despite his clear desire to tear through the house and explore. "I'm here."

"Audrey." She alighted at the top of the stairs, as if she were posing for a magazine spread, dressed in a beige blouse and tan slacks. "It's so good to see you."

I did not look like my mother. She was tall and thin with blue eyes and short silvery-blond hair, whereas I'd inherited my father's darker features—thick brown hair, brown eyes. Despite my childhood dreams of being taller than my mom, I'd topped out at five foot four and by the time I turned fifteen, I'd been too curvy to borrow her clothes.

"Hi, Mom."

Her eyes flicked to Max and I didn't miss the micro-expression of displeasure that crossed her features.

"He's leashed. I won't let him jump up on you or anything."

Max's tail beat against the marble floor as she approached. He dropped to his back and held his paws in the air, hoping for a coveted belly rub.

"I see you still have the dog."

"He's very friendly. He wants you to pet him."

She eyed him again. "Maybe later. How was the drive?"

"Long." I shrugged. "But fine. No traffic or anything."

"Well, don't just stand here in the foyer." She gestured toward the kitchen. "Come in."

My dad's eyes seemed to follow me as I walked by. Creepy.

I went into the kitchen, keeping Max close. I'd have to take him for a walk to help him burn off some of his energy. Poor dog had been in the car too long.

The kitchen was massive, with a huge island, marble counters, and light wood cabinets. A wrought iron light fixture hung above the island with floral frosted glass lampshades and vines twining up to the high ceiling. It was all very winery-esque, down to the big glass jar half-filled with wine corks in one corner.

"Tea?" Mom asked.

"That would be great, thank you."

I walked Max around, letting him sniff. He stopped to lick a spot on the tile floor and a few steps later, found the transition to the carpet in the family room extremely interesting. He could probably smell my mom's cat.

The family room had a fireplace with a flat screen TV mounted above it and a sectional covered with throw pillows in various shades of beige and light blue. The room didn't look like it was used very much. Mom had never been a big TV or movie watcher. She probably only went in there to dust around the photos and nick-knacks on the mantle and shelves.

And then there was the wall of Audrey.

I'd graduated from high school well over a decade ago, but it was still there. An entire wall of me.

I moved closer as Max kept sniffing. In the center was one of my senior pictures. I had no idea what was going on with my hair back then, with the zig-zag part and flipped out ends. Surrounding the photo were awards I'd received, everything from my sixth-grade student of the year certificate, to my varsity letters in cheer and track, to the plaque from my stint as Pinecrest's Junior Miss.

The valedictorian medal I'd worn at graduation hung from a wooden peg and the console table beneath held more photos, mostly milestones from my high school years. Scowling, I picked up the photo from my senior prom. My ex-boyfriend, Colin Greaves, smirked back at me, dressed in his rented tux with a pink bow tie to match my dress.

"I saw Colin the other day," Mom said, her tone thick with the underpinnings of juicy gossip.

"Oh?" I set the photo down.

"He looked great, of course. He's thinking about running for city council."

"Good for him."

"Your dad would have been thrilled."

"I'm sure he would have."

"Although, I hear he and Lorelei have been going through a rough patch."

"Oh, no," I said, my eyebrows knitting together with concern. I walked back to the kitchen and took a seat at one of the island stools and prompted Max to lie down. Thankfully, he actually obeyed. "That's too bad."

"Well, I wouldn't say it's surprising." She pushed a mug of tea toward me. "Everyone knows he rushed off to marry her too quickly."

I could hear what my mom wasn't saying. *He rushed off to marry her after you dumped him. So it's your fault.*

Granted, he had started dating Lorelei almost immediately after our breakup and they'd gotten married just a few months later. I wasn't angry about that now, but it had stung at the time. We'd dated for five years—from our senior year of high school until after I graduated from college—so you'd think he might have needed some time before moving on.

But, unlike my mother who'd never really forgiven me for breaking up with him, I was over it.

"I hope they're okay," I said, and I meant it. I didn't harbor any ill will against Colin. I was glad it wasn't me who'd married him, but I didn't want anything bad to happen to him.

Mom shrugged nonchalantly. "It's probably for the best that they don't have kids. Maybe they need counseling. Although I'm not sure if a counselor could fix the fact that he married the wrong woman."

Time to change the subject before she got into how I'd been the right woman and I should have married him because look at me now, in my thirties and single. "So I start my new job on Monday."

She smiled. "The smartest thing they ever did was hire you."

"Thanks. I'm just glad someone finally did."

I wasn't so sure about this job but beggars can't be choosers. After applying to just about everything I could find, I'd answered the posting for the Tilikum Tribune mostly out of desperation. I'd never worked for a newspaper, but I did have a degree in journalism. To my amazement, they'd called me for an interview and offered me the job on the spot.

Employment problem solved. But I'd been living almost seven hours away, in Boise, for the last several years. Working for a small-town newspaper wasn't a remote sort of job, so it meant packing up and moving.

Tilikum wasn't Pinecrest, but it was close enough. This whole region, from Pinecrest to Tilikum to Echo Creek, all fell under the umbrella of "hometown" in my eyes. And not in a cute, nostalgic way that made moving back a warm and fuzzy experience. In an I-never-wanted-to-live-here-again way that made me feel like a big, fat failure.

But it was fine. This job was a means to an end—a way to get back on my feet. I'd keep looking for another one—preferably at least five or six hours away—and make the best of it until then.

Without warning, Max jumped to his feet. He took off at a dead run and the leash slid right out of my hand.

"Max!" I scrambled off the stool and went after him. "Max, come!"

Spoiler alert: he didn't listen.

I ran to the living room with my mom close behind and found Max trying to stuff his entire head into the two-inch gap below the couch. His face popped up for a second, just long enough to let out a bark, and he was back at it again, shoving his nose under the couch.

"Max, get out of there."

"Oh, no," Mom said. "Duchess."

"That must be it. He saw your cat."

"Don't you let him hurt my baby."

"He won't hurt her. He wants to play."

Max barked again.

"Audrey, he'll eat her!"

"He won't eat her." At least I hoped he wouldn't. "That's his play bark."

Mom clutched her hands against her chest. "Duchess, stay there. Don't come out, babykins. Mommy will save you."

Not that she was actually doing anything to save her cat.

"I'll get him." I got close enough to grab the leash but Max let out a loud yelp of pain. I grabbed the leash and led him away. "What happened? Did the kitty get you?"

He had a small scratch on his nose, just enough to draw blood.

"Oh buddy, that must hurt."

"Duchess," Mom cooed, approaching the couch slowly. "Come out, kitty-kitty."

I moved Max farther away and kept a death grip on his leash. "Maybe she just wants to hide under there for a while."

"No, she needs her mama." She clicked her tongue. "There, there, my precious little kitty-witty."

Crouching down, I checked Max's nose. He wagged his tail and tried to lick my face. It wasn't a bad scratch. It had probably surprised him more than anything. Now he didn't seem to notice.

Duchess finally came out from around the back side of the couch. She was a white Persian with a mass of long fur, especially around her scrunched up face, and amber eyes that, as far as I was concerned, made her look evil.

"There you go, sweet baby." Mom scooped her up and cuddled her. "Don't worry, the mean doggie won't get you."

Max barked.

Duchess hissed.

"I don't think Max is the mean one in this scenario, but okay."

Mom scowled at me. "My precious kitten isn't mean. She

was only protecting herself. And that dog is going to have to stay outside."

"Outside where?"

"In the back."

"It's not fenced."

"Can't you tie him up?"

"Mom!"

"What? Is that wrong? I wouldn't want to be cruel to him, I'm just trying to be practical."

I sighed. "I'll keep him leashed in the house and just take him for walks to get exercise. And there's a doggie daycare up the street from the newspaper, so I'll take him there while I'm at work."

"The leash didn't exactly work as advertised."

"I set it in my lap. I thought the cat was upstairs in your room or something. I'll be more careful to hold on to it."

She snuggled the cat to her face. "Well, okay then. We'll make it work. Let's go, sweet baby cat, and get a treat. You deserve one after that scare. Yes, you do."

I looked down at Max. His cute brown eyes met mine and he wagged his tail.

"Come on, good boy. Let's take a walk and get some of that energy out."

I could still hear my mom murmuring baby talk to her cat as I left. I shut the door behind me and took another deep breath. The air was fresh and warm—not quite the heat of summer, but there was a hint of it.

We walked past my car, full of the stuff I'd packed, and a sense of resignation stole over me. This was what my life had come to. Moving back home to take a desperation job.

I'd have to make the best of it. It was just the means to an end anyway.

CHAPTER 3
Josiah

THE SMELL WAS EVERYWHERE.

I wrinkled my nose. I'd been hoping the stench was mostly in the carpet, but we'd taken the last of that out yesterday. The entire house still smelled like cigarette smoke and something else I couldn't name. I probably didn't want to know. The walls were trashed, there was water damage everywhere, and it seemed like every time I peeled back a layer, I found a new problem.

Still, there was something I liked about this house.

I lowered the sledgehammer and rested my leather gloved hands on the handle. Broken chunks of cheap cabinetry littered the kitchen floor and dust hung in the air. Sweat dripped down my back and I was really looking forward to sitting on my couch with an ice-cold beer tonight. But demo was satisfying work. A chance to let out the beast for a while.

And despite how much work was still left to be done, the house already looked a hell of a lot better than it had when Dad and I had bought it. The previous owners had kept it as a rental and clearly hadn't bothered with maintenance. I was no stranger to the pitfalls of owning rental properties, but this place had been a dump. We also owned the house next door and half the reason we'd bought this one was so we could clean it up and have an easier time renting the other place. It had to help if it no longer looked like the neighbors might be running a meth lab.

But there was still a long way to go before that would be a reality.

I hoisted the sledgehammer and swung. It hit the next piece of cabinet with a satisfying thwack. I swung again, harder, sending a chunk of particle board flying—along with a big piece of drywall.

What the hell?

Stepping closer, I lifted my safety goggles. Some genius had glued the lower cabinets to the wall. I'd taken out a chunk of drywall along with the cabinet. That probably meant the rest of the cabinets were glued too.

Damn. I'd been hoping we could salvage the drywall but it wasn't looking good.

I grabbed the remaining piece of cabinet that was still stuck to the wall and pulled. More drywall cracked and tore open, exposing the framing behind it.

Screw it. I picked up the sledgehammer and swung, hard, letting it rip through wood, particle board, glue, drywall—I didn't care. I swung again. Crack! Cabinets splintered. Again, and I ripped open more of the wall. Over and over, until my back and arms burned, and sweat ran down my temples. Where there'd once been a dated kitchen counter with crappy cabinets, there was now a pile of rubble and a big-ass hole in the wall.

"Are you okay?" a voice asked behind me.

I turned to find my sister, Annika, dressed in a t-shirt and jeans. Her blond hair was up and she had a purse hanging off one shoulder.

"Yeah." I took off my safety goggles and wiped sweat off my forehead. "Why?"

"You'd think that cabinet murdered your best friend."

I grunted.

"Did you mean to take out half the wall or were you just in the zone?"

"Some idiot glued the cabinets to the drywall."

She winced. "That's not good."

My heart still pumped hard but the quick burst of frustration had already subsided. I glanced back at the damage I'd done. Stupid.

But it had felt good.

"You need something?" I asked.

"I was supposed to meet the new tenants for the two-bedroom next door but they bailed last minute."

My brow furrowed. "Why?"

"They had some kind of family emergency. Changed their plans."

"So it's vacant another month."

"Yeah, at least. I'll get a new ad up when I get back to my laptop."

I grunted again. A vacancy wasn't ideal, especially since we were in the middle of another remodel.

Annika used to work part-time for our brother, Luke, at his custom auto shop, but I'd stolen her away to work full-time for me a few years ago. Now she was the face of our business. Dad and I bought the houses and fixed them up. She interfaced with renters, or buyers if it was one we'd decided to flip. My people skills weren't exactly the best, so it worked out for everyone.

She also had like a million kids, so working from home suited her.

Okay, she had four. But still.

"This place looks…" She paused and glanced around. "I want to say it looks better but you'd know I'm lying. Stinks too."

"A coat of Kilz on the wall should take care of the smell. And it has to get worse before it can get better."

"Kind of like life sometimes."

I put my safety goggles back on. "I wasn't trying to be deep."

"Maybe not, but it's true." She gestured toward the sledgehammer. "Be careful how many walls you take out. Some of them are probably important to the structural integrity of the building."

"You think?"

She rolled her eyes. "On second thought, go nuts. Get some of that aggression out."

I grunted again.

"I'll see you later," she said, already on her way out.

I mumbled a barely coherent goodbye. I liked my sister. We'd always gotten along. I just didn't feel like talking.

Granted, I rarely felt like talking. Grabbing the sledgehammer, I got to work on the next section of cabinetry.

An hour later, the rest of the kitchen cabinets were in pieces and there was a lot less drywall. Part of me wondered if I should just rip it all out. We hadn't planned on taking the kitchen down to the studs but it was probably past the point of repair.

My stomach rumbled, reminding me I'd skipped lunch. I'd deal with the walls later. It was time to call it a day.

I left everything the way it was and went outside to lock up. A dumpster took up half the driveway and the outside of the house needed as much work as the inside. Fortunately, the roof was solid, but new paint and a hell of a lot of landscaping were in order.

I'd parked my truck on the street—a dark gray Ford F-150 that I'd bought a few years ago. Apparently it was a Haven thing; two of my brothers had the same truck, just in different colors.

The evening air was pleasantly cool and the sky was clear. It was June, but the heat of summer hadn't hit yet. Which was a damn good thing. I needed to get my HVAC guy in there to service the AC unit soon, otherwise it was going to be a miserable summer.

I left the remodel, drove into town, and found a parking spot across the street from the Copper Kettle. Usually I just ran into the Quick Stop for a prepackaged sandwich when I was hungry but I was in the mood for a hot meal.

A squirrel ran across the road, making a guy in a red pickup truck slam on his brakes. The truck skidded to a halt, the front tire coming within inches of squishing the animal. It ran on, bushy tail bouncing along behind it, apparently oblivious to the fact that it was almost roadkill.

The squirrels around here thought they owned the place.

I tipped my chin to him and crossed to the diner.

The Copper Kettle smelled like comfort food and the clink of dishes mixed with the low hum of conversation. The hostess, Heidi, barely looked old enough to be in high school, let alone working at a diner. But what did I know. Everyone looked too young to me anymore.

"Do you want a table?" She glanced at the packed dining room. "It might be a few minutes. We're pretty busy."

"I'll get something to go."

"Do you know what you want or do you need to see a menu?"

"No, no, Heidi," a familiar voice called from deeper inside the restaurant. "He'll sit with me."

A mild sense of foreboding struck me as my aunt Louise waved from her table.

Louise Haven had long gray hair she always wore in a bun and deep smile lines around her eyes. She'd married my dad's oldest brother when they were both sixteen and they'd defied the odds by staying together for the last fifty-something years. At some point in the murky past, she'd adopted velour track suits as her signature look. I had no idea if she owned anything else or if her closet was simply a rainbow of zip-up hoodies and matching pants. Today's was dark purple.

Aunt Louise had zero filter, but that wasn't the problem. I actually liked the way she said whatever the hell she wanted. The problem was she presided over the Haven family as a self-appointed matchmaker. Her kids were all married, but if you were over the age of twenty-one, related to the Havens, and single, Louise was coming for you.

She'd been trying to tie me down for years.

"I'll take a French dip to go," I said.

"Josiah," Louise called, still waving. "Come on over here, honey."

Heidi looked back and forth between us, as if she didn't know who she should listen to.

"Put in my order to go and bring it to her table," I grumbled and made my way past Heidi to where Louise was grinning at me.

"Well, isn't this a lovely surprise," she said, as if we didn't run into each other all the time in this damn town. "Have a seat."

I pulled out the chair and sat. "I can't stay."

"That's fine, it's nice to say hello anyway." She dug into her purse, pulled out a little mirror, and started dabbing at the corners of her mouth. "Besides, I've been meaning to track you down. Florence Newland was telling me the other day that her granddaughter Aida is coming to visit for the summer."

"So?"

"I immediately thought of you."

"Why?"

She snapped the mirror shut. "I thought you could take her out."

"No."

"Don't be difficult. She's a nice girl."

"Don't like nice girls."

Her eye roll was more amused than annoyed. "Of course you do. We just haven't found you the right one."

"Not interested."

"I do realize you're a Haven, which is a synonym for stubborn. But eventually you're going to have to settle down."

My brow furrowed. "Why?"

She let out a long-suffering sigh. "Aren't you lonely all by yourself?"

"No."

"One of these days, you're going to realize how much better your life would be with a good woman."

I grunted. Easy for her to say. She'd married my uncle George when they were young and still malleable. I was thirty-eight and too set in my ways. I couldn't fathom sharing my space, my time, or my life with another person. I hated having to answer to someone else. Hell, I didn't even want a dog.

Besides, I'd been on the cusp of that once and look how that had turned out. Never again.

"You should focus on a different Haven."

"Believe me, I'm working on those brothers of yours."

"So why not badger one of them into taking out what's her name. Did you try Luke? Or Zachary?"

"Zachary." She practically spit out his name, as if it tasted bad. "He might be the one who finally stumps me. But Luke?" She tapped her lips with her finger. "No, I don't see it."

"If you don't want to foist her on Luke, I have plenty of brothers to choose from."

That was the truth. There were six of us boys, plus Annika. We were a yours, mine, and ours family. Dad had me, Luke, and Garrett with his first wife. Mom—she was the only mom any of us had ever known—had Reese, Theo, and Zachary. Dad had adopted them after they got married and no one questioned the fact that they were Havens. Then they'd had Annika together.

Plenty of single Haven brothers for Louise to annoy. Even Garrett, who'd gotten a divorce a few years ago.

Then again, Reese was the wild card. We hadn't seen him in years. He could be married with seven kids of his own and we'd have no idea.

"You know, maybe I'll see if Theo is interested," she said. "He has a good, stable job."

"Or Garrett," I said, glad to see the wheels of her matchmaking mind turning away from me. "Also has a good, stable job."

Heidi brought my to-go bag and set it on the table. I pulled out my wallet and shoved some cash at her before she could leave. "Keep the change."

"Thanks."

I stood, ready to make a break for it before Louise talked me into staying to eat with her. "I gotta go."

"Good to see you, honey. But don't think you're off the hook."

I just shook my head and left.

Smelling my dinner all the way home made my stomach growl even more. Fortunately, I lived in town, on Meadow Street, the last house on a dead-end road. I'd bought it years ago, intending to fix it up, but hadn't gotten around to doing much of anything with it. It still had the same sad, faded paint and crooked screen door that squeaked when it opened.

Inside wasn't much better. It was livable, just dated and bare. Dull hardwoods needed to be refinished. I'd taken out the old baseboards and trim and hadn't replaced them. Someone before me had painted the kitchen cabinets a terrible shade of mauve and covered the original linoleum with cheap peel and stick tiles. A few were coming loose, but fixing them meant replacing the whole floor, which really meant redoing the entire kitchen.

One of these days, I'd get around to it. Probably when I was ready to sell or convert it into a rental.

I pulled off my work boots, leaving them by the door, and tossed my phone, wallet, and keys on a small folding table. My furniture was as shabby and mismatched as the house. Same couch I'd had for years, a recliner my brother Theo had dumped on me last time he'd moved, and a small table that doubled as a footrest.

I dropped my takeout bag on the table and went to the kitchen to grab a beer. After cracking it open, I collapsed onto the couch and kicked my feet up.

Lonely? Aunt Louise didn't know what she was talking about. Sure, I was alone, but I wasn't lonely. I liked being able to put my feet on the table right next to my food. Sitting on an old couch in a half-finished house. I worked on my own schedule, did what I wanted the rest of the time. The last thing I wanted was someone else I had to worry about.

Alone, not lonely. Just the way I liked it.

CHAPTER 4

Audrey

MY STOMACH TUMBLED with nervousness as I walked up the sidewalk to my new job. It felt like the first day of school. The feeling wasn't entirely unpleasant, although I did wonder if I'd dressed appropriately. Was this a casual office? More formal? I'd interviewed over video chat, so I hadn't been there in person, and nothing in my correspondence with my new boss had mentioned a dress code.

I'd opted for what I hoped was classic—white blouse with a charcoal gray skirt and black pumps. It made me feel a little bit like Lois Lane, which seemed appropriate, given my new job.

Now if only I could find my own Clark Kent. He didn't even have to be Superman. Just a nice guy with a good job, who liked dogs and would fall head over heels in love with me. Was that too much to ask?

My life experience said yes, but I was a hopeless optimist.

I'd left Max at Happy Paws, the local pet store that also offered doggie daycare. It had taken him all of ten seconds to bond with the owner, Missy Lovejoy. Of course, she'd given him a treat. Max's love didn't come at a high price. But at least it was one less thing I needed to worry about.

The Tilikum Tribune office was a block off Main Street, not far from Lumberjack Park. Tilikum had a much cuter downtown than Pinecrest. It had a quaint, let's-walk-around-and-shop quality, with interesting stores and quite a few restaurants.

I skidded to a halt as two squirrels ran across the sidewalk in front of me. It looked like one was carrying a set of keys. I glanced around, wondering if I should chase it down and get the keys back. They had to belong to someone. But a second later, they both disappeared around a corner.

Apparently the Tilikum squirrels came by their reputation for thievery honestly.

I smoothed down my skirt and took a deep breath, then opened the door to the Tribune office and went inside.

The office was wide open with several desks placed at haphazard angles. A closed door at the back had a nameplate that said Editor and another in the corner was a restroom. The opposite corner housed a kitchenette, with a mini-fridge and a coffee maker on the counter. Framed copies of the Tribune decorated the walls and most of them were slightly crooked.

A woman with a gray pixie cut looked up from her laptop and smiled. She was the only other person in the office. One desk was completely empty and, although the other one had a desktop computer and a few odds and ends, no one was sitting there.

"Hi." She stood. "You must be Audrey. I'm Sandra O'Neal."

"Yes, hi." I walked in with my hand outstretched. "Audrey Young."

Sandra took my hand and shook. She was dressed in a black shirt and khakis—more casual than what I was wearing, so I was glad I hadn't opted for a suit jacket.

"Nice to meet you. Lou's in his office." She gestured to one of the desks. "Ledger, the useless intern, sits there. He's not here yet, obviously."

"I'm sorry, did you say *useless* intern?"

"Don't worry, I call him that to his face." She pointed to the empty desk. "You can have that one. Unless you like Ledger's better. We could move his stuff, he probably wouldn't even notice."

"Oh, no, this is fine."

"Great." Her smile faded as she turned her attention to Lou's office and raised her voice. "Lou! The new girl's here."

She paused, as if listening, but I didn't hear a reply.

"I'm sure he'll be out in a minute. You can get settled. I'd show you around, but there's not much to show. We're a pretty small operation. Do you have your own laptop?" She glanced around. "We probably have an extra one around here somewhere but if we do, it's a piece of garbage. I recommend using your own."

"I have my own." I put my bag down on the empty metal desk. It had seen better days. The bottom drawer was dented —I doubted it would open—and there were rust-ringed dings on the legs.

But it was fine. I was here for a paycheck, not for luxurious surroundings.

The front door opened and a lanky guy with a brown mullet and an attempt at a mustache came in. He wore a faded Led Zeppelin t-shirt, skinny jeans, and a thin maroon scarf around his neck.

"Ah, Ledger, you decided to grace us with your presence today," Sandra said. "This is the new girl, Audrey."

"Hey." Ledger barely glanced my direction before dropping into his chair. His phone seemed to appear out of nowhere and he leaned back, already scrolling.

"See?" Sandra gestured toward him. "That's why I call him the useless intern. He doesn't do much."

He glared at her over the top of his phone. "I do work."

"Since when?"

"I did research for an article."

"That was a month ago."

He shook his head, his attention still on his phone. "You guys need to check your expectations. I have a lot of homework."

"It's summer break."

"Yeah, and I deserve a break."

Sandra met my eyes and shrugged. "He surprises us once in a while but mostly he just sits there. Lou doesn't care because he's an intern and we aren't paying him."

I slowly lowered myself into my chair. "Okay..."

"We're probably not making the best impression, but what can I say? We're a small-town newspaper trying to survive in a post-newspaper era. You've got Lou, who's been here forever and won't let the thing die. Then there's me, who thought it would be fun to get a job a few years ago since my kids had to go and grow up on me. And Ledger, here, who's been working on his journalism degree over at Tilikum College for what, six years?"

"Five and a half," he said.

"As you can see, we're desperately in need of someone like you."

"What is my role supposed to be, exactly?" I asked. "Lou wasn't very specific."

"Well," Sandra said and hesitated, like she had to think about it first. "I handle announcements—weddings, babies, obits. I also do the copy editing and proofreading, plus the bookkeeping and other administrative stuff. Lou oversees things from an editorial standpoint and spends most of his time trying to convince advertisers to pay us. Ledger doesn't do much, so that leaves you with– pretty much everything else."

I blinked a few times. "Everything else?"

She smiled. "Don't worry, our readership isn't picky. Do you have a camera? We definitely have one lying around here somewhere, although the camera on your phone is probably better."

"A camera? I'm not a photographer."

Before Sandra could reply, Lou's door opened. He was bigger than he'd seemed during my interview—tall with a mid-section that strained the buttons on his short-sleeved shirt. I couldn't tell if his gray stubble was intentional or if he'd just forgotten to shave this morning and although he still had some hair on his head, it was clearly thinning.

"Good, the new girl's here." His voice was rough as gravel. "Audrey, right?"

I stood, ready to offer my hand. "Yes, hi, it's nice to—"

"Come in."

He disappeared back into his office. I glanced at Sandra. She gave me an encouraging smile, so I followed Lou.

His office smelled pleasantly of paper and ink, calling to mind elementary school paper mâché projects using torn newspaper as our medium. What had to have been some of the earliest editions of the Tribune, dating back to the early nineteen hundreds, hung on the wall in mismatched frames, and his desk was littered with stacks of paperwork and mail. Although he had a computer, a vintage typewriter sat on the console behind his chair, and somehow it looked like it fit the vibe better than any modern technology.

Lou shuffled through the mess on his desk. "I must have given Sandra your paperwork. She does the bookkeeping and payroll."

"Oh, okay. If there's anything else you need, let me know."

He grabbed a folded newspaper off the top of one of his stacks and pushed it toward me. "This is last week's edition. You can get an idea of the layout from here. It's pretty straightforward. The local section is at the back. Not much happens around here, but we print the high school sports schedules, town events, that kind of thing. Any questions?"

I had about a hundred questions, but I wasn't sure where to begin. "What should I... "

His phone rang and he answered it so fast, my question was left dangling in the air. "This is Lou."

He paused, listening, and started to shake his head. "No, no. That's not going to work."

I waited, trying not to fidget in my seat.

"You always do a half-page spread. You've been doing the half-page for twenty-five years. Why change it now?" He put his hand over the mouthpiece and gestured for me to go. "Gotta take this. Go get started."

Get started on what?

He uncovered the phone and kept talking. "I know subscriber numbers are down but these are the times we live in. This is still a great way to reach your loyal customers."

I got up and took the paper, then quietly left his office.

Sandra smiled. "All set?"

"Not really." I went back to my desk and took a seat. "He got a call."

"That's okay. There's always a learning curve on the first day. Not much you can do about it. I'll help you out."

"Thank you." I liked Sandra already, which was a relief, because the rest of the situation had me a little confused. "He handed me last week's paper as if that would explain my whole job. But I have to be honest, I have no idea what I'm supposed to do."

"It's a metaphor for life," Ledger said, nodding sagely. "None of us know."

Sandra laughed. "True enough, Ledger. Maybe you're not always useless."

"Told you," he said, although he still didn't look up from his phone.

"Don't worry," she said. "I'll help get you started. There's a community calendar on the city's official Facebook page that will help. You can get dates for local events there. And I'll send out some emails introducing you to people you'll need to know. Trisha over at parks and rec, Carolyn in the mayor's office, Ed on the city council. But it's rare that anything newsworthy happens around here."

I opened the paper and flipped through the pages. I didn't want to be judgy—and I was certainly no expert on small-town newspapers—but it was all fairly generic. The local section was at the back, when it seemed like it should be front and center. And there wasn't much that was particularly interesting. Just the basic news stories people could see anywhere, a few columns that were clearly reprinted from other sources, and a tiny calendar of events.

Refolding the paper, I let out a long breath. What had I gotten myself into? I wasn't sure what they expected of me, where I should begin, or what I could do—if anything—to help the failing newspaper. Looking at its sad pages, I wondered if it would stay open at all. Or if I'd come to work one morning and find the door locked and my hopes of getting back on my feet torn to pieces, like all that scrap newspaper we used for our art projects.

That feeling that I'd made a big mistake in coming here was back. With a vengeance.

But what could I do? Keep making the best of it, and hope I still had a job next week.

That and find a new job that actually had a future, as soon as humanly possible.

CHAPTER 5

Audrey

MY FIRST DAY didn't get any worse. So at least I had that going for me.

Sandra helped me get started on a few things and before I knew it, it was time to go home. The day had seemed both too fast and too slow, leaving me feeling like a wrung-out washrag.

I said goodbye to Sandra—she was the one bright spot at my new job so far—and went to get Max.

When I picked him up, he did his sacred job as a dog, acting like he was ready to burst with excitement as soon as he saw me. He circled around me, wagging his tail like the crazy dog he was, and gave me some wet face licks when I crouched to pet him.

The drive back to Pinecrest gave me some time to decompress. I didn't quite dread the prospect of going back to my mom's house, but I wasn't looking forward to it, either. Keeping Max away from Duchess was proving to be frustrating. He didn't mean to be so naughty, but the more I kept him away from the cat, the more he wanted to check her out. Her warning scratch had done nothing to temper his curiosity.

Last night, he'd gotten away from me and Duchess had ended up stuck on the top of a bookshelf, unable to get down.

At least, Mom had claimed she was stuck. I was convinced she was just being dramatic.

The grocery store was on the way, so I decided to stop in and get something for dinner. A bit of a peace offering to my mom for putting up with my crazy dog.

Max would be fine for a few minutes while I ran in. I'd never leave him in a car for long—a vehicle could heat up faster than you realized, especially in the sun—but it wasn't hot out and I parked in the shade. I'd be in and out fast enough, he'd be fine.

"Stay here, good boy. I'll be right back."

I went into the store and veered to the right, toward the deli. Thankfully, they had the chicken salad my mom liked. I ordered a medium—probably more than we needed but she could have leftovers tomorrow—and waited while a guy wearing a hairnet over his man-bun filled the container. He handed it to me and I thanked him.

"Well, well, well," an all-too-familiar voice said behind me. "I heard you were back."

I knew this moment had to happen sooner or later. This town was too small to avoid him for long. But I still wasn't quite prepared to see Colin Greaves.

"I guess news travels fast," I said as I turned around.

He was dressed in a pale blue button-down and a pair of dark slacks. Probably stopping at the store on his way home from work, like me. He worked for his father's law firm, the only one in town, and he certainly looked the part. Slicked-back hair, clean shaven, not a wrinkle in his expensive clothes.

One corner of his mouth lifted and his eyes flicked up and down. "You look good."

"Thanks. First day of work."

"Oh yeah? Where are you working?"

I pressed my lips together. I shouldn't have said more than *thanks*. Now I was being roped into an actual conversation instead of a quick hello situation. But I didn't want to be rude. "The Tilikum Tribune."

"Is that thing still open?"

"Well, they hired me and the door wasn't locked when I got there this morning, so I'd say that's a good sign."

"Cute," he said, and I wasn't sure if he was referring to the newspaper or my attempt at sarcasm. "I heard you're living with your mom."

I didn't miss the judgment in his voice. "Just until I find a place."

Looking me up and down again, he crossed his arms. "Who would have thought. Miss Most Likely to Succeed, back home. I thought you said you'd never live here again."

I had said that. At the time, I'd meant it. Adamantly. "Yeah, well, life throws you curve balls." I held up my container of chicken salad. "I should get home while this is still cold."

"Hey, I don't mean to be hard on you." His voice took on the soothing quality he'd always used to get out of an argument. "Is everything okay?"

I lost my job and now I'm living with my mother after I swore I'd never move home; my new job is a disaster, and I'm going to spend all my off-hours trying to keep my dog away from my mom's pampered cat. No, everything is not okay.

Obviously I didn't say that.

"Yeah, fine. I was just looking for a career change and this happened to be where I wound up. Life is funny that way."

He nodded slowly and I could tell he didn't believe me. "Good for you."

"Thanks."

"We should get coffee sometime." He stepped closer and gave me the same flirtatious grin that had given me butterflies back in high school. "Catch up properly."

Why was he looking at me that way? His eyes traveled up and down, lingering on my chest much longer than was polite.

"How's Lorelei?"

For half a second, he froze, and a flash of anger hardened his features.

He reminded me of my father.

That was disconcerting.

"She's great." His expression melted back into his cocky half-grin. "You should stop by. She'd love to see you."

Nice save, buddy. "Yeah, I will. I really do need to get going. My dog is in the car and I don't want to leave him out there too long."

"Of course. Me too. Gotta get home before the old ball and chain thinks I'm running around on her." He winked and a part of me wondered if he *was* cheating on her. Or would, if given the opportunity.

Dang it, Colin, don't be that guy. "Have a good night."

"Bye, Audrey." He paused, locking me in his gaze. "It really is good to see you."

"You, too." I was such a liar. It wasn't good to see him and I would have avoided it for as long as I could.

"I'll see you around." He winked again, then turned and sauntered off.

I let out a long breath and headed for the check out, feeling mildly icky. I'd felt that way when I'd seen him at my dad's funeral, too. Instead of just expressing his condolences, like a normal ex-boyfriend, he'd cornered me and insisted on giving me a long hug. Somehow his offer of *anything I needed* had struck me as inappropriate.

Fortunately, today he hadn't tried to hug me, just asked me to coffee, which could have been perfectly innocent. Maybe he did just want to catch up and see how I was doing.

I paid for the chicken salad and headed back to my car. Max was diligently watching for me as I walked across the parking lot and I could see his bushy tail start wagging as soon as he caught sight of me.

Silly dog.

Out of nowhere, a chill ran up my spine and the hairs on my arms stood on end. I had the strangest feeling that I was being watched, and not just by my dog. The sense was so strong, and so pervasive, it made my heart race, as if I were walking in a dark alley in a big city, not the parking lot of a small-town grocery store in broad daylight.

I couldn't decide whether to look around to see if anyone was actually watching me, or sprint for my car, so I wound up doing an awkward combination of both. My head turned from side to side, too quickly for me to make out much of my surroundings, and I darted forward. I dug into my purse, scrambling for my keys. Where were they?

Max's nose left wet streaks across the glass of the passenger side window. He probably interpreted my dash across the parking lot to mean something fun was about to happen.

I kept waiting for a rag with chloroform to clamp over my nose and mouth or a sharp object to stab me from behind.

It's possible adrenaline gave me an over-active imagination.

I got to my car, pressed the remote to unlock it, and scrambled inside, locking the door as fast as I could.

Max wagged his tail while I tried to catch my breath. My heart pounded and the tingly, I'm-about-to-be-stabbed feeling took a long moment to go away.

I looked out the windows and in the rear-view but didn't see anyone. Not even Colin.

It had probably just been him, pausing outside his car to watch me when I came out of the store. Just my not-dangerous ex-boyfriend. The worst thing Colin would do was eye me inappropriately and suggest we have coffee—and quite possibly cheat on his wife, but I wasn't going to have any part in that.

No reason to fear chloroform rags or being stabbed from behind.

Max put his paw on my arm.

"Thanks, good boy. Your dog-mom is ridiculous. I hope you know that."

He looked up at me with his big brown eyes, as if there was nothing wrong with me at all.

Dogs are the best.

My heart was slowing down and my arms no longer resembled a hyper alert porcupine, so I turned on the car and left. I kept the chicken salad container in my lap so Max wouldn't get too curious. I didn't need to wind up with dinner and dog slobber all over the inside of my car.

I told myself in no uncertain terms that I was not being followed on the drive home. There was literally no one behind me, but apparently my adrenaline-fueled imagination wasn't quite done.

It was just the stress of – everything. My stint with unemployment, the rampant rejection of applying to a million jobs and never hearing back, plus the move home. Not to mention running into Colin. It was a lot.

The sight of my mom's house wasn't exactly comforting but at least I'd made it through my first day of work. I just hoped doggie daycare had worn Max out. I was feeling pretty depleted.

I parked and clipped on Max's leash. Between my bag, the chicken salad, and Max, I had a lot to juggle, so I let him hop out first while I got my things. He ran straight to the door and sat.

"Good boy, Max. Wait there for me."

I gathered up everything and shut the car door with my hip.

The front door opened and my mom poked her head out.

Before she could say a word, Max tore past her and ran inside.

"Duchess!" Mom yelped and darted after him.

"You've got to be kidding me." I hurried in and kicked the door closed behind me so Duchess wouldn't run outside. The only thing worse than Max chasing her would be to let Mom's precious baby get out. "Max! Come!"

I set my things down and rushed to the kitchen, but they weren't there. A muffled scream came from upstairs, so I headed that way.

"Max, you're trained better than this," I shouted as I took the stairs two at a time. "Sort of. Come!"

He popped out of the master bedroom, his eyes wide with excitement, tail wagging like crazy.

"Good boy. Come on."

For a second, I thought he was going to obey. But the lure of his new favorite game—chase the spoiled cat—was too much for him. Training versus temptation; temptation won.

I started to yell for my mom to close her bedroom door, but I was too late. He spun around and charged back in, the loose leash trailing behind him. Mom screamed again, because of course she did, and something crashed to the floor.

"Audrey!"

"I'm right here. Max, no. Come!"

A lamp had been knocked over but it didn't look broken. Mom's face was flushed and she stood in front of her king-sized four poster bed, legs in a wide stance, arms held out to the sides, as if she were ready to sacrifice her body to save her precious feline.

Max finally obeyed his command, coming to sit in front of me, eyes on mine, tail wagging happily. I picked up the leash so he couldn't run off again.

Mom took ragged breaths and her eyes were slightly wild. "He can't keep terrorizing my baby, Audrey."

"I know, I know. I was just grabbing my stuff. I didn't think you were going to open the door."

"It doesn't matter. The leash solution is clearly not working."

"Mom, he's just trying to play. He won't hurt her."

"He's hurting her mentally."

Duchess peered out from under the bed and hissed.

"I'm sorry. He doesn't mean to. He's just excited."

The look Mom gave me spoke louder than words. *Keep him away from my cat.*

"I picked up dinner. It's in the bag I left by the front door." I didn't know what else to say, so I took Max and left, closing the door behind me.

I went to my room and patted the bed, inviting him to hop up.

This living situation was not going to work. I'd never meant for it to be long term, but I'd hoped I could make it work for a few months. It had barely been a few days and I was ready to rip my hair out.

Plus, I didn't like the idea of running into Colin so easily. I'd be nervous every time I went anywhere in this town, wondering if he'd be there.

I needed a place of my own. Even my rampant optimism couldn't make this work much longer.

I put Max in his crate for a little chill-out time—thankfully he liked his den—and went downstairs to get my things. Mom was apparently still upstairs, probably cooing over Duchess after the latest dog-trauma. I put dinner in the kitchen and took my bag back upstairs to my room.

Max was curled up napping, so I left him to sleep and got out my laptop. After the Colin encounter, I really wanted to find a place to live outside of Pinecrest—preferably in Tilikum, so I'd be close to work. But just about anything would be better than here.

I opened my saved search and ran it again, holding my breath.

Please let there be something new.

Several listings I hadn't seen before popped up and hope rose like a warm tingle in my chest.

The first was a two-bedroom apartment. Awesome. It was in Tilikum, near the college. That would work. Recently remodeled with new appliances, that was nice. The rent was within my budget and just when I thought I might have found the solution to my problems, I came to the end. No pets.

Shoot.

The next ad was for a house. Three bedrooms, a little out of my price range, but it did have a fenced backyard. That would be great for Max. Pets were allowed with a deposit, which was fine. I clicked on the map to see where it was and my heart sank. It was in Pinecrest. In fact, if Colin still lived in the same place, it was right around the corner from his house.

Hard no.

That hope I'd felt was fading fast.

I clicked on the last new ad. Two-bedroom house in Tilikum. Rent was in my price range. No mention of a fenced yard, but I didn't necessarily need one. Just a decent place that was clean, not up the street from my ex-boyfriend, and without a pampered white Persian in residence.

The ad didn't say anything about pets one way or the other. Crossing my fingers that the answer would be yes to my silly dog, I called the number.

"Haven Properties," a woman's voice answered. "This is Annika."

"Hi, Annika. My name is Audrey and I just saw your ad for a two-bedroom in Tilikum. Is it still available?"

"Yes, it sure is."

I took a deep breath and crossed my fingers harder. "Do you by chance allow pets?"

"We do on a case-by-case basis, and with a deposit. What kind of pets do you have?"

"Just a dog. He's a medium mixed breed, long-ish fur but I keep him groomed."

"Oh sure, one dog is fine. If you want, I can meet you there tomorrow so you can take a look. Or later in the week if tomorrow doesn't work for you."

"I don't need to see it first. I'll take it."

She paused. "Are you sure?"

"If it allows my dog and isn't in Pinecrest, it's perfect."

"Oh, okay," she said with a laugh. "If you could text me your email address to this number, I'll send you a link to our online rental application. Go ahead and fill that out to get things started. When were you hoping to move in?"

"As soon as possible. I'm temporarily living with my mother and my dog and her cat aren't exactly best friends. Well, my dog thinks the cat is his new best friend—or more accurately, his chew toy—but the cat has other ideas. It's getting stressful."

"I totally understand. The application process won't take long. Just make sure to fill it out completely and that will give me everything I need. Assuming it all checks out, we can get you moved in soon."

I sighed with relief. "Thank you so much. You're a lifesaver."

"No problem. I'll give you a call when things are good to go on our end and we can meet to finalize the rental agreement and get you the keys."

"Thank you," I said again. "So much."

I ended the call and immediately texted her my email address. About two minutes and too much fidgeting later, an email from Annika Bailey appeared with the subject line: rental application.

Bingo.

I filled it out, hoping nothing unexpected would come up

that would prevent me from renting this house. I had a feeling it was going to be perfect.

And if not, at least there wouldn't be a cat to worry about. As for the rest, I'd make the best of it. I was pretty good at that.

June 8th

I saw her today.

Yes, her.

I'd managed to scrub her from my mind. That took a lot of hard work. It took discipline. I was proud of that. Proud of how I didn't think of her at all.

How I'd made her nothing.

Apparently her memory wasn't buried as deep as I'd thought. Just seeing her brought it all back.

It made me angry to see her. So fucking angry. And I don't like it when I'm angry. Anger is too raw and uncontrolled.

Perhaps she's here to test me. That's an interesting idea. Test my discipline. My strength.

Or maybe it's time I consider settling the score, once and for all.

CHAPTER 6

Josiah

THE TIMBERBEAST TAVERN WAS HALF-EMPTY. Odd for a Friday, although it was early. Not quite six. It would fill up as the night wore on. Especially because Rocco, the longtime owner, had inexplicably started doing karaoke on Fridays. I'd be out of there well before that mess started.

I went in and took a seat at the bar, next to a couple of regulars nursing regrets along with their beers. A few locals had claimed spots at the tall tables and a group of women—definitely tourists—took up a large table on the right. They were late-twenties, maybe early thirties, probably in town for a girls' weekend. They were doing a lot of laughing and posing for selfies.

I ignored them. Girls like that were Luke and Zachary's thing. Not mine.

Hayden came out from the back. "What can I get you? The usual?"

"Yeah."

He grabbed a glass and poured me a beer, then slid it across the bar. Hayden wasn't really the new guy anymore, although I still thought of him that way. Rocco had brought him on a year or two ago. Or was it three? Hell, I didn't know.

Younger guy, maybe thirty at most, with shaggy dark hair. He had kind of an emo vibe, but he was a good enough bartender —served drinks without making pointless conversation. Worked for me.

I took a sip and glanced at the time on my phone. I was a bit early, there to meet Dad. One of the perks of partnering with my father was having our business meetings over a couple of beers at the Timberbeast. Mom teased us that it was just an excuse to go to the tavern. Maybe. But we actually got a lot done.

The door opened and I glanced over my shoulder. It wasn't my dad, but I nodded at the guy who walked in. No one batted an eyelash at his entrance, but not that long ago, he wouldn't have set foot in here.

Asher Bailey was a big guy who had a look of danger about him. And rightly so. He was a jiu jitsu coach who'd done time in federal prison for killing the guy who tried to assault his then-fiancée, Grace. I'd never understood how they could have put him away for that. Any man would have done what he did.

But that had been a long time ago, when his family and mine had still been feuding. Although the shots we took at each other had mostly been pranks, I'd been obligated by long-standing tradition to hate Asher Bailey and his brothers. Six years ago, that had all changed, and somehow, Asher and I had become friends.

Although it wasn't all that weird. My sister Annika had crossed feud lines to marry a Bailey. But that was another story.

He took a seat next to me. Hayden came over to take his order. I didn't know where Hayden was from, but he hadn't lived in Tilikum long enough to remember when the Timber-beast had been Haven territory.

"What can I get you?"

Asher gestured toward my beer. "One of those."

"Coming right up."

"What are you doing in here tonight?" I asked.

"Grace and the kids are out with her mom. I saw your truck outside, so I figured I'd stop in."

Hayden gave Asher his beer. Asher thanked him.

We lifted our glasses to each other and took a drink.

"What's new with you?" He set his beer down.

"Not much. Just ripping apart a house."

"How's that going?"

"Shitty, but that's typical. I had to pull out a bunch of drywall earlier this week that I hadn't been planning to replace. But at least we got rid of the smell."

Thinking about the house made me wonder. Did I forget to lock up when I left? That wasn't usually something I'd do, but I had the weirdest feeling that I'd left the back door unlocked.

"It still amazes me that Grace remodeled our house on her own while I was gone."

"Grace is a badass."

He lifted his glass. "Cheers to that."

I clinked mine against his. "What about you?"

"I had a job interview yesterday."

"You thinking of leaving the gym?"

"For this? Yeah. Chief Stanely wants to hire me on at the TFD."

I raised my eyebrows. That was some news. Asher had been planning to be a firefighter before he'd been sent to prison. Once he'd come home, his record had made him ineligible. "No shit?"

He nodded. "The state changed the law. I've gone long enough without re-offending, Chief can hire me. He blindsided me with that news last weekend."

"Not wasting any time, is he?"

"I have a lot of training to catch up on, so he's trying to get the formalities out of the way."

"Your brothers must be excited." Three of Asher's brothers were career firefighters with the TFD, including my brother-in-law, Levi.

"They assumed I was fucking with them at first."

"Naturally."

The door opened again and I glanced back to see my brothers Luke and Zachary waltz in. Zachary nudged Luke and gestured to the table with the girls—because of course he did—before coming over to the bar.

"Hey, Asher," Luke said. "I hear the fire department is lowering their standards."

"How did you know about that?" I asked.

His brow furrowed. "Everybody knows."

"I didn't know."

"That's because you don't talk to anybody."

I shrugged. Fair point.

"Congrats, man." Luke slapped Asher on the shoulder. "I don't know how Chief Stanley is going to handle another Bailey on his crew, but that's his problem."

"He's handled Gavin all these years," Asher said. "That must make him some kind of saint."

"That's a fact," Luke said. "Gavin is nuts."

Asher chuckled. His youngest brother came by his reputation honestly.

"As charming as this all is," Zachary said, his voice thick with sarcasm, "I have more important things to do. Catch you dickheads later."

He went straight for the table with the girls, sauntering over with his hands in his pockets. Z was all confidence with women. It was probably well-placed. I doubted he had much of a problem getting laid.

Asher shook his head, like he was mildly amused. He'd been a family man for years. Picking up girls in a bar had to be the last thing on his mind. It was part of why we got along. I didn't have a wife and kids—nor did I want them

—but I wasn't any more interested in that scene than he was.

Luke leaned a little closer and lowered his voice. "You know, there's a table full of hot girls over there."

"So?"

"I'm pretty sure the blond one in pink has been eying you since we got here."

"Not interested."

"Seriously?" Luke looked at Asher, as if he'd have an answer, but he just shrugged. "Is there something wrong with you? Everything works, right?"

I glared at him. "Do you want me to take you down in front of all those girls?"

Luke grinned. "Not particularly. Look man, I'm just trying to help. You want to be sad and alone, that's fine. I'm going to have a little fun with some out-of-towners."

He strolled off, his cockiness low-key compared to Z. But it was still there. Those two read from the same playbook. Luke was just more subtle about it.

"I'm not sad and alone," I muttered.

"What was that?" Asher asked.

"Nothing. My brothers are annoying."

"Yeah, so are mine, but what are you gonna do."

Dad finally arrived, taking up half the doorway with his broad shoulders. Paul Haven was a big guy from lumberjack stock. His brown hair and beard were peppered with gray and he wore a faded blue plaid shirt and jeans.

He paused, noting two of his sons surrounded by a bunch of women. With a slight shake of his head, he came over to the bar and took the seat on the other side of me.

Asher stood. "I should get going. Make sure I'm home before Grace and the kids get back."

"The beer's on me," I said. "Congrats again."

"Thanks, Haven." He tipped his chin to my dad. "Good to see you, Paul."

Dad nodded. "You too."

Asher left and Hayden brought Dad a beer.

"How's the house looking?" he asked. "I meant to get over there today but I didn't get around to it."

"So far it's in worse condition than we thought."

"How much drywall did you ruin?"

I cracked a smile. "Most of it."

He chuckled. "Figures. We should probably make changes to the budget, then. Find some less expensive options for some of the finishes."

"Probably."

"I'll work on that. Jim Brenner owes me a favor, maybe I can get a deal on the windows."

"Sounds good. And I'll try to finish demo without breaking anything else."

"You do that."

Our meeting, such as it was, didn't take long. He had a lead on another property that might go up for sale. We weren't quite ready to invest in another house, but it was good to keep an eye out. I showed him my sketch for the new kitchen layout to make sure he approved. He did.

My dad was a pretty straightforward guy. Made working with him easy.

While we talked, the question of whether I'd locked the back door of the remodel kept bugging me, like an itch I couldn't reach. It was probably fine, but we'd had trouble with squatters in one of our properties not long ago and I had no desire to go through that again.

I left some money on the bar to cover our tab and tip, then stood. "I need to swing by the house. Might have forgotten to lock the back door."

"Okay, son," Dad said. "Have a good night."

"Tell Mom I said hi."

"I will."

I left the tavern and got in my truck. The days were

getting long as we got into June and the sun was still above the mountain peaks. It was a nice night. If Z and Luke had any sense, they'd take those girls down to the river. Better atmosphere than a grimy old tavern.

But what did I know?

I headed over to the house and parked next to the dumpster. I remembered locking the front door when I left and sure enough, it was secure. Inside was quiet, everything the way I'd left it. A dirty mess. I walked to the back of the house and checked the back door.

Locked.

That was good but I was glad I'd taken the time to check anyway. Tilikum had always been pretty safe, but you never knew.

I went back out the front and locked up behind me. Movement in the corner of my vision caught my eye. Probably just a squirrel—they were everywhere in this town—but why was there a car in the driveway of the two-bedroom next door?

Annika had said the tenants bailed, so it was going to be vacant for another month. Wasn't that just a few days ago? She couldn't have found a new tenant already.

The car in the driveway was a basic sedan. It needed a wash but that wasn't what tugged at my gut instinct. The back seat was jam packed full of stuff. I walked closer to peer inside. The passenger seat was clear, but the rest of the car was stuffed. It looked like someone—or a couple of someones —living out of their car.

Oh hell no. This was exactly what had happened with those squatters a couple of years ago. A random couple with a drug problem who'd been living out of their car moved into one of my vacant rental houses. It had taken months to get them out. Total pain in the ass. I was not dealing with that bullshit again.

Good thing I had a key. I'd get them out before they got comfortable.

CHAPTER 7
Audrey

THE CARPET WAS SOFT.

I laid on my back, looking up at the living room ceiling, and trailed my arms across the floor, like I was making a carpet angel. The rental house was everything I'd hoped it would be and more. It was cute, cozy, clean, and although it was a hair outside my intended budget, the extra expense was worth it. It was already furnished, so I didn't have to worry about getting new stuff. And there wasn't a pampered Persian cat to be found.

Cute neighborhood, too. The house next door looked a bit sketchy but there was a big dumpster in the driveway, so maybe it was being torn down or remodeled or something.

My mom had pretended to be surprised that I'd found a place to live already, but I could tell she was relieved. The feeling was mutual. Even aside from the Max and Duchess situation, my relationship with her was always better if we didn't see each other every day.

"I think we can make this work. What do you think, Max?"

He rolled onto his back, mimicking my posture, his front

paws bent like he was playing dead. I gave him a scratch on the belly.

"Yep, this is perfect. Our own space. Sorry there aren't any kitties to play with but it's for the best."

My application had gone through just fine. Annika had sent me a rental agreement and met me after work to give me the keys. The lease was for a year, which felt kind of daunting, but I'd known going in that most places would require twelve months. That would give me plenty of time to look for another job—again—preferably in another city. I'd make the best of this temporary stopover in the mountains, but that's all it was—temporary.

After a week at my new job, I still felt like I had no idea what I was doing. They already had material for this week's edition, and Sandra had helped me figure out some ideas for my journalistic debut. I didn't particularly enjoy the feeling of flailing around at work while everyone there seemed to assume I knew what I was doing. But today was Friday and I was going to leave work at work for the time being. At least I wasn't unemployed anymore.

"What do you think, should we unpack the rest of the car?" I asked. Max rolled to his side. "And by we, I mean me, since you need all your limbs for walking."

With a big yawn, he stretched his legs in opposite directions.

"I think that means I should relax first. Maybe poke around the house a little more. That's good advice."

I got up and stretched my arms overhead. The living room had a couch and two armchairs around a coffee table. The kitchen was small but fully stocked and there was an eating nook with a view out the back. Down a short hallway were two bedrooms and a small bathroom. The larger bedroom had its own bathroom, which was nice.

I wandered into the bedroom where I'd left my suitcase. The king-sized bed was a bit large for the room but they'd made up for it by choosing narrow bedside tables and a tall dresser that fit in a nook next to the closet. The bathroom was a charming surprise. Tile floor, a nice sized vanity with two sinks, a walk-in shower, and the best part? A freestanding bathtub.

A hot bath sounded so good.

Sure, my car was still full of stuff and I had no groceries, but those sounded like future Audrey problems. I needed a break.

Max jumped up on the bed and curled himself into a dog-ball. Apparently doggie daycare had worn him out today. I turned on the water in the tub and got a towel out of the cupboard. I needed to remember to pick up some bath salts when I went shopping.

Steam rose from the tub as it filled. Temperature felt good. I went back to the bedroom and dug a claw clip out of my toiletries case so I could put up my hair—I didn't want to have to mess with drying it—and put a pair of clean pajamas on the bed.

I left Max on the bed and shut the bathroom door behind me, in case he woke up and got curious. I didn't want him thinking he needed a bath too and jumping in with me. It wouldn't have been the first time.

It felt good to get out of my work clothes. I let my blouse and slacks drop to the floor, along with my bra and panties. I twisted my hair up and secured it with the claw clip. The water was still running but it was deep enough for me to get in comfortably. I checked the temperature one more time. It was just right.

I held onto the edge of the tub and dipped one foot in. Max barked from the other room. It sounded like a happy play bark, but what was he doing in there?

Out of nowhere, the door opened. I whipped my head around, my heart instantly racing, to find a big, burly bearded man in red flannel standing in the doorway.

I screamed. His eyes widened. Max barked again, like this was a fun game, not a potentially life-threatening breaking and entering situation for his human.

"Get out! Who are you? What are you doing here? Get out!"

I was rambling at the top of my lungs, but who could blame me? I was stark naked, bent over with one foot in the tub, holding onto the edge for dear life so I wouldn't fall, and a strange man was in the doorway, looking away as if he were trying to avert his eyes.

But he wasn't a strange man. I knew who he was. Josiah Haven.

The shock of it all destroyed my balance. I tried to stand up and grab the towel off the counter so at least I wouldn't be completely naked, but my foot slipped. I fell forward, face first into the bathtub, and sucked in a mouthful of water.

My arms and legs flailed, slipping on the wet tub, as I tried to right myself. What direction was I facing? Where was the air? I twisted and my butt hit the bottom of the tub. Sitting up, I broke the surface of the water and took a sputtering breath.

Max darted in and started splashing in the puddle of water on the floor.

I hunkered down and gripped the sides of the tub, rounding my back to make sure my boobs were at least partially covered. My hair was plastered to my face and my sinuses ached from the rush of water that had invaded them when I face planted. With a deliberately slow movement, I shut off the faucet.

"Are – are you okay?" Josiah asked.

To his credit, he was keeping his eyes averted.

"Do I look okay? What are you doing in my house?"

"This isn't your house."

"Yes, it is."

"No, it's my house."

"Can we maybe have this conversation when I'm not naked in a bathtub?"

Max stopped splashing long enough to sit at Josiah's feet, tail wagging, and eagerly looked up at him, no doubt hoping for attention.

Josiah glanced at Max, then at me. He looked away abruptly. "Sorry."

He stepped out, shutting the door, and left me with Max in a soaking wet bathroom.

Max put his paws up on the side of the tub and looked at me, panting happily.

"Some guard dog you are. What if he'd been trying to kill me?"

He leaned closer and licked my face.

I scrubbed my wet hair back, unplugged the drain, and carefully stood. The floor was a mess. I got out of the tub, tiptoeing through the puddle, and wrapped myself in the towel.

Opening the door a crack, I peeked out to make sure Josiah wasn't in the bedroom. It was empty and the door shut, so I dried off and put on the pajamas I'd laid out for myself.

I opened the bedroom door and stuck my head out. "Are you still here?"

"Are you dressed?"

"Obviously."

Josiah Haven stood by the front door, as if ready to make a quick getaway. He was dressed in a red plaid flannel shirt with the sleeves rolled up and a pair of faded jeans that had seen better days. He raked a hand through his brown hair and his beard and thick arms gave him a tough, woodsman vibe.

I stopped at the end of the hallway and gave Max a down command, then crossed my arms. "Why did you break into my house?"

"It's my house."

"According to the rental agreement I signed today, it's mine for the next twelve months."

His brow furrowed. "You're the tenant? I thought you bailed."

"I have no idea what you're talking about."

"Who gave you a rental agreement?"

"Annika Bailey."

Recognition softened his features. "You talked to Annika?"

"Yes. I called on the ad, she ran my application, and gave me the keys today."

His hands rested lightly on his hips and he looked at the ground. "She didn't tell me the place was rented. I thought you were a squatter."

"Why would that be your first thought?"

"We've had problems with them before. And your car is full of crap. Looks like you're living out of it."

"Don't judge. I just moved and I haven't had a chance to unpack. And that doesn't give you the right to barge in on me when I'm in the bath. Or ever."

He put his hands up in a gesture of surrender. "I didn't know you were in the bath."

"Well you shouldn't just walk in."

"I told you, I thought you were a squatter."

"And I told you I'm not."

Max seemed to be able to feel the tension in the room. He put his paws over his nose.

"My mistake," Josiah grumbled. "I'll get out of your way."

He was out the door before I could say another word.

Max jumped up and sniffed around the room, following Josiah's scent to the door.

I let out a long breath. Had that just happened? I probably should have been preoccupied with the shock of a man walking in on me naked—not to mention my extraordinarily embarrassing face-plant into a bathtub full of water—but all I could think about was how disappointing it was that he hadn't asked for my name. Or offered his.

Granted, I knew who he was. I wasn't usually good with names or faces, but how could I forget Josiah Haven?

We'd gone to different schools and he'd been two years ahead of me, but everyone knew the Haven brothers from Tilikum. They'd been right alongside the Baileys for being high school famous in the area, mostly because of sports.

And because every last one of them were as hot as a wildfire in July.

Oh yes, I knew Josiah Haven. I'd cheered against his football and basketball teams with my pom poms in hand, and cheered against him from the stands during baseball season.

I'd harbored a secret crush on the forbidden Tilikum high schooler.

He had no idea who I was, obviously. That didn't bother me. How could he? We'd never met, or talked, or even hung out in the same circle. Colin had hated the Haven brothers, simply because they went to a rival school. And they'd beaten Pinecrest High at just about everything.

But my daydreams had been full of him.

I'd seen him since, too. Just a handful of times when I'd been in town visiting my parents. He always caught my eye, made my stomach tingle a little.

And now he'd seen me naked.

Great. I'm sure I'd looked positively alluring while I was falling on my face and flailing around in the bathtub, half drowning.

Awesome first impression, Audrey.

I sighed again and went back to the bathroom to clean up the mess and brush out my tangled hair. So much for a relaxing hot bath. Maybe next time I'd barricade the door to make sure no one came in. Max clearly wasn't going to help in that department.

CHAPTER 8

Josiah

I STALKED out of the house and back to my truck feeling like an idiot. Talk about awkward. I'd gone in full of righteous indignation at the apparent squatters in my house, only to find a naked girl in the bathroom.

A hot naked girl.

I adjusted myself in my jeans.

Dumbass. I should have known better than to barge in when I heard the water running. But it had pissed me off. There was some random asshole in my house—with a dog—and they were taking a bath?

Except it wasn't a squatter and I'd looked like a jackass.

I got in my truck and dug out my phone to call Annika.

"Hey," she answered. "I kind of have my hands full, but what's up?"

"Did you rent the two-bedroom to someone?"

"I sure did." Her voice was annoyingly cheerful. "Quick, right? Did you call to thank me? Because if you did, I don't know why you sound angry."

"Were you going to tell me the place was occupied?"

"Sorry, I just hadn't yet. Wait, why?"

"I just went over there and barged in on some girl because I thought she was a squatter."

My sister burst out laughing. I ground my teeth together in frustration.

"I'm sorry." She took a gasping breath. "Oh my gosh, that's not funny but I can't stop laughing."

"You're right, it's not funny. She was in the bath."

That earned me a renewed bout of hysterical laughter.

"That poor girl. I really shouldn't laugh. You must have scared the crap out of her."

The image of her falling, face first, into the tub was burned into my memory. "Yeah."

"I'm sorry. She came out of nowhere asking to rent it and wanted it as soon as possible. I only gave her the keys a few hours ago and then I had to get home to the kids."

"And you say I'm the one who lacks communication skills."

"Well, you do. Did you apologize to Audrey?"

Somehow it didn't surprise me that her name was Audrey. She'd looked like an Audrey. Not when she was falling into the bathtub. Then she'd just looked like a lot of smooth skin and a very nice ass. But when she'd come out afterwards.

In fact, she'd looked vaguely familiar, but I couldn't place her.

"You know, the tenant," Annika said when I didn't answer. "Her name is Audrey Young. She's from Pinecrest."

"Yes, I apologized." I paused. Had I apologized? "Sort of."

"You should probably go back over there and tell her you're sorry. Just, you know, knock first like a normal person."

"I'm not going back over there."

She sighed. "Sure, leave it to me to do damage control."

"You're better at it than I am."

"True. Although if you didn't barge in on our tenants, we wouldn't have this problem."

"You say that as if I've done it before."

"Haven't you?"

"No."

"Huh. Seems like something you'd do."

I rolled my eyes. "Thanks."

She laughed. "Okay, I gotta go. I'll call Audrey tomorrow and make sure she knows we're not crazy people who won't respect her space."

I grunted in acknowledgment.

"Bye, big brother."

"Bye."

I ended the call and tossed the phone on the other seat. Great way to end the week.

Oh well. She'd get over it.

She wasn't my problem.

I started up my truck and drove home, and when I went to sleep later that night, I closed my eyes to visions of a hot brunette falling into a bathtub.

———

I was not going over there.

My attention kept wavering from the work I was supposed to be doing—pulling up a layer of ugly old linoleum from the kitchen floor—to the house next door.

She'd fallen pretty hard. Had she gotten hurt?

She had seemed okay afterward, but you didn't always feel blunt trauma immediately. Adrenaline and everything. What if she'd hit her head? Had she woken up this morning?

Damn it. She wasn't my problem.

Like the cabinets, the linoleum had been glued down with an obscene amount of adhesive. I was on my hands and knees with a crowbar, pulling up chunks of disintegrating particle board along with the flooring. Small chunks. Every time I thought I'd be able to peel back the linoleum, it would break off, bringing a piece of particle board with it.

This was going to take an eternity.

The only good news in this disaster was that the subfloor underneath it all still looked decent.

I didn't know why whoever had done the work originally had such a hard-on for construction glue. Unfortunately for me, I was the guy who had to deal with it.

This was my problem. Not Audrey.

It was weird that I remembered her name. I generally wasn't good with names. Like the latest girl Aunt Louise had tried to foist on me. No idea what her name was. Not that I cared. It was just odd that the name Audrey rang so clearly in my memory after only hearing it once or twice.

I ripped up another section, swearing under my breath when the particle board split. Complaining wasn't going to help—I had to suck it up and get it done—but nothing was going to stop the litany of curse words coming out of my mouth.

Sweat beaded on my forehead and I lost track of time as I settled into a rhythm, ripping up the godforsaken floor piece by piece. It was slow and tedious work, but also oddly calming. My mind was clear, my arms and back flexing, my muscles hot and tense with effort.

After a while, I looked up. I'd made it about halfway across the length of the kitchen. Not bad. It looked like a bomb had gone off, with chunks of flooring scattered everywhere—not to mention all the dust—but I'd made good progress.

I decided to clear out the debris before I got to work on the rest. I loaded up an armful of linoleum and broken particle board and took it out to the dumpster.

Seemingly out of nowhere, a black and brown dog appeared. He ran a circle around me as I dropped my load on the ground, then stopped, looking up at me with his tongue hanging out of his mouth and his tail wagging so hard it made half his body wiggle.

He'd seemed similarly excited to see me last night, just before I'd walked in on his owner.

"Not much of a guard dog, are you?" I picked up a chunk of flooring and tossed it into the dumpster.

"Max!" Audrey came running after her dog, dressed in a tank top and a pair of cut-offs that showed off her legs.

Nice legs. Not skinny, exactly, but firm.

I tore my eyes away. Looking at her skin was going to remind me of what she'd looked like naked.

"Hi." She flashed me a friendly smile. "Sorry about Max. He thinks everyone is his best friend."

"I can see that."

"I guess we didn't have a chance to actually meet before." She held out her hand. "I'm Audrey Young."

I took her hand in mine. Her skin was soft, her grip firm. "Josiah Haven."

"Yeah, I know. Sorry, that sounded weird. I just mean I remember you. From high school."

My brow furrowed. Was that why she seemed familiar?

"Oh, no, I didn't go to Tilikum," she said, as if I'd asked a question. "I went to Pinecrest but I was a cheerleader and we played you guys in sports a lot. So I remember you and your brothers."

A cheerleader? No surprise. She still had that bubbly, happy girl thing going on, like at any moment she might do a cartwheel and end with her arms in the air, wiggling her fingers.

Bubbly girls were not my thing, no matter what they looked like naked.

"Nice to meet you," I said, hoping to end the conversation quickly. "You can let Annika know if you need anything for the house."

"Oh, thanks. She's your sister, right? She's so nice. She called me this morning to explain – well, you know – you."

I furrowed my brow even deeper. "She explained *me*?"

Audrey smiled and nodded. "Yeah. Just so you know, we're fine. About last night, I mean. It's no big deal."

"Did you get hurt?" I asked before I could stop myself.

"No, not really. I might have a bruise or two." She twisted one arm to examine her elbow. "But I'm fine. That's sweet of you to ask."

It was not sweet of me. I was not a sweet guy. Instead of replying, I just grunted.

Her dog—Max, apparently—dropped a ball at her feet. I hadn't seen him go get it, but I hadn't really been paying attention to him.

Without missing a beat, she picked it up and tossed it toward her house. "What are you doing over there? Remodeling?"

I glanced at the other house. "Yeah. Just getting started."

"I was wondering about the big dumpster. This thing is huge."

Max came back and dropped the ball. She picked it up and threw it.

"It's a gut job," I said. "Outdated everything."

"Did you remodel the house I'm in?"

"Yeah. It's what we do."

"You, meaning you and your sister?"

"She works for us, but I partner with my dad."

"Do you keep them all as rentals when you're done remodeling?"

I picked up another chunk of flooring and tossed it in the dumpster. "Why are you asking so many questions?"

"I'm just curious."

She had brown eyes but despite their dark color, they were bright, shining with pleasant interest.

It was frustratingly endearing.

"Depends on the property."

I'd meant for that to be the entirety of my answer but she kept looking at me with cheerful expectancy while she threw the ball for her dog again. It was like she was drawing me into a conversation against my will.

"We've flipped a few over the years but the market has been slowing down so it's generally better for us to keep them and rent them out."

"Is it frustrating?"

"Is what frustrating?"

She shrugged. "Being a landlord. You have to deal with tenants all the time, fix broken stuff, chase them down for late payments, that sort of thing."

"Annika deals with the tenants."

"Right, because you're bad with people."

"Is that what she said?"

"Something like that." There was that cheerful smile again. Was she teasing me? "You did a great job on the house next door. It's really nice."

"Thanks."

"Sorry, I should quit bugging you. I'm sure you have a lot of work to do." She picked up the ball but kept it tucked against her chest while Max did a circle around her. "I'll see you around."

"Yeah, see you."

Flashing me another big smile, she turned and walked back next door. Her overly excited dog was as bubbly as she was. I was surprised he didn't do cartwheels around her.

It took me a second to realize I was watching her as she left. I shook my head to clear it and went back to tossing old particle board into the dumpster.

There. That was over with. We had a tenant in the two-bedroom and Annika had smoothed things over after my screw up last night. I didn't need to worry about her.

Or think about her in those shorts.

But I did think about her in those shorts. I got back to work, ripping out the rest of the kitchen floor, and no matter how hard I tried, I couldn't stop thinking about Audrey Young and her annoyingly beautiful smile.

CHAPTER 9

Audrey

THE TIMBERBEAST TAVERN looked exactly how I'd pictured it when Sandra had told me where to meet her. She'd invited me out for a drink after work and this place was everything I'd expected. Vintage logging photos, old business signs, and rusty timber equipment adorned the walls, and the guy behind the bar had a thick beard, buffalo plaid shirt, and big hairy arms, making him look more like a lumberjack than a bartender.

In fact, he looked a lot like the cartoon lumberjack on the Timberbeast sign.

I'd gone home after work to take care of Max, grab some dinner, and change clothes. I'd opted for a short-sleeved shirt and jeans with a pair of sandals. It was getting warmer during the day but still cooling down at night—typical mountain weather in June. I hoped my feet wouldn't get too cold, but I'd painted my toenails the cutest shade of pink and I wanted the chance to show them off.

Or at least enjoy them myself, since I doubted anyone in a dimly lit small-town tavern was going to notice my toes.

Sandra waved to me from her table. She'd also changed

since work, into a t-shirt and casual pants. Her silvery-gray
pixie cut was adorable as always.

"I'm glad you made it," she said as I took a seat. "I wasn't
sure if you'd want to hang out with an old lady, so thanks for
indulging me."

"You're hardly an old lady."

"I'm getting awfully close to sixty. That number sounds
significant."

"It's a milestone but that doesn't mean you're an old lady.
You've just leveled up."

"See, this is why I like you. You know how to put a positive spin on things." She turned toward the bar and raised her
voice. "Hey, Rocco. What does a girl have to do to get a drink
around here? Flash her boobs?"

I covered my mouth and laughed behind my hand. Rocco,
the lumberjack bartender, crossed his arms and raised his
bushy eyebrows as if to say, *go ahead, I'm waiting.*

Sandra laughed. "Leave it to Rocco to call my bluff. I'll go
get us drinks. What do you want?"

My first thought was a lemon drop, but I was trying to cut
down on sugar. And this didn't seem like a lemon drop sort
of place. "What are you having?"

"Vodka soda. I used to be a margarita girl, but I can't do
tequila anymore. And Rocco makes terrible margaritas."

"I heard that," Rocco grumbled.

Sandra grinned, pretending to ignore him.

"I'll have the same. But let me get them. I want to celebrate not being unemployed and having the funds to treat a
friend to a drink."

"I won't argue with that. Thanks."

I went to the bar. Rocco was busy with a customer, but
another bartender came out from the back. He was younger
than Rocco, with shaggy dark hair and no beard. He looked
vaguely familiar, but a lot of people around here did. Plus I

wasn't great with faces—or names—unless I knew someone well.

Or if it was Josiah Haven, apparently.

The bartender eyed me with a vaguely annoyed expression. "What can I get you?"

"Two vodka sodas. One with lemon, if you have it."

He didn't say anything. Just nodded.

Okay, so not the chattiest guy.

I waited while he made our drinks. When he finished, he slid them across the bar, along with the check.

"Do you want to start a tab?" he asked.

"Sure, that would be great. Thanks."

He nodded, still looking slightly irritated. Maybe he didn't like his job. I picked up the drinks and took them to our table.

"So how are things going?" Sandra asked. "Are you getting settled in?"

"Yeah, I think so. My house is great. Super cozy. I still feel like I'm flying blind at work but Lou doesn't seem to dislike me too intensely, so I have that going for me."

"He likes you fine."

"I hope so. The last thing I need is to get laid off again."

"Lou is pretty loyal. He won't get rid of you unless there's a good reason. Or if the paper finally shuts down."

"I'm afraid to ask, but do you think that's possible?"

She shrugged. "I imagine Lou will keep it open as long as he can. That paper is all he knows. His wife has been trying to get him to retire for years but he'll probably croak in his office when he's ninety. But small-town newspapers are dinosaurs. The meteor hit, the sunlight's been blocked, and it's only a matter of time before the last of them die off."

"That's kind of sad."

"It is. But time marches on."

I wondered if there was anything I could do. It wasn't like I could actually revive a dying newspaper. But there had to be ways to improve it—to make it more interesting to the readership.

The door opened and the man who appeared instantly pulled my thoughts from all things journalism.

Josiah Haven.

His surly expression seemed to suck all the air from the room. It was like the barstools had made him angry and he'd come to collect his vengeance. That should have scared me. I usually shied away from people who seemed mad all the time. But there was something about Josiah's brow furrow and perpetual scowl that glued my eyeballs to him.

And it wasn't just his face, which probably would have been quite handsome if he actually smiled. His shoulders were so broad, his chest so wide, his arms so thick. His thighs were like tree trunks in those jeans. His physical presence was so intimidating, I couldn't stop staring.

His gaze swept over the bar in a quick arc. I couldn't be sure in the dim light, but it seemed like his eyes might have narrowed when he saw me.

I was probably imagining it. But it left a tingle in my stomach just the same.

Actually, Josiah Haven did scare me. But I kind of liked it.

Sandra let out a dramatic sigh. "If only I were younger."

"You like big burly angry types?"

"Who doesn't?" She laughed. "The Haven boys are all far too young for me, but I do enjoy looking."

I watched, twisting in my chair as Josiah stalked to the bar and took a seat. Rocco came over to take his order. I might have been imagining things, but it almost looked like Rocco was watching Sandra watch Josiah—and he didn't seem too pleased about it.

"I just realized I don't know if you're married." I turned back to Sandra, hoping she didn't think I was rude for the way I'd been staring at Josiah. "You mentioned that you have kids, but I don't think you said anything about a husband."

"Divorced. He thought he could do better elsewhere. Now he's alone after being divorced twice and yes, I'm very smug about that."

"That's too bad."

"It is. I shouldn't have married him in the first place but I was young and stupid. You're smart to wait."

"Tell that to my mother."

"Mothers can be opinionated, can't they? I've tried to let my kids live their own lives but it's not always easy."

"How old are your kids?"

"My daughter is thirty-two and my son is almost twenty-nine. They're both married but neither have made me a grandma yet, unfortunately. Hard to keep my mouth shut about that one but I do try."

"Do they live close?"

"No, they both high-tailed it out of Tilikum as soon as they could. Some people love this place, myself included, but it was too small for them. They both live in the Seattle area. And I don't mind, although it would be nice if they were close enough that I could pop in and annoy them."

A hint of jealousy pricked at me. Sandra's kids had left their hometown and stayed gone.

"I bet your mom is happy to have you living so close," she said.

"Yeah." I paused. "She is."

She tilted her head. "Let me guess. It's complicated."

"A little. It could be a lot worse. I've known people with real mother horror stories. We get along most of the time. I just can't help but think she wishes I would have turned out differently."

"How so?"

"My dad was a politician, so my parents were very image conscious. The most important thing was always how we looked to everyone else in town. And when I was in school, I played into all that. I was an overachiever. You know, the girl who always got good grades and joined all the clubs. I was a cheerleader and in student government. I made them look good."

"But?" she prompted.

"They had very lofty, and very specific, expectations. They encouraged me to go to college, but then I was supposed to come back to Pinecrest to serve in city government and marry Colin Greaves, my high school boyfriend, so we could be some kind of small-town power couple or something."

"Obviously you didn't do that."

"No. I broke up with Colin and declared I was going to have my own life and it was not going to be anywhere near Pinecrest." I sighed. "And yet, here I am."

"Took a hit to your pride in coming back."

"That's an understatement. But I was laid off and I couldn't find a job. Lou was the first person to reply to one of my applications in months. I'm trying not to let that hurt my feelings but it still stings."

"It's tough out there. My son was out of work for a while, too."

"So tough. My old boss was really apologetic when she had to let me go. She kept saying she knew I'd land on my feet, so she wasn't worried about me. Little did she know."

"But you did land on your feet. Just not where you expected."

"I guess that's true. And it's probably good for me to be close to my mom for a while. My dad died a couple of years ago, so I know things have been hard for her."

"I'm sorry to hear that."

"Thanks. It was tough but also not unexpected. His health had been deteriorating for a while."

"How's your mom doing with such a big change?"

"She seems fine. Honestly, this might sound terrible, but in a way, I think she's relieved. My dad wasn't a bad guy, necessarily, but he wasn't easy to live with."

"Wait, Young. Was your dad Darryl Young?"

"Yeah. Did you know him?"

"Not personally. But wasn't he mayor of Pinecrest for years?"

"Oh yeah. Twelve years, I think."

"I remember his name being in the paper. Your mom, too, I think. Patrice?"

"That's her. And yeah, I think press coverage was his favorite thing ever."

The door opened again and I had to do a double take. Colin? What was he doing here?

"Speak of the devil."

"Who's that?" Sandra asked, looking over her shoulder.

"Colin."

"High school ex-boyfriend Colin? You're kidding."

"Nope, that's him."

"His ears must have been burning."

Our eyes met and he flashed me a wide smile as he walked to our table. He was dressed similarly to the last time I'd seen him—button-down shirt and slacks. I wondered if he always dressed like that or if he'd just come from the office.

But what was he doing here?

"Hey, Audrey. We keep running into each other." He turned to Sandra. "Hi. Colin Greaves."

"Sandra O'Neal."

"I didn't think I'd see you here, of all places," he said. "What are you doing here?"

"I was about to ask you the same thing."

He glanced around. "I come down here once in a while. Nice to have a change of scenery. I can't go anywhere in Pinecrest these days without being recognized. Sometimes I just want to have a drink in peace, not give out a bunch of free legal advice to the locals."

I gave him as friendly a smile as I could manage. "I'm sure that gets old after a while. Enjoy your drink."

He grinned, like I'd said something amusing. "I see what you're doing, but you can't get rid of me that easily, sweetheart. We still need to catch up. Sandra, you don't mind if I join you." He was already circling behind her to sit in one of the empty chairs. "How's your mom?"

I felt like I had to answer. After all, he'd known my parents for years. "It's been a tough couple of years, but she's okay."

"Glad to hear that. I've seen her around town. She's certainly stayed active in the community. I'm sure that's good for her."

"She does like to keep busy. How are your parents?"

He leaned back in his chair. "The old man is – well, he's still my old man. He made the mistake of retiring and now he just stays home and drives my mom crazy."

Colin's parents had always seemed like decent enough people, although I'd never gotten the impression that they'd liked me all that much.

I shifted in my chair, finding it impossible to get comfortable. I hoped he'd decide to get up but the silence was a few seconds away from getting awkward and he wasn't moving, so I rushed to fill it. "And how's Lorelei? Is she still working at the library?"

"No." His eyes narrowed for a second. "She's a medical assistant now, which I guess makes her happy. She works a lot of hours, anyway."

His tone was flippant, almost irritated, and I wondered if my mom's gossip about Colin and Lorelei had been true.

"Good for her."

He shrugged, as if his wife and her profession didn't particularly matter. He angled his face toward Sandra and put on a smile. "I'm sorry, Sandra, I don't mean to exclude you from the conversation. How do you know Audrey?"

The skepticism in Sandra's eyes almost made me laugh.

She was clearly not impressed with Colin's attempt to act interested in her. "We work together. And how do you know her, exactly?"

Colin met my eyes and smiled. "We're old friends from high school."

"Old friends?" Sandra asked.

"Well," Colin said, turning his palms up. "We were more than friends. In fact, we almost got married."

That took me aback and I sat up straighter. "We didn't almost get married."

"Of course we did."

"We were never engaged. I think you need to at least be engaged to be able to say you almost got married."

"Most of us thought it was a foregone conclusion that we would get married."

Sandra raised her eyebrows at me, as if to say, *what are you going to do about this guy*?

I wanted to stand up and make a scene. To tell him that I didn't care what everyone else had thought. They'd been wrong. He'd been wrong if he ever thought I'd marry him and he should go home to his wife.

But I couldn't make a scene. I squirmed in my seat. What would all the people in here think? I just wanted to get out of there.

Without thinking about what I was doing, I pushed my chair back. "I'm sorry Sandra, but I should probably get home."

"Audrey, sweetheart." Colin's tone was placating, like he was talking to an upset child. "Don't do that."

"You shouldn't call her that."

My eyes widened at the growly voice behind me. I didn't know when Josiah had gotten up from his place at the bar but I could feel his presence behind me now, dark and menacing.

Colin looked up at him. "Excuse me?"

"I don't think she likes you calling her sweetheart. So how about you go find your own table and leave these ladies alone."

"How about you mind your own business."

"I would love to but you keep bothering them and I don't like it."

My heart raced and I felt like I was glued to my chair. Sandra grinned at Josiah, as if this whole scene was making her night. I cast a quick glance over my shoulder. He towered behind me like a wall of timber, arms crossed and brow deeply furrowed, his eyes locked on Colin.

I had no idea why Josiah was standing up for me. Colin hadn't been harassing us in an obvious way. Sitting at our table and making conversation wasn't that bad.

Except it was. It was making me uncomfortable. In a moment when I'd been about to run away, Josiah Haven, a guy I barely knew, was stepping in to stop it.

Kind of restored my faith in humanity a little bit.

Colin stood, his chin lifted. His eyes flicked up and down, as if he were sizing up his opponent. He probably spent time in the gym every week, but he had to be smart enough to realize that if this got physical, he didn't stand a chance.

And something told me Josiah would have no problem getting physical.

After an agonizing moment, Colin turned to me, his face betraying nothing. "Sorry for intruding, Audrey. It's always good to see you. We'll pick up again where we left off another time."

Josiah growled.

With one last glare at Josiah, Colin turned and left.

Vaguely, I was aware that my eyes had to be as wide as saucers and my mouth was hanging open. Not a great look. But I was too stunned to do anything but slowly twist in my seat and look up at Josiah Haven.

He kept his eyes on Colin's back until the door shut behind him. His gaze moved to me but he didn't say a word. Just glared, like he was mad at me now, and went back to his spot at the bar, leaving me wondering what on earth had just happened.

CHAPTER 10

Josiah

ROCCO SMIRKED AT ME.

I hunched over my beer and locked my eyes on the bar. Why had I done that? I didn't need to get involved. The asshole had been right, it wasn't my business. *She* wasn't my business.

But every word out of that prick's mouth had been like the sound of a fork scraping over a plate. Some people hated fingernails on a chalkboard, I hated a fork scraping on a plate. I could be as clueless as the next guy, but how dumb did he have to be to miss the obvious fact that Audrey had not wanted him there?

I didn't know who he was, although I'd heard the word ex-boyfriend at some point. Not that I'd been eavesdropping on Audrey and Sandra. I'd just been stupid enough to pick a spot at the bar right behind their table. Couldn't help but overhear their conversation.

My back tightened, like someone was turning a screw and stretching my skin across my muscles. Sandra and Audrey were talking but too quietly for me to make out what they were saying.

Didn't care. She wasn't my problem.

I drained the last of my beer and gestured to Rocco for another. I needed to calm down. Wound up this tight, I'd probably punch the first guy who looked at me wrong.

While Rocco poured my beer from the tap, I cast a quick glance over my shoulder. Audrey's back was to me and Sandra had scooted closer to her. Their heads were down in quiet conversation. Sandra's eyes flicked to me and her mouth twitched in a grin.

I looked away. Rocco slid my drink across the bar and I took a long swallow. I could feel other eyes on me, could practically hear the whispers. Great. By morning, half of Tilikum would be talking about how Josiah Haven had chased off some guy who'd been bothering the new girl in town. And the other half would hear about it by lunchtime.

A light touch on my arm wrenched me from my thoughts. Before I even looked to see who it was, I had the offending wrist in my grip.

Audrey's eyes were wide and her lips parted. "Sorry. I didn't mean to startle you."

Feeling like an absolute jackass, I let go. "Sorry."

She rubbed it with her other hand. "It's okay."

"I didn't hurt you, did I?"

"Oh, no." She held up her arm as if to prove it. "I just didn't expect that. I startled you, you startled me. I guess we're even. Except we're not. What I mean is, I want to thank you for getting rid of Colin."

"Sure."

"He lives up in Pinecrest so it's kind of weirding me out that he was here. Anyway, you didn't have to stand up for me like that and you did, so I appreciate it."

I grunted, keeping my eyes on the bar.

"Okay, well, I'll quit bugging you. I probably talk too much when I'm nervous and right now I feel about as calm as a rabbit running through a field full of foxes."

That almost made me crack a smile. "Nice alliteration."

She laughed softly. "I'm going to go before I make this worse. Thanks again, Josiah. I'll see you around."

I tried not to look when she left—and failed. Sandra hesitated, like she was deciding whether or not to say something to me.

She stepped closer. "Thanks for that. She needed it."

"Just do me a favor."

"What's that?"

"Don't tell my aunt Louise about this."

Sandra chuckled. "She won't hear it from me. But we both know she'll hear about it."

I groaned. "I know."

"See ya, Josiah."

I turned back to the bar. What did I care if people talked? Gossip was Tilikum's favorite pastime. Nothing I could do about it.

But something about the whole thing kept eating at me. I met Rocco's eyes and he stepped closer.

"That asshole I chased out of here. Have you seen him in here before?"

He shrugged. "Didn't look familiar, but I don't memorize faces."

I nodded. That was fair enough. But a cocky jerk like that would stand out. Seemed like Rocco would have remembered him.

Did he come down here from Pinecrest once in a while just to have a drink in peace? Or had he been out looking for Audrey? Noticed her car in the parking lot and come in to see her?

And if so, did he go home? Or was he out there waiting for her?

I clenched my hands into fists. Damn it. She wasn't my problem.

But I got up anyway.

I twisted off the stool, my boots hitting the floor with a

thud, and was out the door in a few strides. I hadn't paid for my drinks, but I didn't worry about it. I'd square up with Rocco later.

Empty. Just a handful of parked cars, but no sign of Audrey and Sandra. Or Colin.

Audrey hadn't gone out to the parking lot alone. Sandra had been with her. I knew Sandra O'Neal well enough to know that if Colin had been waiting, everyone in the bar would have known about it. That woman could be loud when she wanted to be.

But what if he'd waited in his car somewhere out of sight, and he was following her home?

I was being paranoid. The guy had probably come down to Tilikum to get a drink by himself, like he'd said, and running into Audrey had been a coincidence. But I couldn't shake the thought that he might have followed her.

She wasn't my problem.

I let out a resigned breath and stalked to my truck. She wasn't, but apparently tonight I was making her my problem.

I drove the short distance to the rental and parked next door, on the other side of the dumpster. Her car was in her driveway and light peeked out from behind closed curtains in the widows. I got out, leaving the truck door open, and looked up and down the road. There weren't any vehicles parked on the street. Nothing suspicious that I could see.

Definitely paranoid. Colin was probably halfway to Pinecrest by now.

Headlights flashed as a car turned onto the street a few blocks away. I locked eyes on it, momentarily convinced it was the asshole. I'd been right, he'd followed her home. He was going to—

Nope. It was just Jim from down the street. He drove right by, offering a quick wave my direction.

What was wrong with me?

Audrey's front door opened and I ducked behind the dumpster.

"Let's go, Max. Time to go potty."

I peeked around the edge. Max tore out the front door and for a second, I thought he was heading straight for me. But he circled around a tree in the front yard, moving back and forth like he needed to find the perfect angle, before peeing on the trunk.

"Good boy. Let's go, back inside."

He stopped, lifting his nose in the air to sniff.

"I know, lots of smells out here. Inside, Max."

He sniffed again, then turned and followed her back into the house.

I let out another breath, relieved that she hadn't noticed me.

Who was the creeper now? I was worried about her ex-boyfriend and there I was, watching her from behind a dumpster.

I was basically stalking her.

How many times was this girl going to make me feel like an idiot?

I had a feeling this wouldn't be the last.

She wasn't supposed to be my problem, but as I got in my truck to head back to the bar and settle up with Rocco, I knew full well that I'd be over there early tomorrow. Not to get a jump on the day, but to make sure she was still okay. I couldn't shake the feeling that Colin still could show up.

Apparently Audrey Young was my problem now.

June 19th

It's not my fault.

None of it is my fault. It's her.

She shouldn't have come back. She shouldn't have come here.

Everything was fine until she reappeared. Visits home were to be expected but this is no visit.

Why does she always have to ruin everything? She's been doing this to me my entire life.

Which means it's not my fault. Nothing that happens is my fault.

It's hers.

CHAPTER 11

Audrey

A COLD, wet nose woke me up. Groaning, I turned over. Max licked the side of my face before I could shield myself with my arm.

"Max, stop."

I blinked a few times and looked at the clock. Six-thirty on the dot. I really wished Max understood weekends.

Maybe if I closed my eyes and kept very still, he'd go back to sleep and then I could too.

For a moment or two, I thought it was working. I kept my eyes shut and waited, feeling sleep beginning to overtake me again.

Until the wet nose poked my cheek.

"Okay, okay."

Reluctantly, I dragged myself out of bed. Max hopped down and waited by the door, his tail wagging.

"Why are you so chipper? Haven't you figured out Saturdays? We can sleep in."

He just looked at me, his eyes bright and excited.

I rubbed my hands up and down my face a few times, then slipped on a pair of gray joggers. I didn't bother with a bra—just kept on the tank top I'd slept in. It wasn't as if anyone else was around. Max certainly didn't count.

Still fighting to wake up, I used the bathroom, then went to the kitchen to start the coffee maker. Max waited not so patiently, his tail still doing double time.

"You have a bladder of steel, I can get coffee going first."

Once the coffee was brewing, I shuffled to the front door. He stood next to me, buzzing with energy like a coiled spring. I paused with my hand on the doorknob.

"You really need to go, don't you?"

He looked up at me, almost frantic.

"Okay." I turned the knob. "I guess when you gotta go, you gotta go."

I opened the door and he shot outside. But he didn't run straight for what had become his pee tree. He stopped a couple of feet from the door to sniff something on the ground.

Wait. What was that?

"Max, no! Leave it!"

I darted out to get hold of his collar before he could grab the dead animal in his mouth. He jumped away, like this was a very fun game, and surged in again to grab it.

"No, that's not a toy. Gross, leave it!"

He circled around the dead thing but I anticipated his move and headed him off. I grabbed his collar and dragged him away, back toward the front door.

With him safely inside, I shut the door and leaned against it, breathing hard. The last time he'd come upon a dead animal, he'd tried to eat it. I shuddered at the memory.

"Whatever that is out there, it's not a snack."

That brought up a good question. What was it and why was it right outside my door?

Max did have a strong bladder but I didn't want to push him too far and wind up with a dead animal *and* dog pee to clean up. I got his leash and took him out back. He refused to pee for what felt like an eternity, as if knowing a dead animal was on the other side of the house was far too interesting to bother with anything else—even emptying his bladder. Finally, he chose a spot and peed, and I brought him back inside.

He immediately went to the front door and wagged his tail.

"Not a chance. Whatever that is out there, you're either planning to roll in it, or eat it, or both."

He looked at me over his shoulder as if to say, *yep, you're right.*

"Nope. Not happening."

I went to the window and looked outside. It was still there —because of course it was, it was dead. When Max had gone after it, I'd been too preoccupied with keeping it out of his mouth to worry about what it was. It was small and gray with a bushy tail—probably a squirrel.

Why on earth had a squirrel died right in front of my door?

There were squirrels everywhere around here. They were up in Pinecrest too, although the Tilikum squirrels had a reputation for being particularly crafty little thieves. They got hit by cars once in a while, but this one obviously wasn't in the road. What had happened to the poor little guy?

And how was I going to get rid of it?

I felt my gag reflex threaten at the thought of disposing of it. I didn't think I could do it. But I couldn't leave it there, either.

The rumble of a truck outside caught my attention. Josiah Haven pulled into the driveway next door.

Perfect. That big flannel wearing grump could help me.

I ran to the kitchen to get Max a treat to distract him. I tossed it down the hall, he ran for it, and I went running out the front door.

Careful to give the squirrel plenty of room, I went across the lawn to the other house.

Josiah was just shutting his truck door. I didn't miss the flash of surprise that crossed his features when he saw me—eyes widening, his mouth parting.

Then I realized I wasn't wearing a bra and it was still chilly.

Great.

Oh well, too late now. Besides, after the tub incident, this wasn't so bad. And I really needed his help.

Still, I tried to casually cross my arms so I wouldn't be nipping out all over the place.

"I'm sorry to bug you, but I'm so glad you're here."

His brow furrowed.

"There's a dead squirrel outside my front door."

"What do you mean, there's a dead squirrel outside your front door?"

"I mean it's there and it's dead and I don't know what to do with it. Max will try to eat it, or roll in it, so I need to get rid of it. And I'm not at all ashamed to say that if I try to do it myself, I'll probably puke."

"But why is there a dead squirrel outside your door?"

It was clearly a rhetorical question because without waiting for a reply, he stalked past me and across the grass. He stopped in front of the squirrel and looked down at it, resting his hands on his hips. I followed.

"What the fuck?"

"Yeah, it's gross. Poor thing. What are the chances it would just keel over and die right here?"

"Almost zero." He glanced around then picked up a stick and poked at it.

I gagged a little. "What are you doing?"

He crouched down and used the stick to turn it over. "You don't have a cat, do you?"

"No, just Max. Why?"

"Cats sometimes leave dead things for their owners. Have you seen a cat around?"

"No."

He kept poking at it and I averted my eyes. I was such a wimp.

Something he'd said bothered me. "What did you mean by that?"

"By what?"

"The chances are almost zero that a squirrel would just die right there."

He stood. "It didn't just die. Something, or someone, killed it."

I winced. "What would have killed a squirrel and left it lying around?"

"I don't know. Have you ever had this happen before?"

"A dead animal on my doorstep? No, definitely not."

He grunted.

I swallowed hard to suppress the rush of heat that burst right between my legs when he made that noise. What was that about?

"The guy at the bar last night," he said. "How long ago did you break up?"

"Colin? Years ago."

"Is it normal for him to harass you?"

"No. He doesn't harass me, really, he just—"

"He was harassing you."

"Okay, he was. But no, it's not normal. Although after I moved away, I went a long time without seeing him, so I guess if he wanted to harass me, he didn't have the chance. He was a little weird at my dad's funeral, but that was two years ago, and it could have been because it was a funeral and everything."

"Do you always make excuses for people?"

I crossed my arms again, feeling suddenly defensive. "I don't make excuses for people."

"You're doing it right now."

I was *not* making excuses for Colin. "Are you asking about him because you think he might have killed a squirrel and left it on my doorstep?"

"The thought did occur to me."

"That seems – I don't know, crazy."

"Yeah, you think?"

I made myself look at the squirrel. "I can't imagine Colin doing something like that."

"How well do you actually know him?"

"True, I don't know him very well now. I don't know how well I knew him back then, either. Then again, how well can you know a guy in his late teens and early twenties? Their brains are still developing until what, twenty-five?"

"Audrey."

"Yeah?"

"You're rambling."

"Sorry." I took a deep breath. "I'm just very grossed out by the squirrel corpse and I'm starting to freak out a little bit that someone might have left it there on purpose."

"Someone being Colin."

"I guess. It still seems odd for him. What would he be trying to accomplish?"

That seemed to crack a hole in Josiah's theory.

"I don't know. If he wants you back, or at least to get in your pants, leaving a dead animal at your door isn't a smart move."

"He's married, he doesn't want me back. Or in my pants."

His eyes lifted to meet mine. "He definitely wants to get in your pants."

"No, he doesn't. I told you, he's married. He got married right after we broke up."

"Sounds healthy."

"Half the time I can't tell if you're being sarcastic. You have the ability to deadpan everything."

"Assume sarcasm."

"Okay. Then you're right, it doesn't seem healthy, but it wasn't my business anymore. And it still isn't."

"Whether or not he did that," he said, nodding toward the squirrel, "don't be surprised if he tries to get in your pants."

I hated the idea that Colin could do that to his wife but I couldn't shake the feeling that Josiah was probably right. "Well, he's out of luck there. I wouldn't even if he wasn't married, but I'd never, ever sleep with a married man."

The corner of his mouth lifted, sending a tingle down my spine.

"Who lived here last?" I asked, trying to change the subject. "Maybe they had an enemy who wanted to terrorize them with dead animals. Or they had a cat and it came back, thinking this is home."

"I'd have to ask Annika."

"I'll keep my eye out for a cat. I like that explanation the best."

He grunted again and took out his phone, then crouched to take a few pictures.

"Gross, why are you taking pictures?"

Ignoring my question, he made a phone call. "Hey. There's a dead squirrel outside one of my tenant's houses." He paused. "No, it's not roadkill. It's right outside her front door. Something slashed it open but there's not a lot of blood on the ground, so it looks like they did it elsewhere and left it here."

He paused again, listening. I wanted to ask who he was talking to, but he didn't make eye contact.

"How the hell would I know? I'm asking you because what if someone did it on purpose?" Another pause. "Okay. Bye."

"Who was that?"

"My brother, Garrett. He's a cop."

My eyebrows drew in. "I don't think this warrants calling the cops."

"I didn't *call the cops*, I called my brother to see what he thinks."

"And what does he think?"

"That it's probably just a dead animal a predator left behind and I should get rid of it for you."

"Okay, then."

His eyes flicked to my chest and he looked away.

Dang it, I kept forgetting I wasn't wearing a bra. I crossed my arms and tried to hunch a little so my nips weren't poking out so much. "Do you mind getting rid of it?"

"I'll do it."

"Wait, what are you going to do with it? Because if you fling it into the woods or even bury it, Max will definitely find it and I'll wind up with a dog covered in rotting squirrel stink."

He sighed, like I was taking up too much of his time. "I'll double bag it and put it in the dumpster."

I glanced at it again, tilting my head. "Should we have a funeral?"

"What?"

"The poor thing deserves better than to wind up in a dumpster with no one to mourn him."

Josiah looked at me like I'd just suggested we eat it for dinner. "It's a squirrel."

"I know but I feel bad. We don't have to do anything fancy. Just get it in the bag ready to go in the dumpster and let me say a few words before you toss it in."

He shook his head and went back to the other house. I thought about going inside to put on a bra but then I'd have to deal with Max. He was at the front window watching me, and as soon as I opened the door, he'd go straight for the squirrel.

At least my tank top wasn't white?

A few minutes later, Josiah came back with a pair of gloves and two plastic garbage bags. I didn't watch while he picked up the squirrel and bagged it. I didn't mean to be such a baby, but I had issues with things like blood and guts and dead stuff.

"Got it," Josiah said. "What do you want me to do now?"

I hated to throw it in the dumpster like garbage, but I hadn't been kidding when I'd said Max would find it or dig it up. I appeased my guilt by telling myself that if we put it in the dumpster, Max wouldn't be able to desecrate the body.

"Let's take it over there but don't toss it in yet."

Josiah's face was stony. At a glance, he seemed irritated with me. And I couldn't exactly blame him. A funeral service for a squirrel was pretty silly. But he was also indulging me, and I wasn't sure why.

I decided not to overthink it and get this over with so he didn't have to keep holding a bag with a dead animal in it.

We walked over to the dumpster. He held the bag just below where he'd tied it closed, keeping it slightly away from himself.

"Okay, I guess I'll start," I said.

"And you'll finish."

That made me laugh a little. "Dearly beloved, we're gathered here today – um – I don't actually know how that's supposed to go. Let me start over." I took a deep breath. "The life of a wild animal, even a little Tilikum squirrel, is hard and fraught with danger. Although this small creature met its end, we appreciate its role in nature. May it rest in a land of abundant nuts."

Josiah cracked a smile.

I about died right there. I didn't even care that he was smiling at an unintended nuts joke like a twelve-year-old boy. That smile could be my undoing.

"Go ahead and put it in its final resting place."

He tossed the bag into the dumpster.

"I guess that's that."

Josiah looked at me again, but his eyes didn't stray to my chest. His brow furrowed slightly, as if he didn't know what to make of me. "Call me if anything else weird happens."

I nodded. "I will, but I don't think I have your number."

He slipped his phone out of his pocket and lifted his eyebrows.

My heart seemed to skip and a pleasant tingle swirled low in my tummy. I gave him my number and he typed something.

"I texted you." He met my eyes again. His were a stormy blue-gray. "And seriously, anything weird happens, call me."

His concern was both sweet and electrifying. My cheeks warmed and I was more aware than ever of the cool morning breeze on my skin—and my lack of bra.

"Thanks. For everything. I really appreciate your help."

"Sure. See you later, Audrey."

"Bye."

With my heart beating a little too fast, I went back home. Max tried to rush out the door but I managed to block him with my body and get him under control. I'd let him out there to sniff around and realize the squirrel was gone later. For now, I had a very silly and very desperate need to see the contents of Josiah's text.

I went to my room and unplugged my phone from the charger, then swiped to his message.

Josiah Haven

Just his name. Not that I'd been expecting a cute message or an emoji string. That wouldn't have been like him at all. But his name on my screen didn't feel impersonal. It was like a declaration, a simple assertion of who he was and the fact that we were connected in a new way.

I suppressed the urge to text him back. I'd already thanked him and I was sure he needed to get to work. He hadn't planned on starting his day with roadkill removal. Or a squirrel funeral. Plus, he wasn't a big talker and I didn't want to annoy him.

Looking at his name on my screen, I realized something. It wasn't just that I didn't want to bother him.

I wanted Josiah Haven to like me.

CHAPTER 12

Josiah

A SQUIRREL. Somehow Audrey Young had reduced me to participating in a funeral service for roadkill.

At least none of my brothers had been around to see it. Or my dad. They'd never let me hear the end of it.

Trying to push her out of my mind, I got to work. And there was plenty of it. The drywall wasn't going to fix itself.

Of course, the more I tried to not think about Audrey, the more I thought about her. And the squirrel.

She didn't seem like the kind of girl to make enemies, not even ex-boyfriend enemies. But I couldn't shake the feeling that someone had put that dead squirrel in front of her house for a reason.

Had it been her ex? Was he still holding a grudge from their breakup? Or maybe it was retaliation for rejecting him at the bar. I'd humiliated him pretty thoroughly; he might have decided to blame her.

Not knowing the guy, I couldn't be sure.

About an hour later, my phone buzzed with a text. For a second, I wondered if it was Audrey. Had something else happened? I hurried to get my phone out of my pocket, but it wasn't her. It was my dad.

Dad: *How goes?*

Me: *Slow and steady.*

Dad: *I won't be able to get over there today. Mom's orders.*

I knew what that meant. Either his back or his knees—or both—were bothering him and Mom had insisted he take it easy.

Me: *Don't worry about it. I have it covered.*

Dad: *Thanks.*

It would mean a couple more hours of work for me, but that was fine. A little hard work had never bothered me.

———

A few hours later, I had the drywall done. It was nice to mentally check off a task. One less thing.

When I went outside, I cast a quick glance at Audrey's place. I wasn't checking up on her. Just making sure no one had left another present in her yard. I didn't see anything out of the ordinary, so I resisted the urge to go knock on her door to make sure she was okay.

She was fine. What was I worried about?

I locked up and left but instead of heading home, I decided there was someone I did need to check up on. My dad.

My parents lived just outside town, in a log home my dad and uncles had built with their own hands. It had a big front porch with a wooden welcome sign and a shop out back, where my dad spent a lot of his time. I hadn't lived there in a long time, but in some ways, it still felt like home.

I parked out front and knocked a few times but didn't wait for an answer. Just opened the door and went in. A hint of citrus was in the air and I caught a glimpse of my mom in the living room.

Although I was old enough to remember my biological mother, Marlene Haven was the only mom I'd ever had.

She'd been in my life since I was pretty young, and adopted me and my brothers when I was about ten, making the relationship official. I didn't need the paperwork to think of her as my mother, but I'd always appreciated that she and my dad had done everything they could to take two broken families and make them whole.

She sat on the couch with a lap full of knitting. She was forever knitting something—blankets, sweaters, hats, you name it. Her brown hair was up in a bun and her blue-framed glasses had slipped down her nose.

"Hi, honey." She looked up and smiled but her needles didn't stop moving. "Looking for your dad? Or something to eat?"

I hadn't come to raid their fridge, but that wasn't a bad idea. "Both?"

"There's leftover chicken alfredo but it has spaghetti squash instead of pasta. I'm trying to get your dad to cut down on carbs."

"I'm sure he loves that."

"He's convinced I'm trying to ruin his life, not extend it."

There was amusement in her voice, but I could also hear the concern. We all shared it. Dad had a few chronic health problems, common to men his age, especially those who'd spent most of their adult life as smokers. He'd quit about a dozen times over the past decade. I was pretty sure this last time was for good; it had been a while since anyone had caught him with a cigarette. But Mom was probably right to clean up his diet, whether he liked it or not.

I went to the kitchen, dished up some leftovers, and waited while they warmed in the microwave.

"So I heard there was a little incident at the Timberbeast last night."

The microwave beeped and I took out my plate. I knew exactly what she was talking about but I decided to play dumb. "What incident?"

"Something about the new girl in town and her ex-boyfriend. Ring any bells?"

I shrugged. "It wasn't a big deal."

"I'm just wondering what really happened. According to Doris Tilburn, you were on a date with the girl and he showed up claiming she was his wife. But Margie Hauser said he was her ex-boyfriend, not her husband, and you threw him out of the bar. Amy Garrett heard it was Zachary, not you, or that you almost started a fight but Zachary stopped it. I know that one's just town gossip, Zachary would escalate a situation, not calm it down."

She wasn't wrong about Zachary. He'd turned escalating situations into an art form. "You know better than to listen to what the gossips in this town say."

"Of course I do. That's why I'm asking you."

I took my plate to the living room and sat in an armchair. "Why do you care?"

"Call it motherly curiosity. You're not exactly forthcoming about what's going on in your life. Whether or not there really was drama at the Timberbeast, it makes me wonder if you were out with a girl."

"I wasn't."

"Then what happened?"

I let out a breath. "Her ex-boyfriend showed up and wouldn't leave her alone."

"And you intervened?"

"Yeah."

"Hm," she said, and I couldn't tell what it meant. "Did you throw him out?"

"I got him to leave."

"Good for you. I'm sure the girl appreciated it."

"Audrey."

The corners of her lips twitched. "So you do know her."

"She's a tenant."

"But you know her name."

"Yeah. She's a tenant."

"Tell me the name of one of your other tenants. Any one."

I went back to my food.

"See? You don't remember names unless they're important to you."

"She's not important to me. She's a pain in my ass. I had to help her hold a funeral for a dead squirrel this morning."

Dad came in through the back door right as I said *dead squirrel*. His brow furrowed. "Where was there a dead squirrel?"

"Audrey's house," Mom chimed in.

"Who's Audrey?" Dad asked.

"The girl Josiah saved from her ex-boyfriend at the Timberbeast."

His thick brows drew in closer. "Why did a girl's ex-boyfriend have a dead squirrel?"

I dropped my fork onto the plate. "That's what I'd like to know."

It was Mom's turn to look confused. "What does the dead squirrel have to do with her ex?"

"The dead squirrel was at the Timberbeast?" Dad asked. "I thought you said Audrey's house. The Timberbeast has had a squirrel problem ever since that Bailey prank all those years ago. Not usually dead ones, though."

"No, dead squirrel, her house," I said, gesturing like I was putting something in a box. "Douchey ex, Timberbeast."

"Then why are we talking about dead squirrels?" Dad asked.

"Because Josiah likes her," Mom said.

I groaned.

"The squirrel?" Dad asked.

"No, Audrey."

"Who's Audrey?"

"One of your tenants," Mom said. "Josiah intervened at the Timberbeast when her ex was harassing her. And he held a funeral for a dead squirrel at her house. Those are separate things."

"So the ex didn't have anything to do with the squirrel," Dad said.

Mom shook her head. "No."

"Maybe," I said.

"Do you think so?" Mom asked, turning back to me.

Dad crossed his arms. "Are you saying we have a tenant whose ex left a dead squirrel at her house?"

"I don't know. But I'm suspicious. He comes to the Timberbeast, I chase him off, then she winds up with a dead animal on her doorstep the next morning."

Mom winced. "That's disturbing."

"You're probably reading too much into it," Dad said. "There are more squirrels than humans around here. Sometimes they die."

"It didn't just die of old age. Something killed it."

"A coyote, maybe?" Dad asked.

"A squirrel would be a snack for a coyote," I said. "I doubt one would kill it and leave it behind without eating it."

"Maybe a bird of prey," Mom said. "It could have been dropped there."

"Right in front of her door?"

"The placement is odd," she said. "But it's not impossible. An owl could have been flying low and something scared it away before it could pick up its prey."

"She does have a dog," I said.

"There you go. I wouldn't worry too much about it. There's so much wildlife out here. It was nice of you to give it a funeral."

Dad's brow furrowed again.

"Don't ask." Hoping to change the subject, I gestured to my half-empty plate. "This is really good, Mom, thanks. Don't even miss the pasta."

Mom beamed at me. "Thank you."

Dad just grunted.

I went back to my food. Dad grunted again, then went to the fridge and took out the rest of the leftovers. I noticed Mom's smirk, but she didn't say a word.

Someone knocked on the door. I half-expected one of my brothers to walk in, but Mom set her knitting aside and got up to answer it.

"I'll get it."

"Who's here?" Dad asked.

"Louise. I invited her for tea."

Dad went back to heating his leftovers.

I thought about making a break for it out the back door. But Mom was already greeting Aunt Louise in the entry.

Too late.

Today's track suit was forest green, making an odd contrast with her bright pink lipstick. As soon as she caught sight of me, her eyes lit up and her lips pressed into a knowing smile.

"Well, well, well. If it isn't the town hero."

I did my best not to groan. "Hi, Aunt Louise."

She swept into the living room and sat on the edge of an ottoman. "I hear you were quite the gentleman last night. Tell me everything."

"There's nothing to tell."

"Don't be so modest. You certainly moved up a few spots on the bachelor hierarchy."

My brow furrowed. "What's the bachelor hierarchy? On second thought, never mind. I don't want to know."

"It's just an unofficial ranking system of eligible Tilikum men."

"I said I didn't want to know."

"We've divided it into age brackets," Louise said, ignoring me. "And points are given for things like job stability, hygiene, style, and personality."

"That's kind of messed up. You know that, right?"

She waved off my comment. "It's all in good fun. And our wagers are never for money."

"You're betting on this stuff?" I turned to my mom. "Do you know about this?"

Mom shrugged. "Aunt Louise and her friends generally leave me out of it."

"You still have too many bachelor sons to be properly unbiased," Louise said, as if this were all perfectly reasonable. "So, tell me about the new girl in town. I saw her coming out of Happy Paws the other day, but I haven't had the chance to meet her yet."

"Her name's Audrey," I said. "She has a dog."

Aunt Louise watched me with raised eyebrows. "And?"

"What?"

"Come on, Josiah, don't be stubborn."

What did she want me to say? She's frustratingly sexy? I'm annoyed with myself for thinking about her all the time?

I stood and took my plate to the kitchen. "I barely know her."

"This is the problem with men. Especially Haven men. Not the best communicators."

Mom set her tea kettle on the stove with a laugh. "Isn't that the truth."

"Hey," Dad said.

"We both know you speak half-English, half-caveman." Mom moved closer and gave him a quick kiss. "Fortunately, I speak both."

He grunted.

Mom shook her head with a soft laugh.

I took advantage of the momentary break in the conversation to head for the front door. Dad seemed fine and Mom and Aunt Louise had plenty of town gossip to keep them busy.

"Bye, honey," Mom called.

I paused at the door and held my hand up. "Bye."

Bachelor hierarchy? I shook my head as I walked out to my truck. It figured there would be a bachelor hierarchy in Tilikum.

And I was not going to ask how I compared to any of my brothers. I didn't even want to know.

Okay, I kind of wanted to know how I rated next to Zachary. But only out of curiosity, not because I was hoping to be the first to graduate off the bachelor list.

I headed home, telling myself once again that just because I was alone, it didn't mean I was lonely.

And I almost believed my own lie.

CHAPTER 13

Audrey

LOOKING at job postings had become so second-nature, I clicked to my saved search while I drank my coffee every Saturday morning without even thinking about it. Yes, I had a job—thank goodness—but working for a small-town newspaper that might be on the verge of closing wasn't exactly ideal.

Although it was growing on me.

Still, I'd come here intending to take some time to get back on my feet, and that's what I was doing. I needed to keep looking ahead to the next step.

And I wondered if I'd just found it.

The ad was for a marketing communications manager for a brewery and restaurant chain. That would be kind of cool. They wanted a background in either PR, marketing, or journalism. Heck, I had all three. And it was in Seattle, which was fine. It wasn't Pinecrest, and when it came to location, that was my main requirement.

I sipped my coffee as I filled out the online application and sent a copy of my resume. I didn't expect much. I'd applied to about a zillion jobs when I'd been unemployed. But you never knew. This could have been the opportunity I'd been waiting for.

My phone rang—my mom—so I picked it up and answered.

"Hi, Mom."

"Did I catch you at a good time?"

"Yeah, just finishing my coffee. What's up?"

"I'm just calling to check in and see how you're doing."

"That's nice of you. I'm doing fine."

"How's work? Are you getting settled in at your job?"

There was a hint of what might have been anxiety in her voice, like she was concerned about my answer. "Yeah, I am."

"That's a relief."

"Why is that a relief?" I got up and grabbed a dog treat for Max from a jar on the kitchen counter and tossed it into the living room for him.

"You just spent a good stretch of time unemployed. I'd hate for you to find this job doesn't suit you, especially since you went to all the trouble to move."

"That's true. I guess I can't say it's my ideal job, but it's going okay so far."

"Plus I'm not sure how I'd explain it if you were to leave right away."

"Explain to whom?"

"Oh, you know, the ladies here in Pinecrest. They're always interested to hear how you're doing."

I leaned against the counter, suddenly filled with suspicion. "What did you tell them about me?"

"There were just some less than flattering rumors going around. Obviously I couldn't let people talk about us that way."

"What way? What were the rumors?"

"Don't worry about it, honey."

"I'm not worried, I'd just like to know."

She took a deep breath. "Just that you'd fallen on hard times and were out of work."

"That's not a rumor, that's true. I was out of work."

"Yes, but only for a minute. I'd hardly call it falling on hard times."

"My bank account would argue with you. And why are you worried about whether people in Pinecrest know I was laid off for a while?"

"You're Audrey Young. People expect things of you. They expect things of us."

I rolled my eyes. "I don't think it's going to ruin your reputation in Pinecrest if people know I was unemployed."

"That's not what I'm saying. Besides, look at you now, associate editor of a newspaper."

"I'm not associate editor. I'm not actually sure what my job title is. Reporter, I guess? But I'm not in charge of anything."

"Let's not argue semantics. It's a very reputable job."

Why did it sound like she was trying to convince herself of that? "Mom, what are you worried about?"

"I'm not worried about anything. I just want to make sure you take full advantage of this opportunity."

"So you don't have to tell your friends that I'm unemployed again."

"That's not what I said."

I rubbed my forehead. I was starting to get a headache. "Mom."

"Being a member of this family comes with certain responsibilities. I know you didn't choose it. But do the royals choose their family? No, of course not. And yet they do what's expected of them. They do their duty."

"We are *not* the royals."

"No, but here in Pinecrest, the Young name means something. It carries a certain weight and it's up to me to see it through."

"And I'm not carrying my weight, is that what you're trying to say?"

"Of course not." Her attempt to sound mollifying made my head hurt. "You're doing a great job. I know that. But sometimes maintaining the right appearance requires a little spin. You worked in PR, you know all about that."

I wanted to tell her that you shouldn't have to do PR for your adult daughter but my conflict avoidance instincts were screaming at me to end the conversation, not argue with her. "Well, everything is fine here, so you don't need to worry."

"I'm glad to hear that. I should let you go. Duchess is giving me the look that means I'm a few minutes late with her snack."

"Okay, Mom. Talk to you later."

"Bye."

I set my phone down and glanced at Max. "I honestly don't know how to deal with her sometimes. Do you?"

His tongue fell out of the side of his mouth, as if he were currently unaware of its existence.

"I didn't think so. Let's go outside."

Max dashed to the door to wait for me while I put on my flip flops. Then I grabbed a ball and took him out front to play.

There was something oddly therapeutic about playing fetch with my dog. Maybe it was the fresh air or the warmth of the sun on my skin. Or Max's pure and unadulterated joy as he chased the ball and brought it back, over and over. Probably all of the above. Regardless, it was a great way to work off stress. Good for me, and good for my dog? Win-win.

Josiah wandered outside and stood next to his truck while he talked to someone on his phone. I tossed the ball for Max and moved toward his driveway. Not so I could get closer to him. I was just trying to maximize my ball-throwing space and make sure I didn't accidentally toss it into the street.

Likely story, Audrey.

"That's not going to happen," Josiah said.

There was a hardness to his voice that made my stomach tingle. It reminded me of the way he'd talked to Colin at the bar the other night. Trying to ignore it, and him, I picked up the ball and threw it again.

"I don't care if it's your most popular color, it's not what I ordered."

Max dropped the ball about six feet from me. He loved playing fetch but he wasn't always good at it. I walked over and tossed it for him again.

"Not my issue," Josiah said, then paused. "This ends in one of two ways. Either you make it right by tomorrow or you refund my money." Another pause. "Good. Anytime after seven."

He ended the call and slid the phone into his back pocket.

That's when I realized I was staring at him. With my mouth open.

"What?" he asked.

"Sorry. Nothing." I glanced around, looking for the ball, but Max had left it by his pee tree and was sniffing the ground. "Is everything okay?"

He hesitated, as if he were deciding whether or not to talk to me. "The flooring place messed up our order."

"That's frustrating. How did they mess it up?"

"They delivered the wrong product. Instead of engineered bamboo in antique java, I have a stack of vinyl plank in tawny oak."

"Tawny oak doesn't sound very appealing."

"It's not."

"And vinyl plank isn't even the same thing."

"Exactly."

Were we connecting? I felt like maybe we were connecting. Or maybe I was just parroting back what he'd said and we were about to run out of things to talk about.

My heart beat a couple more times and neither of us said anything.

This was about to get awkward. What should I say? I wanted him to invite me inside to look at the house but I couldn't seem to make my voice work to ask. He was so broody and intimidating.

"Do you want go in and see the house?" He jerked his thumb over his shoulder.

"Yes." My voice came out as an overly excited squeak. I cleared my throat and tried again, trying to fake as much chill as possible. "I mean, yeah, sure. Is it okay if Max comes?"

"As long as he won't pee on anything."

"No, he's good about that." Max chose that moment to pee on the tree. "And he just went. Let's go, Max."

Josiah turned and I followed him to the front door with Max trotting along beside us. We went in and our steps echoed in the empty space. A few spots in the ceiling had bare light bulbs hanging precariously and the floor was made up of large, rough-looking boards. But despite how unfinished everything appeared, it had a certain charm.

I took slow steps toward what had probably once been the kitchen. "Wow, I didn't know a house could look so naked."

Josiah chuckled, a low noise in his throat that brought the tingles back with a vengeance. Getting a laugh out of him felt like a hard-won victory.

"It doesn't look like much now," he said. "But it's going to be nice."

"Tawny oak would never do." I gestured to the floor. "Not that I really know what tawny oak is, but it doesn't sound pretty."

"It's over there." He pointed to a large stack of long rectangular boxes. "My dad was here when the delivery arrived and he didn't realize it wasn't right."

I looked at the picture on the top box while Max sniffed the perimeter. It wasn't a terrible color. Kind of a light brown.

But it didn't seem to fit this house. "I assume the color your wanted is darker?"

"Yeah, a richer brown."

"Do you pick the colors yourself?"

"Mostly. If I'm not sure, I ask my sister, but I can usually tell what will work and what won't." He pointed to the opposite corner of the house. "The kitchen will be over there. We took out a wall to open things up and create more space."

"It's hard to imagine what it would have looked like with a wall there."

"Too dark and closed off."

I wandered to where the kitchen would be. The walls looked like large portions had been repaired. "What happened here?"

"I got in a fight with the cabinets."

There wasn't a hint of humor in his tone but one corner of his mouth hooked ever so slightly.

"Who won?"

"Me."

I laughed. "I can see that. And the wall was collateral damage."

"Yeah, it's not ideal." He ran his hands over a seam. "More work but there wasn't much I could do."

"What's it going to look like when it's done?"

His eyes brightened a little. "I'm thinking walnut cabinets. Rich without being too dark. We'll do an island here and I might paint it for a pop of color. And a statement light fixture. Something bold enough to be interesting without making it look cluttered."

"Wow. That sounds amazing."

He rested his hands on his hips and glanced around. "It'll be a hell of a lot better than when we bought it."

"I bet. And a lot less naked than it is now. I'm excited to see it come together."

"Yeah." His mouth hooked in that almost smile again. "Me too."

I glanced around, looking for Max, but I didn't see him. "Max? I think he might have gone upstairs."

"That's okay, it's just as empty."

"He's like a toddler. Out of sight and quiet is dangerous."

Josiah led the way up the stairs. The walls were intact but the floor looked just as unfinished. A small landing led to a short hallway with several doors—bedrooms, a bathroom, and what was probably a closet. We found Max sniffing a few tools in one of the bedrooms.

"There you are, Max. Silly dog."

Josiah leaned against the door frame. "So, you work at the newspaper?"

My heart did a little skip at his apparent interest. "Yeah. It's – interesting. I'm still figuring things out."

"Have you always been in journalism?"

"Not exactly. It was my major in college but I've done a few different things, mostly in PR and marketing."

"Then how'd you end up at the Tribune?"

"Weird, right? The truth is, I got laid off from my last job and couldn't seem to find anything. I fully admit, I took this one more out of desperation than because it's my dream job."

"Do you like it?"

"It's not bad. Sandra is a hoot. Lou is kind of grouchy but I don't really blame him. Trying to keep a dying newspaper alive is bound to get old." I shrugged. "It's just temporary, anyway. I'm still looking for something else."

"Here in town?"

"I sure hope not." I laughed but the expressionless mask he wore threw me off. Did he not think it was funny or was that just his face? "Tilikum is fine but I never planned to move back to this area."

"Hm." He turned and headed for the stairs.

"Come on, Max."

I followed and Max came down after me. He caught the scent of something and started following it around the perimeter of the room.

Josiah glanced at him. "Your dog is kind of weird."

That made me giggle. "Oh my gosh, I know. He's a total weirdo."

"Cute, though."

"Isn't he? Come here, Max." He zipped over to me, dropped to the floor and rolled onto his back. I crouched to give him a belly rub. "You're the cutest weirdo, aren't you good dog? Yes, the goodest dog ever!"

I realized I probably looked like as big of a weirdo as my dog. But Josiah just looked at us with that almost smile that made my stomach tingle.

"Anyway." I stood and smoothed out my shirt. "He's a lot of fun. Thanks for letting us see the house. I've been curious about what it looks like inside."

He nodded and his eyes lingered on mine. For a second, it looked like his gaze flicked to my mouth. But I might have imagined it. Still, my nerve endings fired, my lips tingling, and I had an almost insatiable desire to know what it would feel like to kiss that big, bearded man.

Thankfully, he turned away before I did something awkward, like move in closer hoping he might kiss me.

Kiss me? What was I even thinking? He probably wasn't even interested in me. Not like that. Sure, he'd been nice to me, but that didn't mean anything.

I followed him outside, sternly telling my silly heart to be quiet. I didn't need to start wishing for things I'd never have. And Josiah Haven was certainly one of them.

CHAPTER 14

Audrey

THE LIGHT in the office restroom was surprisingly flattering. I washed my hands and glanced at my reflection. My skin didn't look half bad. Maybe the at-home mask that my dog had tried to lick off my face last night had helped.

My hair, on the other hand, was in a state.

I dried my hands and tried to fluff my listless locks. It had been ages since I'd had a haircut. Trips to the salon had been one of the first things to go when I was unemployed. Now the ends were dry and it had no shape.

I came out of the restroom and went back to my desk.

"Are you okay?" Sandra asked. "You look uncharacteristically melancholy."

"Do I?" I sat up straighter. "I'm fine. I was just lamenting my sad hair in the mirror."

"You have pretty hair."

I held up a strand. "I haven't had a haircut in forever."

"I can help with that."

"You do hair too?"

She smiled and picked up her phone. "No, but I know who does. You have to see Marigold Martin at Timeless Beauty. It's right up the street. She's a magician."

Before I could reply, Sandra was already talking to someone.

"Hi, it's Sandra… I'm great, how are you?… Wonderful. You don't happen to have any openings soon, do you? My friend Audrey needs you in her life." She paused for a moment. "Let me check." She lowered her phone. "She had a cancellation. Can you do noon?"

"Today?"

She nodded.

"Oh. Yes, I think so."

She put her phone back to her ear. "She'll take it. Thanks, Marigold! You, too."

"Wow, thanks, Sandra."

"Problem solved. And trust me, you'll love Marigold."

The rest of the morning ticked by with agonizing slowness. I didn't know why I was so excited. It was just a trip to the salon. But it had been so long and it felt like a win, just knowing I could afford it.

Finally, lunch hour arrived. I stood and shouldered my purse.

"It's just up the street that way," Sandra said, pointing. "You'll see it. Have fun."

"Thank you, I will. Bye, Ledger."

He lifted his eyes from his phone. "See ya."

I left the office and walked deeper into the little downtown. Summer heat was beginning to settle over Tilikum. It was probably over eighty but a light breeze kept it comfortable as I headed toward the salon. One thing I did like about this town, and my office location, so much was within walking distance.

Timeless Beauty Salon was a couple of blocks away, and like Sandra had said, easy to find. A little bell tinkled when I opened the door and walked in.

"I'll be right there," called a voice from somewhere in the back.

The décor had a distinct old-fashioned vibe, like something out of a historical novel. The wispy curtains, a velvet chaise, vintage art, and antique bronze mirrors made it elegant without being gaudy. A vase of fresh flowers stood on the front counter, spilling their fragrance into the air.

The woman who came out was taller than me, with a big smile and gorgeous long brown hair. Her outfit—a sleeveless black top with a wide collar and wide legged black pants—was sleek and professional, while still highlighting her curves.

"Hi, you must be Audrey. I'm Marigold, or you can call me Mari." She came closer and instead of shaking my hand, she stepped in for a hug. "It's so nice to meet you."

I hugged her back, instantly loving her. "It's nice to meet you, too."

"Sorry to keep you waiting. Stacey, my front desk person, is out sick today, so I'm juggling all the things."

"It's no problem."

"Come on back and we'll talk about your hair."

She led me to her station and I sat in the chair. "I haven't had a haircut in a long time. I got laid off and my hair paid the price."

"I totally understand." She put a black cape around me, then ran her fingers through my hair. "The good news is it's pretty healthy. The ends are a bit dry and you have some splitting, but that's to be expected if you haven't had a haircut in a while. What are you thinking? Just a trim or do you want more of a change?"

"I don't think I'm up for anything too dramatic. I've had enough change in my life lately."

"Do you mind if I take off a couple of inches?" She held up a lock of hair to demonstrate. "Or are you concerned with keeping the length?"

"That's fine. I wouldn't mind a little less weight."

"Yeah, as is, your hair is weighing you down." She drew

the hair around my face downward, emphasizing her point. "What if we take off about two inches to restore the health of your hair and add in some subtle layers for movement. It won't be a dramatic change but it will still be fresh and vibrant."

"That sounds perfect."

She smiled at me in the mirror. "Great. I'll wash your hair and then get started."

I moved to the washing station and after she shampooed my hair, she gave me one of the best scalp massages I'd ever had. It was so relaxing, I was surprised she didn't lull me to sleep. When she finished, she wrapped my hair in a towel and led me back to her station.

"So, Audrey, tell me about you." She gently dried my hair and set the towel aside. "I know you're new in town and you work for the Tribune. I also heard that your real name is Daisy and you're a billionaire heiress, but I'm pretty sure that one was made up."

"Daisy? Who said that?"

She shrugged as she combed out my wet hair. "I don't remember. The Tilikum gossip line gets a little crazy when a new person moves in. Most of us know to take what we hear with a very large grain of salt."

"I'm definitely not that interesting. I grew up in Pinecrest, moved away and thought I'd never come back. A layoff and a stint with unemployment cured me of that delusion. By the time I applied for the job at the Tribune, I was getting a little desperate."

"If you grew up in Pinecrest, that basically makes you a local. What's your last name again?"

"Young."

"Hmm, it rings a bell but I guess we'd both remember if we knew each other. Unless you do remember me and I'm the jerk who forgot and I'm currently making this situation extremely awkward."

"Not at all. Actually, I'm the worst at that. I forget names and faces so easily, it's embarrassing."

"I'm glad it's not just me. Can I ask how old you are?"

"I'm thirty-five."

"Thirty-four, so we're close. We must have been in high school at the same time, although I don't think I knew many kids from Pinecrest."

"I was a cheerleader, so I mostly knew the other cheerleaders or athletes from Tilikum. Even then, I've probably forgotten most of them."

"I tried out for the cheerleading squad my freshman year. Fortunately for me, I didn't make the cut. I thought my life was over at the time, but it was probably a good thing. I would have been terrible. After that, I embraced my identity as the school bookworm."

"Did you have one of those makeover moments when you got older? Because honestly, you don't look like the school bookworm."

She smiled while she kept cutting. "I was really into historical fiction, so books led me to costuming and fashion, which led me to hair and makeup. And I did get Lasik in my twenties, so that did away with the glasses. But it wasn't so much that I had a makeover moment as learning to make my bookworminess work for me."

"Did the cute boy you'd always had a crush on finally notice you?"

"No, but like my failed cheerleading career, that's for the best too."

"Are you married now?"

"No," she said on a sigh. "Always a bridesmaid. My friends say my standards are too high. I don't think my own Mr. Darcy, complete with title, estate, and impeccable manners is too much to ask for, but they think I have my head in the clouds. Or in my books. I do hair but I'm still a bookworm at heart. What about you?"

"Not married, much to my mother's disappointment."

"Don't get me started on the suffocating disappointment of a marriage and grandchildren obsessed mother."

I laughed. "Tell me about it. And I'm an only child, so all her hopes are pinned on me."

"Same," she said, meeting my eyes in the mirror. "So much pressure. I don't think that helps the situation."

"It really doesn't. My mom still hasn't forgiven me for not marrying my high school boyfriend."

"How dare you," she said with a smile.

"I know, right?"

"Do your parents still live in Pinecrest?"

"My mom does. My dad passed away a couple of years ago."

"I'm sorry to hear that."

"Thanks. What about your parents?"

"They're still here, in the house I grew up in. Honestly, I partially blame them for my unrealistic relationship expectations. They met in preschool, were friends their entire lives, started dating in high school, got married, and have been blissfully happy ever since."

"That's so sweet."

"They really are. My parents are nice, but they don't understand why I'm still single in my thirties." She paused, letting a piece of my hair drop. "Actually, I don't understand why I'm still single in my thirties, but here we are."

"I know the feeling. I've dated and even had a couple of relationships that I thought might be the one. But nothing has ever worked out. Sometimes I wonder what I'm doing wrong. I'd love to get married and have a family but it just hasn't happened yet."

"I feel the exact same way. Are we long lost sisters?"

"I think we might be."

"At least you have the advantage of being the new girl. You're interesting. And you don't have memories of every eligible bachelor in town from when they were still afraid of your girl cooties."

"Have you ever thought about moving somewhere else?"

She shrugged. "Yes, but no. I love living here and I don't particularly want to live anywhere else. Plus I have my salon and it would be hard to start over professionally. I just keep hoping some dashing gentleman will appear and sweep me off my feet with over-the-top romantic gestures and we'll build a house on the river and fill it with babies."

"That's not specific at all."

"I know, I know." She sighed again. "But it could happen."

"It absolutely could. You deserve a dashing gentleman."

"Thank you." She stopped cutting and fluffed my hair, then checked the length on either side of my face. "Speaking of gentlemen, I can't say I know everyone in Tilikum, but I do know a lot of people. If you ever want the inside scoop on someone before you take a chance on a date, let me know. There are plenty of good guys around, but definitely a few I'd need to warn you about."

I felt a nervous flutter in my belly. I hoped Josiah Haven wasn't one of the ones she'd warn me about. Not that I wanted to date him or anything. "Oh, really? Who would you suggest I avoid?"

"Let's see. Joel Decker for sure. He's been divorced twice and he's a jerk in general. His sidekick, Cory Wilcox, is just as high on the jerk scale. I probably don't even need to warn you about those two, though. If you meet them, you'll see what I mean."

"I don't think I've met either of them."

"And I'd be careful of anyone with the last name Montgomery. Some of them are perfectly decent people, but there are some bad eggs in that family."

"Good to know." I waited, wondering if she was saving the worst for last and I was about to find out that Josiah had ten kids with six different women or something. But she didn't continue. "I guess I haven't met a lot of people, now that I think about it. Mostly the people at work and Missy at Happy Paws. And Josiah Haven."

"Oh yeah? How do you know Josiah?"

"I'm renting a house from him."

"You must have met Annika Bailey, then. She's one of my best friends."

"I did. She seems super nice."

"She's fabulous. You'd love her. We've been friends since we were little, along with our other bestie, Isabelle. You'd love her, too. I'll have to see if we can all get together. Although planning things is tricky, since they have six kids between them."

"Wow, six?"

She nodded. "Annika has four and Isabelle has two. I adore their sweet little families."

I heard a hint of sadness in her voice, despite her smile. "I bet it makes the single in your thirties thing a little bit harder, though."

"Does it ever. I feel like I can't admit that to them, though. I love being the favorite auntie and I don't want them to feel like they have to hold things back from me to spare my feelings. But yes, seeing my two best friends living their dream lives does make mine seem a little lonely."

"I totally understand."

"So, Josiah Haven." She met my gaze in the mirror and lifted her eyebrows. "What do you think of him?"

I felt a tiny bit of panic rise from the pit of my stomach into my throat. What should I say? "He's – nice?"

"You think so? That's not what most people say about him."

"Actually, I'm a little bit scared of him. But also not. I don't know how to explain it. Wait, he's not the cute boy you liked who never noticed you, is he?"

"Oh, no. Definitely not. I grew up with the Havens, I knew better than to crush on Josiah."

"Why?"

"Don't get me wrong, he's a good guy. As much as I say I'd love a Mr. Darcy, I'm probably too sensitive to be with a man who's so serious all the time. I'd wind up feeling responsible for his emotional state and stressing about his moods."

"That's very insightful."

"I've done a lot of growing up, especially since I turned thirty. And I've probably read too many self-help books."

"It's weird because the grumpy thing should be totally off-putting to me. I hate confrontation and he's kind of intimidating. I'm not usually drawn to that, but –"

"But?"

I took a deep breath. "I am. He's so broody and mysterious but once in a while, he smiles and it's amazing. By the way, I haven't admitted any of this out loud, not even to my dog. Sorry for pouring my heart out to you when we just met."

"Don't worry, it comes with the job. Sometimes I'm equal parts therapist and hair stylist." She put her comb and scissors down and grabbed a round brush and hair dryer. "And don't worry about the Tilikum gossip line. I hear all the gossip—and I mean all of it—but I don't spread it. What's said in the sacred chair of hair, stays in the sacred chair of hair."

"That's good to know. Thank you."

"As far as Josiah, he's a good guy. I'd wonder why he's still single in his thirties, but that seems to be a theme with the Haven brothers. Plus, I'm pretty sure he almost wasn't."

"Oh, really?"

She nodded. "I think it was about five years ago? He'd been dating a woman named Cassandra for a couple of years. Annika thinks he was going to propose when she broke up with him and moved to California."

"Ouch." I put a hand to my chest. "That's brutal."

"Right? Although obviously it wasn't meant to be. But the poor guy hasn't dated anyone since. Not that I know of, anyway." She paused and fluffed my hair. "Regardless, he's not a guy I'd warn you away from, especially if you like broody lumberjack types."

"I never have before, but let's be honest, my track record stinks. Not that I'm thinking of dating Josiah Haven. I don't even know if he'd be interested in me."

"I'm not saying a new haircut is all it would take, but it wouldn't be the first time a fresh look helped a guy see what's right in front of him." She winked.

"Then I guess we'll see what happens."

She grinned. "Indeed we will."

Marigold blew out my hair and then added some soft waves with a curling iron. It did feel fresh and vibrant, without being too big of a change, just like she'd said. Sandra was right, she was a magician.

Before I left, we exchanged phone numbers, since we agreed we'd become instant friends. I walked back to work feeling fresh, pretty, and invigorated. A new look and a new friend? How could my day get any better?

And then I saw my car.

I'd parked on the street in front of the Tribune office and when I'd left my car there this morning, it had been in perfect condition. Okay, so I was overdue for an oil change and there was a ding on the driver's side from when some jerk had opened their door into mine a while back, and it definitely needed to be washed. But that huge dent in the front? That had not been there.

"You've got to be kidding me."

I glanced around helplessly, as if the person who'd hit my car would somehow materialize and fess up. It was obviously a hit and run. They hadn't left a note. Just backed into my car and drove off, probably hoping no one had seen anything.

But maybe Sandra had seen it. It had to have made noise, my bumper was crunched. I wouldn't have been surprised if she'd taken a picture of the guy's license plate and was already on the phone with the police to track him or her down.

I rushed into the office, my mouth open to ask Sandra if she'd nabbed the culprit, but her desk was empty. She must have gone out to lunch.

Ledger leaned back in his chair with his feet on his desk and didn't look up from his phone. "Hey."

"Ledger, did you see who hit my car?"

He glanced up. "Someone hit your car?"

"Yes, right out front."

"That sucks."

"Yeah, it sucks a lot. They backed right into me. You didn't hear anything?"

"No."

Of course not. His earbuds had probably been surgically implanted into his ear holes. Lou was in his office, but he almost never came out. Not much chance that he'd seen it happen and even less that he'd be able to help me figure out who had done it.

"Nice hair," Ledger said.

That almost made me laugh. "Thanks. I was having such a great day, too."

Josiah's insistence that I call him if anything weird happened crossed my mind. But this wasn't weird, exactly. More like frustrating and stressful. I didn't need to bother him about it. But I probably did need to file a police report or something.

With a heavy sigh, I sat at my desk and looked up the non-emergency number. I didn't relish the repair bill I'd be facing, but it could have been worse. At least my car would still run.

Hopefully.

JUNE 30TH

It was petty. I admit it.

I didn't plan it. The opportunity presented itself and I did what came naturally.

No lists, no notes, no plans. Just action. Bold, decisive action.

I hate her with every fiber of my being, but I have to admit, she's making me better. She's drawing me out of my comfort zone. Pushing me to do things I wouldn't have otherwise done.

Still, caution is warranted. I got lucky. Granted, if I'd been caught, it wouldn't have been the end of the world. I'm sorry officer, it was an accident and I freaked out. I'll make it right and it won't happen again.

People around here are forgiving. It would have blown over quickly.

But next time, I'll have to stick to my plans. Take the proper precautions before I act. We can't have Miss Perfect finding out.

Not until I'm ready.

CHAPTER 15

Josiah

I SHOULD HAVE BEEN DONE an hour ago.

I'd hired Zachary for the day to help me install the flooring and shockingly we'd finished the first floor without anything going wrong—and without killing each other. After I'd tossed him some cash, he'd gone home. Which is what I should have done.

Instead, I'd been second guessing the kitchen layout. After redoing some measurements, I'd started sketching it out on a piece of discarded cardboard. My neck ached from sitting on the floor, leaning over at an awkward angle while I worked, but it was coming together.

It had nothing to do with the fact that Audrey was late getting home. I wasn't waiting for her. Kitchens were the center of a house, the showpiece. Even in a rental, the kitchen had to be done right. I was just making sure we didn't make a mistake we'd regret later.

The sound of a car came from outside, so I got up to look. Still not checking to see if it was Audrey. Just curious to see what was going on out there.

I wasn't a great liar. Not even to myself.

It was her, and as soon as I saw her car, I headed out the

front door. Why did she have a dented bumper? Had she been in an accident?

She got out and Max dashed out behind her. He ran a circle around me, and I gave him a quick pet when he paused. But mostly I needed to know what the hell had happened to Audrey's car.

"What happened?" I sounded angrier than I'd meant to, so I stopped and cleared my throat. "Are you okay?"

"Yeah, I'm fine. Some jerk backed into my car, right in front of my office. Can you believe that?"

"Did you get plates?"

"No." She crossed her arms and that pouty thing she was doing was frustratingly sexy. "I wasn't there and the only one in the office at the time was Ledger the useless intern. Of course he didn't see anything. The guy hardly ever looks up from his phone."

I looked her up and down. Obviously she was fine. I didn't know why I had my hackles up over this. Sure, it was inconvenient, and whoever had done it was an asshole for not leaving a note. But I was furious.

"Did you call the cops?"

"I did, but there's not much they can do. It was your brother who came to take the report. Garrett Haven is your brother, right?"

"Yeah."

"I thought so. Anyway, he was really nice but he basically said without any eye witnesses, it would be pretty hard to figure out who did it and I should report it to my insurance as a hit and run."

I glanced at the damage. Front bumper, one broken headlight. It wasn't terrible but it still pissed me off. "Take it to my brother Luke. He mostly does restorations, but he'll take care of you if you tell him I sent you."

Her lips turned up in a smile. "Thanks. I'll do that."

"But why didn't you call me?"

"For this?" She gestured at the car. "It wasn't like you could do anything about it."

"I know, but I told you to call me if anything weird happened."

"This isn't weird, it's more like frustrating and super stressful."

"And also weird."

"I was parked on the street and some jerk backed into me. That's not weird, it probably happens all the time."

"In context, it's weird. What if it was your ex?"

"Colin? I seriously don't think he'd drive all the way down to Tilikum just to back into my car. What would be the point? To give me a minor inconvenience? There's not even enough damage that I needed a ride home."

That was true, and I couldn't put together why her ex-boyfriend would do something like that. Or the dead squirrel. They were probably unrelated, just a couple of unlucky incidents, not the work of someone trying to harass her.

Still, there was something about it all that I didn't like.

"I don't know, but I mean it, call me next time."

"Can we at least pretend there won't be a next time?"

"You're too optimistic. There's always a next time."

She put her hands on her hips. "Maybe you're too pessimistic."

"I'm not pessimistic, I'm realistic. There's a difference."

She opened her mouth, as if to reply, but stopped and looked around. "Where's Max? Max!"

I didn't see him either. He'd been sniffing around her front yard a minute ago.

"Max, come!" Her forehead creased with worry. "Max!"

"He's probably just around back."

"Yeah, hopefully." She went around the house at a jog, still calling for him.

I followed. No dog.

"Max, come!" She met my eyes. "Where could he have gone? He usually stays close."

It was probably my paranoia, but my first thought was that someone must have taken him. But I didn't remember a car driving by, let alone someone stopping. Plus, we would have seen a person getting out to grab her dog, or even just opening the door to let him in their car.

"Do you think he went across the road in front? Would you have noticed that?"

She paused for a second before answering. "I don't think he did. I would have seen that out of the corner of my eye and called him back."

"Then he probably went up there." I gestured to the steep slope, dotted with pine trees, that rose behind the two houses.

"He must have. I bet he caught the scent of some animal and followed it." She cupped her hands around her mouth. "Max! Max, come!"

We waited. No dog.

"I need to go find him." She started up the hill. "He's not the smartest. He'll totally get lost."

"I'll check the remodel in case I left the door open, then I'll catch up."

"Okay," she said over her shoulder.

I hesitated for a beat. She was in a skirt and heels. Not ideal for hiking. But she was charging up the hill like her shoes didn't matter, so I let her go.

I jogged around to the front of the remodel, but the door was shut. Just in case he'd gone in and the wind had closed it behind him, I gave the place a quick once over, calling for him as I went from room to room. Definitely no dog.

Back outside, I checked the front yard and scanned the street in case he was on his way back. Didn't see him. I called a few times, but still nothing.

Instead of going up the slope directly behind Audrey, I veered to the left so we could cover more ground. I powered up the hill, calling for Max, trying to keep an eye out in all directions.

Damn dog.

"Max!"

I had no idea if he'd come to anyone who called his name or just Audrey. She wasn't far from where I was. I could hear her in the distance and used the sound of her voice to keep track of her while I headed steadily uphill.

"Max!"

Pine needles crunched under my feet and squirrels raced up tree trunks as I ran by. He'd probably chased one of them. Those things were smart. I wouldn't put it past them to lead him into the woods just to be tiny assholes.

Sweat beaded on my forehead and I was breathing hard by the time I reached the top. Still no dog. I paused for a moment to catch my breath, listening for Audrey in the distance. Her voice carried between the pines, and even from here, I could hear her rising panic.

Where was that dog?

If he got himself truly lost, or hurt, or worse, it was going to break Audrey's heart.

Growling in frustration, I kept going. I was not stopping until I found her stupid adorable dog.

The pines grew thicker, the spaces between them littered with debris. I had to duck beneath the branches and sharp twigs reached out to snag my shirt and scratch my skin. I pushed through, still calling for Max.

A rustling sound up ahead caught my attention. I crested the next rise and there he was.

Max's back was to me, his tail in the air, as he dug furiously. Dirt sprayed behind him, making a little mound. He was filthy.

"Max, what are you doing?"

He paused and looked back at the sound of my voice, his tongue lolling out of his mouth. Frustrated as I was at his disappearance—I was sweaty as hell—I almost laughed. He really was cute, in a derpy sort of way.

"Come on, Max. Let's go find your mommy."

He went back to digging, tossing more dirt behind him. Maybe I hadn't said the right thing. Dogs knew commands, not actual English.

"Max, come."

Instead of obeying, he dropped to the ground at a weird angle, neck first, and rubbed himself across something in the dirt.

"Audrey!" I called, hoping my voice would carry far enough that she could hear me. "I found him!"

He twisted and writhed until he was nothing but a ball of fur, undulating on the ground.

"Audrey! This way!"

Since Max wasn't interested in listening to me, I figured I should at least get ahold of his collar so he couldn't run off. I started toward him. "Okay, Max. You're dirty enough. Let's go."

In the distance, I heard Audrey's reply. "I'm coming!"

"Here!" I yelled so she'd know the way.

I approached Max cautiously, not moving too fast. I didn't want him to think I was there for a game of chase. He rubbed himself in the hole he'd dug again, then rolled onto his back with all four legs in the air, twisting back and forth like he was scratching his spine on the ground.

"You're ridiculous, you know that?"

When I got a few steps closer, I stopped in my tracks and wrinkled my nose. Something smelled terrible. Where was that coming from?

I looked at Max. Was he covered in dirt or was that something else?

Wincing at the smell, I got closer. He was caked in something brown, some of which was certainly dirt. But dirt didn't stink like that.

"Fucking hell, dog. Are you serious?"

Audrey rushed through the trees, still in her heels. She had pine needles in her hair and something had ripped the sleeve of her shirt.

"Oh my god, you found him."

I saw the second the smell hit her. She stopped as if she'd run into a solid wall.

"Whoa. What is that? Oh, Max. Oh, no."

"I don't know what he found but it's probably the worst thing I've ever smelled in my life."

Her eyes started to water and she backed up a step. "What is that? No, I don't even want to know. Max, how could you?"

He hopped to his feet and shook. Dirt and – whatever else – went flying in all directions, sending the horrible scent with it.

"Ugh." Audrey plugged her nose with her thumb and the side of her forefinger, using the rest of her hand to shield her mouth. "That's so gross I might puke."

"Don't puke. He'd probably roll in that too."

"Good point. I'll have to hose him down at the house. Is there a hose? I don't have one, so I really hope there's one in the back."

"Yeah, there's a hose. If not, I'll call one of my brothers to bring one over."

"Okay, Max. Let's go home."

He happily obeyed, falling in step beside her as she started picking her way through the pine needles.

Limping. In her heels.

I was at the top of a big-ass hill with a dog covered in either shit or the rotting remains of a dead animal, or both, with a woman limping in her heels who was absolutely not my problem.

Except she was. She really, really was.

Damn it.

"Audrey, wait." I moved in front of her, so I was on the downhill side, and bent my knees. "Hop on."

"You don't have to carry me."

"Just get on."

She put her hands on my shoulders and jumped up. I caught her legs around my waist and hitched her up so she was secure on my back. Then I started down the hill.

Fortunately, Max the stinking dog trotted along with us. Maybe it was my imagination, but he seemed awfully proud of himself.

I was a lot more aware of the instability of the hillside on the way down. Rocks rolled downhill and the bed of pine needles felt slick under my boots. The last thing I needed was to drop her or fall on my ass.

We made it to the bottom in one piece with the dog still following. He ran to a tree in her backyard and peed on it, which seemed both natural and an oddly appropriate end to our dog rescue mission. He had no idea the problem was only half solved. Now we had to figure out how to get him clean.

I set Audrey down.

"Give me two seconds," she said. "I don't want to do this in work clothes."

"He better not run off again."

"I know. But I'm not letting him in the house like that."

"Just hurry."

She ran around the front while I eyed her dog. He seemed content to sniff the grass. How he could smell anything but himself was beyond me.

A few minutes later, she came out the back door, dressed in a t-shirt and cutoffs. Her feet were bare and she had a bottle of dog shampoo and a big blue towel.

The house did have a hose. Max wanted to attack the water and since neither one of us wanted to grab and hold onto him, we did our best. At least he seemed to be enjoying the process. Once he was somewhat clean, Audrey took off his collar. It was caked with shit or dead animal or whatever it was. She tossed it aside.

"I have an extra in the house. I don't think that one's salvageable."

"Agreed. Toss it."

After a good rinse, it was time to soap him up. That part he loved. Not surprising, considering it was like having two people pet him all over simultaneously.

"You better be careful," I said. "He's going to do that again just to get a bath."

"He does love his baths, although usually they're not with freezing hose water."

"I'm just glad he's not running away again."

"Oh my gosh, same." She leaned in and sniffed her dog. "I can't tell if the smell is gone. I think it's just in my nose now, but I'm not sure."

I got close and inhaled deeply. "I don't smell it anymore."

"Are you sure?"

"Yeah, I think we got it all."

She breathed out a long sigh. "Thank goodness. What a nightmare. Sorry about all that."

My clothes were wet, I was tired, and I probably smelled like dog. But oddly enough, I wasn't annoyed.

"It's fine. I'm just glad we found him."

"Me too."

She rubbed him down with the towel and he shook again. We both did another sniff test, just to be sure. All I could smell was the lavender from the dog shampoo.

"Okay, Max, that's enough adventures for one day." She opened her sliding door and shooed him inside. "In you go."

He ran in and she shut the door most of the way, leaving just a crack. With her hand on the handle, she met my eyes. "Thank you."

"You're welcome."

For a second, she didn't move. Then she stepped closer and hugged me.

Without thinking, I wrapped my arms around her and drew her in tight.

Fuck me, that felt good. She was soft and warm and her hair smelled good. Her body pressed against mine, stirring up all kinds of things I wasn't prepared for.

She moved back and, almost reluctantly, I let go.

"Goodnight, Josiah."

"Night."

And with that, she disappeared inside her house, leaving me with an ache in my chest.

CHAPTER 16

Audrey

MY MORNING COULD NOT HAVE BEEN MORE chaotic.

I slept through my alarm and for once in his life, Max didn't wake me up. By the time I rolled over and realized what had happened, I had all of twenty minutes to get ready for work.

The coffee machine wouldn't turn on, despite being plugged in, and I didn't have time to figure out why. I took Max outside to do his business, then came in and discovered I was out of dry shampoo. No time for a shower and no way to make my hair presentable meant it was a do-my-best bun sort of hair day.

My shirt had a stain I hadn't noticed and my favorite pair of slacks were dirty, so it took a couple of harried tries to put together an outfit. Finally, I succeeded. No caffeine or breakfast, my clothes may or may not have matched, and I hoped it wouldn't be obvious my hair needed washing. But I was ready to head out the door with two minutes to spare.

"Let's go, Max. Time to go to work."

The sound of my phone ringing startled me and I almost dropped my purse. I thought about ignoring it, but it was odd to get a phone call this early in the morning. That meant it might be important.

It was the number for Happy Paws.

"Hello? This is Audrey."

"Hi, Audrey, this is Missy at Happy Paws." Her voice sounded hoarse and she paused to cough. "Sorry. I woke up sick and I can't be there today. I tried to find someone to fill in at doggie daycare for me, but we all seem to have gotten the same thing. I'm sorry, I know this is really last minute."

I let out a breath and my shoulders slumped. It was that kind of morning. "That's okay, Missy. I hope you feel better."

"Thanks. Hopefully we'll have coverage for tomorrow, but I'll keep you posted."

"Sounds good, I appreciate that. Get some rest."

"I will. Thanks, Audrey."

I ended the call and looked down at Max. "Well, now what are we going to do?"

Technically, he could stay home by himself. He'd mostly sleep all day. I'd just need to take him for a good, long walk when I got home to ensure he got enough exercise, otherwise he'd be crazy by bedtime. But he'd do better if someone could at least come check on him and take him out to pee once or twice.

"I don't know if I'll be able to make it home during the day today, bud." I had an assignment that was going to have me out of the office for a large part of the day. I couldn't be sure I'd have time to come home and let him out.

I didn't really have friends I could ask for this kind of favor. Sandra had to work, too, although she might be willing to drive over here to let him out on her lunch break. I didn't trust Ledger. He'd probably be so busy scrolling on his phone, Max would run up the hill again and recreate his world's stinkiest dog stunt from the other day. And I definitely didn't know Marigold well enough, although I had a feeling she was the type of person who'd help without hesitation. Still, asking her would feel weird.

I glanced out the window. Josiah's truck was already in the driveway next door. He always got to work early over there.

Not that I was watching for him every morning.

Actually, yes I was.

I kind of hated to ask, especially after he'd done so much to help me the other day when Max had gone missing. No one should have been subjected to that smell, and he'd stuck it out, even helping me give Max a hose bath in the backyard. Not to mention the way he'd carried me down the hill.

Oh my swoon.

But was it really that much to ask? He'd be right next door all day. He could pop by and let Max out to go potty once or twice and that would be plenty.

A swirl of butterflies took flight at the thought of going over there. Why was I being so silly? It was just Josiah. We were basically friends now.

Except I knew exactly what it was. That hug.

I'd fallen asleep to the memory of Josiah's thick arms around me every night since I'd hugged him. I couldn't get the way he'd felt out of my head. He'd smelled good too, like pine and fresh air and man. Big, burly, grumpy man.

Apparently I liked that smell because I'd been craving it ever since.

"Okay, Audrey. Time to toughen up. Yes, he's kind of intimidating and he gives you squishy tummy feelings, but that doesn't mean you can't talk to him without turning red."

Max just looked up at me, wagging his tail.

"Right. Let's do this. Except not you. You stay here." I pointed to his bed in front of the couch. "Go lie down."

His ears drooped a little but he obeyed.

"You'll be fine. I'll be right back."

I went next door and found the garage door open. Josiah

was inside, cutting long boards on a big saw.

Instead of his usual flannel, he wore a t-shirt that showed off the size of his arms. His jeans had a big spot of sawdust on the back pockets and no, I did not notice that because I was looking at his butt.

Fine, yes I was.

I waited until he stopped cutting and the whir of the saw died down.

"Hey."

He looked over his shoulder and the way he furrowed his brow made my stomach flip. Why was that so sexy? I didn't understand it.

Then his features softened and the corner of his mouth twitched. On anyone else, it wouldn't have been a smile. But on Josiah Haven, it was as bright as the sun.

He put the board down and turned to face me. "Hey. What's up?"

Breathe, Audrey. He's not that good-looking.

Liar.

"I hate to do this, but I need a favor."

He raised his eyebrows, which I'd figured out was Josiah speak for *keep talking*.

"Missy at Happy Paws is sick and I guess everyone at Happy Paws is also sick, so there's no one to do doggie daycare today. Max can be at home alone for a while, but it would be best if someone could let him out once or twice to go potty. I don't think I'll be able to make it back today, although I could try, but if—"

"Sure."

His single word of assent stopped my babbling. "Oh. Awesome. Thank you. That's a huge help."

He nodded. "Not a problem."

What I wouldn't give for another hug—to have those thick arms around me again. But I couldn't think of a reason to move closer without making it weird.

"He should be fine until around lunchtime. I'll put the leash by the door so you don't have to worry about him running off again."

He nodded again.

"Thank you. I think I said that already but I really appreciate it. It's been such a hectic morning and Missy's call was the icing on the cake, you know? And I'm new in town and I don't know that many people."

"Audrey."

"Yeah?"

"Go to work. I've got it."

My cheeks flushed. I'd almost made it through this without blushing, but then I had to go and run my mouth like a nerd. "Sorry. Yeah, work. Thanks. I'll see you tonight."

There was that almost smile again and his eyes glimmered with amusement.

Clamping my mouth shut so I wouldn't keep talking, I turned around and went back to my house.

I was such a dork. The mayor of dorksville.

After making sure Max had plenty of water and setting his leash out where Josiah could find it, I left for work. I felt a pang of guilt driving away with Max looking longingly out the window, no doubt wondering why he didn't get to go too. But he'd be fine. I knew from experience he'd get bored in about a minute, go curl up on his bed—or maybe mine—and take a nap. By the time he woke up, Josiah would be coming over to take him outside.

He'd be fine.

My morning flew by. I had to finish two articles, so that kept me busy. Ledger had finished a project for once, so I gave his work a good proofread before passing it on to Sandra. Lou was characteristically gruff, although he did give me a nod and a mumbled good job when he saw the half-completed layout for the next edition.

That was practically a gold star, coming from him.

I had just enough time to grab a quick lunch before I was off to visit the Annual Quilting Show to take pictures. It wasn't exactly hard-hitting journalism, but I didn't mind. I liked the quaintness and slow pace of Tilikum life. Maybe there weren't huge corporate scandals, or crime rings, or massive social unrest, but that was part of the appeal. Reporting on the longest running quilting show in the central Cascades was just so dang wholesome. I liked it.

Afterward, I began my race against the deadline. Newspaper writing was fast and I was still adjusting to the need to pump out an article in barely an afternoon. There were also photos to process and a headline to brainstorm, but at least it kept me busy.

Around three, I checked my messages on my phone. My stomach flipped when I saw a text from Josiah. I wasn't sure if it was a quick burst of worry that something was wrong or simply seeing that he'd messaged me.

Probably both.

It was a photo of Max, curled up on a blanket in the empty remodel. It simply said, *hanging out.*

I sighed. Josiah had brought Max over to hang out with him. He'd even found him a blanket. How adorable was that?

"What's going on over there that has you sighing like that?" Sandra asked.

"It's just a picture of Max. Doggie daycare is closed today, so I asked Josiah if he could check on Max a couple of times. I guess he decided to bring him next door." I held up my phone so she could see.

"What a cutie. So, Josiah. Is there something you need to tell me, Miss Audrey?"

"About Josiah? No. No, definitely not. Not at all."

Ledger snorted.

I glared at him. "What was that about?"

He didn't look up from his phone. "You obviously like him."

"I didn't think you were listening."

He just shrugged.

Sandra raised her eyebrows.

"There's really nothing to tell. I guess we're friends but that's it."

"Okay," she said, going back to her work.

I could tell she didn't believe me.

I wasn't sure that I believed me.

But I wasn't lying. There wasn't anything going on between us. Sure, I thought about him all the time and daydreamed about hugging him—and other things—but nothing was actually happening.

Maybe the point was, deep down, I wanted something to happen. I really liked Josiah Haven and not just because he'd helped me clean off a gross dog, or carried me down the hill on his back, or because he was willing to hang out with Max today. I liked him because he was gruff and stoic and sexy and surprisingly sweet under that surly lumberjack exterior.

I'd half admitted it to Marigold already. Maybe it was time I started fully admitting it to myself.

I decided to take a quick walk to get my head back on straight before I finished up for the day. After a little fresh air and an afternoon coffee from the Steaming Mug down the street, I was able to refocus on work. I finished up shortly after five and it was time to head home.

My heart raced on the drive back to my house. I didn't know why. Was it the anticipation of seeing Josiah that had me all jumpy? If that was the case, this crush I'd developed was escalating out of control way too quickly. I needed to get ahold of myself or I was going to be a babbling idiot.

Calm down, Audrey. You've got this.

When I got home, I parked in my driveway. Josiah's garage door was closed and I wasn't sure if he still had Max next door or if he'd brought him home. I decided to check my house first.

I opened the door and as soon as I peeked inside, I almost swooned. Like a legitimate old-school Hollywood starlet swoon that would have had me on the floor.

Josiah was sound asleep on the couch with Max spread out over his legs. Max cracked one eye open but apparently my arrival wasn't exciting enough to entice him to move from his spot snuggled up with Josiah. I couldn't say I blamed him.

It was so adorable, I quickly fished my phone out of my purse and took a few pictures. Then I set my things down, right as Josiah started to stir.

He blinked and rubbed his eyes, like he couldn't quite remember where he was. He grunted and when he spoke, his voice was husky with sleep. "Oops."

"Sorry if I woke you."

Max grudgingly rolled off him and jumped onto the floor when Josiah moved his legs. Then he seemed to realize mama was home. His tail wagged and he darted around me, sniffing with excitement.

"Hi, Max. Nice to see you, too." I crouched down to give him a good pet.

Josiah grunted again as he sat up, then stretched. "Sorry, didn't mean to fall asleep."

I stood. "That's okay. Max is pretty snuggly. It's easy to do."

He got up and straightened his t-shirt. "He was fine today. Didn't roll in anything."

"That's good. Thanks again for your help."

"No problem."

He moved closer but I was still in front of the door. I stepped right but he shifted in the same direction. Then we both moved to the other side.

"Sorry," I said. "I'm in your way."

He stopped and met my eyes, obviously waiting for me to move.

But I didn't. I got caught in those stormy blue-grays, my heart beating a wish I could scarcely dare to think.

Kiss me, Josiah.

His eyes lowered to my mouth. My pulse raced and excitement swirled in my stomach. Taking the chance, I stepped closer and put my hand on his chest. I let my eyelids close halfway and parted my lips, ready for whatever he wanted to give me.

He cleared his throat and stepped past me. "I gotta go."

I sucked in a quick breath, shock turning my tingly excitement into a roil of nausea. He shut the door behind him, and just like that, he was gone.

For a long moment, I couldn't move. I stood rooted to the spot, as cold as an ice sculpture, my mouth hanging open.

I hadn't faced such a clear and harsh rejection in a long time.

If ever.

Feeling like I'd just been punched, I put a hand to my stomach. "Ouch. That was brutal."

Max wagged his tail. He had no idea what had just happened.

My shoulders slumped. He probably needed to go outside. I decided to take him out back. I didn't want to risk seeing Josiah, even just in his truck on his way out. I was too humiliated.

So much for my crush. That had been misplaced. Badly.

Wallowing in my misery, I took Max outside to go potty, then came in and dug through the kitchen for something unhealthy. Fortunately, I had a container of triple chocolate ice cream in the freezer. I needed to remember to always keep triple chocolate ice cream on hand. One never knew when they'd need to binge on fat and sugar after a depressing rejection.

Those always seemed to come out of nowhere.

CHAPTER 17

Josiah

I SLAMMED the door of my truck, shoved in the key, and started the engine. Music blasted through the speakers and I had to fumble for a few seconds to turn the stupid thing off. Before I could second guess myself, I backed out of the driveway and took off.

My hands gripped the steering wheel and my jaw was tight. I was so pissed at myself and the worst part was, I wasn't sure why.

Was I mad because I'd almost kissed her when I knew I shouldn't? Or because I'd almost kissed her and I should have?

Probably both.

Fuck.

The look of shock on her face when I'd mumbled that I had to go was burned into my memory. I'd only seen it for a second before I'd walked out the door, but that had been enough. I'd hurt her feelings. And I felt like shit about it.

But she didn't understand. She was too nice. Nice girls didn't belong with assholes like me. She was blue sky and sunshine, plucky optimism and happiness. I was a stoic cloud of pessimism and surliness. It would never work.

I drove home and went inside. The weather had been warm and the house was stuffy, so I threw open some windows. The daylight and fresh air mocked me, highlighting the fact that my house was dusty and unfinished. The lack of baseboards and trim had never bothered me before. Why the hell did I care now?

Maybe I needed a dog.

No, a dog would be a hassle. I didn't want to be responsible for something, or someone, else. I liked being able to do what I wanted, when I wanted. Keep my own schedule. I didn't want to answer to anyone, even just a dog who needed to go outside.

I'd stayed single for a reason.

Which meant I'd done the right thing by not kissing Audrey.

That was it. I could stop thinking about her.

I spent the next hour grilling a steak, eating dinner, drinking a beer, and relentlessly pushing all thoughts of Audrey out of my mind. I ate on the couch in front of the TV because I could. I stuck my feet on the coffee table because I could. I left the dirty dishes in the sink because I could. There was no one around to complain. No one around to tell me how to do things.

Just the way I liked it.

No dogs, no women, no hassles. I'd lived this way for a long time and I was going to keep living this way. No matter how tempting Audrey was.

She wasn't going to stay anyway. She'd said so. Tilikum was temporary.

I didn't want to admit—couldn't admit—how much of a problem that was for me. Because if I thought too hard about why that bothered me, I'd have to face things I didn't want to think about. Memories that ate at me from the deep recesses of my mind.

I got up and paced around the house. Maybe I'd run to the

hardware store and get started on the baseboards. It was about time I finished this place. I could work on it in the evenings. That was what I'd always meant to do anyway.

But Tilikum Hardware closed early. I didn't have time.

I plopped back on the couch, trying to resist the restlessness that seemed to have overtaken me. I turned on the TV again, but that didn't hold my interest either.

Finally, I gave up. I needed to get out of the house. I put my shoes back on, grabbed my keys, and headed to the Timberbeast. I'd get a drink and hopefully shake this off.

The parking lot was almost full. I found a spot near the road and when I went inside, I realized why. Karaoke night.

I almost turned around and left. But then I'd be back to where I started. Maybe the crowd and noise would be a good distraction.

The place was packed. Several of my brothers were inside —Theo, Zachary, and Luke. Not surprising. There was probably at least one Haven brother at the Timberbeast on any given evening.

Hayden was helping Rocco tend bar. For reasons that were unfathomable to me, karaoke night always drew a crowd, but with the two of them working, I didn't have to wait long.

"What can I get you?" Hayden asked.

"Just a beer."

He grabbed a glass and started to fill it from the tap. "I heard your girl's car got damaged the other day. Hit and run."

"She's not my girl. And how'd you know about that?"

He raised his eyebrows. "This is Tilikum."

"Good point."

"Any idea who did it?"

"No. Probably some tourist." I wasn't sure if I believed that, although it was the likeliest explanation.

He slid my beer across the bar. "She's not your girl, huh? There's nothing going on with you two?"

"Why?" I couldn't keep the irritation out of my voice. "Are you interested in her?"

A subtle smile curled his lips. "No."

I wasn't sure if I believed that either. "Then why the fuck do you care?"

He shrugged. "You hear a lot of talk doing this job. Sometimes I like to figure out what's true and what's the gossip line gone wild."

I grunted a reply and took my beer. I'd come here to get my mind off Audrey, not chat about her with the bartender.

I hated being the object of town gossip.

There weren't any open tables, so I decided to join my brothers. Thankfully they'd found a spot near the back, farther away from the speakers. I grabbed an empty chair and dragged it over to where they were sitting.

"You guys plan this or did you all just wind up here?" I asked as I took my seat.

"It's karaoke night," Zachary said, as if that explained everything.

"I was bored," Theo said. He was dressed in a Tilikum High School t-shirt and basketball shorts. "What about you?"

"Same. How's your team looking for next year?" I asked. Theo was Tilikum's high school football coach.

"We were just talking about that," Luke said. "I was about to ask if we're actually going to win a game."

"Hey, we won a game last season. Three, in fact."

"Let me guess," Luke said. "It was a building year."

"It *was* a building year," Theo said. "We had a young team."

Luke laughed and patted his shoulder. "I know, man. I'm just giving you shit."

Theo rolled his eyes. "I'll know more after camp later this summer. But I believe in those kids. They're gonna have a good year."

"Thanks, coach." Zachary smirked at him. "We believe in you too."

"Shut your hole, Z."

Zachary just chuckled.

"How's Audrey doing?" Luke turned to me. "Sucks what happened to her car."

"Who's Audrey?" Zachary asked. "And what happened to her car?"

"You know," Theo said. "The new girl."

"Hit and run," Luke said. "Damage to the front bumper, broken headlight. I took care of her."

"There's a new girl in town?" Zachary looked around the bar, as if she must be there. "How did I not know about this?"

"She's in one of Josiah's rentals." Luke met my gaze, his eyes full of challenge. "Cute, too. Dark hair, kinda curvy."

"Stay away from her." My voice was hard.

"Which rental?" Zachary asked.

I pointed at him. "You especially stay away from her."

"I actually agree with Josiah on that one," Luke said.

Theo raised his hand. "Me too."

"What?" Zachary put a hand to his chest. "I'm hurt. If she's new in town, she could use a nice guy to show her around."

"You?" I asked. "Since when are you a nice guy?"

He grinned. "I'm not. But when Luke is done showing her the town, I'll show her something better."

"If you send her a dick pic, I'll kick your ass," I said.

"What am I, a child?" Zachary shook his head. "Dick pic. I'm insulted."

"Yeah, you're a real gentleman, Z," Theo said.

"I didn't say I was a gentleman."

"All of you." I pointed to each of them. "Stay away from her."

Theo's brow furrowed. "What did I do?"

I let out a frustrated breath. Apparently going out for a beer had been a bad idea.

"No one's trying anything with her," Luke said. "It's just fun to mess with you."

"I didn't say I wouldn't try anything with her," Zachary said. "Why is the new girl off limits?"

I leveled him with a glare.

"Oh, she's your girl."

"She's not my girl."

"So she's your girl but she doesn't know it yet." Zachary grinned again. "Nice."

"She's. Not. My. Girl."

"Apparently he doesn't know it yet," Theo said.

"She's—"

"Why not?" Luke asked before I could finish. "I'm not saying you should marry her or something, but she obviously likes you for some reason. Why not take her out?"

"She likes *him*?" Zachary's voice was full of skepticism. "Then yeah, dude, you should definitely take her out. You don't know when you'll get a chance like that again."

"He does have a point," Theo said.

"Why are we talking about this?" I asked. "You guys are as bad as Aunt Louise."

"Hey." Zachary held up a hand. "Aunt Louise is a Tilikum treasure. Don't you talk bad about her."

"You just like her because she bakes you cookies and never tries to set you up with random girls," Theo said.

"Aunt Louise tries to set you up with random girls?"

"Yeah, all the time," Theo said.

Zachary turned to Luke. "You too?"

"Yeah, but it's never a good thing," Luke said. "Trust me."

"Why doesn't she try to set me up with random girls? I feel so left out."

"Don't," I said. "Luke's right, it's never good."

"She wore me down a few months ago and I agreed to a

date with someone she claimed was perfect for me," Theo said. "Turns out the girl was twenty and two years ago she was one of my students. Aunt Louise neglected to mention that. When I called her out, she claimed she thought the girl was older because she seemed mature. The whole thing was mortifying."

Zachary winced. "Yeah, that's a little much, even for me."

"The last Aunt Louise date I went on turned out to be Jill," Luke said.

"Your crazy ex-girlfriend, Jill?" Theo asked. "Damn."

"Yeah. That went over well. Never again."

"Okay, maybe I am lucky to only get cookies from Aunt Louise," Zachary said. "The last thing I need is for someone to set me up with an ex-girlfriend."

I sipped my beer while the conversation turned from Aunt Louise's lack of matchmaking skills to Luke's latest car restoration punctuated by commentary on the karaoke song choices. At least they weren't talking about Audrey anymore.

Not that it kept her out of my head. I couldn't stop thinking about that moment when I'd almost kissed her. She'd been right there, giving me every indication she wanted me to. Hand on my chest, chin lifted, lips parted. And I'd have been lying if I'd said I didn't want it too.

So why hadn't I done it? Was I really so convinced I was too much of a grumpy bastard to even date her?

That was a lie too.

Granted, I *was* too much of a grumpy bastard to date a sweet thing like her. That was true enough. But it wasn't what was stopping me.

Temporary, she'd said. Tilikum was temporary.

Audrey wasn't the first woman in my life to feel that way. And I wasn't letting it happen again.

CHAPTER 18

Josiah

I HELD the door steady while Dad put in the first screw to attach the door to the hinges. Hanging doors always took longer than it should. There were small adjustments to make and nothing was ever truly square, especially in an older house.

We were going with two-panel shaker doors, painted white. Simple and clean. And they were a hell of a lot better than the cheap hollow core doors that had been in here when we'd bought it.

The house still looked empty and unfinished, but it was coming along.

Dad finished screwing in the hinges. I stepped back and he swung the door closed, then opened it again.

"Good fit," he said.

I grunted in agreement.

We moved on to the next door. I held it up while Dad screwed it onto the hinges.

"Everything all right?" he asked out of the blue.

"Yeah. Why?"

He shrugged. "You've been quiet today."

"I'm always quiet."

"Preoccupied, then."

I was preoccupied—by a curvy brunette who wasn't even home. But I wasn't about to admit it. "Just thinking ahead. Tile guys haven't gotten back to us with a date."

"I'll follow up in the morning."

"Thanks."

He set the cordless drill on the floor and stretched his back.

"You want to finish these tomorrow?"

"Yeah." He twisted, cracking his spine. "I'm getting too old for this."

I patted him on the back.

We picked up our tools and brought them to the garage. The last couple of interior doors were propped up against the wall and there was still sawdust on the floor. I needed to spend some time cleaning up in preparation for the next phase of the renovation.

"If you want some dinner, feel free to come up to the house," Dad said.

"Thanks."

The noise of a car approached and I glanced out. Aunt Louise's beige Buick pulled into the driveway behind my truck.

"Damn."

Dad patted me on the back. "Good luck, son."

"You're leaving?"

"She didn't park behind me."

I glowered at him. "Thanks."

She got out, dressed in a hot pink track suit and oversize sunglasses, and waved. "Hi, Paul. Say hi to Marlene."

"Will do, Louise," Dad said as he got in his truck.

"Josiah." She flashed me a bright smile. "Just the man I was looking for."

The passenger side door of her car opened and a blond

woman got out. She was dressed in a tank top and shorts, showing off a lot of tanned skin.

"This is Aida," Louise said, as if that was supposed to mean something to me.

Aida approached with a smile and held out her hand. "Nice to meet you."

My brow furrowed as I looked at her outstretched hand.

"Josiah," Louise chided. "Don't be rude."

I took her hand and shook.

"I'm glad we caught you," Louise said. "Aida needs a ride out to her grandmother's house. You know my good friend Florence. I'd be happy to take her myself, but I don't have time."

"Why not?"

She only hesitated for a second. "I have plans. And you know where Florence lives, it's in the opposite direction."

This was so transparent, it was ridiculous. "Really? Plans?"

"I misjudged the time. I feel terrible about it, but you'll help your auntie, won't you?"

Aida's lips were pressed in a smile. I couldn't tell if she was in on it or if I was being foisted on her as awkwardly as she was being foisted on me.

I let out a frustrated breath. I could stand there and argue or I could take Aida to her grandma's and be done with it. Maybe Aunt Louise would consider her work done and leave me alone for a while.

"Fine."

"You're such a dear." Louise stepped in and popped on her tiptoes to give me a kiss on the cheek. "Have a good evening."

"Mm hmm."

She waved to both of us as she scampered back to her car. "Goodbye, you two! Don't get into any trouble."

"Of course not, Louise," Aida said. "It was nice to see you."

She got in her car, backed out of the driveway, and left.

"Well, that was interesting," Aida said. "I swear, I didn't know what she was up to."

"Whatever. Just get in."

"Hold on." She came closer and sucked on the end of her thumb, then swiped it across my cheek. "She got lipstick on you."

My back stiffened. I didn't particularly want her touching me. She wiped my cheek again and shifted closer, right as Audrey pulled into her driveway.

Shit. Shit, shit, shit.

I tried to move but Aida had me backed up against my truck.

"I didn't know what she was up to, but I'm glad she did it. I saw you at the bar the other night and I couldn't help but wonder about you."

My brows drew in and I was painfully aware that Audrey was watching this.

"I'm just going to be blunt," Aida continued, inching closer to me. "I know Louise and my grandma have been conspiring to get us together. It's cute. But I also know that Louise probably told you I'm a nice girl." Her eyes swept up and down and she licked her lips. "I'm not a nice girl, Josiah."

I felt like a caged animal. Audrey called for Max. From the corner of my eye, I could see her as she led him inside. I wanted to run over there. Tell her this wasn't what it looked like; it wasn't my fault.

But I hesitated. And a second later, her door shut behind her.

I wanted to give Aida a ride about as much as I wanted a hole in the head, but I couldn't tell her to walk. Her grandma lived off the highway south of town. Which was obviously why Louise had dropped her off. She knew I'd do it and figured a drive together might get me to ask her out.

"Let's go," I said, before Aida could try to give my face another spit bath. I brushed past her and went for the driver's side while I swiped the back of my hand over my cheek, both to rid myself of the last vestiges of Aunt Louise's lipstick and to wipe away Aida's saliva.

Aida got in the passenger's seat and shut her door. "Are you okay?"

No. The girl next door who I'm not supposed to have feelings for just saw me with another woman, which shouldn't matter because I didn't kiss her for a reason. But now I feel like garbage about all of it. "Yeah."

"Are you sure? If you don't want to give me a ride, I can—"

"It's fine." I turned on the engine and backed down the driveway.

"Sorry if I came on too strong. I just like to be up front with people. I'm only staying for another few weeks, so obviously I'm not interested in anything serious." She paused. "I thought that might be appealing to you."

"It probably would be for a lot of guys."

"But not you."

I shook my head.

"You're kind of fascinating, Josiah Haven. You realize that, don't you?" She seemed to expect a reply, but when I didn't give her one, she kept going. "You're exactly the type of guy I usually go for. Dark and brooding, averse to commitment. Emotionally unavailable but probably an animal in bed. And down to a man, they always want exactly what I want. But apparently not you."

"Guess not."

"What do you want?"

Audrey. I wanted Audrey.

Damn it. No, I didn't.

"To be left alone."

"I really want to ask who hurt you but I doubt you'll tell me."

"What are you, a therapist?"

"Actually, yes."

That made me chuckle a little. "Figures."

"Listen, I appreciate the ride and I'm sorry you got stuck with me. After I saw you at the bar, I thought I had a pretty good read on the kind of guy you are. So when Louise mentioned you, I egged her on a little bit. I wanted a shot at being alone with you and thought I could indulge her at the same time."

"Don't worry about it."

She folded her hands in her lap and I hoped she was done. She wasn't.

"But really, who hurt you?"

"No one."

She laughed. "Come on, Josiah. We both know that's not true. Emotionally unavailable men aren't born that way."

"What made you like emotionally unavailable men so much?"

"Touché."

Thankfully, she left it at that. I didn't really want to know.

I drove her across town to her grandma's house. Florence lived down a gravel road that gave my shocks a workout. I stopped in front of the house, put the truck in park, and waited for her to get out.

"Thanks again for the ride."

"No problem."

"I won't try to give you my number because I don't think you'll take it. But if you change your mind, the offer's on the table."

I grunted a noncommittal reply.

"Have a good day, Josiah."

"You too."

She got out and I waited until she opened the front door before I turned the truck around and left. My mom had drilled that into me.

Marlene, not my biological mother. If there'd been anything that woman had wanted to teach me, she hadn't stuck around long enough to do it.

I headed back through town, fully intending to go home. I was done working for the day. There wasn't any reason to go back to the remodel.

As for Audrey, I didn't know what I was so worried about. She wasn't my girlfriend. Why did I care if she'd seen me with Aida? We hadn't been doing anything.

Audrey wasn't my problem.

Except that was a big-ass lie.

She was very much my problem.

A sense of hard resolve poured through me. It was time I stopped lying to myself. That wasn't getting me anywhere.

I turned toward Audrey's house, not quite sure what I was going to do. I didn't have a plan. I just knew I needed to see her.

Now.

CHAPTER 19

Audrey

"ICING ON THE CAKE, MAX."

I paced around the kitchen, opening and closing cupboards and taking things out of the fridge. I didn't know what I was doing but I couldn't seem to slow down long enough to figure it out.

Max watched and I wasn't sure if he looked concerned or just confused.

"Of course there's someone else. Why wouldn't there be? You'd think he would have told me he had a girlfriend." I got a jar of pickles out of the fridge. No idea why. "Although maybe she's not his girlfriend. Maybe there are a lot of someone elses. She could be one of many."

I put the pickles back.

"He probably has a bunch of girls. That could be why he didn't kiss me last night. He thinks of me as a friend and he doesn't sleep with his friends, just girls like that." I gestured vaguely toward the house next door. "I don't know what that means. She's probably fine. And he probably doesn't even think of me as a friend. I'm just the weirdo next door."

I'd been very stern with myself today. I was not going to think about Josiah Haven. Nothing had happened between us, and my little crush had been silly. Totally misplaced. I didn't like him at all. I'd been inadvertently hypnotized by the power of his surly brow furrow.

He was completely wrong for me.

It didn't matter that he'd helped me give a squirrel a funeral or that he'd found Max when he'd gone missing and helped me wash him off. And the whole thing with Colin at the bar? He'd probably do that for anybody. It didn't make me special, and it certainly hadn't turned my interest into a full-blown crush.

"Who wants a guy like him anyway?" I got out a pan. "He doesn't like anyone. Who needs that kind of negativity in their life?"

Max cocked his head to the side.

I rolled my eyes, like he'd called me out on a lie. "I know he's not that bad. He's just very serious and yes, I realize I actually like that about him. Come on, Max, I'm trying to make this situation okay. Help a girl out, here."

He wagged his tail.

"I know you like him too." I stomped my foot. "No, not *too*. I don't like him. That's what I'm trying to say. I can think he's mysterious and interesting and oh my gosh, so gorgeous, but that doesn't mean I like him. Because obviously he doesn't like me."

My phone rang, startling me. I sighed as I dug through my purse to find it. It was probably my mother.

Exactly what I needed right now.

I pulled out my phone and it didn't hit me that it wasn't my mom's number until I'd already swiped to answer. It said restricted.

"Hello, this is Audrey."

Nothing.

"Hello?"

Max watched me curiously.

I sighed. It was probably one of those robo-caller things

and it hadn't clicked over to the telemarketer who was about to try to sell me something stupid. It was the third or fourth time I'd gotten a call like that in the last week.

So annoying.

"Sorry, no thanks."

There was sound, almost like a click, but no voice. I looked at my phone and the call had disconnected.

I put the phone down and looked at the counter. For some reason, I'd pulled out a package of frozen chicken, a box of spaghetti noodles, a frying pan, a can of vegetable soup, and a spatula.

"What am I even doing?"

Max didn't have an answer any more than I did. With a deep breath to calm down, I started putting things away. I didn't feel much like cooking, but I was hungry, so I got out a few things that actually made sense together and started throwing together a meal.

While my dinner cooked, I fed Max. Like usual, he inhaled his food, then happily trotted into the living room to curl up on the couch.

I'd stopped ranting but I couldn't stop thinking about seeing Josiah with that girl. It had felt like a punch to the stomach. I couldn't decide what was worse, the way he'd walked out so abruptly last night or seeing a woman practically pressed against him, touching his face.

I couldn't be mad. I didn't have any claim on him. But it still made my stomach hurt.

Maybe I wasn't hungry after all.

The rumble of a vehicle came from outside. Max jumped off the couch and stood by the front door, tail wagging furiously.

I turned off the stove right as someone started pounding on my door. Hard.

"Audrey?" came Josiah's muffled voice.

What was he doing here?

Max let out a happy bark.

I opened the door and Josiah stood there, looking like a storm about to break.

And all the mixed-up feelings I had about him coalesced into a tight ball of mad.

"What are you doing here?"

He came in.

"Excuse me." I crossed my arms. "I didn't invite you inside."

"I'm coming in anyway." He shut the door behind him.

"Rude."

"I'm sorry, I'm not trying to be rude. I just need to talk to you."

"Oh, I see. Now you need to talk?" I was about to start word vomiting and I knew it. But I couldn't seem to stop. "Last night you just took off. We could have talked then. But no, just right out the door without a word."

He took a step closer. "Audrey."

"I don't know why you want to talk to me anyway." I was really going off the rails, gesturing wildly with my arms. "You obviously had someone else to keep you busy. She's probably more your type, anyway. I'm not tall and blond and super skinny. My mom is, but don't even get me started on how much I look like my dad. Lucky me."

He took another step. "Audrey."

"No, it's fine. I don't even know why I'm upset. You're just the guy working on the house next door who was nice to me a few times and apparently I'm that desperate. I get a tiny bit of attention from a guy who's just trying to be a decent human and suddenly I'm like, oh Audrey, he's so hot, and oh Audrey, what if he kissed you. I'm the ridiculous one and I know it, so you don't have to say anything."

He came closer, but this time didn't stop, backing me into the wall. His arms caged me in and he leaned down until our noses almost touched.

"Audrey."

"Yeah?"

"Shut up."

His lips crashed down on mine. The shock of hot contact left me breathless. He wrapped one hand around the back of my neck, threading his fingers through my hair, while the other went to the small of my back. He pulled me against him and held me in a firm grip while his mouth worked magic on mine.

Despite how much I wanted that kiss, anger welled up inside me. I planted my hands on his chest and shoved.

He let go, dropping his hands and separating his mouth from mine. But instead of pushing him back halfway across the room like I'd intended, he only moved a few inches away.

"You can't just come in here and kiss me like that." My voice was embarrassingly breathless. "Especially if you were just kissing someone else."

"I wasn't."

"You looked awfully cozy."

"That wasn't my fault. My aunt Louise made me give her a ride home."

"What I saw was not you giving her a ride home."

He moved closer again, planting his hands on the wall on either side of me. "What you saw was me turning her down."

Some of my anger evaporated, leaving confusion in its place. "Josiah, I'm confused. I don't know what's happening here."

He stared at me, his gaze so intense I felt like I might melt. "I've been trying really hard to not like you."

"If that's supposed to make me feel better, it's not working."

"It's just the truth. I didn't want any of this. I didn't want to care about you or worry about you. I liked my life the way it was before you showed up in my town."

I had no idea what to say to that, so I just waited for him to continue.

He leaned in. "But it's impossible to resist you."

With his palms still planted on the wall, he kissed me again. This time, I put up no resistance. My eyes fluttered closed and I sank into his kiss. His lips were soft and warm, his beard rough against my skin.

He shifted closer, slanting his mouth over mine. I slid my hands up his broad chest and pressed myself against him. His arms wound around me as his tongue delved in, sliding against mine.

He took the kiss deeper, devouring me like a man starving. I was practically limp in his arms. Nothing could have prepared me for what it would be like to kiss Josiah Haven.

I lost track of time but eventually, he gently pulled back. We hesitated there for a long moment, just breathing.

"I've been trying really hard to not like you, too," I said. "But mostly just today."

His eyes darted to the side, drawing my gaze in the same direction.

Max sat watching us with his tail wagging.

"Your dog is being weird again."

"I know."

"I should let you get back to whatever you were doing."

"So that's it?" I asked. "You just came over here to kiss me?"

"Yeah."

"Did you plan that out beforehand, or–"

"No."

His short, straightforward answers made me like him so much. I smiled at him. "I'm glad you did."

"So we're good?"

"Yeah, we're good."

"Are you going to the festival tomorrow?"

"I have to for work."

"Good." He stepped back. "I'll see you then."

I watched him go, shaking my head in bewilderment. Had that just happened? Had Josiah just barged into my house to kiss me, and then left?

Of course he had. That was so him. He'd wanted me to know something, and he'd communicated more with that kiss than words could possibly have done.

The fact that it left me wanting more—so much more—was exciting rather than frustrating. I'd see him tomorrow.

And who knew what that would bring. For now, Josiah Haven liked me, and knowing that made my day.

CHAPTER 20

Audrey

I'D ALMOST FORGOTTEN how cute a small-town festival could be. When I was a kid, I'd always looked forward to the little festivals and events in my hometown. In middle and high school they'd become less enjoyable, probably because they were times I was expected to be "on."

Smile, Audrey, but don't stand in front of your father.

Wave, Audrey, we need to make a good impression.

Still, I had fond memories of ice cream and honey sticks. Of parades and balloons and farm fresh produce.

But Pinecrest's events had nothing on the weekend-long Tilikum Mountain Man Festival.

The town was bursting with people, as if every man, woman, and child in a hundred-mile radius had come for the festivities. Several downtown streets had been closed to traffic and were lined with vendor booths. It was like a farmers market on steroids. People were selling everything from the usual, like flats of luscious red strawberries and bunches of cut flowers, to the unusual, like squirrel repellent and yard art made of old car parts.

The market was just the beginning. Lumberjack Park, in the center of town, was also the center of the action. Men and women lined up to compete in a series of games and as far as I could tell, the prizes were nothing more than bragging rights. There was an archery tournament, wood chopping and log pulling contests, and other competitions showing off feats of strength.

It was riveting. I'd been to the festival with my parents when I was a kid—most Pinecrest residents went—but it was even better than I remembered.

Sandra nudged me. "You should take the occasional break from staring to take a picture or two."

"I wasn't staring." I lifted the camera and took a few photos of the ongoing wood chopping contest. "I was just watching."

"Yeah, right."

It didn't help that it was Josiah going head-to-head with his brother-in-law, Levi Bailey. Two shirtless men furiously chopping wood while the crowd around them cheered like it was a professional sports game? How could I not stare?

I zoomed in on Josiah and took another picture, wondering if it was possible to capture the way sweat glistened on his taut skin as his muscles flexed.

Just to be fair, I took a picture of Levi, too. After all, I wasn't here to hang out, I was here to cover the event for the Tribune. I couldn't spend all my time watching Josiah.

"This puts me in a very awkward position," Sandra said.

"How so?"

"I'm either drooling over a married man or drooling over your boyfriend. It was easier when Josiah was single. He's such a lumbersnack."

"I don't know if he's really my boyfriend."

"Oh fun, are we playing the denial game?"

"I'm not in denial, I'm just saying this isn't middle school where you hold hands at lunch once and that means you're *together*. So yeah, he kissed me, but that doesn't mean we're in a relationship."

"He's showing off for you."

"No, he's not. He's just competitive."

"He keeps glancing up to see if you're still watching."

Just then, his eyes lifted. It was only for a second, while he raised the splitting maul to swing again, but she was right.

My stomach fluttered and I had to press my lips together to hide my smile.

"You're so cute," Sandra said. "Quit it, I'm getting jealous."

"I'm sorry."

"Don't be. I'm just coming to terms with the fact that there aren't any decent eligible men my age in this town."

"Of course there are."

She raised her eyebrows. "Who?"

"I don't know, I'm still new here. But there must be. This town isn't that small."

"Miracles do happen, I suppose."

A tingle ran down my spine and the hairs on my arms stood on end. I glanced over my shoulder, wondering why I suddenly felt like I was being watched. There were people everywhere, of course eyes would be on me. That didn't mean someone was intentionally watching me.

I didn't see anyone, but the image of Colin stepping behind a group of people to stay hidden came to mind.

No. He wasn't there. No one was watching me. I was just being dramatic again.

The crowd started counting down from ten, drawing my attention back to the competition. Josiah and Levi chopped faster, their piles of split wood growing.

Five, four, three, two, one!

They both dropped their splitting mauls and held their arms up. I wasn't sure exactly how it would be determined who won—presumably by the amount of wood they'd chopped, but their piles looked about the same to me.

The crowd quieted while two judges picked through the

wood, then conferred with each other. Finally, they brought Josiah and Levi in front of the chopped wood with one of the judges in between them. He held each man's wrist, like it was the end of a boxing match, then raised Josiah's arm in the air.

Cheers erupted. I let the camera dangle from the strap around my neck so I could clap and scream.

Levi smiled and shook Josiah's hand, bringing him in for a back-slapping bro hug. It was pretty adorable. He moved off to the side where his wife and kids waited for him. They were such a cute family, it made my ovaries ache.

Josiah met my eyes and the corners of his mouth turned up in a subtle smile. A thrill swept through me and heat rushed to my cheeks.

"Here, give me the camera," Sandra said. "I'll hold it while you go love on your sweaty boyfriend."

"I don't know if he's my—"

"Just go," she said with a laugh.

I lifted the camera strap over my head and handed it to Sandra, then crossed the grass to meet Josiah.

He did smile then and it made my heart feel like it could burst.

I was in so much trouble.

"Hey," he said.

"Hi." I popped up on my tiptoes to kiss him. "Nice work, champion."

"I'm surprised I kept up with him. He beat Luke again last year, so my brothers goaded me into competing this time." He pulled his t-shirt on over his sweaty body.

I was slightly disappointed.

"Do you win something or just the honor of being the fastest wood chopper in town."

"Oh yeah, I get pie."

"Pie?"

He looked at me like I was weird for questioning that.

"Yeah. I guess if you've never had Gram Bailey's pie, you wouldn't understand."

"Will you share some with me so I can experience this magical pie?"

"I don't know if I like you that much." The corners of his mouth lifted and he slid his hands around my waist to the small of my back, pulling me against him. "Then again, maybe I do."

"That's very generous of you."

"Will you go out with me tonight?"

Coming out of nowhere, the question caught me by surprise. "What?"

His eyebrows drew in. "I thought that was how you asked a girl out."

"No, that's right, I just didn't expect it."

"You didn't expect me to ask you out?" He pressed me tighter against his muscular body. "What are we doing, then? I've been out of the loop for a while, but I thought that was how dating worked."

I laughed. "Sorry, you just keep taking me by surprise."

"I told you I'm bad with people."

"You're not bad with people. Sometimes you're just kind of blunt or abrupt."

"So, yes or no. I'm not good with subtle cues, you're going to have to be straightforward."

Smiling, I draped my arms around his neck. "Yes. Definitely yes to a date."

"Good. I'll pick you up at six."

"Sounds good." As much as I could have stayed there all day, wrapped in Josiah's arms, I was technically working, even though it was a weekend. "I should probably go do some interviews and take more pictures. This is kind of my first really big assignment and I don't want to mess it up."

He leaned down and planted a firm kiss on my lips. "Go get `em."

Reluctantly, I stepped away, my head swimming. How was I supposed to focus on being a reporter after *that*?

But I did have a job to do. I went back to Sandra and she handed me the camera.

"Not sure if he's your boyfriend, huh?"

"Yeah, well, we got off to a confusing start. I didn't want to assume and wind up looking like a bigger dork than usual." I put the camera strap around my neck. "Where should we head next?"

"This is your gig. You lead the way."

I looked around at the festival in progress. Lou hadn't given me much direction. Mostly he'd just grumbled about how no one was going to read it anyway, so I could do what I wanted.

Not exactly an optimistic attitude, but I didn't really blame him.

Still, if I could make the piece interesting, maybe it would give us a little boost.

"People always like talking about themselves," I said.

Sandra looked confused. "What?"

"I'm thinking out loud. If people like to talk about themselves, I bet they'd like to see themselves in print. I think that's the problem with the Tribune. It's trying to be something it isn't. We put all the Tilikum stuff in the local section in the middle of the paper. We should lead with it. We're a small local newspaper, so we should act like it."

"If you can convince Lou."

"I'm not going to convince him, I'm going to show him."

"I love your optimism."

I smiled. "Sometimes it's all I've got."

The idea forming in my mind wasn't so much a plan—that sounded too organized—as a loose concept. But I was confident it would work. We needed to make the Tribune unique, offering Tilikum residents something they couldn't get elsewhere. Otherwise, the readership was going to keep declining and eventually, it would have to close. Lou meant well, but he was too set in his ways. Too stuck to see the possibilities.

So I'd have to show him.

Which meant I needed to get some great photos and interview a few interesting people.

I left Sandra and set off on my journalistic quest. The games were an obvious place to start. I took photos of the log pull and got some great shots of the women's archery competition.

In between photography sessions, I focused on simply talking to people. Who were they and why had they come to the festival? What was their favorite event? Had they found any unexpected treasures in the market?

I talked to a family of five who didn't live in Tilikum anymore but brought their kids to the festival every year. It was one of the highlights of their summer. I talked to an elderly gentleman who'd lived in Tilikum his entire life and told me all about the feud that had once existed between the Haven and Bailey families. I chatted with a group of firefighters, with an older woman named Mavis who clearly loved looking at said firefighters, and a recent high school graduate who'd decided to stay in town and attend Tilikum College in the fall.

After stopping to take a bunch of notes in my phone—I had so many ideas—I walked to the other side of the park, toward where I'd left my car. I had plenty of material for an article about the festival, as well as some ideas for making it, and the Tribune as a whole, more interesting for locals.

The strange tingly feeling hit me again, like I'd just been touched on the back. My heart rate kicked up and I cast a wary glance over my shoulder.

Was that Colin?

As soon as I looked, a group of people walked in front of him, blocking him from view. Had it been him? I'd only seen him for a second, so I couldn't be sure. But it had looked a lot like him, and whoever it was, he'd been facing my direction.

Was Colin here, watching me?

The people walked past, and the man was gone.

A shiver ran down my spine. I kept looking around, but I didn't see Colin among the crowd. The park was teeming with people, but no one seemed to be paying attention to me.

Maybe it had been my imagination. Colin had a sort of generic businessman look to him. It could have been someone else and I was jumping to conclusions.

I figured I could blame my childhood. My parents had been so concerned with our image, they'd drilled a certain amount of wariness into me whenever I was in public. That was probably what was making me jumpy now.

The ghost of my father still loomed over my life.

I kept walking. It was a reminder of why I'd left my home-town. Why I'd been so determined never to come back.

But this wasn't Pinecrest. People here didn't know, or care about, Audrey Young, daughter of Darryl and Patrice. I was just Audrey, the new girl who worked for the newspaper.

Plus, I had a date with Josiah Haven tonight. That was enough to chase away the unsettled feeling trying to worm its way through me.

July 5th

I hate seeing her happy.

Hate it.

Seeing her at all twists my gut with anger but seeing her happy makes it so much worse. She's always happy. Always with that fucking smile. Because no matter what, her life is great. It's perfect.

Always better than mine.

Maybe I shouldn't have taken those pictures. But now that I have them, I can't stop staring at them. She's on her tiptoes, reaching up to kiss that hairy Neanderthal mountain man. I don't know what she sees in him and I don't really care.

I just hate seeing her so fucking happy.

I have to do something about that. She came here. She's the one who came back. Everything was fine before. I don't want her here. Can't stand it.

I need to make her leave. She needs to go.

CHAPTER 21

Josiah

I WASN'T NERVOUS.

A guy like me didn't get nervous for a date. I'd been on tons of them. Maybe it had been a while, but that was by choice, not for lack of opportunity. Hell, Aunt Louise tried to set me up on dates all the time.

But there was something going on inside me when I pulled up to Audrey's house. A buzz, like from a shot of good tequila. I kind of liked it.

I got out and went to her front door. Max stood with his front paws on the windowsill, bushy tail wagging like crazy.

"Tell your mommy I'm here, okay?"

I didn't know why I was talking to her dog through the window. Maybe she was rubbing off on me; she talked to him all the time. I knocked and Max disappeared for a few seconds before reappearing in the window, wagging his tail even faster.

The door opened, revealing Audrey dressed in a moss green t-shirt, black bike shorts, and hiking boots. Her hair was up in a ponytail and she had a jacket draped over her arm.

"Does this work?" She gestured to her clothes.

I was pretty uninterested in a regular dinner date. So I'd told her to dress for the outdoors and if she was up for it, we'd go on a hike.

"Perfect." I looked her up and down, appreciating the way the bike shorts showed off her curves and sexy legs. "It's not a hard hike, but those shoes aren't new, are they?"

"Oh, no, I've had them for a while."

"Good. I wouldn't want you to get blisters and have to pack you in on my back."

She smiled and my buzz increased. "Come on, giving me a piggy-back ride down a treacherous slope was so fun."

"Especially with a stinky dog."

"That was not our best evening. But don't worry, my shoes are broken in. Carrying me on your back shouldn't be necessary."

"Good." I glanced at the dog. "Ready, Max?"

"Is Max coming too?"

"Does he like to hike?"

"Yeah, he loves it."

"And do you want to bring him?"

"Well, yeah."

"Then he's coming."

I didn't know why she was looking at me all starry-eyed, like I'd just done something surprising or whatever. We were going on a hiking date. Of course her dog could come.

Besides, I kind of liked him.

We loaded up in my truck. There was room for Max in the back seat and he managed to stick half his body in the front by standing on the center console. I had to admit, his happiness was contagious. He posed with all the joy of a creature who couldn't imagine anything better in life than to go for a truck ride with his mommy. And me, apparently, but I figured his doggy happiness was mostly due to the drive.

I took us out to a back road that led toward the far end of Lake Tilikum. Audrey watched the scenery go by with a small smile on her face. And it was pretty. Pine trees were interspersed with wildflowers blooming in clumps where the ground got enough sun and the tall grasses were still green from the spring snow melt and rain.

The dirt road ended in a small clearing with just enough room to turn around. I parked, turned off the truck, and reached for my backpack.

I glanced at her bare legs. There was a lot of skin showing with those sexy little shorts of hers. "Hang on. You're going to want bug spray."

"Ew. Good call, thanks."

I gave her the bug spray and we got out. Max was eager to explore but to his credit, he stayed close. She sprayed her arms and legs and I went ahead and sprayed my arms. I was dressed in long pants but my arms were bare and being attacked by biting insects had a tendency to ruin an otherwise enjoyable evening.

"Ready?" I asked, slipping the backpack on.

"Yep. Where are we going?"

I pointed toward the trail. "That way. It's an out and back, only about a mile."

"What's at the end?"

"You'll see."

She smiled again. Damn, I liked making her do that. Her whole face shined.

"Okay, then lead the way."

We started off down the trail. It was wide enough to walk side by side and I was glad for the work my brothers and I had done to keep it open. Of course, given that we were still a bunch of single guys, I had a feeling I wasn't the only one who'd use it for a date. Especially with the spectacular scenery at the end.

"How did you know about this trail?" she asked. "I didn't see any signs."

"There aren't any. It's private property."

"Are we allowed to be here?"

"Yeah, it's my family's property."

"Wow. This is amazing."

"It's nice. Actually if you went up the hill behind your house and kept going, you'd come out over there somewhere." I gestured vaguely in the direction of the hiking trail that ran along the river.

"Does anyone live out here?"

"No. We kind of inherited a bunch of land about six years ago. We sold a lot of it but kept this parcel. That's how Dad and I got started with our business."

"It's so neat that you work with your dad. You must have a good relationship with him."

"He's a good guy."

"What about your mom? What's she like?"

"She's great. Technically, Marlene is my stepmom, but I think of her as my mom."

"Has she been with your dad for a long time?"

"Yeah, I was pretty young when they got together."

"Is it okay if I ask what happened to your biological mom?"

I was quiet for a moment, as our feet crunched on dry debris, wondering how to answer. Or whether I wanted to answer.

"She pretty much just left."

"Oh, I'm sorry. Do you have any contact with her?"

"No."

"That must be hard."

I shifted the backpack strap. "She made her choice and it wasn't us. Not much I can do about that. And my mom, Marlene, she always treated us like her own kids. So I didn't miss out on having a mom."

"Your mom, Marlene I mean, sounds awesome."

"Yeah, she is. What about you? What are your parents like?"

"My mom is, I don't know. She's kind of high strung. My dad was really active in local politics, so she was always in the spotlight with him. I can't figure out if she loves the attention or just got so used to it, she doesn't know how else to live. And my dad died a couple of years ago. He had some ongoing health problems and didn't take care of himself at all, so it wasn't a huge shock."

"Sorry to hear that."

"Thanks. I hate to admit it, but I wasn't devastated or anything. I was sad, but more for my mom than for me. My dad wasn't easy to live with. I wanted a better relationship with him, but it was like I barely knew him. There was the guy he was in public, the guy everybody loved. And then there was the guy he was at home, and he was so different. He didn't seem very interested in me in private, you know? I was good for his reputation, so in front of other people he pretended to be this really involved father. But in private, he mostly wanted me to leave him alone."

I wasn't sure what to say to her. Making people feel better wasn't really my area. "That sucks. I'm sorry."

She stopped and looked up at me. "Thank you."

"For what?"

"For saying that it sucks and not trying to fix it or make excuses for him or tell me I should have tried harder. I swear, every time I open up to someone about my issues with my father, I get the weirdest responses. It's like people can't handle hearing something uncomfortable and they want to fix it. But he's gone, there's no fixing it. I didn't have a great relationship with him and I never will and yeah, that sucks."

"You're right. It does suck."

"And so does the fact that your mom left you."

I glanced off into the trees. I didn't like talking about her.

It was easier to pretend it didn't matter. "Yeah, it sucks a lot, actually."

Part of me wanted to say more. To admit that it hurt. That I hated knowing I wasn't enough to make her stay.

But I didn't. I couldn't get the words out.

Audrey took my hand and squeezed. "I'm sorry."

I met her eyes. She was right, there was something comforting about that simple reply. She wasn't going to try to convince me I was enough, or tell me my mom had been a terrible person for leaving her husband and three kids, or that I should just be glad I had Marlene. She wasn't telling me how to feel. Just acknowledging the ache.

I nodded and squeezed her hand back.

We kept going while Max circled around us. He sniffed through the pine needles and stopped now and again to pee on a tree trunk. Instead of being awkward, the silence was comfortable.

The trail ascended in a gradual slope then hooked to the right and turned downhill. The roar of water rose in the distance.

"What is that? Is that water?"

"You'll see. It's just up ahead a little farther."

We came around another bend and the trail opened onto the pristine waters of the lake. A waterfall plunged from its rocky height, sending up white spray into the evening air.

"It's so beautiful," she said, her voice filled with awe. "I can't believe this place isn't packed with hikers."

"Not many people know about it." I pointed at the rocky cliff face. "My brothers and I use to come out here and climb, then jump."

"You're kidding. How did you not die?"

"It was stupid. We had to get as close to the waterfall as we could. It's deep there, but on either side, it's just rocks."

Max ran to the edge of the lake and sniffed the water.

"Audrey?"

"Yeah?"

"Does Max know how to swim?"

"Yes, but—"

Whatever she was about to say, it was too late. Her dog dashed into the water and started paddling around.

"Oh, no. He's going to make your truck smell like wet dog."

I chuckled. He looked so pleased with himself, I couldn't even be mad. "That's okay. Are you hungry?"

"I'm starving, actually. Did you pack dinner?"

"Of course." I took off the backpack and set it down. "What did you think we were doing out here?"

"Just a hike, I guess. A picnic by a waterfall is so –"

"What?"

"Romantic."

"Should I be insulted that you didn't think I could be romantic?"

She laughed. "No. I just wasn't sure what to expect on a first date with Josiah Haven. You keep surprising me."

Surprising her felt good, just like making her smile.

I found a flat spot and unpacked the picnic I'd brought. In hindsight, I should have brought a blanket, but I hadn't thought of that. Still, I had sandwiches from the Copper Kettle, raspberries I'd bought at the festival market, and a bottle of wine that I'd wrapped in a towel to keep it secure. I didn't have wine glasses, but Audrey didn't seem to mind drinking wine out of plastic cups, so I didn't worry about it.

She called Max out of the water before we sat down to eat. Fortunately for us, he did most of his shaking by the edge of the lake and we only got hit by a bit of the spray. He did smell like wet dog, though. I'd brought a bully stick for him and he settled down to gnaw on it while we sat to eat our dinner.

I had a thing for the sound of water. It tended to undo the knots in my back and make me feel peaceful. I'd never brought a date out there before and I was glad it was Audrey.

The dull roar of the waterfall as a backdrop to our first date felt prophetic, somehow. Like it meant something.

That made me nervous, but I pushed it aside. It was just a date. I didn't need to worry about where this was going or how long she was really going to stay.

Easier said than done, but the food was good, the company was better, and the setting was serene.

We talked as we ate, about her job and mine. About the house I was remodeling and my plans for it. About my nieces and nephews and the old Haven-Bailey feud. About pranks and squirrels and the weirdness of Tilikum life.

I kept gazing at her while she talked. She had ideas to help resurrect the newspaper, but she could have been talking about anything and I would have been mesmerized. I liked hearing her voice, watching her mouth move, seeing her smile.

Eventually, cool air started to nip at us as the sun went down behind the mountain peaks. I packed up the remains of our meal and we started back down the trail, leaving the roar of the waterfall behind.

I held her hand. It felt good.

Max trotted happily around us, zig zagging back and forth across the trail. The sun was still up when we reached my truck, but only just. Audrey got in with a contented smile and I preened a bit. I'd pulled off a damn good date, if I said so myself.

Hell, even I'd enjoyed it.

I wasn't thinking too much about where tonight was going as I drove back to Audrey's place. A little—I'm a guy, after all. But if we said goodnight outside and that was it, I was okay with it. As much as I would have loved to get her naked, I was also hesitant to jump into something too soon.

Although when I pulled into her driveway, that buzz came back—the sense of anticipation hit me like the blast of heat from a bonfire.

Until I saw her door.

"Oh my god," she said. "What is that?"

Even in the waning light, it was clear. Someone had scrawled the word *bitch* in big letters across her front door.

And based on the rust color, I had a feeling they hadn't used paint.

CHAPTER 22

Audrey

"STAY HERE."

Leaving the keys in the ignition, Josiah got out and shut his truck door behind him. My heart raced as I watched him cautiously approach the house and the sight of that word scrawled across my door made my stomach churn with fear.

Who would do something like that? And what had I ever done to them?

Max seemed to sense the tenseness of the situation. He hopped onto Josiah's seat and whined a few times.

"We need to wait here for a few minutes. I don't know what's out there."

As if he understood me, he sat.

Josiah inspected the front door and surrounding area. He held up a hand for me to stay where I was, then made a circuit around the house. I didn't like waiting while he was out of sight, so I locked the doors until he came around the other side.

Finally, he came to my side of the truck. I rolled down the window.

"There's another squirrel. Let me get rid of it before you let Max out."

"A squirrel?" I stared in horror at the door. "Does that mean –"

"Looks like it."

Someone had killed a squirrel and written on my door in its blood?

This could not be happening.

"Actually, I probably shouldn't move it," he said. "I need to call Garrett. Do you have a leash so you can take Max inside?"

"Yeah, I brought one in my bag." I pulled out Max's leash. "Are you sure it's safe?"

He looked around. His jaw was set in a hard line. "Seems to be and I didn't see any sign of forced entry. You locked your door when we left, right?"

"Yes. I'm sure I did."

"It's still locked and so is the back door. I don't see anyone around. Looks like they did this and took off."

"In broad daylight? The sun isn't even all the way down."

"It's ballsy, I'll give them that."

"Ballsy and horrible."

I didn't ask the question. I knew we were both thinking it. Who did this?

Was it Colin?

"Let's just get inside," Josiah said. "I'll walk you in and we can call my brother."

I clipped on Max's leash and with my stomach jumping, got out. Josiah took my hand and led me to the front door. I kept Max close so he wouldn't have a chance to even sniff the poor little squirrel that had been left behind.

With the front door safely shut behind us, I let Max off his leash. He didn't tear through the house, sniffing, which seemed like a good sign. If someone had been inside, he would have caught their scent. He wasn't much of a guard dog, but he was curious. He'd have at least followed where the scent led.

Josiah still did a sweep of the whole house, checking every room. Probably not necessary, but it made me feel better.

He came back and pulled out his phone. I sat on the couch while Max curled up next to me.

"Hey," Josiah said. "Do you have a minute?"

I petted Max, stroking his soft fur. It helped me start to calm down.

"I'm putting you on speaker." He tapped his screen and held the phone out. "I'm at Audrey's. We just got here and someone vandalized her house."

"What kind of vandalism?"

"Someone wrote on her door in squirrel blood."

"Josiah, that's not funny."

"It's not a joke. The word bitch is scrawled in big letters and there's a dead squirrel out there. *Another* dead squirrel."

"Where are you now?"

"Inside."

"You should have stayed outside. The perpetrator could be there."

"Doors were still locked. I don't think he got in." He glanced at Max. "The dog would have noticed, right? If someone had been here?"

"Yeah, he would have chased the scent of someone he didn't recognize."

"You still shouldn't have gone in, but since you did, stay where you are," Garrett said. "I'll be there in a minute. Which house is it?"

"Next to the new one."

"Got it. On my way."

He ended the call and slipped his phone back in his pocket. "Are you okay?"

I took a deep breath and kept petting Max. "Yes? No? Maybe? I don't know, I'm kind of freaking out. But also not, mostly because you're here."

His expression softened and he came over to sit next to me. "You're safe with me. I won't let anyone hurt you."

Some of the tension in my body melted. I believed him.

"Do you think this means the other squirrel was on purpose?" I asked.

"Yes."

As if he could read my mind and knew I needed his touch, he clasped my hand. His were warm and strong.

I was so glad he was there.

"I don't understand why someone would do this. I don't have any enemies. I know you're thinking Colin, and maybe you're right, but why would he do this now? Our relationship ended so long ago and he's been married for years."

"Yeah but you didn't live here. Now you're back."

"But I'm not even in his town. He can still strut around and be the biggest fish in the tiniest pond in Pinecrest and I'm not there to bother him."

"It doesn't make sense to me either."

"I guess it wouldn't. We're talking about someone who's willing to murder poor defenseless animals."

"You're worried about the squirrels in all this?"

"Of course I am. They didn't do anything to deserve being a pawn in some madman's horrible game. What did they ever do to anyone?"

"They're Tilikum squirrels, so they're probably thieves."

"But even that doesn't mean they deserved to die. Theft isn't a capital crime."

He squeezed my hand. "You're right. They didn't deserve to die."

I wasn't sure if he was saying that to keep me calm or if he meant it, but it probably didn't matter. I did feel terrible for the poor squirrels, but thinking about them was mostly a distraction from the fact that someone had vandalized my house.

A car pulled up in the driveway. I waited on the couch

while Josiah checked to make sure it was Garrett. It was, so we left Max in the house—thank goodness all the swimming and hiking had tired him out so much—and went back to the crime scene.

My house as a crime scene? This couldn't be happening.

Garrett Haven was a tall guy with arms that gave his deputy uniform a workout. He had dark blond hair and stubble rather than a full beard like Josiah. He paused a few feet from the door and looked up and down.

"What the fuck?" he muttered.

"Exactly." Josiah gestured to the poor little squirrel. "That's about where they left the other one."

Garrett crouched to inspect the squirrel. He pulled a pen out of his pocket and turned it over. "This isn't roadkill."

Josiah pointed at the door. "You think?"

"I just mean someone could have found a dead animal and used it. But this was a precision kill."

"Is Colin a hunter?" Josiah asked.

"I don't think so. He didn't used to be at least."

"Colin is the ex?" Garrett asked.

I nodded.

Garrett stood and turned his attention back to the door. "Not very subtle, is it? Have there been any other incidents? Times you might have been followed or noticed something strange or out of place here at home?"

"Not really." I paused, wondering if I should even mention the weird feeling I got at the Mountain Man festival. "There's nothing I can point to with any certainty, at least."

"What do you mean?"

"It's just that when I was at the festival earlier today, there were a few times when I felt like maybe someone was watching or following me. I know that doesn't give you anything to go on. I thought I might have seen Colin, but I didn't get a good look."

"Even if you did, thousands of people go to that festival," Garrett said. "Is that all?"

"I guess there have also been some phone calls."

"Phone calls?" Josiah asked. "What phone calls?"

"Hang up calls. They came from a restricted number and if I answered, no one would be there. I figured it was telemarketers or something."

Josiah and Garrett shared a look.

"If this hadn't happened, I'd tell you not to worry about the calls," Garrett said. "But this did happen, so we need to look into it. I need to get our crime scene crew over here. Give me a few minutes."

Garrett walked away and got on his radio. I heard him use the words *potential stalker situation.*

It sent a chill down my spine.

I hugged my arms around myself. "He thinks I have a stalker."

"You obviously have a stalker."

"What if it's not me?" The pitch of my voice started rising. "What if whoever did this got the wrong house? Or it was meant for someone who used to live here and they don't know they moved?"

Josiah put his hands on my arms, holding me in a gentle but firm grip. "We'll find out who did this, okay?"

I nodded, desperately wanting to believe him.

Garrett walked back over. He wanted Colin's full name and any contact information I had, so I gave it to him.

"We're going to need to process the scene," he said. "What did you touch?"

"Just the doorknob," Josiah said. "Didn't touch or move anything else."

"The squirrel was there when you found it?"

"Yeah, I wasn't in a hurry to pick up another dead animal."

"Fair enough. I don't know if we'll find much. Seems like

whoever did this would have worn gloves, but you never know. And we'll check with the neighbors. See if anyone caught something on a front door camera."

"I'm installing one of those tomorrow." Josiah shook his head. "I should have done it after the first squirrel."

"What are you going to do with the squirrel's body?" I asked.

"We'll bag it up and take it down to the station to be examined."

"And then what?"

Garrett's brows drew together. "What do you mean?"

"She wants to make sure it gets a proper funeral," Josiah said.

He turned his confused look on his brother. "A funeral?"

Josiah sighed. "Can we just have it back when you're done with it?"

"Probably." Garrett sounded more bewildered than ever. But he didn't say anything else. Just shook his head and walked back to his car.

"Thanks." I could feel my lower lip protruding in a pout, but I couldn't help it. I'd gone from deliciously happy after our date to horrified in the blink of an eye. I glanced at the door again and turned away. I didn't want to look at it anymore.

"Stay at my place tonight," Josiah said. It wasn't a question.

"Are you sure? I don't want to impose."

He moved closer and placed his big hand on my cheek. "You're staying at my place."

I breathed out a sigh of relief. "Okay. Thank you."

He lifted my chin and kissed me. I still felt queasy, but kissing Josiah helped. A lot.

Even more than petting Max.

"Go ahead and get whatever you need for you and Max. Then we can get out of here."

I packed a bag, grabbed a few things for Max, and we got back in Josiah's truck. As much as I hated the idea of someone driving me out of my own house, even for a night, I was filled with relief that I didn't have to stay.

By the time we got to Josiah's house, darkness had fallen. I clipped on Max's leash before we got out of the truck. With all the scents of a new place, I didn't want him taking off on us. The last thing we needed was another wild dog chase.

Josiah took my things and led us inside. He shut the door behind us, flipped on a light, and paused.

"Sorry."

"For what?" I asked.

"I don't have people over."

I glanced around. It wasn't exactly neat and tidy, and I could tell he was partway through fixing it up, but it wasn't gross or anything. "Don't worry about it. It's fine."

He gave me a quick tour and I let Max wander around sniffing everything. Even though it was unfinished, it had a lot of potential.

And it was definitely a bachelor pad. Considering Josiah had an eye for not just construction, but design, he hadn't used it at all in his own home. I wondered if he just hadn't gotten around to it or if he didn't plan on staying in the house long enough to bother. He had the basics—furniture in the living room and one of the bedrooms and a small table off the kitchen. But the other bedrooms were empty and the light in the extra bathroom didn't work.

He finished showing me around and took my things to his bedroom. "You can sleep in here. I'll take the couch."

I tried to hide the wave of disappointment that swept through me. It wasn't that I was ready to jump into bed with him, not in that sense. Sure, I was wildly attracted to him, and that rough lumberjack of a man could probably ravage me in a hundred different ways. But that wasn't where my head was. I was tired and upset and I didn't want to be alone.

But what was I supposed to say? Could you please let me sleep in your bed with you without having sex?

That would be too weird, right?

"Unless–" He paused, as if he were trying to find the right words. "I won't push you into anything."

Deciding to take a chance and ask for what I wanted, I met his eyes. "Will you stay in here with me? Even if it's just to sleep?"

The corners of his mouth lifted. "Yeah."

Pleasant warmth spread through me at that smile.

It wasn't late but I was happy to go to bed early. I took Max outside for one last potty break, then came in to get ready for bed. I felt a little awkward, being in Josiah's space. I didn't want to get in his way. But we navigated the process of getting ready for bed without too much weirdness, and the simple intimacy of it was oddly exhilarating. There was something about standing next to him in the bathroom while we brushed our teeth and almost bumping into each other reaching for a towel that felt familiar and sweet.

My heart beat a little faster when we got into bed together. Max jumped up and decided on a spot—he tended to be a foot of the bed sleeper and didn't seem to care that we weren't home and there was another person in bed with his mommy.

Josiah turned out the light and for a moment, it felt like I couldn't quite breathe. Then he reached over and pulled me close, tucking my back against his front. He took a deep breath and with his exhale, the tension in my body melted. He was warm and strong and close, and I could have stayed in bed with him forever.

And as I fell asleep, warm and safe in his arms, I fell a little bit in love with Josiah Haven.

CHAPTER 23

Audrey

LIGHT PEEKED through the bent blinds and it took me a second to remember where I was. Josiah's house. Not just his house, I was in Josiah's bed.

I took a deep breath and let that sink in.

The reason I was there threatened to dull my moment of bliss. But I pushed reality away just for a moment so I could bask in the feeling of waking up next to Josiah Haven.

Since I had my back to him, I shifted a little so I could peek, hoping to catch a glimpse of him sleeping.

I was not prepared for what I saw.

Josiah was on his side, facing me, and between us was Max. My dog lay stretched out, belly up, tucked alongside Josiah in blissful doggie sleep. It was the cutest thing I'd ever seen. Josiah, who'd been somewhat indifferent to Max at first, was basically snuggling him in his sleep.

If I hadn't fallen for Josiah a little bit the night before, I would have then.

Max seemed to sense I was looking at him. He opened his eyes and was wide awake in the space of a second. He jumped off the bed, tail wagging.

"I'm coming," I whispered. "Give me a second."

I cast a longing glance at Josiah. He looked so big and warm and comfortable. I would have loved to tuck myself against that burly body, but I didn't want to test the limits of Max's bladder. I got up, careful not to wake him, and took Max outside.

Considering everything that had happened, I decided to give my mom a call. I didn't want to worry her, but I also knew she'd be upset if I didn't fill her in. It was early, but she'd always been an early riser. I knew she'd be up. While Max sniffed around the yard, I took out my phone and called her.

"Hello?" she answered.

"Hi, Mom. Sorry it's so early."

"Is it? I've been up for a while. How are you?"

"Fine. Sort of. Actually, something creepy happened last night. I figured I should call and let you know what's going on."

"Are you all right?" she asked, her voice suddenly laced with concern.

"Yeah, I'm fine. It was disconcerting but I'm not hurt or anything."

"What happened?"

"This is going to sound crazy, because it is, and I don't know how else to tell you other than just coming out and saying it. Someone wrote a swear word on my door. In squirrel blood."

"I'm sorry, what did you say?"

"I got home last night and someone had written a swear word in big letters in squirrel blood. The poor little squirrel was left in front of the door."

"Who would do such a thing? Did you call the police? Have they found them yet?"

"I don't know, and yes, and no."

"They must have done it to the wrong house. Someone wouldn't target you like that."

"That's one of my theories, too, but I just don't know. There was another dead squirrel outside the house not long ago, but I didn't think much of it. There's a lot of wildlife around here, I thought it had just died there. But now I'm not so sure."

"You need to move home. Immediately."

I rolled my eyes. "While I appreciate the offer, I don't think that's a good idea."

"Audrey, you can't stay in that house."

"The police came and they're doing everything they can."

"You still can't stay in that house."

"Mom, I have a lease. And one act of vandalism that could have been random or a mistake isn't going to get me to move."

"It might not have been random or a mistake."

I followed Max toward the driveway. "I know."

She took a deep breath, like she was about to tell me something important or possibly difficult to hear. "You know your father was loved and respected in Pinecrest, but anyone who enters politics makes enemies."

I paused to consider what she was really saying. "So you think someone from Pinecrest found out where I live and wrote 'bitch' on my door in animal blood to get back at my dad who passed away two years ago?"

"Stranger things have happened."

"Mom, has someone been targeting you? Has your house been vandalized and you didn't tell me?"

"Oh no, certainly not."

"Well, it seems like if Dad had enemies who would do this kind of thing, they'd go after you first."

"Perhaps. Although my security system could be enough of a deterrent. They could have tried to get to me and settled for you instead."

Was my mother really suggesting I was a second-choice vandalism victim? I couldn't help but sigh. "I'll mention

Dad to the police in case they want to follow up on that lead."

"Be sure you do."

Although there was no way I was going to suggest to my mother that Colin might be the perpetrator, I did wonder if she'd seen him lately and if he'd been acting any different.

"Speaking of people from Pinecrest, you haven't seen Colin lately, have you?"

"I see him now and again. Why?"

"I was just wondering. I ran into him not that long ago and something seemed off."

"We both know what's wrong with Colin."

I rolled my eyes again. "I know you think he married the wrong woman but they've been together for a long time. I'm sure they're fine."

"They're hardly fine. Everyone knows she's having an affair with her boss."

If Pinecrest and Tilikum went head-to-head over which town had the biggest gossips, it would be anyone's game. Something "everyone knew" in Pinecrest could be true or a total fabrication. It was impossible to tell.

"That might just be a rumor."

"Rumors are usually rooted in truth. I feel terrible for the poor man."

I wanted to tell her what had happened when I'd seen Colin at the Timberbeast. He had not been acting appropriately for a man who was married to someone else, regardless of whether or not his wife was being unfaithful. But she'd just make excuses for him like she always did.

"Look, I can't really worry about Colin's marriage right now. I have bigger problems."

"Indeed you do. Audrey. I mean it, tell the police this was probably aimed at you because of your family."

"Okay, Mom, I will."

"Good. Are you sure you're safe there?"

There was also no way I was telling her that I'd stayed with Josiah last night. At some point, I'd tell her we were dating, but she didn't need to know I'd slept in his bed. She'd just find a way to lecture me about it.

"Yes, Mom. I'm safe. And I have friends in town where I can go if I need to."

"You can always come here. I mean it. Even with the dog."

I smiled, my expression softening. I knew she actually meant that. "Thanks, Mom. I'll keep it in mind."

"Okay. Keep me posted on what the police find."

"I will. Talk to you later."

I ended the call. Mother-daughter relationships were so complicated sometimes. Her insistence that this might have had something to do with my father was so frustrating. Of course she'd make it about them, rather than me. But I could hear the concern in her voice, especially when she offered to let me come stay again. She wasn't perfect and things between us weren't always the best, but she was still my mom, and she cared.

"Let's go inside, Max."

He followed me in and I got him his breakfast. As much as I would have loved to have crawled back in bed with Josiah, I had to go to work.

———

The high school gym was packed. Rows of folding chairs had been set up in front of the stage and most of them appeared to be taken. The noise of dozens of conversations echoed off the cavernous walls and there was a buzz of energy in the air.

I'd gone back to Josiah's house after work and he'd told me there was an emergency town meeting in an hour. That had given me just enough time to change and grab a quick bite to eat.

He took my hand and led me into the gym, past knots of people who hadn't yet taken their seats.

"Is this a normal turnout?" I asked.

"Depends. Something obviously has everyone riled up."

"But your dad didn't say what this was about?"

"No." He paused and craned his neck, looking out over the crowd. "There they are."

He led me to the front where I recognized his dad, Paul. I hadn't met him yet, but I'd seen him at the remodel a few times. He was a big guy with thick, hairy arms and a beard shot through with gray. A woman who had to be Marlene stood with her hand tucked in the crook of his arm. She wore blue rimmed glasses and a dress with daisies on it.

"What's going on?" Josiah asked.

"The squirrels," Paul said.

"What?"

"Two squirrel killings, and both at one of our properties. People are concerned."

"Someone vandalized Audrey's house and the town is worried about the squirrels?" He glanced at me. "Oh, this is Audrey."

"I'm Marlene, this is my husband Paul," she said. "Sorry we're meeting under less than ideal circumstances."

"It's still nice to meet you."

She smiled. "You too."

A tap on the microphone caught our attention and the chatter in the room began to fade.

"Good evening." An older man dressed in a blue shirt and tan pants stood on the stage. "Can everyone hear me?"

"We can hear you, mayor," someone said from the back.

"Excellent. If everyone could take their seats, we'll get started." He gestured toward the back. "Are there enough chairs? We can bring in more if necessary."

He waited a moment while people sat. Paul gestured for us to sit next to him and Marlene in the front row.

"Tilikum residents, thank you for coming tonight," the man on stage said. "If you don't know me, I'm Bill Surrey, and I have the honor of being the mayor of this fine town."

The crowd responded with a polite round of applause.

"Thank you. As you all know, there have been some disturbing incidents here in Tilikum. Miss Young, a newcomer to our town, had her house grotesquely vandalized." He focused on me. "Miss Young, my sincerest apologies. We pride ourselves on the safety of our community and I assure you, Sheriff Cordero and his highly capable team are doing everything they can to find the perpetrator of this heinous crime."

He gestured to a man in uniform, standing off to the side. He was every bit as intimidating as Josiah. Older, with gray in his hair and beard, but there was no mistaking the look of danger. He looked like a sheriff, all right, and one I wouldn't want to cross.

I wasn't sure if I was supposed to get up and say something or just acknowledge what he'd said. I nodded and that seemed to be the right call because he continued.

"With the human aspect of the crime in the hands of the law," he said, gesturing to Sheriff Cordero again, "we can have complete confidence that the criminal or criminals involved will be apprehended and charged to the fullest extent of the law."

The crowd applauded again and a few cheers of, "*Sheriff Jack!*" rose up behind me.

"But that leaves us with another problem, and the reason for this emergency town meeting tonight. So far, two squirrels have lost their lives at the hands of this criminal or criminals. The good sheriff and his deputies have their hands full dealing with the crime. That means it's up to us to come up with solutions that take our squirrel population into account."

"Protect the squirrels!" someone yelled from the back.

Mayor Bill pointed. "Exactly. I know the squirrels can be a

nuisance, but based on the feedback my office has been getting, it's clear that we need to act."

"It wasn't me!" a rough voice called out.

Heads swiveled. I looked behind me and saw a man in a worn leather vest and wide brimmed hat, standing in the middle of one of the rows. He had a shaggy beard and deep lines around his eyes.

"Who's that?" I asked Josiah.

"Harvey Johnston. He's not exactly all there. Used to hate the squirrels but now he builds them tiny picnic tables and stuff."

"Thank you, Harvey," Mayor Bill said, raising his hand in a placating gesture. "We all know you and the squirrels have had your differences. But the past is in the past."

Harvey nodded gravely and took his seat.

I leaned closer to Josiah again. "It was just two squirrels. I'm surprised the town is so serious about this."

"Who knows with these people."

"At this time, I'd like to open the floor for comments and ideas for what we can do to address the situation," Mayor Bill said.

"I have an idea," someone said.

"Go ahead, Earl."

"We build a squirrel zoo. Then we can round them all up and keep them in an enclosure."

"Good idea," someone else called out. "Then we can charge admission."

"Okay, that's an idea," Mayor Bill said. "We're brainstorming, folks, so we'll sort through the ins and outs later. How about you, Miss Hembree, I see your hand raised."

"What if we outfit them with tiny bulletproof vests?"

"Huh, okay. I'm not sure if we think there's much danger of the squirrels being shot." He turned to Sheriff Cordero. "What do you think, Sheriff?"

He shook his head. "We're not concerned about gun violence against squirrels at this time."

"All right, good to know. Thank you, Sheriff. If you couldn't hear that, folks, there's not a reason to be concerned about gun violence against the squirrels. Anyone else?" He pointed. "Fiona Bailey."

"I just want to say we can't put them in a zoo or an enclosure. They need to be free."

"That's good feedback, Fiona, thank you." He pointed to another person in the crowd. "Go ahead, Mrs. Doolittle."

A tiny old lady in a pink house coat stood. I'd talked to her at the Mountain Man Festival. "We could ask the firefighters for their help. They're a group of big, strong men. I'm sure they could keep the squirrels safe."

"Thanks for that, Mrs. Doolittle. Your admiration of the fire department is well known and appreciated."

Josiah leaned closer. "Mavis Doolittle has a thing for firefighters. She used to call in false reports just to get them to come to her house until they threatened to fine her."

"Anyone else?" Mayor Bill asked. "Go ahead, Harvey, did you have something else to add?"

Harvey stood and took off his hat, placing it against his chest. Oddly, he looked right at me. "We form a squirrel protection squad."

The mayor nodded slowly, as if he were digesting the idea. "I like that, Harvey. That has potential. We could get volunteers to run patrols. It wouldn't be foolproof, but some action is better than none at all. What do you think, Sheriff?"

I couldn't tell if Sheriff Cordero looked amused or irritated or a combination of both. "If you want to form a volunteer squirrel protection squad, you're more than welcome. Just make sure everyone knows not to interfere with our investigation."

"Will do, Sheriff. All right, folks, we'll get a sign-up form going for those interested in running some patrols."

"Can we get t-shirts?" someone asked from the back.

"We can look into that, sure."

Mayor Bill finished up with a few more announcements—unrelated to squirrels—before thanking everyone for coming. A line formed at the front where someone had started a signup sheet for people interested in the squirrel protection squad.

"They're really serious about this, aren't they?" I asked.

"Only in Tilikum," Josiah said with a shake of his head.

Paul and Marlene stood. I noticed Paul give Marlene a quick kiss on the cheek. It was very cute.

"That went well," Marlene said.

Paul's brow furrowed in a scowl. It reminded me a lot of Josiah. "I'm just glad they're not laying the blame on us. Besides, they're just a bunch of rodents. Don't know why we have to worry about protecting them."

Marlene put her hand on his arm. "We both know that's not all they're doing. Forming a group to protect the squirrels is just an excuse to get the townsfolk involved in protecting Audrey. Everyone is shook up over what happened to her. They want to do something about it."

Paul grumbled something I didn't understand, but Marlene seemed to. She smiled at him. He kissed her on the cheek again, then went to stand in line to sign up for the squirrel protection squad.

"Audrey!"

I turned to see Marigold approaching. She looked stunning in a sleeveless high-necked blouse and floral skirt. She clasped my hands, pulling me into a tight hug.

"I'm so glad you're okay." She let go and stepped back. "I heard what happened. It's horrifying. Do they have any idea who's behind it?"

"Not yet."

"That must have been so scary. If you're not comfortable

staying at home, you're more than welcome to stay at my place. I have a guest room that's all ready if you need it."

Josiah slipped an arm around me. "Thanks, Mari, but I've got her covered."

She gave me a sly smile. "I see. That's very gentlemanly of you, Josiah."

He grunted in reply.

"That's so nice of you to offer," I said. "I'll let you know if anything changes, but I'll be fine."

"Just be careful. We're all so worried about you."

We hugged again and said goodbye. Josiah put his hand on the small of my back and led me outside.

He stopped next to his truck and lifted my chin so I was looking up at him. "Are we sleeping at my place or yours?"

A thrill ran through me. I loved that he didn't consider it an option; he was staying with me and that was that.

"Either way is fine with me."

"Yours, then."

"Sounds good."

He opened the passenger door for me and I got in. Maybe I shouldn't have been so giddy, considering everything that had happened. But I was. None of it was quite so scary when I had Josiah to protect me.

CHAPTER 24

Josiah

AT NINE IN THE MORNING, it was already hot. Summer had officially arrived in the mountains and it felt like it would be a scorcher. Fortunately, the air conditioning in the remodel was working. Once I got the camera installed at Audrey's, I'd be out of the weather for most of the day.

Max sat near her front door, watching me while his tail wagged. I'd offered to keep him with me today. Figured I might as well. I kind of liked having a work buddy and it would save her money on doggie daycare.

"I hope the asshole is stupid enough to show up here again. Hell, he doesn't even have to be stupid, just arrogant."

Max kept wagging his tail.

I put in the final screw and checked my handiwork. Looked straight. The doorbell camera was one of three I'd decided to install on her house. The other two were covering areas this one wouldn't see, including out the back door. There were blind spots, and I wasn't ruling out putting up another camera or two. But realistically, these covered the driveway and entrances to the house.

Still, going overboard was tempting.

"I'll help her set up the app on her phone when she gets home."

I had no idea why I was explaining everything I did to Max. It wasn't like he could understand me.

My phone rang, so I pulled it out of my pocket to answer. It was Garrett.

"Yeah."

"Just checking in, although there's not much of an update. We didn't pick up any prints or fibers, so that's a dead end."

"What about neighbors? Anyone see something?"

"Not a thing. It doesn't help that there aren't any houses directly across the street. The Campbells up the road have a doorbell cam, but it doesn't show anything useful. Too far away. And Mrs. Cutter next door wasn't home that day. She was visiting her daughter."

"Damn."

"I know. We contacted the ex-boyfriend but he has an alibi."

"What if he hired someone?"

"Yeah, he could have. I'm not ruling him out, especially because Audrey doesn't seem to have any enemies. I hate to admit it, but this one has me stumped. Writing on her door in animal blood is pretty extreme."

"No shit."

"Did you get cameras installed?"

"Yeah, just finished with the last one."

"Good. That will be a deterrent if nothing else."

"I don't really expect the guy to walk up to the door again now that there are cameras. But you never know. If he's arrogant enough, he might."

"Let's hope if he does, she's not home. Is she staying at your place?"

"She did the first night. I'm staying at her place now."

"Good. I don't want her to be alone if we can help it."

"Trust me, that's not happening."

"I'm going to get in touch with her mom today. See if there's anything she can tell us. There might be something Audrey isn't saying or hasn't thought about. An old rivalry or something like that."

I didn't think Audrey was hiding anything on purpose, but he had a point. She'd lived out of the area for a long time and moving back could have triggered someone holding an old grudge. Especially if that someone was already unhinged.

Because seriously, a guy had to be unhinged to kill a squirrel and write on a door with its blood.

Zachary and I had cleaned it up for her once the cops had given us the okay. Some had seeped into the wood, so I'd sanded and painted it after the emergency town meeting. Now all traces of it were gone.

"Keep digging," I said. "We need to find this guy before he does something worse."

"Agreed. I'll keep you posted."

"Thanks."

I ended the call and pocketed my phone.

My blood surged with anger when I thought about that psycho. I wanted to rearrange his face for what he'd done to my girl. Not just the vandalism, but the fear and stress he was causing her.

Audrey was literally one of the sweetest, kindest people I'd ever met. Who would want to fuck with her like this?

The more jaded part of me did wonder if she was hiding a secret.

I didn't want to doubt her. But I wasn't an idiot. I knew people could keep secrets, even otherwise good people. I just hoped I wasn't setting myself up to get burned.

A good reminder. Take things slow. I was sleeping at her house, next to her in bed, and the desire was there. I wanted her. Badly. But it was probably smart that we hadn't gone there yet.

I needed to be careful.

"Nothing more we can do over here," I said to Max. "Let's go next door."

Max followed me to the remodel and promptly curled up in a corner for a nap. Apparently watching me install cameras had been tiring work for a dog.

The baseboards were in and about half the windows were trimmed out. I needed to finish the windows and get started on the door trim.

After second-guessing the trim package, I'd finally asked Audrey what she thought. She'd liked the four and a half inch baseboards with stepped detailing at the top. Now that they were in, I had to say, she'd nailed it. The white looked great against the wood floors and the height set off the room perfectly.

The windows were looking good, too, with trim that echoed the lines of the baseboards. I got to work, measuring, cutting, and installing. Once in a while Max would get up and want some attention or need to go outside. A bit after one, I decided to take a break. He hopped in the truck with me and we ran into town to grab some lunch.

I stopped by Audrey's office to make sure she was okay. She came outside to say hi to me and Max, but couldn't stay long. She was in the middle of wrapping up an article for next week's paper. Still, it was good to see her—and kiss her. And Max was thrilled to see his mama.

He really was a cute dog.

After lunch, I went back to work. The afternoon went quickly and I made good progress on the windows and doors. It was finally starting to look livable.

Which reminded me, I needed to make a decision on the countertops. My cabinet guy was already working on the kitchen and bathroom cabinets, but I wasn't sure what to do about the counters. I'd originally thought quartz, but granite was also a possibility. However, the granite samples I'd grabbed weren't doing it for me.

Maybe I'd ask Audrey about that too.

Max jumped up from his spot in the corner and ran for the front door.

I glanced at the time. Already after five. "Is your mommy home?"

He looked at me and wagged his tail, as if to say, *let's go see her*!

I couldn't help the smile that stole over my face. If I'd had a tail, I'd have been wagging it too.

Damn. I was in trouble.

I brushed the sawdust off my hands and went outside.

Audrey got out of her car with a smile already on her face. It was such a cliché, but the woman was sunshine. I could feel her warmth from where I was standing.

Max ran to greet her, tail wagging so hard I wondered if he'd throw out his back.

"Hi, Max." She crouched to scratch him while he gave her excited dog kisses. "I missed you too."

I let the dog have his moment while I walked across the grass. Her eyes lifted to meet mine and I took her hand to help her stand. "Hi."

"Hi," she said with a smile.

I pulled her close and kissed her lips. It was possible Max had just licked her face but I didn't care. I needed her mouth on mine, the warm feeling of our tongues sliding together. She tasted like mint and a flavor that was distinctly her.

It was starting to get addicting.

She moved back and licked her lips. "Wow."

"How was your day?"

"What? My day?" She blinked a few times. "Sorry, you just scrambled my brain. My day was fine. How was yours?"

I liked the dazed look in her eyes—that I'd done that to her. "It was good. Got a lot done."

"Can I see?"

"Cameras are in." I pointed to her front door. "There's one there, another over the garage, and a third in the back."

"That's a lot of cameras."

"I'm tempted to put in more, but this is a start. I'll show you how to use them later."

"Thanks for doing that."

"Of course." I jerked my thumb over my shoulder. "Do you want to see the house? Trim is almost done."

"Definitely."

I led her next door and walked her through, showing her how great the trim she'd picked was looking. The paned windows and two-panel doors added a touch of detail and the trim set it all off perfectly.

"This looks incredible. You got so much done today. I'm glad Max wasn't in your way."

"Nah, he's fine. He mostly naps in the corner while I work. The noise of the saw in the garage doesn't even bother him."

"That's good. So what's next after you finish the trim?"

"Carpet goes in the bedrooms soon, then I can finish the baseboards upstairs." I grabbed the samples and laid them out to show her. "Which one do you think?"

She crouched down and ran her hands over the samples while Max sniffed them. "I like this one." She tapped the dark beige. "The color is neutral, which I think is good if you're going to rent it out, and it's so soft. You want really soft carpet under your feet when you get out of bed in the morning."

I mentally checked that off my list. "Agreed. Thanks."

She stood and smiled at me. "You're welcome."

Since we were there, I figured I'd ask her about the countertops too. "Do you mind giving me another opinion?"

"Not at all."

"Kitchen counters." I grabbed the samples and laid them out. "Those ones are granite and the others are quartz. What do you think?"

"Definitely that one." She pointed to a simple creamy white quartz. "It's so pretty. The granite ones are nice but they're so busy. I love the simplicity of this. And it will contrast with the floors which I think will be gorgeous."

She was spot on. Plus, for reasons I couldn't explain, I wanted her to like this house. "Great. One less thing I have to worry about."

"I can't wait to see how it looks when it's installed."

"You and me both."

"Is that it?"

"Yeah, for now. Let's go, Max."

We went back to her house and as soon as we were inside, something shifted inside me. Truthfully, it had been building. Not just since the vandalism and the last couple of nights sleeping next to her, although that had kicked things into overdrive. It had been building since the first time we met.

I wanted her.

And I wanted her now.

A part of me didn't want to want her. I wanted to keep her at a distance so if this crashed and burned, I could walk away unscathed.

But as I watched her set down her purse and step out of her shoes, I knew it was too late for that. I stared at her, desire flooding my veins—watched her like a predator locked on his prey.

"What?" she asked, a small smile playing on her lips.

I'd always been a man of few words and now wasn't the time for talking. I strode over to her, ran my hands through her hair, and pulled her mouth to mine. She whimpered slightly as I kissed her deeply.

I pulled away and flicked a quick glance at Max. He'd curled up in his spot on the couch and didn't seem particularly interested in what we were doing.

Good dog.

I kissed along her jaw toward her ear, then spoke, my voice low. "Bedroom?"

"Oh yes," she breathed.

That was all I needed to hear.

I picked her up and tossed her over my shoulder. A bit caveman—or maybe mountain man—of me, but let's be honest, I'm not exactly a refined gentleman.

In her bedroom, I shut the door behind us and dropped her unceremoniously on the bed. It took us mere moments to tear off our clothes. I kissed and licked her skin as I undressed her, pausing only to let her pull my clothes off me.

It wasn't the first time I'd seen her naked, but it was the first time I was able to appreciate her natural beauty. She was soft and curvy with slight definition in her legs, probably from all the hiking she did with her dog.

Perfection.

Her hands were silky against my rough skin, her mouth eager. I took care of the condom situation but I didn't rush. My body ached for her but I wanted to savor this. Touch her, taste her, experience every curve.

Her hands roamed over me, fingers digging into my flesh as I explored. Her gasps and whimpers spurred me on until I couldn't take it anymore.

Groaning, I slid inside her, reveling at the feel of her body joining with mine. It was all I could do not to explode right there.

We found our rhythm, moving in sync like this wasn't our first time together. I felt her let go, opening up to me, sighing and moaning with the pleasure I was giving her.

I wanted to take all of her, devour her completely. I couldn't get enough. Possessiveness and the instinct to protect her flared to life, adding intensity to every movement. Every thrust felt like a chorus of *mine, mine, mine.*

The heat between us built to a breaking point. I saw her climax begin to overtake her, watched her eyes roll back and her lips part. She was so fucking beautiful, I couldn't hold back any longer.

I unleashed inside her, groaning as the tension released in hot waves. When it was over, I paused to catch my breath.

"Wow," she said, her lips curling in a dreamy smile. "That was amazing."

I preened a little at her compliment. Hell yeah, it was amazing. I gave her a half-grin and gently kissed her.

I got up to deal with cleanup and she took the bathroom after me. I was about to pull my clothes back on when she came out and crawled back into bed. Normally I wasn't much of a cuddler. The sex had been great, we'd both enjoyed it, couldn't we get on with life?

But the little eyebrow raise she gave me, the nonverbal please, was irresistible.

I got back into bed and pulled her close. She took a deep breath, relaxing into me. I felt my muscles loosen, the tension in my body melting away at the feel of her nestled against me.

I was calm and sated, and although I was a bit afraid to admit it, maybe even happy.

July 8th

Tilikum is filled with idiots.

I went to their so-called emergency town meeting. No one noticed me. I'm good at that; going unnoticed. It's a useful skill.

But it was a hollow victory. Who cares if I can slip in and out without calling attention to myself.

She's still here.

I should have known my present wouldn't be enough to drive her away. She still has her job to consider. And the mountain man.

I'm not worried about him. I don't care who she dates or who she fucks. She can fuck half the town if she wants to.

It just makes me hate her all the more.

CHAPTER 25

Audrey

A FEW WEEKS went by and three things didn't happen. One, Lou didn't put up much resistance to my ideas for the newspaper. I wanted to focus not only on local news, but on the locals themselves. Feature them, in all their quirky, Tilikum glory. So we came up with Hometown Spotlight, a weekly piece that would focus on the people of Tilikum.

I thought it was a pretty good idea, if I did say so myself. Hopefully the readership would like it.

Two, I didn't get a reply to the job I'd applied for in Seattle. Boo.

And three, no one wrote anything in animal blood on my door, or performed any other creepy acts of vandalism. That was a yay.

The biggest yay? Josiah Haven.

We'd stopped discussing whether or not he was going to sleep at my place. He just did. It wasn't like he was moving in. Not exactly. But a toothbrush and a few other things did appear in my bathroom and instead of taking everything home each day, a few clothing items made their way onto the chair in my bedroom.

Josiah's presence in my life eased the sting of not getting a reply from the Seattle job. Despite how great it had sounded, it was also hours away, and it wasn't a remote position. When I'd applied, starting a relationship here in Tilikum hadn't even been on my radar.

But now? Things were changing. Fast.

That didn't stop me from my usual Saturday morning routine of checking online job listings and noting the ones that might be worth pursuing. But my heart wasn't in it. I took a sip of my coffee as I sat at the kitchen table and scrolled through the postings.

Could I fathom staying in Tilikum for good? Was I crazy for worrying about it? Just because Josiah and I had taken things to the next level didn't mean it was going to work out in the long run. I'd been swept up in the beginning stages of a relationship before. The newness, the excitement, the constant butterflies. None of those things meant we'd go the distance.

I'd been disappointed before. As much as I didn't want to experience that again—didn't want to jump into something that didn't have forever potential—I couldn't put that kind of pressure on Josiah.

So, Josiah, do you think the amazing sex means you might want to marry me at some point?

Yeah, no.

I took another sip of coffee and kept scrolling. Although Max had woken me up early, I'd managed to get up without waking Josiah. He hadn't emerged yet and Max had gone right back to sleep on his doggie bed after going outside. Silly dog.

Thinking about jobs and the future and Tilikum and Josiah, I had to ponder the big question. What did I want?

Did I want to go the distance with Josiah? If he told me he thought we had a future together, what would I do? How would I feel about that? Could I be satisfied with a life here?

Big questions and I didn't know the answers. I really liked Josiah. Maybe too much, considering things between us had only heated up recently. I loved being with him, sleeping next to him—and with him. He made me feel safe and protected.

But his whole life was here. His business was literally rooted to the ground of Tilikum. I very much doubted he'd relocate if I got a job somewhere else. And I didn't blame him. This was where he belonged. I couldn't ask him to do that.

As for me? I didn't know where I belonged. Maybe I never had.

I heard the bedroom door open and my heart did a little flip. Just the anticipation of seeing him gave me a rush of endorphins. As if I hadn't been tangled in the sheets with him all night.

He walked into the kitchen in nothing but pajama pants, with messy hair and still blinking away sleep. He was so sexy, with that hairy chest and lumberjack beard, I wanted to eat him.

"Morning." His sleepy voice was ridiculously sexy. So rough and growly. He leaned over and kissed my head.

"Morning." I closed my laptop and resisted the urge to jump up and climb him like a tree. "There's coffee if you want some."

"Thanks."

Max came over to get his obligatory morning pets. Josiah gave him a few scratches. That seemed to satisfy Max and he went back to his spot.

I took him in as he poured his coffee. The hard lines of his body. The muscle built on hard work. His rough hands that could be both possessive and surprisingly gentle. He was a marvel. So sturdy and stoic, yet with a softness on the inside that he rarely let anyone see.

He sat down across from me and took a sip. "Why are you always up so early?"

"Max." I nodded my head toward my derpy dog. "He doesn't understand weekends."

Cupping his mug in his hands, he nodded.

"Are you working on the house today?"

"I probably should. And I need to run up to my parents' place at some point." He took another drink. "Wanna come?"

He said that so casually, like it was totally not a big deal that he'd just invited me to his parents' house. I'd met them, of course, but going to their house seemed like a thing.

Although maybe it wasn't a thing. Maybe he was just being practical and it didn't say anything about our relationship.

"Sure, I'd love to."

He didn't say anything else. Just nodded.

A man of few words. It was refreshing.

I decided to take Max for a hike while Josiah worked on the remodel. He protested, telling me he didn't want me to go alone. He had a point, so I promised to stay close to home and not go where my cell signal would drop. Based on his expression, he still wasn't happy about it, but he didn't argue.

Max and I set out and did a couple of laps around the neighborhood. Then I took him out back and we climbed the hill behind the house. I let his leash out so he could sniff around the trees and the steep slope gave me a good workout. When we got to the top, I stopped and checked my phone. I had a signal, but just barely, so we made our way back down.

Josiah was still working next door when we got home. I gave Max a bully stick to chew and hopped in the shower. I took the time to wash my hair—too many dry shampoo days in a row probably wasn't a great idea—and exfoliate with sugar scrub. I got out feeling fresh and clean.

After getting dressed, putting on a little makeup, and blow drying my hair, Josiah came back. He stopped just inside the doorway and the corners of his mouth hooked ever so slightly. Max ran over to greet him.

"You look good." He absently petted Max's head.

"Thanks."

Of course, my preparations had nothing to do with going

to his parents' house. I wasn't nervous or anything. It was probably just a quick stop. I didn't even know if I'd go inside.

"Ready to go?" he asked.

"Yep."

"What about him?" He nodded toward Max.

"He can stay here. After our hike, he'll just pass out."

Josiah didn't shower, but I didn't mind. I liked the way he was often a little dirty and he always smelled amazing. I brushed the sawdust out of his beard and off his t-shirt and we headed out.

Nervous energy thrummed through me as we drove to the Haven family home. They lived up a long gravel driveway that snaked its way up a small hill. The trees opened up on a gorgeous log home with friendly lights in the windows.

"Do they know we're coming?" I asked, fighting the tremor in my voice. "Do they know I'm coming? Is this going to be weird? I'm probably going to make it awkward somehow, just warning you."

"Audrey." Josiah's voice was low but gentle.

"Yeah?"

He didn't say another word. Just leaned over and kissed me.

It helped.

With a deep breath, I hopped out of his truck and steeled myself to step into his family's world.

He didn't knock, which struck me as sweet. Upon opening the door, he walked right in. "Mom? Dad?"

No one answered. "They're probably out back."

I followed Josiah inside. The décor was cozy and welcoming. A couch and denim armchairs faced a wood stove and there were photos in mismatched frames all along the mantle. Lots of smiling little boys in various states of rough and tumble disarray.

There were more on the walls and one photo in particular caught my eye. Six boys lined up on a couch with what had to be Josiah in the middle, holding a newborn baby. It must have been their sister, Annika.

They were all looking at the baby dressed in pink, as if she were the most exciting thing in the world. It was so precious it made my heart ache. As an only child, I'd never known what it would be like to have siblings.

Maybe six brothers would have been a lot to handle. But it would have been nice to have had one or two.

"Is this you and all your siblings?" I asked.

"Yeah, right after Annika was born."

"Tell me about your brothers. What are they like?"

"Pains in the ass." He cracked that almost smile of his and pointed out each brother in turn. "You've met Garrett. He wanted to be a cop from the time he was a kid. He was married for a while but she was the worst. They got divorced a few years ago, thankfully. Now he's raising their son, Owen."

"He seems like a nice guy."

"He's solid. This one is Zachary. He's the smartass of the family. Despite the fact that he's a man-child, he does well for himself. He's an electrician; owns his own business. And that's Theo. He played professional football for about a minute but he got injured. Now he's the high school football coach. That one is Luke. You met him, too. He inherited our great-uncle's custom auto shop."

"Who's that one?" I pointed to a boy on the far left. He was a little chubbier than the rest of them, with round cheeks and a bit of belly showing beneath his shirt. The type of kid well-meaning grown-ups referred to as *husky*.

"Reese."

"That's so weird, I knew who your other brothers were, but I don't know if I've ever heard his name. What's he like?"

He paused for a long moment. "I don't know. He left Tilikum a long time ago. Hasn't been back."

Before I could ask why, he walked away, toward the

kitchen. I understood. He didn't want to talk about it. Despite my curiosity, I decided not to press the issue.

The back door opened and Marlene came in. She smiled warmly and adjusted her glasses. "Hi. Sorry, I was in the shop with your dad, I didn't hear you drive up."

"No problem," Josiah said.

"Nice to see you again, Audrey."

"Thanks. You too."

"Is Dad around?" Josiah asked.

"He was right behind me."

The door opened again and Paul came in. He was like an older version of Josiah, with the same perpetually furrowed brow and thick arms stuffed in flannel. He tipped his chin to me but didn't say anything.

Yep. So much like Josiah.

"Audrey, are you responsible for the new Hometown Spotlight section in the paper?" Marlene asked. "Because it's so charming."

"Yes, that's me. I'm glad you like it. My editor was a little stubborn about taking up front page real estate with something that's not breaking news, but I convinced him to try it for a few weeks at least."

"I loved it," she said.

"Thanks. I'm hoping to interview the sheriff soon. I heard he's originally from Seattle, so I want to know what it's like to go from big city law enforcement to a small town."

"Sheriff Cordero is such a good man," Marlene said. "Hopefully you can pin him down. If not, let me know, I'll put in a good word with his wife."

"That would be great, thank you."

Paul grabbed a towel and wiped off his hands. "I got the tile samples."

"Let's take a look," Josiah said.

He slid a box closer and started taking out square tile samples. "You said neutral, so that's what they gave me."

Josiah moved them around, as if putting them in order. Some were in varying shades of beige, others gray. He slid a dark slate gray tile away from the others. I agreed. It was too dark.

He turned to me. "What do you think? Master bathroom floor. They'll be larger than this, we're just looking at color."

That was easy. I pointed to the one I liked, a cream color. "This one. It will brighten everything up in there."

"Agreed." Josiah handed it to his dad. "Let's do this in both upstairs bathrooms."

"Done and done." Paul's eyes moved to me. "Good choice."

I smiled. "Thank you."

"That will be pretty," Marlene said. "What if we used that in our master bathroom?"

"Are we putting new tile in our bathroom?" Paul asked.

She smiled at him. "It doesn't have to be right away but it would be nice."

He leaned over and gave her a light kiss. "Anything for my bride."

Oh my gosh, they were so adorable, I could have died.

There was a knock at the front door and I realized I was staring at Josiah's parents, kind of dreamily. Thankfully, they didn't seem to have noticed.

"That must be Louise," Marlene said. "She's picking up a casserole to take to Doris Tilburn. She's recovering from gall-bladder surgery."

"Oh good," Josiah said, his voice flat, "you get to meet my aunt Louise."

I couldn't tell by his tone if he was actually glad or if he was being sarcastic.

He'd said to assume sarcasm, so I went with that.

Marlene answered the door and an older woman in a bright red velour track suit swept in. Her long gray hair was in a ponytail and her lipstick matched her outfit.

Josiah made a noise that was a cross between a throat clear and a groan.

"Hi, Louise." Marlene hugged her and they came into the kitchen. "Have you met Audrey?"

She turned to me and smiled. "I haven't had the pleasure. I'm Louise Haven but you can just call me Aunt Louise."

"It's nice to meet you."

"You as well. You're even prettier up close." Her eyes flicked to Josiah, then back to me. "Here meeting the family? I love that. Welcome. It's not my house, but welcome."

She was so effusive, I wasn't quite sure how to respond. "Thank you."

"Well done, Josiah. I was hoping you'd snap this one up before someone else got to her."

"What?" Josiah's voice sounded uncharacteristically shocked. "You've been trying to push your friend's grand-daughter on me."

Louise waved her hand, as if batting his comment out of the air. "Aida? I wasn't trying to push her on you."

He raised his eyebrows, disbelief clear on his face.

"I wouldn't do that. She's not good enough for you."

"You said she was a nice girl."

Louise shrugged. "I shouldn't have listened to Florence. You can't believe a word that woman says, especially about her grandchildren. Makes up stories like you wouldn't believe."

"Then why did you drop her off at my remodel so I had to give her a ride home?"

She sighed, as if the answer should be obvious, but she'd explain anyway. "If you must know, I was trying to push you toward Audrey."

"How would trying to get me to go out with another woman push me toward Audrey?"

"Don't question my methods, Josiah." She patted his cheek. "Besides, it worked, didn't it?"

I pressed my lips together so I wouldn't laugh out loud. This woman was hilarious. Although Josiah was clearly not amused.

Marlene handed her a casserole dish wrapped in foil.

"Thank you, dear. I'm afraid I can't stay. I have to get this to Doris. But it was so good to meet you, Audrey." Her eyes moved to Josiah. "Seal the deal on this one quick, before she gets away from you."

I tried to suppress another laugh.

Josiah just shook his head.

"Ta ta!" As quickly as she'd come, Aunt Louise disappeared out the front door.

"That reminds me, I don't have anything defrosted for dinner," Marlene said. "Paul, what sounds good?"

"Let's go out. Date night." He headed for the back door. "I'll pick you up at seven. Wear something pretty."

She beamed at him as he walked out and shut the door behind him. "I guess that means I'm not inviting you to stay for dinner."

"That's fine. We need to get going anyway." Josiah grabbed my hand. "See you later, Mom."

"Have a fun date night," I said.

"We will. Bye, you two. Have a good evening."

We left and got into Josiah's truck. On the way home, I was almost as jumpy as I had been on the way there. Which didn't make any sense. It had been a fun visit. His parents were amazing and I'd adored his aunt Louise.

So why did I feel so tangled up inside?

Because I really liked Josiah and I really liked his family. And that combination was starting to scare me a little.

CHAPTER 26

Josiah

AUDREY NESTED AGAINST ME, all smooth skin and soft curves. I wasn't tired enough to sleep but I wasn't motivated to get out of bed, either. She did that to me. Settled me down enough to want to stay in bed with her after sex.

Damn woman was turning me into a cuddler.

Her slow, deep breath loosened the tension in my back. I kissed her neck a few times, enjoying the feel of her body tucked against mine. I was sated and relaxed, although if she'd wanted another go, I'd have been up for it.

She did that to me, too.

"Have your parents always been like that?" she asked out of the blue.

"Like what?"

She rolled onto her back and I propped my head on my arm.

"So cute."

"If by cute, you mean gross, then yes."

She laughed. "They're not gross. They're in love. That's amazing."

"Yeah, I guess that's better than the alternative. Although I've seen an unhealthy number of butt grabs in my life."

"You just don't know how lucky you are. My parents were never affectionate around other people. Come to think of it, I have no idea if they were affectionate in private."

"They made you."

"Yeah, but that doesn't mean they were affectionate toward each other. I never saw them hug or kiss or anything like that. I definitely never saw my dad grab my mom's butt."

"You're not missing anything."

"I'm sure it would have grossed me out. But I kind of wish I had been grossed out." She paused for a long moment. "It makes me wonder what their marriage was really like. So much of what I saw was just for show."

"That sucks."

"Yeah."

A soft whine came from the other side of the door.

She laughed. "I guess we should let him back in."

Strangely, I didn't mind. There were some things her dog didn't need to see, but I liked having that furball around.

We let him in and he hung out while we got ready for bed. And there was something about all of it that I really liked.

———

A wet dog nose in my face was not my favorite way to wake up. I didn't know how he chose which one of us to torture in the early morning, but he seemed to pick one and leave the other alone. Unfortunately for me, today was my turn for the morning potty trip.

Actually, I didn't mind too much. It would give Audrey a little extra sleep.

I grunted an acknowledgment that I was awake and peeled myself out of bed, careful not to wake her. Max jumped down, full of energy, and waited by the door while I used the bathroom and tugged on some sweats.

He followed me to the front door. I didn't bother with

shoes. His morning trips outside were always the same—a mad dash to the pee tree and right back inside.

But when I opened the door, he didn't run for the tree in the middle of the front yard. He paused, ears perking like something had caught his attention. His nose lifted a few times as he sniffed the air. Then he took off at a run and disappeared around the side of the house.

"Damn it, Max."

I followed. Thankfully when I turned the corner, I found him furiously sniffing the ground.

"What are you doing?"

I was still half asleep, so maybe that was why it took me a few seconds to notice the words on the side of the house.

You don't see me.

Instantly awake and wary, I checked my surroundings. No sign of anyone but I still had the unsettled feeling of being watched. Max kept sniffing the ground and followed the scent toward the street in front of the house. He definitely smelled whoever had been there.

"Max, come."

Amazingly, he obeyed. Or he wanted to sniff where the scent was strongest and that just happened to coincide with what I wanted him to do. Hard to tell, but at least he didn't take off.

I stepped closer to the house. The words were in red, but it was brighter than the animal blood had been. It looked like paint. I touched one of the letters with the tip of a finger. Mostly dry but still tacky. Hard to tell how long it had been there, but it must have been some time in the night. We'd been out with Max before going to bed and there hadn't been a scent for him to find then.

Damn it. I needed to tell Audrey and call Garrett. And obviously install a lot more cameras. I could already tell whoever had done this had figured out the blind spot. Maybe that was what the message meant. He wanted her to know that he could still get to her, despite my precautions.

Fucker.

"Let's go, Max."

We went inside and I sent a text to Garrett to give him a heads up. Then I went to the bedroom to wake Audrey and deliver the news.

She looked so cute, all snuggled up in the covers. She'd rolled to my side of the bed, probably to absorb the warmth I'd left behind.

I hated that this was happening to her. Hated that I couldn't make it stop.

I sat on the edge of the bed and brushed her hair back from her face. "Audrey."

She took a deep breath and stirred but didn't open her eyes.

"Audrey, honey. Wake up."

The fact that she smiled before even opening her eyes hit the soft place in my chest that I wanted to pretend wasn't there.

"Morning."

I loved her sleepy voice. "Morning. Sorry to wake you, but we have a problem."

Her eyes opened wider. "What's wrong?"

"Someone spray painted the side of the house."

"Spray painted? Like graffiti?"

"It just says, *you don't see me.*"

She sat up. "This is good. Maybe the camera caught him."

I shook my head. "We'll check but I'm almost positive he stuck to the blind spots. Obviously I'm installing more cameras today."

Her shoulders slumped. "I thought maybe it was over. It's been weeks."

"Me too."

"I just wish I knew why they were doing this. And who it is."

"I think we know who."

"Colin?"

"Yeah, obviously."

She let out a breath. "I don't know."

"Who else would it be? He already proved he still has a thing for you."

"I guess, but why would he start vandalizing my house?"

"Because he's pissed at you."

Her voice started to rise. "What did I ever do to him?"

"Gee, I don't know, Audrey. Maybe breaking up with him?"

She fell back onto the pillow. "That was so long ago. And it's not like he was that heartbroken. He married Lorelei right after."

"That was probably his first act of revenge."

"Why does it have to be my ex? Couldn't it be one of your exes?"

"I don't have any exes who hate me that passionately."

"Colin doesn't hate me that passionately either. He's not necessarily the nicest guy but he's not a criminal. I can't imagine him sneaking over here in the middle of the night to spray paint my house. That's insane."

"Well someone did."

"Maybe my mom is right and it's someone who hates my dad. My dad's not around anymore, so he's harassing me instead."

I hesitated, not sure if I should say what I really thought. "Look, I don't know your mom, and I don't want to talk shit about her, but it's weird that she's trying to make this about her."

"She's very good at that."

"Then why are you listening to her?"

"I'm not, I'm just wondering. At the time, it seemed like everyone in town loved my dad, but he was a politician. He had to have made enemies. They all do, don't they?"

"Seems like it. But I still don't buy it."

"Why are you so sure it's Colin?"

"Because it fits. You break up with him, bruise his ego, so he runs off and marries someone else. Years go by and he doesn't think about you because you're not around. Suddenly you move back and he's reminded of how you rejected him. Maybe you're the only woman who ever has. He's holding a grudge. At first he thinks he'll just manipulate you into bed, take out his anger on you that way. But that doesn't work and he can see it won't. So he gets creative."

"If it's so obvious it's Colin, why haven't the cops arrested him?"

"They just don't have enough evidence yet. Maybe he finally screwed up this time and his wife will admit he left the house in the middle of the night."

She sat up again and tucked her hair behind her ears. "I guess."

A jolt of anger made my back stiffen. "Why do you keep defending him?"

"I'm not."

"Yeah, you really are. Every time he comes up, you have another excuse as to why he couldn't have done it."

"It just doesn't seem like him."

"How would you know?" My voice was rising and part of me knew I shouldn't yell at her. But I was pissed and my self-control on the verge of snapping. "You don't know what kind of person he is. Maybe when he was twenty-one, he wouldn't have gone psycho on you, but he's different now. Maybe he's just that fucking angry at you."

"It's not like our breakup was traumatic. We only stayed

together as long as we did because it was what everyone else expected of us."

"So you're saying when you told him it was over, he was totally fine with it."

"No," she said, as if reluctant to admit it.

"What did he do?"

Her eyes darted away and she didn't answer.

"Audrey, what did he do?"

"He got mad."

"And?"

She let out a long breath. "He got really mad. I don't remember everything he said, but he yelled a lot and told me no one breaks up with him."

I raised my eyebrows.

"I get it, our breakup wasn't exactly smooth. But he didn't do anything after that. He didn't call or text or drive by my house or try to see me. It was like I'd dropped off the face of the earth. He started dating Lorelei right away and it was obvious he was over me."

"Dating another woman doesn't mean he was over you."

She rolled her eyes. "I don't know how he felt about it then or why he started dating Lorelei so fast. But they got married and they're still together. Now he's a super successful attorney who probably lives in a mansion and gets to strut around town like a big shot. That's everything he ever wanted."

"Are you being blind to this whole thing on purpose or are you really that naïve?"

"Excuse me?"

"You have no idea what's going on in this guy's head – what seeing you again might have done to him or what he's willing to do to you." I stood and started pacing. "And for some reason that I can't fathom, you won't even entertain the possibility that he's the one behind all this stuff. So I'll ask you again, why are you defending him?"

"I'm not."

"You are and you need to stop."

Her back snapped straight and she clutched the covers to her chest. "You need to not tell me what to do."

Still pacing, I groaned in frustration. "I'm not telling you what to do."

"You literally just did."

"But this doesn't make any sense. You have someone seriously fucking with you and you've convinced yourself the most obvious suspect is innocent." I needed to walk away before I said something stupid. With another frustrated groan, I rubbed my forehead. "I have to go get more cameras."

Audrey called after me as I walked out—something about it being too early. She was right—nothing was open yet—but if I stayed, I was going to screw this up.

I was mad, but I didn't want to do anything to mess things up with her.

Max didn't try to follow me out. He wasn't the world's most brilliant dog, but he seemed to realize I was not in the mood—and his mom needed him more.

I checked my texts. Garrett would be there soon. And Audrey was supposed to go to some breakfast thing with her mom. I didn't like the idea of her going to Pinecrest alone but she was going to the country club. She'd be in public and so far, this guy's MO seemed to be keeping to the shadows and messing with her at home.

Plus, I could just drive up there and follow her.

That's what I'd do. Keep an eye on her and make sure she was safe.

I'd figure out what to do about fighting with her later.

CHAPTER 27

Audrey

I WAS IN A TERRIBLE MOOD.

First, I'd woken up to the news that my house had been vandalized again. While we'd been sleeping. The reality of that was so unsettling. I'd been sound asleep next to Josiah, feeling for all the world like I was perfectly safe, and someone had avoided the cameras and spray painted another message on my house.

It made me wonder what else they could do and whether or not anyone could keep me safe.

As if that hadn't been bad enough, Josiah and I had gotten in a fight. It was basically our first fight, which meant I was stuck wallowing in uncertainty, since I didn't know how this would end.

Had he walked away because he'd decided I wasn't worth all this trouble? Or was he a walk away and cool off kind of guy and that was how he coped with conflict? Would he come back and apologize, or come back at all?

The scenery between Tilikum and Pinecrest was pretty but I didn't notice any of it as I drove north. Because sometimes life was just that unfair, I had to attend a breakfast with my mom. Today of all days, when I had another act of vandalism and a fight with Josiah weighing heavily on my mind.

But canceling would have caused more stress. I'd already taken a half day off work and I'd have to find a way to make it up to her if I didn't go. It would be easier to get it over with. Then I could move on with my day.

Garrett had come to check things out and the forensics team had been on their way when I'd left. Poor Max wanted to go out and play with the nice cops, but I had to leave him inside. I couldn't take him with me, either. The Pinecrest Country Club wasn't a dog-friendly establishment. Too fancy for that.

And let's be honest, my mom wasn't really dog friendly either.

I parked outside the large building fronted with beige stone. Golf carts were parked in specially labeled parking spaces and the landscaping was so well-manicured, it looked too perfect.

Sort of like my childhood.

Before I got out of my car, I took a few deep breaths, steeling myself for what was essentially a public appearance. The Pinecrest Women's Club was made up of mostly middle-aged to retirement-age women. Some of them were business owners. Others were married to local politicians or prominent businesswomen. On the surface, they were all about supporting education and community programs to help those in need. In reality, they were the queen bees of Pinecrest—the grown-up version of the popular girls in high school.

I could still remember when my mom had been offered admission. Forget her wedding day or the birth of her only child. I was certain that had been the happiest day of her life.

With one last breath, I got out. Despite the chaos of the morning, I'd remembered to dress appropriately. I'd chosen a simple yellow dress with a scalloped hem and nude heels.

What I hadn't remembered to do was check for dog hair. I dug a lint roller out of my purse and did my best.

I went inside and veered toward the restaurant. The one good thing about these events was the food.

I'd make the best of it.

Mom was already there, looking slender and perfectly put together in her white pantsuit. She smiled warmly when she saw me and I felt a little guilty for wondering how much of that smile was real and how much was for show.

"Hi, Mom."

"Audrey, dear." She kissed next to each of my cheeks. "You look lovely. I'm so glad you could make it."

"Thanks. It's actually been a little bit crazy but—"

"You remember Mrs. Sheffield, don't you?"

Smiling like she hadn't just cut me off, I turned to greet the woman. She had white hair and was dressed in a hot pink blazer and beige pants. "Hi, Mrs. Sheffield. Nice to see you again."

Her hand was cool and dry when we shook but I managed to keep any reaction off my face.

"It's been a while, hasn't it?" She didn't let go of my hand. "How have you been? On second thought, I see Jessica O'Malley just walked in. We'll catch up later."

She dropped my hand and moved past me to greet someone else.

Okay, then.

The next twenty minutes or so were spent making the rounds with my mother. She introduced me to a long list of women I was probably supposed to know but didn't really remember. I'd never been great with names or faces. They either appeared disinterested in me, which elicited an even cooler response from my mom, or they gushed about how accomplished I was and how proud my mother must be. There wasn't much in between.

And accomplished? I had no idea what they were talking

about, but I could guess. There was no way my mother would have admitted to any of these ladies that my career hadn't gone very far, that I'd spent months unemployed, or that I'd taken a job at a rinky dink newspaper so I could pay rent and keep buying dog food.

Mom's version must have sounded a lot better than reality.

Finally, the buffet opened. Mom hesitated, watching as people found places at the round tables. A moment or two later, she seemed to decide and gestured for me to follow. After placing the cloth napkins on the backs of our chairs, claiming them as ours, we went to the buffet to dish up.

The food did look good and miracle of miracles, my mother didn't say a word about what I put on my plate. I decided to be thankful for small blessings and took my breakfast back to my seat.

After putting down my plate, I peeked at my phone, hoping for a message from Josiah.

I was disappointed.

"So, Audrey," one of the women across from me said. "Patrice tells us you're living in Tilikum. How do you like it?"

I'd already forgotten her name. I had a fleeting wish that they wore name tags at these things, but the women in this group were accustomed to everyone knowing who they were.

"It's nice. I like it a lot."

"And how is your new job?"

"I finally feel like I know what I'm doing, so that's good."

"You were always such a go-getter. I bet you'll be in charge soon."

Mom touched my arm. "I agree."

The subtle pressure was so familiar. *Put on a good show, Audrey. Make us look good.*

I took a bite of mini-pancake topped with a slice of strawberry. If my mouth was full, I wouldn't have to do as much to keep up the conversation.

"Do you remember Alexa Wilcox?" She didn't wait for me to reply. "She moved back to the area recently as well. I think she has four children now? Is that right?"

"I believe so," Mom said.

"Yes, four," the woman sitting next to her answered. I couldn't remember her name, either.

"She keeps naming them after spices," the first woman said. "Rosemary, Sage, Lavender. I don't recall the name of the fourth."

"Poppy?" the other woman offered.

"That sounds right," Mom said.

"Audrey is so smart to be stable in her career before settling down," she said, her eyes on my mom.

"Oh, I agree," Mom said, her voice smooth. "I won't pretend I don't want to be a grandmother, but I'm proud of her for waiting."

As if I'd waited on purpose and it wasn't mostly bad luck in relationships. I stopped myself from rolling my eyes.

"I hear you're dating one of the Haven brothers," she said.

There wasn't any judgment in her voice, at least that I could detect, although Josiah Haven was definitely not country club material. Maybe because I wasn't her daughter, she didn't have to worry about what a burly, bearded lumberjack of a man would do to her family's reputation.

"Yes, I am." I was mad at him, but I couldn't help but smile. "But it's a new relationship."

"He seems like a decent man," Mom said. "I'm looking forward to meeting him."

I glanced at my mom in disbelief. Did she mean that? I'd told her about Josiah over the phone and her voice hadn't betrayed anything. For all I knew, she was just glad her daughter was finally dating someone, and didn't care who. Maybe she'd finally given up hope that I'd marry someone from the right family.

"He's a very good man," I said. "Mom, speaking of my

personal life, something happened this morning and I just want to keep you updated."

Most people wouldn't have noticed her reaction, but I knew her too well. Her fork dropped a little too quickly, clinking against her plate. And her eyes darted to me a little too fast.

"Of course, dear, we can talk about it later."

I didn't want to talk about it later. But habit took over. *Don't make a scene, Audrey.*

So I got up to get more mini-pancakes.

It occurred to me as I dished up more food that the ladies at the table hadn't mentioned the squirrel killings or the vandalism. Maybe they were too preoccupied with the goings-on in their own town, they didn't pay attention to the news from Tilikum. I was glad. I didn't want the fact that I had a stalker to be the topic of their conversation.

The rest of the breakfast passed in painful slowness. The food wasn't enough to make up for the dull conversation, most of which centered around Pinecrest gossip. Husbands, children, and other family members of the attendees were paraded out, as if they were on display, their various life choices and accomplishments—or lack thereof—the morning's entertainment.

There was a vicious undercurrent of judgment to the conversation that made me push my plate aside and decline the server's offer of a mimosa. Instead, I sipped coffee and waited until I could reasonably make my exit.

When my mom seemed to have finished her breakfast, I decided it was time to escape. "Mom, this has been lovely, but I'm afraid I can't stay."

"You have to leave already?"

"I do. I need to get to work." That wasn't entirely true. I'd taken half the day off, so I didn't need to be in the office until noon. But still.

"Of course," Mom said. "It's a weekday, and you have so much responsibility. I'll walk you out."

I gathered my things and Mom walked to the car with me. It was already hot out; today would be a scorcher. I stopped by the driver's side door but paused before opening it.

"Thanks for inviting me, Mom. It's good to see you." And it wasn't even a lie. She wasn't perfect, but she was still my mom.

"You're welcome. Are you all right? You seem stressed."

"Yeah, well, someone vandalized my house again. We found it this morning."

Her eyes widened. She took a step closer and lowered her voice. "What happened?"

"They spray painted *you don't see me* on the side of the house, right where the new security cameras have a blind spot."

"Spray paint is certainly better than animal blood."

"It's not as gross, and I'm glad whoever did it didn't kill an animal this time. But what's going on? Why would someone do this to me?"

"I tried to tell the police that they should be looking for connections to your father."

"And I'm sure they are. But Mom, really, why are you so sure it has to do with Dad? Did something like this happen to you guys and you never told me?"

"No, nothing like that."

"How do you know I didn't make a bunch of enemies in Boise and one of them followed me here to become my stalker?"

"Did you?"

I rolled my eyes. "No."

"No one ever wrote things on our house but we did have people try to heckle your father in public or smear him in the press."

"That's pretty normal politician stuff though, right?"

"It comes with the office."

"But aside from being a politician, did Dad make any enemies? Did he secretly take down a local crime family or something?"

"Honey, this is Pinecrest."

"I know, but this is getting intense. If you think it's because of Dad, you must have a reason. What aren't you telling me?"

Once again, most people would have missed it, but I'd grown up learning to read my mother's cues. Usually they meant things like, "don't speak unless spoken to", or "smile wider and wave". But that brief movement of her gaze to the side, breaking eye contact with me, meant there was something she didn't want to talk about.

"I wish there was something specific I could point to, because then I could tell the police and they could find this terrible person," she said. "I just know better than you how many hidden dangers there are when you're a political family."

Maybe she really was just making this all about her.

"Okay, well if you think of anything that might be relevant, call me. I need to go to work and then see if there's a way to remove spray paint or if I just have to paint over it."

"Take care of yourself." She touched my arm. "I worry."

"I know you do. I'll be fine. It doesn't seem like this person is interested in hurting me. Just scaring me for some reason."

"It could still escalate. Stalkers are known for both repetitive and escalating behaviors."

Was it weird that my mom knew facts about stalkers? "I'll be careful."

I hugged her and we finished our goodbyes. She went back into the country club to finish her socializing. I took a deep breath of the fresh air, tasting my freedom, and checked my phone.

Still nothing.

Feeling defeated, I was about to get in my car when I had the strangest feeling that I was being watched.

This time, I was right. Across the parking lot, I caught sight of Josiah sitting in his truck.

What was he doing here?

I didn't know whether I was annoyed that he was here or glad to see him. I decided it would depend on why he was here. If he'd followed me because he thought I was going to see Colin, I'd barrel right past annoyed and straight to mad.

He got out of his truck and shut the door as I walked across the parking lot toward him. His expression didn't betray a thing, but that was normal for Josiah. He always looked on the verge of being angry, even when he wasn't.

"What are you doing here?" I asked, stopping in front of him.

"You have a stalker."

"So you're going to follow me everywhere?"

"Maybe."

I was trying not to smile, but it was hard. "Sounds like you're the stalker."

"Yeah, I'm clearly out to get you," he deadpanned.

"What did you think was going to happen to me?" I gestured to the building. "It's a country club in the middle of the day."

"Probably nothing. But my tile guy postponed, so it was either this or paint bedrooms."

"So following me was just a less boring alternative to watching paint dry."

He glanced away. "I'm worried about you, okay? Maybe you're right and Colin doesn't have anything to do with it, but someone has a big-ass problem with you."

"I'm honestly not trying to defend Colin. I don't have any reason to. If it bothers you because you think I still have feelings for him, I promise I don't."

He stepped closer and tucked my hair behind my ear. "I know you don't. It's just, sometimes the most obvious answer is the right one."

"Sometimes. And sometimes it isn't. But either way, don't we need to trust the police on this? If it is him, they'll find the evidence, right?"

"Hope so. I trust Garrett. But whoever it is, they're being careful. We checked the camera footage. There's nothing."

I didn't know why that, of all things, made me tear up. I already knew the cameras hadn't caught the stalker. They alerted us every time a car drove by and we had tons of incidental footage of Max running around the yard.

Maybe the reality of the situation was sinking in. Someone really, really hated me, and they were willing to go to great lengths to show it.

Trying to pull myself together, I swiped away the tears that fell. In an instant, Josiah's arms were around me. He held me tight against his solid body, sure and strong. I relaxed into him, taking comfort in his embrace. And something else sank in.

He really had followed me out here to keep me safe.

And in that moment, I fell a little bit more in love with Josiah Haven.

July 26th

I don't know why it took me so long to figure it out. I blame her. She riles up my emotions, makes me too angry to think straight. It doesn't help that she's everywhere. Always running around with her camera, playing intrepid reporter.

Too bad the pretty little journalist can't crack her own story.

Showing her that I can still get to her, no matter what the mountain man does, is only one piece of the puzzle. I need to sever the ties that bind her here. Cut off her connections. Take away her reasons to stay.

She thinks a little spray paint is bad? I'm going to dismantle her life, piece by piece. I'm going to ruin her.

And I'm just getting started.

CHAPTER 28

Audrey

NO ONE in the office could see my laptop screen, but the urge to close it was there. It felt weird to be looking at an email from another company, especially when the purpose of the email was to invite me to interview for a position.

I wasn't as excited as I thought I'd be. When I'd received a similar email from Lou, offering an interview for my current position, I'd celebrated like I'd just won the lottery.

This job was a better fit and it paid more. So why wasn't I jumping out of my chair or rushing to answer as quickly as I could?

Probably because it was in Massachusetts.

It was just a request for an interview. It didn't mean I'd get the job. And if I did get the job, I wouldn't necessarily have to take it.

Who was I and what had happened to Audrey? A few months ago, I would have been salivating over this job, especially because it was in Massachusetts. Now I couldn't imagine saying yes to a cross-country move.

I knew what had happened. Josiah Haven.

Was I really going to decline an interview for a good job?

Yes. Yes, I was.

Because I already knew I wouldn't take it if they offered it to me. And I didn't want to waste everyone's time.

Was I crazy?

Yeah, maybe.

I typed a polite response and tried not to think about the implications of the decision I'd just made. Maybe I'd regret it. Maybe Josiah and I would fizzle out or he'd get tired of me or I'd realize I was nuts to think I could happily stay in this town.

But, at least for now, I was going to let my heart lead the way. And my heart wanted Josiah.

Sandra came in balancing a drink carrier filled with coffees and a bag in her other hand. Ledger didn't seem to notice, so I got up to help her with the door.

"Thanks," she said as I held the door for her. "In case you didn't notice, the coffee maker broke. I figured that meant we needed muffins, too. They had blueberry."

"I love blueberry muffins. Thank you."

"Thanks for your help, Ledger," she said, her voice laced with sarcasm.

He took out one of his earbuds. "What?"

She put the drink carrier on her desk and picked up one of the coffee cups. "I got you a latte. Maybe the caffeine will motivate you to get some work done."

He grinned, clearly ignoring her familiar insult, and grabbed his coffee like a happy toddler. "Thanks."

She lifted another cup and handed it to me. "For you. Help yourself to a muffin. I'll take Lou his coffee."

Sandra placed her coffee on her desk, then took Lou's to his office. I grabbed my cup and a muffin and took them to my desk.

Ledger held out a napkin toward me. "Here."

"Thanks."

Mayor Bill walked by the front window and peeked in. He was wearing a Squirrel Protection Squad t-shirt. They'd even put their names on the back, like sports jerseys. He spotted me and waved.

I waved back. Someone from the SPS walked by at least once a day. It was heartwarming to realize they weren't just looking after the squirrels.

"So, has your stalker struck again?" Sandra asked on her way back to her desk.

"Not so far."

It had been almost a week since the spray paint incident. Sometimes I wondered what was worse, finding the stalker had struck again, or the anticipation of what he might do next.

"It sucks that someone's doing that to you," Ledger said.

"Thanks. It's so frustrating. I wish I knew why."

"Have you considered that it might be a jealous ex? I don't mean yours, I mean one of Josiah's."

"I've certainly thought about it. He doesn't think he has anyone in his past who hates him that much."

Sandra tilted her head, as if she were thinking about it. "He might be right."

"How would you know?"

"It's a small town. Not a lot happens here that we don't all know about. Seems to me, Josiah has been burned a time or two. Women who thought they were too good for Tilikum."

I picked at my muffin, glad I'd just declined that interview in Massachusetts. "I guess I don't know a lot of details about his dating history."

"It's easy to forget he ever let anyone past those grumpy defenses of his. Until you, it had been a while. He took his role as a loner pretty seriously."

That made me smile. So did he. "That doesn't surprise me."

"Well, despite what people in town are saying, I think one of you has an enemy you don't know about. Someone who's out for revenge."

"Wait, what are people in town saying?"

"That you're keeping a terrible secret and your stalker is going to expose it."

I blew out a breath. "Great. So glad to know I'm now the town liar."

"I think my favorite theory is that you're the daughter of a crime boss and you're trying to hide out in Tilikum. But your father's enemies have already found you."

"That is a good one," Ledger said. "Not that I believe it, but it would make for a good story."

"I'm definitely not the daughter of a crime boss. Although my dad was a politician. But a small-town politician and everyone in Pinecrest loved him."

"He could have had enemies," Ledger said.

"Yeah, that's what my mom keeps insisting. She either knows something she isn't telling me or she's just trying to make this about her. I'm leaning toward the latter."

"How about some good news to balance out all this bad juju," Sandra said.

"Yes, please."

"Subscriptions are up for the first time in about a decade. So are newsstand sales. Convincing Lou to lead with the local interest stuff on the front page looks like it's paying off."

"Really?"

She smiled. "Yeah. And I think it's more than just the local focus. We've done that before. But no one wants to read a boring recap of the event everyone in town saw in person. Your idea for the Hometown Spotlight was brilliant. They say bad news sells, and it does, but so does heartwarming human interest stuff, especially when it's something readers can relate to."

"That's what I was thinking. It doesn't all have to be bad to be compelling."

"Seems you were right. If this keeps up, who knows. We might be able to afford to pay Ledger."

He pulled out his earbud. "What?"

"Never mind."

Out of the blue, Lou's office door opened. He always made me jump when he did that. So far, Lou had been nice enough. But he spent so much time in his office, it made him seem broody and mysterious.

Not in a sexy Josiah Haven way. In a make-me-scared-of-him way.

So when his furrowed gaze turned on me, my stomach did a flip.

"Audrey. Can I see you in my office?"

His gruff voice was so ominous. I glanced at Sandra, but she didn't seem concerned. She just shrugged and took a bite of her muffin.

"Yeah, of course."

I got up, feeling shaky. It occurred to me as I walked into Lou's office that he was probably so intimidating because he reminded me of my father. That dark brow, protruding belly, and booming voice were so much like my dad.

Swallowing hard, I took a seat across his cluttered desk while he sat in his big office chair.

I knew if I spoke first, I'd start rambling, so I kept my mouth shut and waited. My heart beat uncomfortably hard and I clasped my hands in my lap, trying to keep still.

"We have a problem," he said. "It's partly my fault. When I hired you, I didn't bother checking your references. Your resume looked good and you didn't annoy me in the interview. That was enough for me. But it seems that there are some things you failed to disclose."

I had no idea what he was talking about. "I'm sorry, I don't know what you mean."

He held up a piece of paper. "When you filled out the online application, you didn't make it clear that you'd been fired from your last job for cause."

"I wasn't fired. I was laid off."

"Yeah, that's what everyone says. But I've been told that you were fired for some very serious offenses, including theft."

"What? I never stole anything."

"I'm not going to report you to the authorities or anything like that. But some very serious allegations have been brought against you. I need to look into it."

"Who did you talk to?"

"That's confidential information."

"If someone is accusing me of a crime, I have a right to know who it is."

"I can't tell you at this time."

"Do you even know who it is?"

He hesitated. "They have asked to remain anonymous but they were able to verify that their information is reliable."

"How?"

"Look, this is an internal matter, and I have to do my own digging to see if it's true."

"Lou, I swear, I didn't get fired from my last job. They were downsizing and I got laid off. And I never stole anything. I've never even been accused of stealing."

"My source has provided evidence that suggests otherwise."

"Have you talked to my old boss? She can clear this up in two seconds."

"I haven't been able to reach her yet. She's not with your previous employer anymore." He tapped his desk with a thick finger. "Audrey, just tell me the truth. I mean it, I won't involve the authorities."

"I am telling the truth." Suddenly it dawned on me what must be happening. "Lou, someone's been harassing me. You know all about it; everyone in town does. They vandalized my house twice. I bet that's who contacted you."

"I know about the vandalism. But this person didn't seem

to have anything personal against you. They were just passing along information they thought I should have."

"Of course they didn't act like they had anything against me. They're trying to not get caught." I sat forward in my seat. "Lou, who was it? The person who contacted you might be the one doing all this to me. They might be the stalker."

"I can't tell you. Not until I figure out what's what."

"Then at least tell the police. You can call Garrett Haven, he's been working on the investigation."

"What I do with the information I have is my business. And until I figure out what's going on, you can go on home."

"Wait, what? Are you firing me?"

"I'm not firing you. But I can't have you here until I find out the truth. I'm putting you on leave for a few days."

It felt like I'd been kicked in the stomach. The air rushed from my lungs and I slumped in my seat.

What was even happening?

I didn't say anything as I got up from the chair and turned for the door. But then something sparked inside me and I did a very un-Audrey thing.

I fought back.

"Lou, this isn't right. And it's not fair. I'm going to go home and you do what you need to do while I'm gone. But I'm just going on record by saying I disagree with how you're handling this and I think it's wrong."

I didn't wait for him to reply. Just walked out and shut the door behind me.

Sandra hadn't looked worried when I went into Lou's office, but she did when I came out. Even Ledger seemed concerned. He took out one of his earbuds and raised his eyebrows at me.

"He's sending me home."

"What?" Sandra asked. "Why?"

"Someone told him I got fired from my last job and that I lied to him when I applied. And something about being accused of theft. It's all a lie. But he thinks he needs to investigate the accusations himself."

"Well that's a load of bullshit," Sandra said, already getting up from her desk. "I'm going to tell him what I think of—"

"No. Don't, Sandra. I don't want you to lose your job because of me. He'll figure out the truth. And I told him what I thought about how he's handling this. Let's just leave it at that."

"I don't like this, Audrey."

"Neither do I, especially because it has to be the same person who wrote on my house. If you do anything, convince him to talk to the police. I'm calling them as soon as I get to my car. I just hope they believe me."

"He'll talk. I'll make sure of it."

I put my laptop in my bag and put the strap over my shoulder. "I guess I'm off for a few days. I'll see you guys later."

They watched me go. Feeling defeated, I went to my car and got in. Realistically, I knew this was temporary. I hadn't been fired and I'd never stolen anything. Lou would find out the truth and I'd be back to work.

But who was doing this to me? And why?

Not knowing was the worst.

CHAPTER 29

Josiah

PAINTING WAS one of my least favorite jobs. But I was reluctant to hire it out simply because it was so easy. I could knock out a few bedrooms in a day or two, especially if I had help, so why waste the money paying someone else to do it? Every dollar counted on these projects.

My dad often helped paint but he was busy fixing a plumbing problem at home. Which was just as well because Audrey's asshole of a boss had sent her home yesterday. She wanted something to do, since she couldn't go to work, and I certainly didn't mind the company.

Not when it was her.

Plus, her painting clothes were hot.

She stood next to me, rolling out the off-white satin finish on the bedroom wall, dressed in a worn tank top and cut-off jeans. Her hair was in a ponytail and all that exposed skin, even with all the drips and splatters of paint on it, was very tempting.

Especially those legs. I wanted them wrapped around me.

Despite the fact that we spent virtually every night together, I couldn't get enough of her. She was turning me into an addict. Insatiable.

"Am I still doing this right?" she asked, jarring me from thoughts of her naked body.

"Looks fine. Just make sure you roll over any drips."

"Did I mention before we started this morning that I've never done this before?"

"You've never painted a wall."

"Nope. Not once."

"Why would you, I guess. You're doing fine."

She smiled and dipped the roller in the paint tray.

I didn't know how she was still so damn happy. We hadn't caught her stalker and it was only a matter of time before he struck again. There was no doubt in my mind he was behind the call to her boss. The fucker had hit her car, vandalized her house, and now he was trying to get her fired.

Yet there she was, humming to herself while she painted a bedroom.

I wasn't so calm.

In fact, I was seething. I was mad on her behalf, but there was nothing I could do. Garrett said they were following up on everything, including who might have contacted Lou. But I was getting awfully tired of waiting for the cops to do their job.

Tired of feeling like I was chained up, being held back from taking care of this myself.

Not that I knew what I'd do, exactly. But it wouldn't have been painting a stupid wall.

"Do you think Max is okay?" I asked.

We'd left him next door since there was a one hundred percent chance that he'd walk through the paint trays and we'd spend the rest of the day cleaning up dog footprints.

She pulled out her phone and checked the time. "We should probably wrap it up sooner rather than later."

The paint was going on easily and we were almost done, which was good news because the carpet guys would be here in the morning. My tile guy was still out sick, but he planned to be here over the weekend so he could get caught up. That meant the vanities could go in the bathrooms later next week. Not quite on schedule, but close. And close was as good as it got in this business.

Audrey had picked the vanities. They weren't identical to the kitchen cabinets, but had a similar vibe. I'd also had her pick the tile for all three bathrooms, as well as the lights and fixtures. I was basically designing the house to her taste, rather than erring on the side of neutral like I usually would for a rental. Maybe it wasn't the best business decision, but there was something about seeing her vision for the house come to life that I liked.

Plus, she had good taste.

"We're almost done anyway. Do you feel like going out after this, or staying in? I was thinking we could get a drink at the Timberbeast."

"I like that idea." She smiled. "But do you mind if I invite Marigold? We don't have concrete plans, but we did talk about hanging out tonight."

"Sure."

She moved closer, popped up on her tiptoes, and kissed me. "Thank you."

"I'll finish up here if you want to go shower."

"Am I dirty?"

I set the roller on the edge of the paint tray so I could hook an arm around her waist and drag her against me. "You're covered in paint splatters."

"Oops."

"You did a good job but you made a mess." I leaned down and kissed her, slow and deep. Her mouth was soft and warm against mine.

So good.

"Sorry about the mess," she said.

"Don't be. I just hope you planned on those being your permanent painting clothes."

"They are now." She smiled again.

Damn, that woman. Her smile was going to be the death of me. I dipped my mouth to hers and kissed her again, indulging in her taste.

I managed to let her go without ripping her clothes off. But only just. I finished the last part of the wall and cleaned up while she went next door to take Max outside. Concern pressed at me as soon as she left. I didn't like it when she was out of my sight. So far, the stalker hadn't attempted to hurt her directly. But that didn't mean he wouldn't.

A peek out the window reassured me. She was wandering behind Max while he sniffed the yard. I waited until he did his business and they both went inside.

Cleaning up after a day of painting always took forever. I got everything washed out and put away in the garage, then went next door to get myself cleaned up so we could go out.

I was glad she'd agreed to a drink at the Timberbeast. I was too restless to stay in. Painting was physical enough work, it should have helped me burn off some of my excess energy. But it hadn't. I hated feeling so useless. Like her stalker could do whatever he wanted and I had no way to answer back.

I kind of hoped he'd be at the bar—finally show himself in public. Then I could give him what he deserved.

———

The noise of voices and music spilled out into the parking lot when I opened the door. At a glance, it looked crowded but not packed. I could live with that. At least it wasn't karaoke night.

I put a hand on the small of Audrey's back as we walked in. A light touch, but it held a message for every man in the bar. Don't even think about it. She's mine.

Audrey checked her phone. "Marigold is on her way. I'll just save her a seat."

That was fine with me. Marigold had been one of my sister's best friends for years. Nice enough girl. Probably too nice for most of the guys in this town.

There was an empty table on the left side, so I led Audrey to it and pulled out a chair for her. "I'll get drinks. What do you want?"

"A vodka soda, with lemon if they have it."

I scanned the crowd as I walked to the bar, practically glaring at everyone. I was looking for Colin, half-expecting to find him there attempting to blend in. No matter what Audrey said, I didn't trust that guy. Even Garrett had admitted they hadn't ruled him out as a suspect.

But there was no sign of him. There were a handful of unfamiliar faces—probably tourists—but most were towns-folk. No pompous, self-important asshole.

Rocco and Hayden were both working the bar but it was Rocco who came to take my order. He was dressed in his typical uniform—red buffalo plaid flannel with the sleeves rolled up over his thick forearms. I ordered a beer and Audrey's drink, then leaned against the bar while I waited.

I kept an eye on Audrey. Before our drinks were up, someone approached the table. I was half a heartbeat away from barreling over there when I realized it was just my brother, Zachary.

He was a troublemaker, but he wouldn't mess with my girl.

"Do you want me to start a tab?" Rocco slid our drinks across the bar.

"Sure. But don't let Z charge anything to it."

"Make sure he simmers down tonight or he'll wind up in the parking lot."

"What'd he do now?"

"Nothing tonight. Just tell him to watch himself."

"Will do. Thanks, man."

Hayden glanced my direction as I picked up our drinks, so I tipped my chin to him. He nodded back, although he looked kinda pissed. Not that I blamed him. He probably dealt with all kinds of shit in his line of work, especially on a busy night.

I took our drinks to the table and glared at Zachary until he got up and moved to one of the other chairs. Obviously I could have sat on the other side of Audrey, but sometimes a guy had to put his younger brother in his place.

"Where's my beer?" he asked as I sat down.

"Get your own."

"Jerk."

"What kind of trouble have you been getting into lately?" I asked. "Rocco said to make sure you simmer down."

Z pretended to look shocked. "I have no idea what he's talking about."

Audrey snickered.

"I'm serious. I'm a perfect gentleman."

I snorted. "You? Hardly."

He turned to Audrey. "Can you believe this guy?"

"I'm inclined to believe Rocco." She gestured toward the bar. "He doesn't look like a guy who messes around."

"True enough," Zachary said. "Did he threaten to kick me out again?"

"Yeah," I said. "Don't test him. He'll do it."

"Wouldn't be the first time."

"Aren't you getting a little old for that?"

He grinned. "Probably."

Luke appeared, pulled out the other chair, and sat. He had grease under his fingernails and his hair was disheveled.

"What happened to you?" I asked.

"Two of my mechanics are out and we have a deadline. Means I have to get my hands dirty."

"Good," Z said, practically spitting out the word. "You spend too much time all cozied up in your office."

"How would you know?"

Z just shrugged, as if he didn't care enough to argue his point.

"What's going on with the stalker situation?" Luke asked.

"Other than someone's trying to get her fired, nothing," I said, not bothering to keep the frustration out of my voice. "The whole thing is bullshit."

"Do you think the patrols are helping?"

"No more dead squirrels," Zachary said.

"Whoever it is still walked right up to her house and spray painted it in the middle of the night."

"But at least he didn't kill another squirrel," Audrey said brightly.

If one of my brothers had said that, I would have glared at him hard enough to melt his face. But coming from her, it was so cute I almost smiled.

"Good attitude," Luke said.

"I like to focus on the bright side."

I loved that about her and I wasn't about to rain on her parade by reminding her there wasn't much of a bright side to any of this.

Although it had given me an excuse to sleep at her place every night.

Maybe there was a bright side after all.

I took a sip of my beer. Someone near the door caught Audrey's eye and she waved.

Marigold came to the table, dressed in a pink shirt and floral skirt. Her hair always looked nice, which made sense, considering what she did for a living. She looked at the full table and took half a step back.

"Hey. Busy in here tonight." She tucked her hair behind her ear. "I can go find somewhere else to sit."

Maybe it was just me, but she seemed almost nervous. Which was weird.

But it was probably just me. I kept assuming everyone was keeping secrets or harboring ulterior motives.

"No, we can make room," Audrey said.

Zachary stood. "I have to be at work early. Later." He unceremoniously sauntered off toward the front door.

"Damn it, Z's my ride." Luke got up and offered his chair to Marigold. "You look beautiful tonight, Mari. Sorry I can't stay."

She smiled and took his seat. "Thanks."

He pushed her chair in before saying goodbye.

Audrey looked at me, her eyebrows lifted, as if she were trying to ask, or maybe tell me something. She flicked her eyes toward my departing brothers, then toward Marigold. I still didn't know what she was getting at.

She sighed.

Marigold reached for Audrey's hand. "Tell me how you're doing. I heard about Lou. What was he thinking?"

"He's just trying to do his best in a confusing situation."

"He's being a dick," I said. "He should be giving you the benefit of the doubt."

"I agree," Marigold said.

"At least I'm on paid leave. Once he gets in touch with my old boss, I'm sure she'll clear it up. I bet he calls me Monday morning and asks me to come back."

"This whole thing is so crazy," Marigold said. "You still don't have any idea who's behind it?"

"Not really," Audrey said. "But with all the cameras Josiah put up at the house, no one's getting close without us knowing about it. And the SPS patrols seem to be helping. At least there haven't been any more squirrel murders."

"That's one good thing."

I rolled my eyes. I didn't want animals to die—I wasn't a monster—but it was not the squirrels I was worried about.

"I'm not going to lie, Audrey," Marigold said. "I keep thinking it must be that ex-boyfriend of yours. The one who lives up in Pinecrest? I know you said you don't think it's him, but I just have a feeling."

I met Audrey's gaze and raised my eyebrows.

"I know, it might be," she admitted.

"He could have hired someone to do the dirty work. He's a suit, right?"

Audrey nodded. "He's an attorney."

"That seems like that type to have a henchman. He probably has the money. Or maybe he has a shady client who can't afford to pay him, so he struck a deal. The guy harasses you and your ex will make sure he gets a lighter sentence. Or maybe I've been reading too many romantic suspense novels lately."

"Hiring out the dirty work isn't a bad theory," I said. "It would explain how he always has an alibi."

"The cops would have thought of that, right?" Audrey asked.

"It seems like it," Marigold said.

I didn't know what Garrett and the other guys on the case were doing. They wouldn't tell me shit. Which was probably just part of the job, but it still pissed me off.

Sandra came in and waltzed directly to our table. She plopped into the empty chair with a smug smile.

"What's going on?" Audrey asked. "You look very suspicious."

"I quit."

Audrey's eyes widened and Marigold's mouth opened in surprise.

"What?" Audrey asked. "Please tell me you didn't quit because of me."

"Damn right I quit because of you. Lou had no right to believe some random person over you. I don't care what kind of supposed evidence they claimed to have. He should have taken your side. So I walked out. Ledger did too."

"Are you going to come back if he takes me back?" I asked. "I can't work there without you and Ledger, especially now."

"If Lou apologizes properly, like a man, then I'll consider it. And you better not go back unless he grovels. Make him work for it, Audrey. Don't accept anything less."

"I know, you're right," she said. "It's just that I kind of need a job."

"Oh come on." Sandra waved off her concern. "You said this job was just to get back on your feet anyway. Maybe this will be the kick in the pants you need to find something better. Besides, it's not like your landlord will kick you out if you can't pay rent."

Audrey laughed and met my eyes. "Yeah, but I can't take advantage."

"I'm with Sandra." I placed my knuckle under Audrey's chin so she wouldn't look away. "He needs to make it right with you if he wants you back."

She gave me a little nod. "Okay."

"It's been a big day," Sandra said. "I need a drink. Anyone else need a drink? Where's Rocco?"

He appeared next to the table as if by magic. "What can I get ya?"

Sandra looked him up and down with a slight twitch of her lips. "A big grouchy bartender, if you're offering. Or maybe just a vodka soda. Marigold, sweetie, do you need something?"

"Just a glass of chardonnay for me. Thanks, Sandra."

"You can put it on my tab," I said.

He tipped his chin in acknowledgment and went back to the bar.

"Why do you get table service?" I asked. "Rocco makes everyone else order at the bar."

"I think he likes her," Audrey said.

"In my dreams," Sandra said on a sigh.

"I'm serious, Sandra, I think he likes you," Audrey said. "You're always teasing him but maybe you should see if he wants to go out for real."

"Oh my gosh, you two would make the cutest couple," Marigold said.

"If Rocco wanted to ask me out, he's had more than enough opportunities."

"Maybe he needs a little push," Marigold said. "He could be shy on the inside."

Audrey glanced toward the bar. "I think you're right. He acts all gruff and intimidating but maybe he's secretly afraid of rejection."

Marigold clutched her hands to her chest. "He's been harboring a crush on you for years but the more time that goes by, the more he thinks it must not be in the cards. I bet he's pining for you, Sandra."

She rolled her eyes. "You read too much."

"I know, I really do. It's given me very unrealistic expectations. But I still think he secretly likes you."

"He totally does," Audrey said.

"You girls are sweet, but I'm too old for that kind of love story."

Marigold gasped. "No you're not."

"What do you think, Josiah?" Audrey asked.

I glanced at the three of them. Audrey and Marigold watched me with expectant eyes, as if I were about to say something profound to settle the argument. Sandra's expression was full of skepticism.

"I'm not getting involved in this conversation."

Audrey laughed and lightly smacked my arm. "You're no fun."

"I never said I was."

Audrey and her friends chatted over their drinks. I was content to drink my beer, more or less in peace.

But one thing that Sandra had said stuck in my head like a splinter. *You said the job was just until you got back on your feet.*

Temporary.

I knew Audrey hadn't moved here with plans to stay. That was why I should have steered clear of her in the first place.

But I hadn't been able to stay away from her.

And I couldn't help but wonder if I'd made a mistake.

CHAPTER 30

Audrey

SOMETHING WAS WRONG WITH JOSIAH.

It wasn't the fact that he'd been quiet that tipped me off. He was usually quiet. If he had something to say, he'd say it, but otherwise, he didn't fill the silence. It was refreshing, reminding me that I didn't have to fill every awkward silence either.

But today was different.

I sat at the kitchen table in my house, picking at the remains of my breakfast, my laptop open but powered down. He walked by and didn't stop to kiss my head or my cheek, like he usually did.

"Are you okay?" I asked.

"Yeah." He poured a cup of coffee. "Tile guy will be here any minute. I need to go let him in."

"Okay."

He left without another word. And without a kiss goodbye.

Maybe I was being too sensitive. Nothing had happened. He couldn't be upset with me. Maybe he was just distracted, thinking about the remodel next door.

It was coming along. Painting with him had been fun and

we'd gotten a lot done. It was amazing how much different it looked from the first time I'd seen it. Now it had most of the flooring, new windows and doors, baseboards and trim. I couldn't wait to see the kitchen when it was finished. It was going to be gorgeous.

I pushed my plate to the side, brought my laptop closer, and turned it on. Despite my plucky attitude when I'd talked to Sandra about my job, I was worried. What if Lou expected me to come back without any sort of apology? I couldn't let this go without standing up for myself. But I really needed this job.

What if he didn't ask me back at all? He might blame me for Sandra and Ledger walking out and decide to replace all of us.

Or he might finally close the paper down.

That made me oddly sad. Why did I care if the tiny Tilikum newspaper finally closed its doors. It was inevitable, wasn't it?

But, for a moment at least, it had felt like we were making headway. Giving the community something they wanted and were willing to pay for. It seemed a shame for all that work to go to waste.

I checked the Tribune website. It hadn't been updated. It didn't say the newspaper had closed, but that wasn't a good sign.

For a second, I felt a pang of guilt. But this was not my fault. And I was not going to shoulder the blame, even just in my own mind.

If anyone was to blame, it was whoever was stalking me.

My phone rang, startling me out of my thoughts. Assuming it would be my mom, I picked it up to answer. But it wasn't her number on the screen. It said restricted.

It had been a while since I'd gotten one of these calls. I'd stopped answering them and whoever was behind it never left messages.

I didn't know why, but I answered. "Hello?"

Silence.

"Hello?"

I waited. Still nothing.

"Why are you doing this to me?"

I didn't expect an answer and I didn't get one. The call ended.

Clearly I was becoming desensitized to the whole stalking thing. I wasn't even upset. I put my phone down and went back to my laptop, like nothing had happened.

Although to be fair, a hang up call was small potatoes compared to messages written in animal blood on my door.

What I needed was an alternative in case my job at the Tribune really did vanish. The hang-up call hadn't upset me, but the thought of being unemployed again sure did. My stomach twisted with dread at the thought of the stress. The desperate searching, waiting to hear back, wishing someone would at least give me an interview.

But how was I going to find another job in this town? The job market wasn't exactly hot around here.

I thought back to the interview I'd declined for the job on the east coast. Had that been a mistake?

The problem was, everything hinged on Josiah. And I didn't truly know how he felt.

That was the trouble with the strong, silent type. He was so hard to read.

Maybe I could find something remote. Or mostly remote with a little bit of travel. I could handle something like that.

I knew it would make me feel better to spend some time looking and at least get a feel for what my options might be, both for local jobs and remote ones. I set my search criteria and started scrolling.

I'd bookmarked three or four that had potential when Josiah nearly made me jump out of my chair. He stood behind me, his expression characteristically difficult to read.

I put my hand on my chest. "You scared me. How long have you been standing there?"

"Not long."

"How did I not hear you come in?"

He shrugged. His eyes flicked to my computer screen, then away again. Without a word, he stalked away.

Quiet and broody was one thing, but this was getting ridiculous.

I got up and followed him into the living room. "What's going on?"

"Nothing."

"It doesn't seem like nothing. You've been acting weird since last night."

"No, I haven't."

I put my hands on my hips. "Yes, you have. Are you stressed about the remodel? Or something financial? Or is it the stalker thing? I wish you would just talk to me because I'm afraid it's none of those things and the problem is me."

"You're not the problem."

"Then what is the problem? You show about as much emotion as a rock but I can see it simmering inside you."

He glanced away. "What are you going to do if the job doesn't work out?"

"I'm not sure. Is that what you're worried about? I have a little saved so even if I can't find a job right away—"

"I'm not worried about money."

"I just mean I'll try really hard not to get behind on rent."

"I don't give a shit about that," he snapped.

"Then what's wrong?" I yelled back.

"I don't want you to leave."

His reply was so unexpected, I just stared at him, my lips parted.

"My life was fine," he said. "I didn't have to answer to anyone. I did what I wanted, when I wanted, and I liked it that way. Then you showed up."

I wasn't sure what to say to that. "Sorry?"

"I'm not good with people, Audrey. I don't know how to do this."

"Keep trying because I'm not sure I understand what you're trying to say."

He hesitated, his eyes stormy. "I didn't think I wanted this. But I do. Every morning when your stupid dog wakes me up with his wet nose in my face, I look at you sleeping next to me and I can't imagine losing you."

"Why do you think you'd lose me?"

"You're not here because you want to be."

"What, in Tilikum? It wasn't exactly my first choice, but that doesn't mean I'm looking to leave at the first opportunity."

"You sure about that?"

"I really want to be on the same page with you, but I feel like we're still talking past each other. Is this because you saw job postings on my laptop just now? Why are you jumping to conclusions that I'll just up and leave?"

He opened his mouth like he was going to reply, but a flash of pain passed over his features.

"What? Josiah, for the love of everything, please tell me what you're thinking. Why are you so convinced I'm going to leave you for a freaking job?"

"Because she did." His voice boomed but I could tell he wasn't yelling at me. "They both did."

He didn't say anything else right away, so I just waited, hoping he'd continue—hoping he'd open up.

"Cassandra, my ex-girlfriend, she did me a favor. I had a ring in my pocket the night she broke it off, but it would have been a mistake. She clearly wasn't in love with me and I don't think I was really in love with her. Just comfortable, so it seemed like the thing to do. She chose a promotion over me. Didn't even give me the chance to decide for myself whether or not I'd go with her. My mother, though– "

My breath caught.

"She didn't do my dad the same favor. She took his ring, married him, had three kids. Then she decided she had dreams that didn't include a husband and three little boys in a tiny-ass town in the mountains. So she fucking left. Tilikum wasn't enough for her. My dad wasn't enough. And neither was I."

Realization washed over me and my heart broke for him. Of course his mother would have given him abandonment issues. And his ex-girlfriend would have torn that wound open again. If I knew him, that was probably the first time he'd ever admitted to anyone how much it hurt.

I marched over to him and threw my arms around his neck. His wound around me, like an automatic response, but his body was still stiff.

"What are you doing?" he asked.

"Sticking to you like Velcro." I squeezed him and felt him start to relax. "I'm not leaving you unless you make me."

His arms tightened around me. For a long moment, neither of us said a word. We just breathed together, existing in the same space, holding each other.

Finally, I pulled back and trailed my hands down his chest. I figured I'd be the one to keep going but he surprised me by speaking first.

"I want you to stay." His voice was low and soft. "Stay for me."

As if I could have refused him anything. "Of course I'll stay. I don't want anything else. I just want you."

"Really?"

"Yes, really." The vulnerability in his face was so disarming. "I know I didn't move to Tilikum because I wanted to be here. But I do now. Because this is where you are. I can't imagine my life without you, either. I already turned down an interview on the east coast because I didn't want to leave."

"Why didn't you tell me?"

"About the job I turned down or that I want to stay with you?"

"Both."

I laughed. "What was I supposed to say? Hey Josiah, we haven't been together very long, but I'm thinking about rearranging my life so I can stay here with you. Are you up for that kind of commitment?"

"Yes, that's exactly what you should have said." His tone was vehement. "Then I'd know. You have to be straight with me. I don't get subtlety."

"So total honesty, no hiding anything?"

"Yes."

I met his eyes, and with a deep breath, I said it. "I'm in love with you."

All at once, he picked me up off the floor and kissed me. Hard. I held on, my arms around his shoulders, and let him devour me. He could have it all, every bit of me.

He set me down, his face still close, his nose brushing against mine. "I'm so in love with you."

His next kiss was both softer and needier. The contrast made my head spin. In seconds, we were backing into the bedroom. Thankfully, Max was napping on his bed and didn't seem to notice us leave.

We couldn't get our clothes off fast enough. Josiah took control, moving me to the bed. I opened for him eagerly, desperate to feel his skin on mine. His lips, his tongue, his strong body. I wanted it all.

And he gave it to me.

With him inside me, all thought vanished. I could only feel. We moved together, the intensity increasing fast. This was hardly our first time, but it was different somehow. It was as if our innermost selves were on full display, nothing hidden. Physically and emotionally, we were one.

He rolled me over and I rode him hard, digging my fingers into his chest. My inhibitions gone, I moaned with his rhythm. His brow furrowed and he grunted and growled. I loved this side of him, so sensual and raw.

My climax built fast. So much pressure and heat, it took my breath away. I let go, swirling in the heights of pleasure. He grunted again with his release and it was nothing but bliss.

I slumped on top of him, breathing hard. He caressed my back and kissed my shoulder.

"I love you," he murmured.

"I love you too. So much."

He held me tight, and he didn't have to say anything else. My man of few words had said the only ones I'd really wanted to hear.

CHAPTER 31

Audrey

ALTHOUGH IT WAS A SATURDAY, Josiah was already at work on the remodel. The kitchen cabinets had been delivered and his dad and brother Zachary had come to help with the install.

I was excited to see how it was going to turn out.

That left me and Max to enjoy a leisurely morning together. I'd taken him for a walk—sticking close to home and not going where my cell would lose signal, of course—and I had plans with Marigold later.

I didn't know what was going on with my job, or whether I'd still have one in the coming days, but I wasn't worried anymore. I had Josiah and that was all that mattered.

I also still didn't know who was stalking me or why. That was a little harder to set aside, even as I basked in the glow of newly declared love. A sense of foreboding followed me wherever I went. I knew it wasn't over and I doubted the attacks would simply stop. From what I'd read online, stalking behavior often escalated. It made me wonder what was coming next.

Max looked up at me from his spot on the couch. I set my

empty coffee mug on the side table, trying to gather the motivation to go take a shower.

"Don't look at me like that," I said. "Sometimes lazy days are nice."

His eyebrows twitched from side to side.

"I know we need dog food. You had your breakfast, you'll be fine. I'll go to the store after I shower and you'll have dinner right on time."

He kept looking at me.

"Stop judging. I know I don't usually run out of your food, but I've had a lot on my mind."

Finally, he put his chin back down and closed his eyes.

My phone rang and I glanced at the screen before answering. It was my mom.

"Hi, Mom."

"Hi, dear. I was out watering flowers and they made me think of you, so I thought I'd call."

"Aw, that's nice."

"I remember when you were little, you used to love to pick flowers and bring them inside to put on the table. Do you remember that?"

"I do."

"I had to plant you your own little flower bed to pick from so you wouldn't disturb my roses."

"I remember that too. I liked gardening with you. It was one of the only times you let me get dirty."

She laughed softly, then her voice grew serious. "Sometimes I wonder if I was too hard on you."

That was a surprising admission. I wasn't quite sure how to respond. "You did your best."

"I tried. Although what would have been so bad about letting you pick some roses?"

"Mom, are you okay?"

She sighed. "I suppose I'm just feeling nostalgic. How was your week?"

"Honestly? Ups and downs. Someone's trying to get me fired."

"What? What do you mean?"

"My boss got a call from someone claiming that I lied about my last job. That I'd been accused of theft and fired."

"That's nonsense."

"I know but try telling that to my boss. He sent me home until he can do his own investigation."

"Is he going to fire you?"

"At this point, I don't know what's going to happen. My other two co-workers walked out over it, so I don't know if the newspaper will even come out this week. For all I know, this will be the straw that breaks the camel's back and Lou will just close the paper entirely."

"Oh Audrey, that's terrible."

"It's definitely not ideal. But don't worry about me. I'll figure it out. I don't have another job lined up but if there's one thing I have a lot of experience in, it's job hunting. I'll find something else."

She didn't reply. I fiddled with a string on the hem of my tank top, trying not to get upset. But the last thing I needed right then was a lecture about how it was up to me to uphold the family reputation for excellence and another stint with unemployment was unacceptable.

"Mom, I know this isn't a great situation, but—"

"I think I should come over."

"Wait, why?"

"You've had a hard week and I haven't seen your house yet. That seems like a good enough excuse. Do you mind?"

The woman was going to give me a serious case of emotional whiplash. "No, I don't mind. What time?"

"What works for you?"

"Maybe give me a couple of hours? I haven't showered or anything and I need to run a quick errand."

"That's fine. I'll see you in a couple of hours. Love you."

"Love you, too."

I ended the call and let my phone drop onto the cushion next to me.

"Well, Max, I guess our lazy morning is over. Grandma's coming."

His only acknowledgment was to crack open an eye, then close it again.

"Yeah, I know, not very exciting news for you. I just hope she's not coming down here to lecture me in person."

Leaving Max to enjoy his couch nap, I got up to shower and get dressed.

———

I had about an hour before my mom would arrive. Plenty of time to run to the pet store for dog food. I probably would have had time in the afternoon before my plans with Marigold, but I wanted to get it done. Plus, if I stayed home I'd just stress about the state of my house. It was decently clean and neither Josiah nor I were all that messy, so a quick tidy had done the trick. And to be fair, my mom was a lot of things, but judgmental about cleanliness wasn't one of them. She had a blind spot for pet hair at least, probably because of her affection for long-haired felines.

Josiah was still next door, so I decided to pop by and let him know I was heading out—and get a sneak peek at the kitchen.

I found him in the garage, shirtless and sweaty.

"Hey," I said, trying not to salivate too much. "How's it going over here?"

"It's hot. AC stopped working and my guy can't get over here to take a look until tomorrow."

"That sucks." I moved closer and, heedless of his sweaty body, threaded my arms around his waist.

"Don't do that. I'm gross."

"I really don't care."

He leaned down and pressed his mouth to mine. I tasted the hint of salt and flicked out my tongue to lick his lower lip.

The low growl in his throat gave me a swirl of desire.

"Ugh, gross," a voice said behind him.

"Shut up, Z," Josiah said and kissed me again.

"Dad, Josiah's making out with his girlfriend in the garage," Zachary called.

Josiah just chuckled and kissed me again. "Ignore him."

"Fair enough," I said. "I'll let you get back to work. I just wanted you to know I need to run to the pet store."

His brow furrowed. "Can you wait? I'll go with you later."

"My mom is coming over for a surprise visit in about an hour and I have plans with Marigold after that. It'll just be a quick trip."

He growled again. "I don't like you going out alone."

"I won't be alone. I'll bring Max."

"As if that will help. If your stalker shows up, he'll roll over and ask for belly rubs."

He wasn't wrong. "True. But you can't come with me everywhere I go. I'll run into town and come right back."

"I still don't like it."

I lifted myself up to kiss him. "I'll be fine."

He cupped my cheeks and kissed me again, deeply this time. Apparently Zachary had gone back inside because there were no more brotherly groans. I sank into his kiss, heedless of the sweat he was leaving on my clothes. My head spun with the pleasure of it—the warmth of his mouth and the tenderness of his touch.

Who knew this rough man could be so gentle.

When he finally pulled away, I glanced around to make sure Max hadn't wandered off. He was sniffing the ground near the garage door.

"Hurry home," Josiah said.

"I will. Wait, can I see the kitchen first?"

The corner of his mouth lifted. "Not yet."

"Really? You're not going to let me see it?"

"Not until it's done."

My shoulders slumped. "Fine. But is it turning out the way you wanted?"

"So far."

"That tells me nothing."

"You just have to see it."

"I want to see it, but you won't let me." I stuck out my lower lip.

He leaned down and grazed his teeth along my pout. "Later."

I loved the pleasant tingle that raced through my veins. There was more to his promise of later than just a tour of the new kitchen.

I couldn't wait.

We said one more goodbye, then I peeled myself away from him and loaded Max into the car.

On the way into town, I found myself looking at the surroundings with a fresh set of eyes. I'd made a decision last night. Primarily, for Josiah. I wanted him more than any job or place to live. But I'd also made a decision for Tilikum. This quirky little town was not where I'd envisioned myself ending up. But as I drove past the shops and pine trees, with the mountain peaks in the background, I felt a surprising sense of peace.

I liked it here. And it was getting harder and harder to remember why coming back to the central Cascades had felt so much like failure. So what if I'd once declared that I'd never live here again? Audrey in her early twenties hadn't known what she wanted. All she'd known was what she didn't want—the life that had been expected of her.

This wasn't that life. This was a life of my own making,

my own choice. And it was shaping up to be better than anything I'd imagined.

When I pulled into a parking spot outside Happy Paws, I was in a great mood. The sun was shining, I was in love, and best of all, Josiah Haven loved me back.

My phone rang. Restricted. I decided I wasn't going to let a stalker bring me down.

"Hi, this is Audrey. Are you going to say something this time, or just keep hanging up on me? Because I don't think the weird hang-up calls are doing what you hope they'll do. I'm not scared of you."

No reply but the call remained connected.

"Maybe we could just talk this out, like adults. What do you think? You tell me what's behind this and we can find a way to resolve it."

Still nothing.

"Would that really be so bad? Listen, just last night my boyfriend and I finally said the things we needed to say and I have to tell you, it was amazing. Simple honesty goes a long way."

I waited. It wasn't that I expected a reply, but I'd never stayed on the phone with whoever this was for so long. I opened my mouth to keep talking—because why the heck not—when I got the shock of my life.

"I hate you."

The voice was low, definitely male.

"Why?"

The call ended.

I swallowed hard, a sick feeling swirling in my stomach. That voice. I didn't recognize who it was, but the malevolence had been unmistakable. Whoever he was, he'd just told me the truth. He hated me. Deeply.

As much as I didn't want to let him steal my joy, it was with a subdued sense of happiness that I got Max out of the car. I glanced over my shoulder, unable to escape the feeling that I was being watched.

Maybe I shouldn't have gone out by myself after all.

But I was there, so I decided to go in and get the dog food. Then get home as quickly as possible. I needed to tell Josiah about the phone call.

"Hey, Audrey," Missy said when I walked in. She looked a little older than me, probably forty-ish, with strawberry blond hair and freckles, and was one of the biggest animal lovers I'd ever met. Max adored her.

I veered toward the checkout counter first so Max could say hi. "Hey, Missy. I just need to pick up some dog food real quick."

She crouched down to spoil Max with attention. I left him with her and found our preferred brand, then brought it to the check out. I spotted some cat toys on the way and decided to pick up a little present for Duchess. My mom would appreciate it.

"Is that all for you?" she asked.

"Yep, this will do it." I grabbed a pouch of sweet potato dog treats—his favorite—and got out my wallet.

I glanced out the front window while she rang up my purchase. Max happily wagged his tail next to me. I didn't know what I was looking for, exactly. I couldn't see my car from where I was standing. Did I think I'd see the stalker, peeking in the window, watching me?

The voice on the phone had unsettled me. I just wanted to get out of there.

Missy handed me a small bag with the cat toys and dog treats. I grabbed the dog food and settled it on my hip, then grabbed the rest. "Thanks, Missy. I'll see you later."

"Have a great day. Bye, Max!"

My heart beat uncomfortably hard as we walked out of the store. The sidewalk on this side of the street was empty, just a few cars parked nearby. A couple walked out of a store two doors down, but otherwise, no one was around.

I took a deep breath. I was fine. Just feeling jumpy after that phone call. I shouldn't have answered it in the first place. That had been stupid.

The leash jerked as Max hit the end of it. His nose was to the ground and he pulled toward my car.

"Hang on, Max. I know you want a treat, but you can wait."

He half-dragged me to my car where he kept sniffing furiously.

"Was there a squirrel?" I adjusted the bag so I could get out my keys. There was a squirrel, chittering at us from the roof of the building. "It's gone now, silly dog."

Max didn't stop sniffing. He tried to do a lap around the car, but I kept a tight grip on the leash while I opened the passenger door.

"Max, seriously, stop. I need to put your food in the car."

I tossed the stuff onto the passenger seat and shut the door, then let Max do his lap.

"See? The squirrel is go—"

I was about to say gone, when I realized Max hadn't caught the scent of a squirrel.

There was a folded piece of paper on the windshield of my car, tucked beneath the windshield wiper.

Taking slow steps around the car, I moved closer to the driver's side. My back prickled and my heart hammered in my chest. With quick, darting movements, I checked my surroundings. But I already knew I wouldn't see him. I'd have bet anything that he'd either left immediately or was hiding, watching me from afar.

My hand shook as I reached for the note. It was a piece of printer paper. No handwriting and if it was anything like the vandalism incidents, there wouldn't be any fingerprints. It was typed in a basic font, probably Times New Roman. No smears of blood or letters cut from newspaper and magazine clippings. Just the words, *I hate you*.

"Max, let's go."

With my heart in my throat, I loaded him up and headed home.

CHAPTER 32

Josiah

FIVE MINUTES AFTER AUDREY LEFT, I regretted letting her go alone. She was right, it was probably fine, and I couldn't shadow her every move like a bodyguard. But I still didn't like it.

Despite the heat, the cabinets were going in without too much drama. My dad wasn't as young as he used to be but he was still as strong as an ox. And despite the fact that Zachary was generally a pain in the ass, he was a good worker. Motivated by his paycheck more than brotherly loyalty, probably, but that was fine with me.

We'd put in the uppers first and so far, everything was level and square. My cabinet guy did good work. I'd go back through later and install all the doors and shelves.

Dad stepped back and mopped his head with a blue bandanna. "Looking good."

Zachary handed him a bottle of water. "Yeah. Doesn't suck."

It was true. It didn't suck. In fact, it looked great. Probably my favorite of all the houses I'd remodeled so far.

Audrey had good taste.

Of course, she was with me, but maybe it was just her taste in men that was questionable.

I was a lucky bastard.

Dad checked his watch. "Mind if we finish tomorrow? I have a few things to get done at home and then I need to get cleaned up. Your mom wants me to take her dancing."

"Dancing?" I asked. "Since when do you dance?"

"Since your mom wanted to learn." He shrugged. "We've been taking lessons."

Zachary looked him up and down. "I can't decide if that's awesome or weird."

Dad's mouth lifted in a crooked grin. "First one. She always comes home in a great mood, if you know what I mean. Take notes, boys."

"Did he just give us sex advice by referring to Mom?" Zachary shuddered. "I gotta go shower that off."

"Yeah, go." I shooed Dad out. "We can finish tomorrow. I'll lock up."

He chuckled on his way out.

Zachary followed. I cleaned up a bit and shut the garage door, then went outside, locking the door behind me. It would have been nice to get the rest of the cabinets in, but I wasn't worried about it. The countertops weren't scheduled for another few days, so we had time. And the heat was brutal. I didn't want Dad to overdo it.

Audrey pulled up and parked in her driveway. Her door opened and Max bounded out of the car ahead of her. I took one look at her face and I knew something was wrong.

I jogged over to her while Max jumped around and tried to get my attention. "What happened?"

"He called. Right when I got to the pet store. I answered and started babbling at him because he never says anything. Just hangs up, right? But this time, he talked back."

"What did he say?"

"'I hate you.'"

White hot anger seared my veins. I clenched my fists and my jaw hitched. "What?"

"That was all he said. Then he hung up. And no, I couldn't tell who it was. I didn't recognize his voice, but it also sounded like he was disguising it on purpose. Remember the Batman movie with the growly voice guy? He sounded like that."

I hooked an arm around her waist and pulled her against me. I didn't blame her for being upset by the phone call, but by the look on her face, I'd thought it was something worse. "Baby, I'm sorry that happened. But you're safe."

"That's not all."

"What else?"

She held up a folded piece of paper. "This was on my car when I came out of the pet store. Tucked under the windshield wiper on the driver's side."

I took the note and unfolded it. *I hate you.*

It took an act of self-control not to crumple it up in my fist. I needed to save it for Garrett, but fuck this guy.

"He left this on your car? Just now?"

"Yeah. It wasn't there when I left home. I would have noticed. And Max caught his scent when we came out of the pet store. He was sniffing around the car like crazy. Josiah, I was only in the store for a few minutes. Five at the most. How did he know I was there?"

"He followed you."

Her eyes glistened with tears. "I knew this was bad but I didn't think he was following me around."

"Maybe he wasn't before." I scanned the street for any sign of someone who shouldn't be there. But I already knew this guy was good at not being seen. "But he is now. And he wants you to know it."

"Why is he doing this? Why does he hate me so much?"

I knew exactly why this guy hated her so much, just like I knew who it was. Fucking Colin. He was taking his grudge against his ex-girlfriend pretty damn far, but clearly he was unhinged.

However, I didn't want to argue with her about it.

"I don't know." I pulled her against me again and held her tight. "But we're going to figure it out and get rid of the asshole."

"That scared the crap out of me. I thought I might throw up on the way home."

"Glad you didn't. Max would have tried to roll in it." That got a laugh out of her and I kissed the top of her head. "Is your mom still coming over?"

"Yeah, she'll be here soon."

"And then you're hanging out with Marigold? Where?"

"We were going to go out to eat but I might ask if she wants to stay in. Just hang out here."

"I won't tell you what to do," I said, in preparation for doing just the opposite and telling her what to do. "But stay in. You're safer here than anywhere else."

"You're right. At least here there are plenty of cameras. I thought they were overkill but now I'm so glad you put in too many. Even though the squirrels keep setting them off."

"The squirrels are annoying as hell, but I'd rather that than give this creep an opening."

She pulled away and glanced around. "Do you think he's watching us right now? I've never been so creeped out in my entire life."

I wasn't sure why, but my gut told me he wasn't. That he'd bolted after leaving the note. "He could be, but I don't think so. It seems like he's good at staying hidden but I think he's just a coward. He put that note on your car and took off."

"Or maybe he got someone else to do it for him."

"Maybe. Hard to say."

She tucked herself against me again and took a deep breath. I kept an eye out for Max, but he was busy sniffing her car. Probably still smelling the stalker.

"I should go in," she said. "I need to call Garrett and let him know about the call and the note. And my mom will be early. She's early for everything."

We went inside and Max went straight for his water dish, then to his favorite spot on the couch. He curled up and closed his eyes. Apparently his adventure to the pet store had been enough to tire him out.

Audrey got out her phone to call my brother. "Hi, Garrett. Yeah, there's been another incident."

I waited, listening while she relayed the information to my brother. When she finished, she put him on speaker so I could hear what he had to say.

"I'm sorry that happened, Audrey. Do you still have the note?"

"Yeah."

"Stick it in a plastic bag for me. Based on the other incidents, I doubt we'll get anything off it, but we'll take a look anyway."

"My fingerprints are all over it. I let Josiah touch it, too. Sorry."

"It's okay. We already know he's careful."

"What about the phone calls?" I asked. "Can't you trace those?"

"We're doing our best, but the guy knows what he's doing. Every call originates from a different number, probably a different phone, and he's using offshore VPNs."

"Who would know how to do all that?" she asked.

"Anyone with internet access could figure it out," Garrett said.

And a lawyer would be familiar with what the police could or couldn't do, what they could track and what they couldn't.

I kept that to myself.

"So you didn't see anyone?" Garrett asked. "No one walking or driving away."

"Not really," Audrey said. "I didn't realize there was anything on the car at first. Max was going crazy because of the scent and I had my arms full of stuff."

"Okay. Well, we're doing everything we can."

"That's it?" I asked.

"What do you want me to say?" Garrett asked and I didn't miss the irritation in his voice. "I want answers as much as you do."

"I doubt that."

Audrey put a hand on my arm. "Josiah."

"No, this is bullshit," I said. "This guy keeps getting closer and closer to her and all I hear from you is what you can't do. Can't trace the calls. Can't find fingerprints. Can't find anything to identify who's doing this. Do we have to wait until he fucking murders her before we find him?"

"I know you're worried about her. So just trust me and let me do my job."

I was so angry I wanted to put my fist through a wall. But then I'd have to fix it and I hated repairing drywall.

So I just shook my head and stalked into the kitchen.

Audrey finished up with Garrett while I seethed. I was fucking sick of this. Sick of handing everything to the cops, hoping they'd come up with a lead. Sick of waiting for someone else to take care of my girl.

I was done.

Audrey put a gentle hand on my arm and while her touch didn't calm me down, it did harden my resolve.

I knew what I had to do.

"So your mom will be here soon?" I asked.

"Yeah, ten minutes or so."

"And then Marigold is coming over?"

"I haven't called her yet, but I'm sure she won't mind coming here. We can order in."

I touched her face and met her eyes. "You're not going anywhere else, right?"

"No. I ran my errand and the last thing I want to do is go into town right now. Why?"

"I have to go do something. I don't want to leave you alone, but as long as you stay here, you'll be fine. And you'll have your mom and Marigold to keep you company."

"What do you have to do?"

I could see the suspicion in her eyes. I hated to lie to her, but I couldn't very well tell her the truth. Not yet.

I'd tell her when it was over. It wasn't lying, exactly. Just delaying the explanation.

"It's just stuff for the house. If I can manage to get everything ready, the countertop guys can install sooner. That puts us back on schedule. I just need to run out and grab a few things to make that happen."

"Oh." She seemed to relax. "Okay. That's great about the counters. I can't wait to see them."

"They're going to look great."

She smiled. "I'm so sorry about all this. You're supposed to be working and here you are worrying about me."

I pulled her in again and wrapped my arms around her. "Don't apologize. This isn't your fault."

It was Colin's fault. And I was going to put an end to it. Now.

CHAPTER 33

Audrey

MAX POPPED up from his brief nap and went to the front window, his tail wagging. I glanced outside and saw my mom's car. I wanted to be happy to see her—excited to finally show her my new place—but after the note on my car, it was hard to feel anything but a vague sense of dread.

I wished Josiah hadn't left.

Granted, I had a feeling it was for the best. I didn't quite understand why my mom had decided to come visit but it didn't feel like the best time to introduce her to Josiah. He wasn't in a good mood, and neither was I. I didn't want to deal with the anxiety of whether or not my mom would approve of my boyfriend.

Especially now. We'd cross that bridge later.

Besides, she was stuck with him, no matter what she thought.

"Max, go lie down."

He gave me the most forlorn puppy dog eyes you could ever imagine.

"I know. It seems like it's always good news when someone comes over. But Grandma needs to warm up to you. Give her space."

Obviously he didn't understand a word of my explanation, but he did partially obey. He stood on his dog bed. Not quite what I asked him to do, but I'd take it.

I opened the door for my mom and she handed me a plastic box of cookies from the grocery store in Pinecrest.

"I thought I'd bring something sweet, but you know I don't bake."

"Thanks, Mom." I let her in, shut and locked the door, then hugged her with my free arm. "Do you want coffee or tea?"

"Tea would be lovely."

"I can do that. Good boy, Max."

He wagged his tail.

"He is a nice boy, isn't he?" She walked over to Max and started petting his head. "Good doggie."

I hesitated in the doorway to the kitchen, watching my mom initiate friendly contact with my dog, probably for the first time. It was oddly endearing.

He dropped to the ground and rolled onto his back.

"He wants belly rubs," I said. "That's his favorite."

"What a good doggie." She leaned over and rubbed his belly.

"Speaking of pets, I bought something for Duchess." I fished the cat toys out of the bag I'd left on the counter. "You can take them when you go."

"That's very sweet of you. Thank you."

"You're welcome."

Mom gave Max a few more pets, then followed me into the kitchen. I started the water and got two mugs out of the cupboard.

"Well," Mom said, looking around. "The house is very nice."

"Thanks. I like it."

"How long do you think you'll be here?"

"That's a good question. For the foreseeable future, I guess."

She wandered back into the living room, showing herself around. Evidence of Josiah was everywhere, but she didn't comment on any of it. I wasn't worried about what she'd think, but I decided to address what could become the elephant in the room.

"You've probably noticed Josiah's stuff. He doesn't officially live here, but he might as well."

"Things are serious, then?"

I couldn't help but smile. "Yeah. Things are serious."

She smiled back. "I'm happy for you."

"Thanks, Mom. I'm happy for me too. He's a great guy."

"Is he?" There was something odd in her voice—a wistfulness. It didn't sound like she doubted me. It was more like she was hopeful that I was right.

"Yeah, he really is. He's very serious, or maybe stoic is the right word. That might put some people off, but to me, that's part of his charm. He's honest. You always know where you stand with him."

"That's priceless."

"It really is." I got a few boxes of tea out of the cupboard so she could choose what she wanted. "I'm kind of crazy about him, I have to be honest."

"You're in love."

"I really am. But why do you sound sad?"

"Do I?" She perked up and I recognized her *everything is fine* face. "I'm not sad in the least. I'm thrilled for you."

I believed her, but I also sensed that something else was on her mind. "Are you sure?"

"Of course. All a mother wants is to see her child happy."

I wasn't sure I believed that—at least not coming from her—but I let it go. "I'm definitely happy with Josiah. Very happy."

"Good."

The water came to a boil. She chose jasmine tea and I made a cup of the same for myself. I put a few cookies on a plate and set them on the table, then we each took a seat.

"So," Mom said, "how is life here in Tilikum? I've always liked this town."

"It's nice. I like it here a lot, actually. I didn't think I would, but it's grown on me."

"I dated a boy from Tilikum when I was younger."

"Did you really?" I knew next to nothing about my mom's life before she was married to my dad. Nothing specific, at least, particularly about her dating life. "Who was he?"

"A young man named Daniel. I was in high school at the time. We didn't see each other for very long. Just a few dates, really."

"What happened?"

Her expression shifted, becoming neutral, like she was trying to hide her emotions. "Your father happened."

"Oh. I guess the other one wasn't meant to be."

"No." She patted my hand. "And we had you, so it was worth it."

The implications of that statement were intriguing. This was the most in-depth conversation I'd ever had with her about my father or their marriage. I honestly had no idea how she'd really felt about him. Had she truly loved him? Did she miss him now?

I had so many questions, I hardly knew where to begin.

"Did you love him?"

"Who?" she asked. "Your father or Daniel?"

"Dad."

She looked down, as if the answer were on the surface of her tea. "Yes."

"Is that a qualified yes, or a straightforward yes?"

"I did love him. Even when I shouldn't have."

This was getting stranger by the minute. She got up,

taking her tea with her, and wandered to the sliding glass door at the back.

"It really is pretty here, isn't it? Is there anything on the other side of that hill?"

"No, just woods."

"What kind of flowers are those?" She pointed to something outside. "I don't think I've seen those before. Did you plant them?"

"No, they just grew."

"Such a pretty color. You would have loved picking those when you were little."

"You're very nostalgic today. What's going on?"

She paused, still looking outside. "I've just been thinking about a lot of things."

"Like what?"

"The past."

"Are you okay? You're not about to tell me you have a terminal illness, are you?"

She shook her head and turned to face me. "No. I'm not sick."

"Then what's going on? You decide to come visit out of the blue and then you're talking about things we've literally never talked about as if it's no big deal. I had no idea you dated anyone before dad. For all I knew, he was your first love."

"Oh, he was. I didn't love anyone before him."

"Okay. That's sweet, but I still feel like there's something you're not telling me."

"There are many things you don't know, Audrey. Things I had to keep from you. It was always for your own good. You must understand that."

The sudden urgency in her voice made me nervous. "What things did you have to keep from me?"

She started pacing, although slowly. "Your father wasn't a bad man. He was good at heart. He loved his community. I'm sure every politician has a certain love of power, and he was no exception. But he did care about the people of Pinecrest."

I wasn't sure where she was going with this. "Okay?"

"I really didn't know what I was getting into when I married him. He was older than me, and so sure of himself. Such big dreams. It was all very attractive. Even before he was in politics, he was very popular. Everyone loved him."

"That's not a surprise."

"And he was good to me, for the most part. He gave me a comfortable life. And he certainly ensured a very comfortable life for me now that he's gone."

She stopped again and set her tea on the table. I didn't know what to say.

"But there were temptations. Every man in power faces them. Most, if not all, succumb at some point."

My eyes widened and a sick feeling spread through my stomach.

"He did succumb, for a time, at least."

"Mom, what are you saying?"

She took a deep breath and squared her shoulders. "Your father had an affair."

Maybe it shouldn't have surprised me as much as it did, but her words sliced through my heart like a knife. I stared at her, dumbfounded. Heartbroken. Devastated.

"He what?"

"She was his secretary, if you can believe it. Some clichés exist because there is truth to them."

"How did you find out?"

"He admitted it."

"And you stayed with him?"

Her expression hardened. "You've never been in my shoes, so you have no room to judge me."

"I'm not judging you, I just can't imagine."

"I had a young child and at the time, I hoped we'd have more. He confessed and made amends. We went to counseling. We decided it was in the best interest of the family if we made it work."

"Why are you telling me this now?"

A spasm of pain crossed her features and she looked away. "I didn't think I'd ever need to tell you. Especially after he passed away. I thought, well, it's all over now. He was never perfect, but who is? He made his mistakes and I made mine and it's all in the past."

"But?"

She pressed her lips together for a long moment, as if steeling herself for what she was about to say. "They had a son."

How I didn't fall backward onto the kitchen floor, I had no idea. It felt like I'd just been hit in the face with a board. "What?"

"She got pregnant. He did the right thing. He supported them financially until the child was eighteen."

"Did you know? From the beginning, did you know about all this?"

"Yes."

Unable to keep still, I got up from the table. "Are you telling me I have a brother I never knew about?"

"Technically speaking, yes."

"Technically?" It was hard to keep my voice from rising. "That's not a technicality. Dad had a son, that makes him my brother. How old is he?"

"You were five when he was born."

"Where did he live? Did I ever meet him?"

"He grew up in town. We took care to keep you apart, and with the age gap, you wouldn't have crossed paths very often."

This was so much to process, I didn't even know where to begin. But there was a particularly nagging question at the forefront of my mind.

"Why are you telling me this now? Is the mom demanding

money or threatening to go public or something?"

"No. His mother moved away from Pinecrest a number of years ago. I don't know where she is now."

"Then what's going on?"

"I've decided to go to the police."

I was about to ask why, when it dawned on me what she was saying. "You think he's the stalker, don't you?"

She nodded.

"Who is he? Does he live around here?"

"His name is Jeffrey Silva. And I heard he'd moved to Tilikum a few years ago."

I searched my memory, trying to place him. Five years younger meant we wouldn't have attended middle or high school at the same time. I didn't remember him from Pinecrest, but had I met him since moving to Tilikum? His name didn't ring any bells.

"Does he know who his father was? Does he know about me?"

"I can only guess what his mother told him. But I suspect he knows exactly who his father was and who you are."

"But what makes you think he's the stalker?"

"Who else would hold such a grudge against you?"

I couldn't believe I was about to argue for this when I'd been so adamantly against the idea when Josiah had brought it up. "Well, Colin for one."

"Colin isn't stalking you."

"How do you know?"

"He wouldn't."

I rolled my eyes because that had been the extent of my argument. "I know it seems like that, but we don't know. He might."

"Fine. I acknowledge it's possible. But I don't think Colin is capable of that kind of madness."

"Mom, I think he would have cheated on Lorelei with me if I'd been willing."

"That doesn't mean he's stalking you. Besides, Lorelei is cheating on him. Everyone knows that."

The burn of bile hit the back of my throat and I almost gagged. "How can you be so nonchalant about that?"

"Because he cheats on her. Everyone knows that too."

My stomach churned and I moved toward the sink in case I did vomit. This was all too much for one afternoon, especially in the wake of the *I hate you* note on my car. "I can't take all this. They're cheating on each other and everyone knows it? And this is not a big deal to you?"

"There's nothing I can do about it."

"But you keep implying that I should have married him. Why would you imply I should have married a cheater?"

"I'm sure he wouldn't have cheated on you."

"Mom." I stared at her in disbelief. "Are you really that naïve?"

She took a resigned breath. "No. You're probably right. It's for the best you didn't marry him."

"Wow, did it hurt to admit that?"

"Don't blame me for all this. I did the best with the cards I was dealt. We were an important family in Pinecrest and your father left it to me to hold our image together. When it came to you, he had expectations. And he expected me to make sure they came true."

"You mean Dad wanted me to marry Colin so he put pressure on you to make it happen."

"And blame when it didn't."

I shook my head. "This is all nuts. You realize that? Dad had an affair, resulting in a child I didn't know existed until five minutes ago. And now you think he's the one stalking me— because reasons?"

"Because he hates your father."

"Dad isn't here. Why would he be stalking me? He just decided to transfer his hatred to his next of kin? Like a crappy inheritance?"

"Yes," she said, as if it were the most obvious thing in the world.

"All right, fine. Maybe you're onto something. But you've talked to the police. Why didn't you tell them before?" As soon as the question left my lips, I knew the answer. Because no one knew. And now they would. "Your friends don't even know, do they?"

"Of course not." She seemed shocked at the very notion. "How could I possibly tell anyone such a thing? What would have become of us?"

It would have caused a scandal and who knows how much damage to Dad's career. Not to mention, their pristine reputation in town would never have recovered.

But what a horrible secret to keep. And for what? Image?

It was so sad, I couldn't even be angry at her. What an awful way to live.

I'd tasted that life myself. I'd been so ashamed of coming home, when I'd thought I was meant for bigger things. And what had that been? Just vanity. The desire to look successful in other people's eyes.

The apple hadn't fallen as far from the tree as I would have liked to think.

But at least I could see it now.

"I wanted you to hear it from me," she said. "I don't know how much anyone will care at this point, since it's been so long, but it could cause gossip. Probably not here, but certainly in Pinecrest."

I moved closer to my mom and took her hands. "I'm so sorry you have to relive this. It must be painful."

She sniffed a little and straightened her shoulders. "I'll be all right. I've persevered this far."

"Of course you have. But, you know you don't have to just persevere through everything. It's okay to admit that you're hurt."

"Well, now I have admitted it." She slipped her hands out

of my grip and smoothed down her blouse. "I should have gone to the police with this immediately, but I didn't want to face it. I admit that and I apologize. I know I've made mistakes, but I love you. I truly do want what's best for you."

"I know you do."

"I should go." Just like that, she'd transformed into the poised, businesslike woman I knew so well. "I have things to do this afternoon and I'm sure you do as well."

I didn't argue with her. She needed space to gather her courage to talk to the police. Whether her theory was right or wrong, I appreciated that she'd finally told me the truth. I'd grapple with the reality that she'd kept this from me for my entire life later.

Sometimes mothers were complicated.

"Yeah, I have plans with a friend. Which reminds me, I need to call her. Anyway, thanks for coming over and telling me the truth. I know that wasn't easy."

Her emotion was gone, hidden behind the mask of the competent politician's wife. "You're welcome. I'll talk to you soon."

I walked her out and she gave me a quick hug before leaving. Max watched her go, his tail wagging.

"Max, I don't even know what to do with what just happened." I shut the door and locked it. "I have a brother. Do you think he's the stalker?"

Max just kept wagging his tail.

"I'll take you out in a few minutes. I need to sit down."

I went to the couch and dropped onto the cushions. Max jumped up next to me. I absently petted him as I leaned my head back, trying to absorb the shock.

It was a lot and I had no idea what to do with any of it.

CHAPTER 34

Josiah

THE THIRTY-MINUTE DRIVE to Pinecrest gave my rage time to cool, hardening like the edge of a blade. That was good. Going in hot wasn't going to solve anything. And, I had to admit, could get me hurt—or worse. I didn't know what kind of resources this Colin asshole had, or what he'd be willing to do.

He'd gutted a squirrel but that didn't necessarily mean he'd gut a human.

Or it might.

But I wasn't going to let that stop me. I wasn't going to wait for him to hurt Audrey. I had to take care of this now.

Not that I was going to kill the bastard, satisfying as that might have been. I'd seen what Asher Bailey had gone through and I wasn't about to do time on account of this piece of shit.

But I was going to get him to admit everything and turn himself in. Even if I had to hog tie him and toss him in the back of my truck.

That, I was more than willing to do.

Finding where he lived had been all too easy. Property

ownership was public record. The question was, would he be there?

He, or someone he'd hired, had been in Tilikum to follow Audrey and leave the note on her car. If it had been Colin himself, I was convinced he'd left immediately. Maybe he'd stayed long enough to watch her find the note, but I doubted it. He didn't have the guts. And he'd want to secure his alibi.

And if he had hired someone, which seemed pretty likely, my gut told me he'd be home with his wife all day. Make sure he was seen by his neighbors, show his face somewhere around town. All to be sure no one could tie him to the stalker terrorizing his ex-girlfriend in neighboring Tilikum.

His house was every bit as douchey as I expected. The circular driveway had a fountain in the center surrounded by neatly trimmed hedges. A balcony jutted out from the second floor, supported by fluted columns that flanked the front entry. I half expected a butler in a black suit to appear.

There wasn't a butler but a peacock strutted through the grass. A fucking peacock? Who had a random exotic bird just wandering around the yard?

Unreal.

There weren't any cars out front, but there was a four-car garage with closed doors. It was very possible he was home.

I didn't creep around the edges of the property, measuring the angles of the security cameras, like a coward. I walked my ass right up to his front door and knocked. Hard.

A woman dressed in a leopard print tank top and mini skirt answered the door. There was no way her platinum blond hair was natural, her nails were at least an inch long, and it looked like she was wearing stage makeup. Maybe under the glare of spotlights, she would have looked normal, but in regular daylight she looked like her face had been painted on.

"Can I help you?" she asked. Her eyes were a little glassy and her speech had the hint of a slur. Definitely day drinking.

"Are you Mrs. Greaves?"

"Yeah." She shifted her weight onto one leg and put a hand on her hip. "Who's asking?"

"Is your husband home?"

"Maybe."

"Can I see him?"

"Who are you?"

"Josiah Haven."

"Is he expecting you?"

"No."

"Are you a client? Clients aren't supposed to come here."

"No. This is personal."

"Oh." She looked me up and down. "Did he bang your wife?"

"No."

"Are you sure? Because you wouldn't be the first."

"I thought you're his wife."

"I am." She shrugged.

I raised my eyebrows.

"He has his fun and so do I. We both come back. Anyway, what do you want with him? You look very menacing."

"I always look like this."

"Oh." She sighed, as if she were bored, and turned. "Colin!"

"Has he been home all day?"

She turned back to me, her head wobbling, like she was having trouble keeping it on straight. "What?"

"Has your husband been home all day?"

"Now you sound like a cop."

"I'm not a cop."

She groaned, like a petulant teenager who'd just been reminded of her curfew. "I don't know. He might have gone out earlier. But maybe that was yesterday."

"Got it." I stepped past her into the house. "If you point me in the right direction, I'll find him."

"Suit yourself. He's either in the study or out practicing his golf swing. Study is down that hall and there's a door to the back."

"Thanks."

The entryway had a wide double staircase leading to a landing on the second floor. A crystal chandelier hung above, taking up too much space. It was the type of thing newly wealthy people bought because they thought it made them look rich. It just looked tacky.

My boots clicked on the marble tile. It was white with streaks of black, almost zebra striped. The walls were sea foam green, a shade that clashed with the dark cherry baseboards and trim.

Whoever had designed this place had done an absolutely horrible job.

But I wasn't there to critique their design choices, tasteless as they were. I found the study and went in through the already open door.

It was empty. The room wasn't as gaudy as the entry. At least the colors coordinated. The wood paneling was good quality—and expensive—and the walls were a deep forest green. Cherry furniture, leather executive chair, shelves filled with law books.

Double French doors led to a patio. The outdoor furniture looked like it was rarely used, covered with a light sheen of dust, and a set of stairs led to an upper deck.

And on the grass, a short distance away, was Colin.

He had a driving range, complete with a green and a large net to catch his golf balls. Not a bad setup, although I hated golf.

And I hated this guy more.

I walked, as casually as I could, to where Colin the douchebag stalker was hitting golf balls.

"Colin Greaves?" I asked.

He jerked, like I'd startled him, and put a hand on his

chest. "You scared me, I didn't realize anyone was out here."
He narrowed his eyes at me. "I'm sorry, who are you?"

"Josiah Haven."

"And what are you doing here?"

"We need to talk."

He set his golf club end down and held the handle in
both hands. I was very aware of how dangerous a weapon
it could be. "I'm afraid I don't know what you're referring
to. If this is a legal matter, you need to make an
appointment."

"It is a legal matter, but I don't need a lawyer. You probably do, though."

Recognition seemed to dawn on him. "Wait, I remember
you. You're the guy from Tilikum."

"The one who threw you out of the bar."

"I wouldn't say you threw me out, but you didn't exactly
extend a warm welcome."

"You weren't welcome."

"Is that why you're here? That was a while ago and in case
you haven't noticed, I haven't been back. Audrey was a sweet
piece of ass back in the day but no pussy is worth that much
trouble."

I wanted to rearrange his face for that comment, but I
decided to let it go. He had much bigger things to answer for.
"I know what you've been up to."

He looked around, like he was confused. "I've been up to
a lot of things. Busy legal practice. Pillar of the community."
He tilted his head. "Fucking a few girls on the side, but I
doubt you care about that, since I'm sure you don't know any
of them. But maybe you can help me narrow it down."

"I know what you've been doing to Audrey."

"Oh, right. The stalker. It's not me. I admit, I can see why
you'd think so, especially if you thought Audrey broke my
poor innocent heart back in the day. Trust me, she didn't."

"No? She said you were angry."

"In the heat of the moment, maybe. But I got over it. I was already fucking Lorelei on the side, so it wasn't hard."

"Then why did you come looking for her at the Timberbeast?"

"She was back in town." He shrugged. "I thought she might want a go for old time's sake. Apparently not, but it's her loss. Like I said, not worth it. After that, I forgot she existed until the cops started showing up at my office asking questions."

I hated to admit it, but I almost believed him. Was this a guy who hated Audrey? Who'd been holding a grudge for years and finally decided to unleash his anger?

Something didn't fit.

"So even though you two have history, you don't give a shit that she's back."

"Not a one." He took a step closer and I was still well aware of how dangerous that golf club could be if he decided to use it on me. "She didn't matter that much to me back then. She certainly doesn't now."

"Colin!" His wife's voice carried across the grass. "What are you doing out there?"

"She's lucky she's still hot," he said, with a you-know-what-I-mean wink. "Just talking, precious."

"Come inside!"

"Did she answer the door?" he asked.

"Yeah."

"Was she drunk already?"

"Probably."

"What do you think? Too drunk to fuck? It's important to 'Goldilocks' the situation with my wife. Too sober and she just bitches about everything. Too drunk and she passes out. I need her just right."

I stared at him, disgust turning my stomach. "She knows you cheat on her."

"Yeah."

"And you know she cheats on you."

He nodded, completely nonchalant. "Judge away, my friend, but I hit the jackpot with Lorelei. Any other woman would get all pissy about my side pieces. That life would suck balls. Lorelei? She doesn't give a shit as long as I fund her bank account, and the liquor cabinet, and fuck her senseless a few times a month."

"So aside from that, you just fuck whoever comes along?"

He paused, like he was thinking about it. "Whoever's convenient, yeah. Lorelei's here and apparently wants some action. My newest lay can't get away until later, so fuck it."

This guy didn't hate Audrey. He wasn't holding a grudge. He was a spoiled child. He'd try to grab a shiny new toy—or shiny toy from the past, as it were—if it was right in front of him, but otherwise, he didn't care.

This guy wasn't out to get anyone. He just wanted to screw whoever would drop their pants for him.

I was so grossed out, I didn't bother saying anything else. I needed a shower—or maybe ten showers—after just being in their house.

As I hurried back to my truck, I was all too aware of what this meant. If Colin wasn't the stalker—and I really didn't think he was—the stalker was still out there. And I wasn't with Audrey.

CHAPTER 35

Audrey

TO SAY I was overwhelmed would have been the understatement of my life.

I didn't know how much time I'd spent staring at the wall, trying to process everything my mom had told me. Minutes? An hour? My sense of time was skewed as I grappled with my new reality.

An affair. A sibling. Enormous secrets kept for so long.

I wondered if my mom felt better after telling me. Did revealing the truth ease the burden she'd carried for so many years? I hoped so. I didn't agree with her choice to keep me in the dark my whole life, but I couldn't help but feel sympathy for her.

On some level, I'd always known their marriage hadn't been great. I'd seen the contrast between how my father behaved in front of others versus at home without an audience. He'd never been mean to my mother—didn't fight with her or belittle her, at least that I saw.

He'd kind of ignored her. Paid attention when he needed something but otherwise, he wanted to be left to his own devices.

I'd received the same treatment. It had been so confusing,

to have him act like a loving father in some circumstances and brush me off in others. My relationship with him had been little more than a performance, and it had varied depending on who was watching. In public? Loving father and devoted daughter. In private? Busy and distracted father who expected his daughter to stay out of his way.

Deep down, I'd felt like an inconvenience to both my parents.

How much worse must Jeffrey Silva have felt?

Obviously, I didn't know anything about his childhood. But as I sat there, staring at the wall, I tried to imagine what it would have been like to grow up knowing Darryl Young was your father. He had to have seen him sometimes or at least read his name in the paper. Maybe that was how he found out. Dad's photo on the front page, prompting a sad and awkward conversation with his mother. *He's your father, but we don't talk about it. He'll stop paying child support if we do.*

Was it possible that this Jeffrey guy really was stalking me, like my mom thought? Or was this another instance of my mother finding a way to make a situation about her, or about the family name?

Why would he hate me so much? He didn't even know me. And he had to know that wasn't my fault.

Too many questions without answers. All I could do was guess.

Had he known who I was when we were growing up? It hadn't just been my dad in the papers regularly. I had been, too, either because the local press liked to talk about the Young family as a whole, or for my accomplishments in high school, like that wall my mom still had, the shrine to teenage Audrey. Had he been aware of me?

Did he have any idea how false our reputation was?

Absently, I petted Max's head. The more I thought about it, the more I wanted to talk to him face to face. If I could find him. Of course, if my mom was right and he was stalking me,

I'd have to be careful. Anyone who'd write in animal blood on someone's house was dangerous.

But if he wasn't the stalker? Maybe he'd be open to a relationship with his half-sister.

"I hope Josiah gets home soon."

Max looked up, probably at Josiah's name.

"He's not going to believe all this. I'm still not sure if I do."

Max's tail beat a rhythm against the couch cushion and his eyes were hopeful.

"You probably need to go out." I let out a long breath. "Okay, we'll go."

I left the untouched cookies and the mugs. I'd clean them up later. I used the bathroom and put my hair in a ponytail. It was hot out and I wanted it off my neck. Max waited not-so-patiently by the door, his whole body vibrating with excitement.

"I know, I know, I'm moving kind of slow." I slipped my feet into a pair of flip flops and grabbed my phone in case Josiah called. "Let's go."

I opened the door and Max dashed outside, straight to his pee tree. He lifted his leg, did his business, then started sniffing around the grass.

I'd been right about the heat. It had to be at least ninety. Even in the shade, the air felt heavy. It made me think about popsicles and sprinklers. Max liked water; I wondered if he'd have fun with a sprinkler in the yard.

He ran toward the street, so I called him back. A car drove by and I waved. The driver lifted his hand as he passed. The simple gesture of friendliness brought a smile to my face. How nice to live in a place where people waved to each other. Even Josiah did it, and he wasn't exactly sociable.

My phone rang and a swirl of dread spread through my stomach. If it was the restricted number, I wasn't going to answer. I wouldn't make that mistake again.

Thankfully, it was Marigold, and I realized I hadn't called her yet.

"Hey, I keep meaning to call you but I've had a really weird day."

"There must be something in the air. So have I. Are you okay?"

I picked up a ball and tossed it for Max. "Yes and no. It's complicated. I'll fill you in when we can talk in person. Are you okay?"

She sighed. "Physically, yes. But I was in an accident."

I gasped. "Oh no. What happened?"

"I was just leaving the salon and a car came out of nowhere. Slammed right into me."

"But you're not hurt?"

"Not really. I got knocked around a bit, so I'll have some bruises. My car, on the other hand, is probably totaled."

"I'm so sorry."

"Thanks. I hate to cancel on you, but I have to figure all this out."

"Of course. Don't worry about it at all. We'll make plans for another time." I grabbed the ball Max had dropped at my feet and threw it again. "What happened to the other driver? The one who hit you?"

"He drove off. Can you believe that?"

The echo of my own hit and run incident made my back tighten. It had to be a coincidence. "He left?"

"Yep. Slammed into me, then took off. The cops are trying to track him down."

"Did you recognize the car?"

"No. But here's what's really weird. I could have sworn it was Hayden. You know, the bartender from the Timberbeast?"

"Hayden? That's weird."

"Yeah. There was this split second where our cars were facing each other and he looked right at me. I thought he was about to get out of his car to come see if I was okay but then he backed up and left. I don't understand why he would do that. He knows me. In fact, I just saw him last night."

"Where?"

"At the Timberbeast. I met Annika and Isabelle for a drink and Hayden was working. We almost called you, actually, but I thought you might be busy. Anyway, it's just so odd. He's always seemed so nice. He was talking to us last night. But maybe he just freaked out when he hit me. Some people don't deal with sudden stress very well."

"I'm so sorry that happened to you. Are you sure you're okay?"

"Yeah, I'll be fine. What about you?"

"Honestly, I had a very shocking conversation with my mother, but I'll tell you in person. Don't worry about me, deal with your car situation."

"Okay. Take care and I'll talk to you soon."

"You too, Mari."

I ended the call and slipped my phone in my back pocket. The feeling of being watched was back, so I moved closer to the house to make sure I was within range of the cameras. Without really thinking about it, I picked up Max's ball.

"Max?" My voice came out like a squeak, so I cleared my throat. "Max, come!"

He didn't appear, which jogged my frozen brain back into action. He'd been right by the house just a second ago.

"Max, come here."

I jogged around the side of the house, hoping he hadn't found another dead animal or something equally stinky to roll in.

No Max.

Oh, no.

"Max?"

I looked up the hill. There was one thing that would ruin

his mostly reliable recall. A scent he couldn't resist. It had certainly happened before.

I did a lap around the house and checked around Josiah's remodel next door. No dog. No humans, either.

A bark carried on the breeze. I ran behind the house again and looked up the hill. "Max?"

Nothing.

Then I heard a yelp, a distinct cry of pain. The last time I'd heard that sound, my mom's cat had swiped her claws across Max's nose.

Whatever Max had found, it was no pampered cat.

I took off up the hill at a run.

CHAPTER 36

Josiah

SEEING Audrey's car in the driveway took my sense of panic down a few notches. At least she hadn't gone anywhere.

I went to the front door and steeled myself to tell her the truth about confronting Colin. I just hoped she wouldn't be too furious with me.

The door opened. It was unlocked.

Why was the door unlocked?

That wasn't good. We'd been keeping it locked in case the stalker decided he didn't care about being on camera.

More alarming than the door, Max didn't come running to greet me.

He always came running.

"Audrey?"

No answer.

I shut the door behind me.

"Max?"

Still nothing.

She might have been in the shower or something, although that didn't explain Max. The bedroom door was open and no one was there. The bathroom was empty.

Where the hell was she?

"Audrey?" I called again, although the house wasn't that big. There wasn't anywhere for her to go where she wouldn't hear me.

I checked the garage. Dark and empty.

There was no sign of them outside. A couple of Max's balls were in the front yard, but that wasn't unusual. And it told me nothing.

I ran next door to see if she'd gone in to get a sneak peek of the kitchen cabinets, but the house was dark and quiet.

I took a deep breath. I didn't need to lose my shit. I just needed to call her. I got out my phone and called, but it went straight to voicemail.

Damn it. Either her phone was off or she was in a dead spot. I swiped to my messages to make sure I hadn't missed a text from her, telling me where she was. Nothing.

She had plans with Marigold. That meant they'd probably gone out to get food somewhere and she'd simply forgotten to lock the door behind her. Surprising that she'd forget something like that with everything that had happened, but it was possible.

I didn't have Marigold's number. I was about to call my sister to ask for it when I realized I was being an idiot.

The cameras.

There wasn't an inch of ground around her house that wasn't being recorded. I'd turned off the notifications because the damn squirrels kept setting them off, but it kept a recording of every incident of movement. However she'd left, she'd have been on camera. If Marigold had picked her up, there'd be footage of her leaving.

I flipped through the footage. Squirrel. Another squirrel. More fucking squirrels.

Then Max. One of the front cameras had recorded him going out to pee. Normal enough. Audrey was outside with him. She got on her phone and I could see her talking to someone. She wandered a little, pausing to toss the ball for Max a couple of times while she talked.

Then she stopped. The footage was grainy and there was no way to see her face, but I would have bet anything she'd just heard something that startled or surprised her. She seemed frozen in place for a long moment. It almost looked like the video itself had paused.

Except for Max. He not only kept moving, he took off around the side of the house.

And she hadn't seen him.

Audrey didn't react to Max's sudden disappearance. If she'd seen him go, she would have moved in the same direction, calling him back as she went.

I fast forwarded through the next couple of minutes, although I had a feeling I already knew what had happened. One of the back cameras had caught Max's flight up the hill. And a short time later, Audrey went after him.

I didn't think. Just sprang into action, barreling up the hill.

She was probably fine. Just chasing her damn dog and hoping to get to him before he rolled in something disgusting again.

That's what I wanted to believe.

But the feeling in my gut told me I was wrong and Audrey was in danger.

CHAPTER 37

Audrey

FLIP flops were not good hiking shoes, but at least I wasn't in heels this time. My legs burned with the effort of rushing up the hill and I was glad I wasn't completely out of shape or I'd have been on the ground gasping for air.

I pushed on, hoping to see or hear some sign of Max. I had no idea if I was on the right path or if he'd veered off in one direction or another. Or trotted back home, happily covered in dead animal stench. There was no way I could cover every possibility, so I kept climbing, hoping he'd hear me and come running.

That yelp had me worried. Especially because I didn't hear anything now.

"Max!"

The ground was littered with dry pine needles. They kept getting caught in my shoes, poking and scratching my feet.

With all the squirrels in Tilikum, I really needed a yard with a fence. They were just too tempting for Max.

"Max! Where are you?"

I came to the top of the rise where the land leveled out. I slowed, pausing to catch my breath and get my bearings. If I remembered correctly, Josiah had found Max not too far from here the last time he'd run off.

"Max, come!"

I waited, hoping to hear the sound of him running through the pine needles.

Nothing.

Sweat dripped down my back and I swiped the moisture off my forehead. It was hot, even in the shade of the pine trees.

I pulled out my phone, wondering if Josiah was back yet. I could have used his help. No signal. Because of course there was no signal.

Stupid phone.

I slid it back in my pocket and kept going.

Instead of running headlong through the trees, I slowed my pace, listening for any hint of my dog. What I wouldn't have given to have his sense of smell so I could follow his trail. I called for him every so often, pausing to see if he came running.

Still nothing.

The hill descended, then leveled out again. This was probably farther than I'd gone last time, but it was hard to be sure. I didn't want to get myself lost in the process, but I couldn't just turn around and go back without Max.

Not yet, at least. I'd go a little farther. He had to be around there somewhere.

"Max!"

This was the worst. I'd probably passed him already. Or he'd gone home and he was sitting at the front door, wondering where I was. Indecision gnawed at me as I made my way deeper into the woods, up another small rise. The trees were thicker, the shade darker.

I probably needed to go home before I got completely lost. I'd find Josiah and we'd go back out and search for Max together.

Another hill rose in front of me and it seemed like there might be a clearing at the top. I decided to forge ahead a little farther and if I didn't see or hear anything, I'd turn back.

My stomach knotted with worry for my dog. He had a great nose but he was kind of derpy. What if he chased a squirrel in so many circles, he couldn't find his way home? Or that yelp meant he was injured and couldn't walk? People hunted around here, could there be traps or snares? What if he was caught in something, miserably hurt and wondering why his people weren't rescuing him?

The trees opened at the top of the hill but there wasn't much to see. It wasn't high enough to get the lay of the land, just an unshaded spot, baking in the summer sun. My mouth was dry with thirst, I was drenched with sweat, and if the rest of me was even a fraction as dirty as my feet, I probably looked like a forest creature.

"Max?"

I shook my head, fairly certain that I'd gone too far and missed him.

As I turned around to go back, I slammed my toe on a rock, hidden beneath the bed of pine needles.

"Ow!" I shifted my weight to my other foot and sucked in a gasping breath. Why did something as small as a toe have to hurt so much?

The pain throbbed in time with my heartbeat. Blood mingled with the dirt. No wonder it hurt so much. I hadn't just stubbed my toe; I was bleeding.

A dog's bark in the distance carried through the trees.

"Max?"

The sound had come from deeper in the woods. I waited, hoping he'd bark again. Birds chirped and danced through the sky above me, but I didn't hear my dog.

With my bloody foot still throbbing, I followed what I hoped was the direction of his bark. It definitely hadn't been the way I'd come. I had to keep going.

"Max, where are you?"

I couldn't keep from limping and I vaguely wondered if I'd broken a toe. Another bark came from up ahead and it was definitely Max. What was he barking at? If I could hear him, he could certainly hear me. Was he barking to get my attention? Another image of him caught in some sort of trap came to mind, although I didn't hear yelps of pain.

"Max!"

With every step, I thought he'd come running out of the woods ahead of me. But he didn't. Was he so preoccupied with whatever he'd chased? I had a sinking feeling that he'd actually caught a squirrel and was currently dismantling its poor little body the way he tore open stuffed toys and pulled out their squeakers and stuffing.

This could be very messy.

He barked again and this time, it was close. Another noise grew and I realized I was hearing the rush of water.

Was it the river? Or the waterfall?

Josiah had said you could hike to the waterfall from the other side of the hill behind my house. Had I really gone that far? I didn't know the area well enough to be sure, but I could definitely hear water.

That was good. The river would mean trails and I could find my way back to civilization, or at least to a spot where my phone would get a signal.

But why wasn't Max coming?

I slowed to a walk because I had a feeling I knew.

Someone had him. It was the only thing that made sense.

My heart started pounding, harder than it had when I'd been climbing the hill. Maybe it wasn't him. Maybe Max had come upon a hiking trail and a nice hiker was hanging onto him for me, realizing that it would be easier to find a stationary dog.

I didn't really believe that. I just wanted it to be true.

"Max?"

He barked in answer. It sounded like he was just over the next rise.

I didn't want to be stupid, the proverbial girl in a horror movie who ran up the stairs when she should have gone out the front door. I knew what was probably waiting for me on the other side of the hill.

But if he had my dog, I couldn't just leave him. Whoever he was, he'd already killed two squirrels. I doubted he'd hesitate to hurt Max. And I loved my derpy dog. I was his human, I couldn't walk away if he was in the hands of a monster.

With a deep breath, I limped up the hill. The river flowed by, its waters churning as it approached the drop of the waterfall.

Max was right on the bank, restrained by a leash that wasn't mine.

Holding it was a guy I recognized. But it didn't make sense. It was Hayden.

CHAPTER 38

Josiah

THE PINE TREES all looked the same.

I'd grown up in these woods, I knew how to keep my sense of direction. Getting lost wasn't the problem.

The problem was I had to guess which way Audrey had gone.

Straight up the hill? That made the most sense. She wouldn't have known whether Max had veered to one side or another, so getting to the top and going from there would be the smart move.

But that didn't tell me where she'd gone from there.

The heat baked the pine forest and gritty dust coated my mouth. My shirt was already half-soaked with sweat by the time I got up the hill. And I had no idea which way to go.

I paused to look at the forest floor, hoping to see evidence of a trail. But the pine needles were so thick and long dried out from the summer sun, it was hard to see where they'd been disturbed.

"Audrey!"

No answer.

Birds chirped overhead but the air was oppressively still. I swiped the sweat off my forehead, picked a direction, and kept going.

"Audrey! Max!"

I wondered if Max had a good enough memory to retrace his route back to the hole of stink where he'd gone last time. Even if he'd started out chasing a squirrel up the hill, he would have lost it up a tree pretty quickly. Something else had to have caught his attention, otherwise he'd have gone back to Audrey.

She'd know that, so it made sense she'd try to find that spot again. I didn't remember exactly where I'd found Max before, but I had a rough idea. And that seemed better than running aimlessly through the trees.

The back side of the hill wasn't as steep, but the trees were thicker. Shade did nothing to cut the heat, but I ignored how quickly my mouth dried out. It didn't matter. I just needed to find her.

Trying to channel her perpetual optimism, I told myself she was fine. Probably trying to drag Max away from something gross and we'd have to spend the afternoon hosing him down again before he was fit to go inside.

I didn't believe it, though. Not really.

"Audrey!"

My shoe caught on something hidden by the blanket of pine needles and I almost fell on my face. I stumbled a few steps to catch my balance.

Damn it.

"Audrey! Max!"

Still nothing.

The ground rose again so I pushed up the hill, sweat dripping down my temples. Both urgency and dread spread through the pit of my stomach. There was too much I didn't know—too much I couldn't control.

Who had been stalking her? And why? What was he willing to do to her?

Was he after her right now?

It could all be a coincidence. The call. The note this morning. Max running off. He'd chased a scent up the hill before. It didn't have to mean the stalker was using the dog to lure Audrey into the woods.

But what if it did?

A potent mixture of rage and panic tightened my chest. I was not going to let him hurt her. I was not going to lose her.

I couldn't. I'd tear that fucker limb from limb if he so much as touched her.

The instinct to protect my woman was deep and primal. It awoke something in me, flooded my veins with adrenaline. I was going to find her and bring her safely home. There was no other option.

"Audrey!"

A rustling sound came from my left, so distant I almost missed it. I stopped in my tracks. There it was again, same direction.

"Audrey!"

She didn't answer, but I headed toward the sound. If it was Max, he might be able to find her faster than I could.

I raced through the trees, kicking up pine needles and dust, ignoring the scratches on my arms. The woods thinned, finally opening onto a sunbaked meadow filled with dry, brown grasses.

"Max?"

Three turkey vultures took off from the midst of the grass, their big wings flapping. They didn't go far, just rose into the air and circled, waiting for me to get away from their meal.

That meant there was something dead over there. I couldn't imagine Max rolling in an animal carcass that was being eaten by carrion birds, but he also had no sense of his own mortality, so maybe big birds wouldn't have scared him.

I jogged over to where the birds had taken flight. The remains of something—not big enough to be a deer but larger than Max—lay in the grass. It was so picked apart and dried out, it didn't look like much of anything. Definitely not fresh.

And no Max.

Fuck.

I checked the sun and the time on my phone to orient myself. I was pretty sure I knew how to get back. Worst case scenario, if I kept going, I'd hit the river. Then it would be a matter of following the water until I found a trail or the waterfall.

But where the hell was Audrey? How far had I gone wrong?

At this point, she could have been anywhere. My instincts weren't enough to take me in the right direction and I hadn't seen any signs that I could follow. Not that I was an expert; I easily could have missed them.

I figured I was probably closer to the river than home. My phone didn't have a signal, but if I got to a hiking trail, I'd find a spot where it would work. I could keep searching and call my brothers to get out here and help.

There was nothing else to do but keep pushing through and hope we were both on a wild dog chase we'd laugh about later.

Because the alternative was unthinkable.

Ignoring the heat and discomfort of dehydration, I started off again, heading for the river. I kept my phone out, checking it in between yelling Audrey's name, ready to call whoever would answer as soon as my phone connected again.

My sense of urgency grew with every step. She was in danger. I didn't know how I knew, but it wasn't my imagination gone wild. I wasn't jumping to the worst-case scenario.

I knew.

My heart pounded in my chest and blood rushed in my ears. A wasp buzzed past and thankfully I had enough presence of mind to look out for the hive. I circled wide around it, cursing the damn things for being in my way.

Finally, I heard the rush of water. I wasn't sure what part of the river I was hitting, but at least I'd found it.

Maybe Audrey had too. She'd know to follow it downstream.

Hoping against hope that I'd see her in the distance, I crashed through the trees and stopped near the bank.

Still swollen from the spring melt, the river rushed by in a mass of white foam and blue-green water. I looked up and down but I didn't see anyone. No Audrey. No Max.

No stalker.

With a deep breath of resolve, I started downstream toward the falls.

CHAPTER 39

Audrey

"YOU?" I asked.

Hayden's expression was unreadable. If he was the stalker, his face showed none of the malevolence I'd have expected from a man who'd gutted a helpless animal and smeared its blood on my door. He just watched me, silent and passive, holding the leash in his hands.

It was terrifying.

Max wagged his tail but it was tentative. I could see the nervous tension in his furry body. He was glad to see me, but he knew something wasn't right.

I reached out a hand, trying not to let Hayden see how much I was shaking. "Can I have my dog, please?"

He pulled what looked like a dog treat out of his pocket and held it out to Max. "Your dog is an idiot."

Max didn't take it. He whined and shifted on his feet.

Hayden tossed the treat to the ground. "Your loss." His eyes lifted to meet mine. "Walk."

He turned and led Max down the bank. I had no choice but to follow.

"Where are we going?"

Hayden didn't answer. Max walked beside him, glancing back at me. I wanted to reassure him that he'd be okay. But I had no idea what Hayden was planning to do.

The noise of the waterfall grew. I could see where the cliff began up ahead, the crumbling drop-off I'd seen from below on my first date with Josiah. I tried not to think about how high the waterfall had looked or what Hayden leading me and Max to the edge probably meant.

"Did you hit Marigold's car today?" I wasn't sure why I was asking that question, when I had so many others, but I just hoped he'd stop before he got to the drop-off.

He paused and glanced over his shoulder. "Yes."

"Why?"

"To get her out of the way. But is that really what you want to know?"

"Maybe this is a stupid question at this point, but has it been you all along?"

"That is a stupid question."

"But why?"

He turned to face me. Max looked back and forth between the two of us. "You really don't know, do you? You're that self-centered, you don't even know who I am."

He'd always looked slightly familiar, but so did a lot of people in Tilikum.

"My first name is Jeffrey. Jeffrey Hayden Silva. I started going by my middle name after high school. Specifically, after I found out the sperm donor picked my first name."

"You're Jeffrey Silva?"

Max tried to come to me and he jerked the leash, making Max whimper. "I wasn't allowed to use the Young name. Not that I ever wanted to."

"I didn't know."

"Obviously."

"No, I mean I didn't know you existed. They never told

me, so if you're mad at me for not acknowledging you, it's not my fault. I had no idea."

"Of course you didn't."

"So this is all a big misunderstanding."

"I haven't misunderstood anything."

"But why?" I wrapped my arms around myself, my stomach churning with fear. "Why do you hate me so much?"

"Another stupid question."

"Is it because of Dad? That's not—"

"Dad?" He practically spat the word. "In case you hadn't noticed, he's not my dad. Sperm donor at best, but never Dad."

"Okay, so hate him. What do I have to do with it?"

His hands tightened on the leash. "Everything."

"Why? What did I ever do to you?"

"Nothing!" He took a deep breath and smoothed his expression. "You did nothing. So of course nothing is your fault. After all, you're the golden child."

"What are you talking about?"

"You have no idea what it was like, growing up in the shadow of the perfect older sister. You didn't even know I'd been born, that's how insignificant I was. Your fucking father couldn't be bothered to acknowledge my existence. Instead, he paraded you around town like a princess, right in front of me."

I didn't know what to say, so I waited to see if he'd keep talking. Maybe if he got everything out, he'd change his mind about whatever he'd brought us out here to do.

"Audrey Young, teenage superstar. Smiling at everyone in that goddamn cheerleading uniform, waving your pom poms. Standing on the stage with your piece of shit parents at every parade. You won every award, every ribbon, every trophy. The morons in that town worshiped you like royalty."

"It didn't mean anything."

"You're right about that. It didn't mean shit. You were a big fish in a very tiny pond. Didn't fare so well on your own, did you? Couldn't hack it without Daddy's influence smoothing the way for you."

The truth in his words cut deep. I had been a big fish in a tiny pond and once I'd swam out to the ocean, I'd basically drowned.

"Growing up, I was so jealous," he continued. "I'd ride my bike past your house, that fucking mansion you got to live in, and throw rocks at it. What made you so special that you got to live there?"

"It wasn't all it seemed."

"No? You weren't living across town in a shack because your mom spent all her money on liquor."

"No, I wasn't."

"You were everywhere in that fucking town. Mocking me. Always in the newspaper for your pointless accomplishments. More popular than the athletes who actually played the games, and all you did was shake your ass on the sidelines. Even when you were in college, I couldn't get away from you. The high school had your fucking picture on the wall next to your student of the year award. I had to walk by that fake smile every goddamn day."

Max whined and tried to circle around him. He jerked on the leash and Max sat.

I clenched my teeth. Anger mixed with fear.

"But you know what? It was fine. Because eventually, you did leave. And people forgot. You wouldn't believe how quickly they forgot you, Audrey. Because you were never special. It was all bullshit."

"I never thought I was special."

"Don't lie. Of course you did. But you know the truth now, don't you? You were never royalty, not even the princess of a small town."

"Okay, so we both agree I'm not a princess and I never was. Can I have my dog now?"

His face changed, his controlled façade burning away, the heat of his hatred suddenly blazing in his eyes.

And I realized the awful truth. He was going to kill me.

CHAPTER 40

Josiah

AS SOON AS I caught sight of her, I stopped. Relief hit first. She was alive.

Then rage. She wasn't alone.

But why the fuck was she standing there talking to Hayden? What did the bartender have to do with any of this?

He had Max on a leash. The dog was agitated and afraid. This wasn't a case of Max running off and Hayden happened to be the one to find him. Something was wrong. I could practically smell it.

I ducked behind a tree before Hayden could catch sight of me. I didn't need to know why he was the stalker to realize the truth—it had been him the whole time. There was no other explanation, no other reason for the scene unfolding in front of me.

As close as they were to the cliff, I also had no doubt as to his intent. They weren't over there for the view.

I clenched my fists and ground my teeth together, trying to keep a lid on my temper. If I charged in from here, he'd see me and have plenty of time to push her off. I couldn't risk that.

Which meant I needed to slow down and think.

There was no way to get close enough without being seen. The roar of the waterfall would keep him from hearing me, but there weren't enough trees. I'd have to be out in the open for too long. No matter how fast I ran, he'd get to her first.

And he was going to push her off. I could see his face and the hatred in his expression was undeniable.

He'd brought her there to kill her. Maybe try to frame it as a suicide.

Fuck that.

They were talking but I couldn't hear what they were saying. Max sniffed the air and I wondered if he'd caught my scent.

My eyes kept going back to the cliff. I knew what was down there. A hell of a lot of wet rocks. I'd almost fallen a dozen times when my brothers and I—

Without another thought, I veered away from the river, darting from tree to tree, keeping an eye on Hayden to make sure he didn't see me. I hated to let Audrey out of my sight, even for a few minutes, but there was no other way. I couldn't come in from behind her.

Which meant coming up the cliff.

I'd done it before, so I knew exactly how dangerous it was. I no longer had the luxury of being a teenage idiot with no sense of mortality. I also couldn't take my time. I'd have to free climb up that bastard as fast as I could.

What would I do once I got to the top? I didn't think that far ahead. I was making this up as I went along. I wasn't some action hero who'd grab her wrist as she went over the edge, saving her from falling. We'd both go down if it went that far.

So I'd have to make sure he didn't have the chance to push her.

Thankfully, I knew the route and it wasn't far out of my way. The trail was every bit as steep as I remembered. I dug my heels into the dry ground, but I slid down, displacing rocks and kicking up dust. I didn't want to go all the way to the bottom. Just far enough that I could climb over and come up from behind Hayden.

I didn't think about the danger or what my head would look like if I fell. I turned to face the cliff side, found a foothold, grabbed a small ledge of rock with one hand, and started to climb.

A rainbow glistened in the waterfall spray. The rocks were wet and slippery, every hand hold precarious. My brother Reese had almost fallen, right about where I was. Not over the deep pool we used to dive into, but over the deadly rocks below me.

That was a weird memory to have at that moment.

My teenage body had been more agile, but now I was more determined. I climbed as fast as I could while still making sure my feet were stable before shifting my weight. It felt painfully slow, but I knew only a few minutes had passed.

Finally, I got close enough to the top that I could hear their voices over the sound of the water. Hayden's, at least. Audrey might have said something, but it was hard to tell.

My left foot slipped on the wet rock. I sucked in a breath and held on, my fingers and forearms aching with the effort. By some miracle, my right foot stayed put and I carefully found another toe hold.

Against my better judgment, I glanced down.

Bad idea.

I was high. Stupidly high and the safety of the pool was well to my right. If I went down here, I'd be hamburger.

So would Audrey, if he pushed her.

Resolve burned away all fear. Audrey was mine and I'd do whatever it took to protect her. If I died saving her, so be it. But I was taking that fucker down with me.

CHAPTER 41

Audrey

FACING the stark possibility of my death was different than I would have imagined. I was afraid. Sick to my stomach with it, in fact. But it was almost too surreal to process. Hayden's murderous glare couldn't be real. This couldn't actually be happening.

But it was.

"You had to come back, didn't you?" he said, his tone dripping with venom. "You couldn't just move away and stay gone. You had to be as big a failure as I always knew you would be."

I opened my mouth to reply, but he kept talking, his voice rising with every word.

"I was fine. I was normal, just living my life. I didn't need to be a big fish in any size pond. I wasn't you, I didn't need to have people adore me. I had a good job and a decent life and I never thought about you. You left and it was like the weight of the world left my shoulders. I could finally fucking breathe. You didn't even exist."

His fury made my heart race.

"I left Pinecrest so I didn't have to see the sperm donor

and your bitch of a mother and everything was good. Do you know what I did when he died?"

I shook my head.

"Nothing. I didn't celebrate and I certainly didn't mourn. I just went to work because it didn't fucking matter to me."

"It seems like it matters to you now."

"Because you should have stayed away. None of this is my fault. If you'd just stayed away like you were supposed to, I wouldn't have had to do all this." His eyes grew wilder by the second. "I was a normal guy before you moved back. I never hurt anyone. I never would have. You came back and you made me do it."

"I didn't make you do anything."

"Yes, you did." He stepped backward, closer to the edge. "I don't know how you did it, but you broke me open. You unleashed the darkness that was always inside me. The sperm donor gave that to me, by the way. So it's his fault too. But it would have stayed dormant if you hadn't come back."

"I didn't know who you were, Hayden. I never knew."

"Don't pretend you would have cared."

"You don't understand. I always wanted a bro—"

"Don't call me that!" Spittle flew from his lips. "Don't fucking say that word. I'm not your brother."

Max whined with fear. Hayden took another step back.

A part of me wanted to tell him that I'd never been our father's golden child. That everything he'd seen had been for show. He hadn't been throwing rocks at the house of a happy, perfect family. We'd been broken too, just in a different way.

But I had a feeling that wasn't what he wanted to hear. And he wouldn't believe me anyway.

"I'm sorry for what happened to you and I'm sorry he treated you like that. It isn't right."

"Too late now. What's done is done."

"Can you please move away from the edge? I don't want you to fall."

"Oh, no. That's not what's happening here." His lips curled in a cruel smile. "I'm not going to end as the sad, pathetic bastard son of a crooked politician, throwing himself off a cliff because he can't go on. We're not out here because I'm suicidal."

I swallowed hard. I already knew the answer, but I asked anyway. "Then why are we here?"

"I've thought about this long and hard, I want you to know that. I liked my life before you showed up. I'd finally found peace. I just want my life back."

"You have your life. It doesn't have anything to do with me."

He shook his head, almost sadly. "No, I don't. I was in control before, but I'm not now, and I won't be if you're here. I thought it would be enough to make you go away but that just leaves the door open for you to come back again. Besides, I'm smart enough to realize I don't want to grapple with that mountain man you've been fucking."

Josiah. His name ran through my mind, almost like a prayer. Tears sprang to my eyes at the thought of leaving him. There was no doubt in my mind Hayden wanted me dead and the pain that would cause Josiah was more horrible than the possibility of being murdered.

"He did me quite the favor by leaving you alone today. I thought I might have to wait longer for this opportunity. And if you're wondering whether you'll survive the fall, I can assure you, you won't. It's nothing but rocks at the bottom." His lip curled again. "I've tested it."

I didn't want to know what poor creature, or creatures, he'd thrown off that cliff.

Could I outrun him? I was in flip-flops and probably had a broken toe. He was taller than me and undoubtedly faster. And would he push Max over the edge if I ran?

"So you're just going to throw me over?"

He reached behind him and pulled a knife out of his back pocket. "After I kill your dog in front of you."

"You're crazy."

"No, I'm thorough. Trust me, the suicide note is very convincing, as is the journal confessing all the mental health problems you tried to hide. And no one will find Max's body. They'll come to the conclusion that you jumped and your dumb dog ran off and probably got eaten by a cougar." His eyes narrowed and he held up the knife. "If you run, I'll kill him slowly—make sure it hurts."

"Why are you telling me all this? Why didn't you just do it?"

"I like seeing the fear in your eyes. It's quite a rush. You unleashed the darkness, Audrey, and I don't know if I'll ever put it back."

It felt like I was watching the birth of a serial killer. They'd say later that I'd been his first victim—the one who gave him a taste for it.

Maybe I would be. But I wasn't going down without a fight.

Out of nowhere, Max spun around and barked. Hayden jerked the leash to turn him around, his face contorting in an ugly grimace.

"Fucking dog."

There was movement behind them. Max tried to turn around again and it took me a split second to realize what I was seeing.

An arm reached over the edge, followed quickly by a shoulder. My eyes widened as Josiah muscled himself over the cliff, right behind Hayden.

Our eyes met, and in that instant, we were one. He didn't have to give me a signal or yell out instructions. I knew. He knew. And we both sprang into action.

I dove forward, hitting the ground so hard it almost

knocked the breath from my lungs. But I grabbed the leash and bent my knees to get my feet under me.

Hayden's snarl of hatred as he tried to keep his grip on the leash was interrupted by a surprise from behind. Josiah tackled him to the ground and the knife flew out of his hand.

Max tried to attack my face with licks. He had no idea this wasn't over. I unclipped the leash from his collar so Hayden couldn't yank him over the edge with it and painfully scrambled to my feet.

Josiah and Hayden struggled on the ground, close to the edge of the cliff. Hayden clawed at the ground, his fingers almost reaching the knife.

I ran for it to kick it away but Hayden got to it first. His fingers curled around the handle and I watched in horror as he whipped his arm around and plunged the blade into Josiah's thigh.

Josiah roared. But the knife in his leg didn't slow him down; it only seemed to make him angry.

I staggered back to stay out of the way. Josiah rolled Hayden onto his back and punched him. The sound of his fist hitting flesh and bone carried above the noise of the waterfall. I flinched at the violent contact, then Josiah hit him again.

Hayden groaned, writhing on the ground. I watched with my heart racing as Josiah got to his feet.

"Stay down," Josiah growled through clenched teeth. He looked at me. "Are you okay?"

I nodded. "Yeah. Are you?"

"Yeah." He didn't even look at his leg.

Hayden didn't listen. He rolled over and pushed himself to standing. Blood streamed from his nose and hatred seethed from his narrowed eyes. He looked absolutely unhinged. Josiah charged but Hayden was fast. He shifted to the side and slammed into Josiah's leg, right where the knife still protruded. Josiah's leg buckled and he crumbled to the ground with a howl of pain.

Max barked like I'd never heard him bark before. With an aggressive snarl, he charged. He jumped on Hayden, teeth bared, and bit his arm.

Hayden shook him off and delivered a swift kick to his side. Max yelped as he rolled across the ground, and Hayden turned his furious gaze on me.

"I'll fucking kill you."

I tried to run but Hayden caught me by the wrist. I fought back, hitting and kicking, but he dragged me across the ground, relentless. His grip was too strong. I couldn't get free.

Finally, I landed a kick that loosened his hold. I scrambled backward just as Josiah surged in and smashed him across the face.

Hayden staggered under the force of the blow. His feet slipped on the rocky edge and he teetered, almost falling backward.

Josiah reached out and grabbed his wrist.

Hayden looked down, as if contemplating the rocky depths below him. Then his gaze turned to me. His eyes narrowed, seething hatred on full display, and before Josiah could grab his other arm, he wrenched his wrist free and fell.

Gasping, I ran to the edge and screamed. Josiah wrapped his arms around my waist and pulled me back before I could see. Tears streamed down my face and I sobbed, the horror of it all washing over me in an overwhelming wave.

Josiah held me tight and we sank to the ground. I took shaky breaths and let his strength envelop me. Minutes passed as I cried. Josiah didn't let go.

"You're hurt," I said finally, pulling away. "Are you bleeding very much? We need to get you help."

"It's fine." He cupped my face and looked at me. "Are you okay? Did he hurt you?"

I probably had a million scrapes and bruises, but I couldn't feel a thing. "I don't think so. Nothing serious. Where's Max? Is he okay?"

As if on cue, Max burrowed into our embrace, tail wagging furiously.

"I don't think he's hurt," Josiah said. "That fucking bastard."

"Good boy, Max. Good job getting the bad guy."

Josiah put his arms around me again and hauled me against him. "I thought he was going to kill you."

"He tried."

"Fuck, I can't calm down. He could have killed you. I swear, I'm never letting you out of my sight." He kissed my hair. "I love you. Damn it, I love you so much."

"I love you, too."

"I mean it, Audrey. I'm shit at romantic stuff but I love you and I'm going to marry you."

I sputtered. "Do you think maybe you're getting ahead of yourself?"

"No."

"So you'll still mean it even when we haven't just experienced intense trauma together?"

"Yes."

I blinked at him. He really was serious. "How about I say yes now and we can have a rational conversation about it when we're calm and you don't have a knife sticking out of your thigh."

"I can live with that. But I'm still marrying you."

I shook my head, but not in disbelief. I believed him. He was just the most straightforward and yet perplexing man I'd ever met.

I loved him so much.

"But why was the bartender stalking you? Did you even know him?"

"It's a long story that involves my father having an affair." I glanced toward the cliff. "Can I tell you the rest later?"

He touched my face. "Yeah."

"What do we do now?" I asked. "We need to call for help but my phone doesn't get a signal out here."

"We'll go that way." He pointed. "The hiking trail isn't far. As soon as we get a signal, we'll call Garrett."

"And an ambulance."

"Oh." He glanced at his leg. "Right. Yeah, that's starting to hurt."

"How about you, Max?" I asked. "Are you okay?"

He licked my face.

Josiah started to get up but winced.

"Let me help." I got to my feet and he steadied himself against me as he stood. "Can you put weight on it?"

"Enough. I'll be able to walk."

I glanced at the cliff but Josiah touched my chin and moved my gaze to him.

"Don't. You don't need to see it."

My eyes welled up with more tears. "Why did he do that? He didn't have to fall."

"I don't know. Sometimes people choose darkness."

"It's like he was obsessed—too twisted with hatred to see another way. It's just all so unnecessary."

"There's nothing you could have done, Audrey." He kissed my forehead. "Let's get out of here."

I draped his arm over my shoulders so he could lean on me if he needed to. Max trotted along beside us as we made our way toward the trail. Even with both of us limping—and the pain of all my scrapes and bruises starting to demand my attention—it didn't take long before we found our way. His phone got a signal first, so he called Garrett. He told us to wait where we were, help was on the way.

We sat down on the side of the trail. Josiah put his arm around me and held me close.

"Thank you for saving me," I said, my voice barely above a whisper.

"Always."

CHAPTER 42

Audrey

MAX DIDN'T UNDERSTAND days off any more than he understood weekends—even when I'd almost been thrown off a cliff a few days ago. He woke me up at six-thirty sharp, so I took him outside to go potty.

I stretched my arms over my head while he did his business. The bruises I'd predicted had definitely come to pass. But I didn't let the aches and pains bother me in the least. It could have been so much worse.

The events at the falls had sent shockwaves through our little community. And for once, there weren't any wild rumors. Apparently the truth was dreadful enough on its own.

Garrett and two other deputies searched Hayden's house and what they found told the story of his obsession. He had a box of old photos and newspaper clippings, mostly from my adolescence in Pinecrest. They'd largely been defaced, most with the words *you don't see me*, or, *I hate you* written over my name or image.

He'd printed more recent photos of me and hung them on a bulletin board in his bedroom. Some were grainy, like they'd been taken from a distance and blown up. Others were disturbingly clear. He had hundreds more on his phone, plus photos of my house, both before and after he'd vandalized it. It seemed as if he'd taken some kind of sick pleasure in the planning and documentation of his crimes.

They also found the fake suicide note he'd written, intending to pass it off as mine. The journal he'd told me about was still on his laptop, also written as if it were me. He'd really believed he could frame my murder as a suicide; really thought he'd get away with it.

Thankfully, no one doubted the truth of our story. From the moment the emergency crew had found us on the hiking trail and brought us to the hospital, we'd told everyone the truth, and they'd believed us. The evidence they found at Hayden's house merely backed up what we'd already told them.

It was a reminder that you never know what a person is truly going through. We all carry burdens that others can't see. Unfortunately, Hayden let his poison him from the inside.

I had sympathy for him—for the kid who'd had a crappy childhood through no fault of his own. But I wasn't going to make excuses for him, either. He could have chosen a different path. He chose the darkness that ultimately ended his life. I couldn't take responsibility for that.

"Come on, Max. Let's go inside."

My toe was indeed broken, but I was only limping a little bit. And although Max didn't understand sleeping in, he did seem to adapt to the slower pace of life the last few days. He'd been content with games of fetch in the front yard in lieu of our normal longer walks or hikes. But I was healing fast, so we'd be back out there, tromping around in the woods, in no time. Especially now that I didn't have to worry about being followed or what I'd find when I got home.

Josiah was in the kitchen when we went in, getting the coffee started. He was shirtless and I could see a dark bruise on his back where he'd hit the ground. His arms had scratches but the worst injury was the knife wound in his leg. Although it was deep, it hadn't done any damage that wouldn't heal with time. I could tell he was favoring it by the way he stood and walked, but for the most part, the injuries he'd taken saving me weren't slowing him down.

"Morning." I slipped my arms around his waist and leaned my cheek against his back.

His sleepy voice was rough and gravelly. "Morning."

"How does your leg feel?"

"Sore. But it's okay."

A wave of emotion swept through me and I held him tighter. He'd risked his life for me. I loved him so much.

"You okay?" he asked.

"Yeah. I just have a lot of big feelings right now."

He gently loosened my grip and turned around to face me, then gathered me into his arms. I relaxed into him while he let me feel my feelings. A burst of sadness for Hayden, the boy who could have been my brother, followed by relief that our ordeal was over. And above all, gratitude and love for the man holding me.

"I love you so much," I whispered.

He kissed my head. "I love you, too."

I took a deep breath and pulled away. The sting of tears subsided. "Sorry. I'm okay now."

He smiled and kissed my forehead.

Max had been waiting, tail wagging like crazy, for his breakfast, so I fed him while Josiah made coffee. We sat down together on the couch, both wincing a little as we took our seats. Fighting for your life on the edge of a cliff was no joke.

I'd talked to my mom shortly after our rescue and again since we'd been home. To her credit, she'd been a lot more concerned about us than the fact that my dad's affair had become public knowledge. I knew it would be hard for her to face her friends in the coming weeks, but she'd assured me she would be fine. And I tended to believe her. She'd seemed lighter, somehow, like she'd freed herself from the prison of lies she'd lived in for so long.

I hoped it meant a better future for our relationship. I still didn't agree with how she'd kept the truth from me. But I'd decided to forgive her for it. It didn't excuse what she'd done, but if I'd learned anything from Hayden, it was not to hold onto anger and resentment. It would just fester and wind up poisoning me.

My phone buzzed over on the kitchen counter. As much as I didn't want to move from my spot snuggled next to Josiah, it might have been my mom. She'd been checking up on me frequently over the last few days.

I would have been doing the same in her shoes.

"I wonder who's texting you this early," Josiah said as I got up off the couch.

"Probably Mom."

I put my mug down and grabbed my phone. But it wasn't my mom.

"It's Lou," I said. "He wants to know if I can meet with him this morning."

"About time."

"I'm going to say yes. He's probably just going to tell me he's closing the paper."

"Maybe. Although he wouldn't have to do that in person."

"True." I typed a reply to Lou. "Who knows, maybe I'll still have a job."

"Make him work for it."

I smiled. "You know what, I actually will. After everything we've been through, I'm not going to settle."

He twisted so he was looking at me. "Before you go, ask yourself a question."

"What?"

"Do you still want the job?"

I nodded slowly. He was right, that was something I

needed to consider. Was a small-town newspaper the right place for me? Surprisingly, the answer came easily.

"Yes. I actually do still want the job. Not if he's going to act like a jerk and pretend that he didn't do anything wrong. But if he's going to keep the paper open, and we can get past what happened, then yes, I do want to work there. I actually like it a lot."

Josiah nodded. I understood. He'd support me, whatever I decided to do.

I was so lucky to have him.

———

The empty newspaper office looked so sad. My desk was the way I'd left it, with a pencil cup, a stack of random paperwork and mail, and a framed photo of Max. Sandra's was empty. Apparently she'd cleaned out all her things, as if she really didn't ever intend to come back. Ledger's desk looked like it always did when he wasn't there—messy. But his absence was felt all the same.

Lou appeared in the doorway to his office as soon as I walked in. "Hi, Audrey. Come on back."

I went into his office but this time, I wasn't nervous. He was either going to apologize or he wasn't. From there, it would be up to me to decide what was best. I didn't relish the idea of being out of a job again, but there were some things I couldn't control. All I could control was me.

"Thanks for coming," he began and I didn't miss the uncharacteristic softness in his tone. He paused to clear his throat. "Obviously I owe you an apology. I won't make excuses. I should have trusted you. I'm sorry. I was wrong and I hope you can forgive me."

The simplicity of his apology betrayed its sincerity. "Thank you. I appreciate that."

"And I'm sorry for everything that happened to you. Are you okay?"

"Yeah, I am. It's been a lot, but I'll be all right."

"Good," he said, nodding. "How do you feel about coming back to work?"

"That depends."

"On what?"

"Are you going to bring back Sandra and Ledger?"

"If they're willing. Sandra hasn't replied to my messages yet. And I figure Ledger will probably wander back in at some point."

"He probably will. And I bet Sandra will come back if I do."

"Hope so. I never meant to drive everyone away." He met my eyes. "Like I said, I won't make excuses. This mess is my fault."

"Well, you're doing what's right to clean it up."

"So will you come back?"

I smiled. "Yes, I'll come back."

"Good. I have plans for the paper and they won't work without you."

"What do you mean?"

"I'm aiming to retire in a couple of years. I'd hate to see the Tribune close. I know newspapers aren't what they used to be, but I think the town still needs us. So I'm hoping I can teach you to take over."

"Me? Why not Sandra? She has more experience."

"Sandra is the backbone of this place in a lot of ways, but what the Tribune needs is someone like you. Someone with vision who's willing to take risks. You've already done more for this paper than anyone in decades."

"I don't know about that. You've kept it going."

"Barely. I get too focused on all the problems, I can't see the solutions. Or even the possibilities. That's your gift. And I know running a small-town paper might not be your professional dream, but you're good at it and I think this place would thrive with you at this desk."

My heart was so full, I hardly knew what to say. Maybe a small-town paper hadn't been my dream, but that didn't mean it wasn't meant to be. It was better than anything I'd ever dreamed up for myself.

"I don't know nearly enough to be in charge, but it's an amazing opportunity."

"Don't worry. I'm not going anywhere yet. We have plenty of time to get you up to speed."

With a smile, I held out my hand to seal the deal. "Then I accept."

He shook my hand in a firm grip. "Good. Now can you please call Sandra for me?"

"Absolutely."

"Thanks, Audrey. And I really am sorry."

"Thanks, Lou. We're good."

He waved me out the door. "Go on, get outta here and get to work."

I smiled and shut the door behind me. He was right. We had a lot of work to do.

———

The Timberbeast was almost empty. But it was a little after four o'clock on a Thursday, so that made sense. And it was kind of nice to have the place mostly to ourselves.

Josiah scooted my chair closer and put his arm around me. Sandra had bought us all a round of celebratory drinks and Ledger had actually taken his earbuds out and his phone was nowhere in sight.

Sandra held up her glass. "Cheers, friends."

We all clinked our glasses together and took a drink.

Sandra had agreed to come back once I called her and let her know Lou had sincerely apologized and I was back at work. Ledger had indeed just wandered back in, shortly after lunch. I wasn't sure if he didn't remember that he'd walked out last week or if he'd heard through the grapevine that the paper was open again. It was hard to tell. But he'd actually done a little bit of work.

Maybe there was hope for our useless intern yet.

We'd decided to leave early and come to the Timberbeast to celebrate our new beginning.

Rocco, dressed in his usual plaid shirt, came over to our table. He rubbed his thick beard. "Audrey, I just need to say that I didn't know Hayden wasn't right. I just thought he was one of those cynical types who act all dark and depressed because they think it makes them cool. Figured he'd grow out of it eventually."

"That's okay. Of course you couldn't have known. Heck, I didn't know he and I were related and I saw him here all the time."

"I'm just glad you're all right. Josiah really climbed up that cliff to save you?"

"He really did."

He nodded to Josiah, admiration plain on his face. "Well done, sir."

"Thanks, Rocco."

"I hear your dog gets some credit, too."

"Max is a hero," I said with a smile. "Who would have thought. And we'll pretend it's not kind of his fault that I was lured into the woods in the first place."

"He's a dog," Sandra said. "It's not his fault he thinks everyone is good at heart."

"He's also easily bribed by treats."

"Next round is on me," Rocco said. "Least I can do."

"Thanks, Rocco. That's so nice of you."

"Happy to. By the way, any of you know someone looking for a job? I'm in need of a bartender."

"Nobody comes to mind," I said.

Josiah shrugged and Sandra shook her head. Ledger didn't know anyone either.

"I'll find someone eventually," Rocco said. "Let me know when you're ready for another round."

He went back to the bar and I didn't miss the way Sandra eyed him as he walked away.

"Are you ever going to go for it with him?" I asked.

She rolled her eyes.

"I'm serious. Can't you just ask him out? You know you want to."

"I've thought about it. But I'm too old-fashioned. I need a man to make the first move. And he's obviously not going to."

Josiah's brow furrowed and he looked between Sandra and Rocco a few times. "Hey, Rocco."

Rocco looked over. "Yeah?"

"You want to go out with Sandra?"

It was hard to tell in the dim light, but I could have sworn Rocco actually blushed a little.

"Well, yeah."

"Then would you hurry up and ask her out? This is getting stupid."

Grinning, he shook his head. "All right. Sandra, you free on Sunday?"

"I am, as a matter of fact."

"Good. I'll call you."

"Okay," she said. "I'm looking forward to it."

Rocco went back to work. Sandra reached over and smacked Josiah's arm.

"Ow," he said. "What was that for?"

"Thank you," she said.

"I do not understand people," he said.

Ledger nodded. "Tell me about it."

I snuggled up next to Josiah. "That was sweet. A little blunt, but your heart was in the right place."

The front door opened and Marigold came in. She was dressed in a floral sun dress and took off a pair of sunglasses as she walked to our table.

I stood so I could hug her. "Hey."

She squeezed back. Marigold gave the best hugs. "Hi, lovely. I saw Josiah's truck outside, so I thought I'd pop in and see if you were here. But you guys are obviously having a thing. I don't want to intrude."

"No, join us," I said. "We can squeeze in another chair."

Josiah pulled up a chair and Ledger scooted over to make room. I'd seen Marigold once since the Hayden incident. She'd come over the next morning with breakfast, which had been so sweet of her.

"Does this mean the paper is coming back?" she asked. "Everyone's been talking about how it didn't come out on Sunday."

"We're back and better than ever," Sandra said.

"I'm so glad to hear that."

"What's the story with your car?" I asked. "Can it be fixed?"

She sighed. "No. Luke took a look at it for me and he said there's no way. He did offer to help me find a new one, so that's good at least."

I nudged Josiah. "That's nice of him."

Josiah glanced at me and his brow furrowed. He didn't get it.

But I had a feeling Marigold had a crush on Luke.

Or was it Zachary?

That night she'd come to the Timberbeast when they'd been sitting at our table, something had been going on. I was sure of it. She'd been flustered and blushy and although that wasn't totally out of character for her, I was certain one of them had caused it.

I just didn't know which one.

It had to have been Luke. Didn't it? Zachary wasn't her

type. Then again, Luke wasn't exactly a suit-wearing gentleman, but he did have better manners. Zachary was probably a good guy under all his cocky bravado. But it was hard to picture him with someone as sweet as Marigold.

Then again, Josiah and I were total opposites, and we complemented each other perfectly.

I also might have been imagining the whole thing. I wanted to ask her, but I'd wait for a better time. I wasn't going to put her on the spot in front of other people.

Besides, I had other things to occupy my mind. Like Josiah's almost-proposal out at the falls.

We'd decided to talk about it when the craziness was over. But we hadn't.

I didn't doubt for one second that he loved me. He'd risked his life to save mine. But things still felt unfinished between us. And I wasn't sure if I should bring it up or wait for him to do so. Maybe he was planning an actual proposal, with a ring and everything, and if I asked him about it, I'd ruin the surprise.

Then again, what if he was rethinking the whole thing? He'd blurted out that he wanted to marry me under traumatic and emotionally charged circumstances. Had he spoken too soon? Now that the dust had settled, maybe he needed more time before making that kind of commitment.

Out of nowhere, he leaned over and gave me a quick kiss on my temple. I smiled back at him. I knew he loved me, and I didn't want to rush him. But of all the things I wanted in this life, becoming his wife was what I wanted most of all.

I just hoped he wanted it as much as I did.

CHAPTER 43

Josiah

I HAD A PROBLEM.

Fortunately, my problem was no longer a psychopath stalking my girl. That had been solved, and I had the aches and pains to prove it. Not that I cared about my injuries. I'd have gone over that cliff with him if had been necessary.

Anything to keep her safe.

My problem now was the same problem I'd had my entire adult life. I was bad with people. And that included the beautiful, sweet, way-too-good-for-me woman who'd somehow fallen in love with me.

I'd meant it when I'd told her I was going to marry her. My timing had been crap, but I stood by it. But despite our decision to talk about it later, we hadn't yet.

And I had no idea what I was doing.

It was hard not to think back to the last time I'd had a ring, intending to give it to a woman. That would have been a mistake. Although I'd been hurt at the time, she really had done me a favor by choosing a job over me.

This time, I wanted to do things right. Not for me, but for Audrey.

But that didn't change the fact that I wasn't great at this

stuff. I was too blunt—too unemotional. I was basically the most unromantic guy on the planet, trying to plan what should be the most romantic moment of Audrey's life.

I'd bought a ring. And I'd almost just handed it to her in the kitchen that very day. That would have been fine, right? She loved me for me, she didn't need me to pretend to be someone else with a big over the top proposal.

Except in that moment, when I'd been standing in the kitchen with a ring in my pocket, I'd realized I wanted to do better. My lack of emotional expression was a sorry excuse to deprive her of a romantic moment.

This was a once in a lifetime thing. Even I understood that.

But I needed an assist.

The internet had been no help. All the ideas I found online had been stupid. My brothers were no help either. The only one of them who'd ever proposed was Garrett, and that marriage had fallen apart. The rest of them were as stubbornly single as I'd been for so long. What would they know about proposals?

Which was why I was pulling into Asher Bailey's driveway on a Friday morning while Audrey was at work.

His wife Grace was outside, sitting in a lawn chair under an umbrella while their two little boys ran through a sprinkler. One hand rested on her pregnant belly and she lifted the other in a friendly wave.

"Hi, Josiah."

"Hey, Grace. Is Asher home?"

"Good timing, he just got off duty. Feel free to go in."

"Thanks."

I went inside and stepped over a few discarded kids' shoes and a toy truck. Small jackets hung from hooks by the door and the mantle was full of photos, both of Asher's kids and their growing group of cousins. I had to give it to them, the Baileys were fertile.

For the first time in my life, I felt an ache in my chest at the sight of someone else's happy family and didn't push it away. Could I imagine a mantle like that in my own house? Filled with tiny smiling Havens?

Yeah, I really could.

"Hey, Asher?"

He came out of the kitchen dressed in his TFD uniform. "Morning. What are you doing here?"

"Do you have a minute?"

"Sure. Want some coffee?"

"I'm good for now."

He brought his cup to the dining table and I sat across from him.

"How's the leg healing up?" he asked.

I flexed my leg under the table, feeling the ache that still lingered as it healed. "It's fine. Could have been a lot worse."

"You were smart not to pull the knife out yourself. That could have been bad."

"Yeah, bleeding out on the forest floor is not my idea of a good time."

"No shit. How's Audrey?"

"Resilient as hell. It's a lot, you know? But she's handling it."

"You probably have a lot to do with that."

I glanced away. "I don't know."

"Own it, man. You're good for her." He paused for a moment. "That's our job. Our calling."

"You ever feel completely ill equipped for it?"

"All the time."

I nodded in acknowledgment. "Glad it's not just me. I don't know, man, sometimes I wonder what she sees in me. I'm like a block of concrete and she's cotton candy."

"Yeah, I get it. But that's the thing. Sometimes it's up to us to be hard so they can stay soft."

That resonated deep inside me. I was hard—always had

been. I had no idea how my sharp edges didn't constantly bruise Audrey's tender heart. But maybe that was the reason. She wouldn't always need me to protect her from being murdered—hopefully that had been a one-time deal—but she would need me to protect her softness. Her sweet nature that made her who she was.

I could do that. I could stand in the gap for her. Protect her from the world. Obviously I couldn't protect her from every hurt that might come her way, but I could do my best to keep her safe—not just her body, but her heart.

It was my calling.

"I want to marry her," I said, cutting to the chase. "She knows that. I told her when we were at the falls. Not the best timing, but I meant it."

Asher smiled. "Good for you."

"That's why I'm here. I want to do it right. Give her the moment she deserves. But I'm an idiot when it comes to this stuff. I have no idea how to propose to her other than just handing her a ring and asking."

"Do you have the ring already?"

"Yeah, I've been carrying it around with me."

He paused for a long moment. "I wound up having to propose twice. The first time was a big show. I put a banner on a fire engine, asked her in front of the whole town."

"I remember hearing about that."

"It was a cool moment, don't get me wrong. But when I asked her again, no one else was around. It was just for us. And it was right; it was what we both needed."

I nodded slowly, thinking that through.

"That's not very specific advice, but I'd say trust your gut. You know her. If a big show would make her happy, put on a big show. If not, just think about what would be meaningful to her. It doesn't have to be complicated."

"Okay. Thanks, Bailey."

I stood and he offered me his hand. We shook.

"No problem. And congratulations."

"Thanks. I'll let you get back to your day."

"Yeah, I need to go change so I can take over for Grace for a while."

"Sounds good. I'll see you later."

I left and said goodbye to Grace and their boys, still turning things over in my mind. Would Audrey want a big show? A banner across Main Street or a full-page ad in the newspaper?

No. Now that I thought about it, that would be the last thing she'd want. Too much of her life in Pinecrest had been for show. She didn't want to be the center of attention. Not like that.

She'd want something personal. A moment that represented us and our future together.

I got in my truck and that was when it hit me. The future. Our life together.

My girl did need something big, but not for show. She needed more than a ring and the funny thing was, it was like I'd been preparing for this all along.

I just hadn't realized it until now.

CHAPTER 44

Audrey

THE HOUSE WAS ODDLY QUIET.

Josiah had kept Max with him all day while he worked on the remodel next door. The two of them were still over there. I kept expecting them to come home any minute, but Josiah must have been busy finishing some last-minute project and didn't want to stop until it was done.

The kitchen cabinets and counters were all in and the bathrooms were finished. In fact, as far as I knew, as of yesterday, the entire house was basically done. And I had yet to see it because Josiah had forbidden me to go inside.

He'd said he wanted to show it to me himself and I had to wait until he was ready.

I was dying to see it. I could still remember what it looked like the first time Josiah had taken me on a tour. It had been little more than a beat-up shell. Fortunately for me, I hadn't been subjected to the smell before they'd done all the demo work. Apparently it had stunk worse than Max after he'd rolled in something gross.

When I'd come home, the landscaping crew had still been hard at work. I glanced out the front window and saw them putting their tools back in their truck. I couldn't see the whole yard from here, but it was looking great.

Finally, the front door opened and Max dashed inside. He circled around me, then sat with his tail wagging happily.

"Hi, Max. How was your day?"

"He was a good boy." Josiah came inside and shut the door behind him.

I smiled, relishing the warm feeling that spread through me at Josiah's subtle smile. He walked straight toward me and wrapped me in his arms.

"I missed you today," he said.

"I missed you too. What have you guys been up to over there?"

He stepped back and his almost-smile that I loved so much still graced his lips. "Want to see?"

I gasped. "Do I get to see the house? Finally?"

"Yeah. It's ready."

I popped up on my tiptoes and gave him a quick kiss. "Yes! Show me!"

He took my hand and led me outside. Max followed, bounding along beside us, ready for whatever adventure awaited. Even if it was just going back to the place he'd been two minutes ago. For a dog, everything is fun.

From the front, it looked amazing. The huge dumpster was long gone and instead of weeds and bare patches, the yard was a friendly mix of native plants, decorative rocks, and grass. The pine dotted hill rising behind it gave it a cozy, protected quality.

The outside had been freshly painted just the other day, and of course I'd seen that. We'd decided on sage green with white trim. The new front door had been stained a warm chestnut brown and the contrast complemented the façade perfectly.

Josiah paused with his hand on the door handle. "Ready?"

I was practically bouncing with excitement. "Yes! Oh my gosh, don't make me wait."

He opened the door and I gasped.

The once empty, run-down house had been completely transformed. Big, new windows let in lots of light and the warm brown of the antique java hardwood looked incredible. The color palette was neutral without being boring, the walls, floors, and trim coming together to create the perfect backdrop for someone's dream home.

Instead of leading me deeper into the house, so I could see the kitchen and dining area, he started up the stairs. They were the same wood as the downstairs with a white railing to match the trim. So pretty. The wood continued onto the landing and down the short hallway. We peeked in three of the bedrooms. I could totally picture bunk beds and kids' toys strewn around. Maybe one for a guest room.

Some family was going to be so happy here.

He led me to the master bedroom and I immediately slipped off my shoes.

"What are you doing?" he asked.

"I want to feel the carpet."

I walked around barefoot, pausing to flex my toes and feel the softness. It was perfect. Not so high a pile that it would hold onto every bit of dirt, but thick enough to feel good beneath your feet.

I couldn't tell if Josiah was amused or just confused as he watched me test the carpet. "Well?"

"I like it. You should try this, it's very relaxing."

"I'm good."

"Your loss. Let's check out the bathroom."

He gestured for me to go ahead.

The master bath wasn't large, but what it lacked in size, Josiah had made up in style. The double vanity had lots of storage and the framed mirrors were a nice touch. There was a big glass shower and much like next door, a nice free-standing bathtub.

"This is so pretty," I said. "Whoever lives here better take advantage of that bathtub."

"I hope they will."

"Okay, what's next? Can I see the kitchen yet?"

In answer, Josiah gestured toward the door.

Max ran ahead and started sniffing things while Josiah and I went downstairs. Without furniture, the entryway and living areas were wide open. There was a small room at the front of the house that would be great for a den or little library. In the back, there was a big living room with a wood stove they'd kept from the original. I could just imagine cozying up in front of its warmth on a cold winter day, watching the snow fall through the big windows and new French doors that led to the back yard.

But the kitchen. I rounded the corner and my jaw dropped.

"Oh my gosh, Josiah. It's gorgeous."

The wood cabinets were simple but lovely and the cream quartz counters contrasted beautifully. He'd built a small island and painted it sage green—a touch I wouldn't have thought of but thank goodness he had, because it was amazing. A light hung over the island, antique bronze with a textured glass shade. The sink was huge and the stainless-steel appliances blended right in.

"Look at all this." I wandered around slowly, turning in a circle. "It's the prettiest kitchen I've ever seen."

"Which house do you like better? This one or next door?"

"Well this one, obviously. Don't get me wrong, my house is adorable. But this is everything I'd want in a house. It's like I designed it myself."

"You kind of did."

"That's true, isn't it." I walked over and threaded my arms around his waist. "Thanks for letting me help. This was fun."

"There's one more thing."

I stepped back and looked up at him. "What, the back yard? We don't have to go back there, I see it all the time."

"No, there's something in the cupboard over there." He pointed.

"Ooh, is there hidden storage for small appliances?" I walked over to the cupboard. "That would be handy."

"Just open it."

Inside I found an envelope. My name was written on the back. "What's this?"

Josiah didn't answer, so I opened it. There was a white notecard, blank on the outside. I took it out and opened it. In blue ink, it read, *Welcome home.*

"Welcome home?" I looked up and met his eyes. "What does that mean?"

He smiled, then. The biggest, most genuine smile I'd ever seen on Josiah Haven. "It means this house is for us."

My mouth dropped open and my eyes widened. I sputtered, trying to say too many things at once and failing at all of them. "This is – What? Ours? You mean – I don't know what to – Are you serious?"

"Yes, I'm serious. I didn't realize it at first, but I think I've been getting it ready for us the whole time."

I dropped the card on the counter and was about to throw myself into his arms out of pure joy, but he held up a hand. "Hang on."

"What?"

"There's one more thing."

"You said that already and it was a *house.*"

He dug into his pocket and pulled out a small box. Before he opened it, I knew what it was. If I'd sputtered nonsense before, I was completely speechless now.

While my eyes filled with tears, he approached. I watched in awe as he slowly lowered himself to one knee. He looked up at me, his stormy blue-gray eyes intent on mine, and in true Josiah Haven fashion, he kept it simple.

"Marry me?"

"Oh, yes. Oh yes, yes, yes."

My body was vibrating with excitement like my dog when he was about to get a treat. Tears of happiness streamed from the corners of my eyes while Josiah took the ring out of the box and gently placed it on my finger.

He rose and I almost jumped into his arms, but didn't want to make his injured leg buckle. So I threw my arms around him. "Oh my gosh, I love you so much. You saved my life and you're going to marry me and you got me a house and I'm sorry I can't stop because I'm just so happy I don't know what to do."

His arms were strong around me. He didn't stop me from babbling. Just laughed softly while I went on and on, waiting for me to wear myself out.

When I finally stopped talking, he pulled back enough to kiss me. His lips were warm, his beard so rough and familiar.

"Are you calm now?" he asked, his voice low and quiet.

"Yes. But there's one thing I don't know."

"What's that?"

"You really did save my life, and now you're giving me everything I've ever wanted. Better than everything I've ever wanted. How can I ever repay you?"

His brow furrowed, like I'd asked a silly question. "That's easy."

"What do you mean?"

"I'm a simple man, Audrey. I just need one thing from you."

"What's that?"

"Just love me."

I placed my hands alongside his face and looked into his eyes. "I will always love you."

He pulled me close and kissed me again, slow and deep. I

would always love him. There was no question. I'd wondered if I'd ever meet the love of my life. If things like marriage and a home and one day a family were in my future, or if I'd missed the boat.

I certainly hadn't imagined I'd find everything I'd been looking for in a little town in the mountains. But here he was, kissing me, loving me. Ready to start a life with me.

My life hadn't followed the path I'd expected. But I'd landed exactly where I was meant to be.

With him. Forever.

Epilogue

JOSIAH

HERE'S THE WEIRD THING. I didn't hate wedding planning.

There were parts of it that didn't require my participation or opinion. The flowers, for example. Audrey could have whatever flowers she wanted. It wasn't that I didn't care, I just didn't have a preference. They all looked the same to me, so whatever made Audrey happy was fine.

But the day we spent at Salishan Cellars winery, touring the facility and listening to the wedding planner's ideas? It was actually kind of fun. Mostly because Audrey was as excited as a puppy. I couldn't get enough of her big, bright eyes and her smile. It was like she was happy enough for both of us. And anything that made her happy was worth it.

So I went along with her when she asked me to, and stayed home when she didn't. Thankfully, my presence wasn't required for the choosing of bridesmaid dresses, and she'd gone with Sandra, Marigold, and her mom to try on wedding dresses. Apparently I wasn't allowed to see that one until the big day, so whatever. I worked on my old house. I needed to get it ready to put on the market as another rental.

Plus, she had Marigold, who was, in Audrey's words, a wedding expert. Which didn't make sense to me, considering Marigold had never been married, but what did I know? Maybe it just meant Mari liked weddings. And when I thought about it, she had helped plan my sister's wedding, so apparently it was just her thing.

Too bad she'd never been married, though. She was a nice girl. Seemed like there ought to be a nice guy out there for her.

When it came to cake tasting, though, that was a given. I was going. It wasn't that I had strong opinions about cake flavors. She could have whatever she wanted. But it was cake, and they'd let us sample them? Count me in.

I was meeting her at the bakery at five-thirty. I checked the time. A little after five. Zachary and Luke had come over to the house—the one I'd been living in before—to help me install new kitchen cabinets. Zachary was usually down for an extra paycheck, especially if he was free, and Luke had been at my parents' house when I'd asked Zachary. He helped out on my remodels once in a while and he'd offered to lend a hand. I appreciated it. Things would go quicker with three, especially since Dad was busy.

We'd decided on white cabinets, since the kitchen was small and anything else would be too dark. The house already looked considerably better than when I'd been living in it, which was slightly embarrassing. To be fair, I hadn't cared all that much. But now that I lived in a house that was actually finished, the contrast was clear.

Luke and I brought one of the lower cabinets in from the garage and set it down.

He brushed his hands together. "Almost done."

"I need to call it a day," I said. "I have somewhere to be."

"Sounds good. I can come back tomorrow if you need more help. At least for a few hours."

"Thanks. Z, what about you?"

Zachary chewed a piece of gum. "Sorry, can't. I have a job."

"I thought you were bitching that your client canceled on you," Luke said.

"No, this is new. Some wealthy out-of-towner building a mansion on the river north of town."

"Nice. How'd you score that?"

Zachary shrugged. "He looked me up. Called and asked if I'd work for cash. Obviously yes."

"Why is some rich dude paying you under the table?" Luke asked.

"I don't know," Zachary said. "Don't really care."

"Sounds sketch."

"It's fine," Zachary said.

He was probably right. But a rich guy building a mansion outside town? I was surprised I hadn't heard about it. That was the kind of thing to get the Tilikum gossip line buzzing.

Then I remembered I didn't talk to people. That explained it.

Luke pulled his phone out of his pocket and scowled.

"What's up?" Zachary asked.

"Aunt Louise. She will not leave me alone about this girl."

"What's wrong with her?"

"I don't know and I don't want to find out," Luke said. "After the Jill incident, I don't trust her."

Zachary snickered.

Luke glared at him, then pocketed his phone. "What time tomorrow, Josiah?"

"Eight."

"Got it. See you then."

I pulled some cash out of my wallet and gave it to Zachary. "Thanks."

He held up the bills. "No, *thank you*. And if I get done early, I'll call. Make sure this gets done."

"Thanks, man. See you later."

I followed my brothers out and locked up, then left. I probably should have given myself more time so I could go home and change before meeting Audrey at the bakery. Too late for that. I gave my armpit a quick sniff. I wasn't exactly clean, but I didn't stink. It would have to do.

Angel Cakes Bakery was downtown, in a building painted to look like a fancy dessert. Audrey was already there. I parked next to her car and went inside.

If heaven has a smell, it smells like Angel Cakes Bakery. It washed over me as I walked in, sweet and sugary with a hint of vanilla.

Audrey was waiting by the front counter with Max on a leash. He saw me first and jerked forward, apparently forgetting he was tethered to his mama. He almost pulled Audrey across the lobby.

"Whoa, Max," she said with a laugh. "Careful."

I scratched his head, then slid an arm around Audrey's waist, bringing her close so I could kiss her. With a deep inhale, I breathed her in. She smelled better than the bakery.

"Hi," she said. "I missed you."

"I missed you too." I kissed her again.

"Oh good, you're here." The owner, Doris Tilburn, came out with a big tray of cake samples. She had to be at least seventy, but she didn't show any signs of slowing down. Her gray hair was braided and she wore a white apron that said Angel Cakes on the front. "Take a seat over there and we'll get started."

We sat at a small table. Audrey tried to get Max to sit but he kept popping back up, his tail wagging, every time his butt hit the floor.

"I have something for you, good boy." Doris pulled a dog treat out of her apron pocket. "You knew it was there, didn't you? That's a good boy."

"That was sweet of you," Audrey said. "Thanks, Doris."

Max settled down with his treat and Doris set the tray of samples on the table.

"Take your time," Doris said. "The little cards will tell you the flavors. And keep in mind, we can mix and match some of these if you want. Let me know if you have any questions."

She went back behind the counter, leaving us with the cake samples.

We tried them one by one. They all tasted good. Mostly I just liked watching Audrey take each bite, her lips closing over the fork. Her eyes would close briefly, as if she needed all her concentration to decide whether or not she liked it.

When she tasted the lemon, she let out a moan that made me want to take her home. Immediately.

"You like that one?" I asked.

She paused with the bite still in her mouth and her eyes rolled back. "So good." She swallowed. "I thought for sure I was going to be boring and want vanilla, but this lemon is amazing. Did you taste it yet?"

"Yeah. It's good."

"Do you like it? Is it your favorite? Or you do like another one better?"

"The lemon is great."

"You didn't answer my questions."

I gently grabbed her chin and leaned over the table to plant a kiss on her lips. "The lemon is good and if it's going to make you moan like that again, we should take some home with us."

She laughed. "Do you want to help pick out the design or is this a whatever Audrey wants is what Josiah wants decision?"

"The second one."

"Okay," she said brightly. "That makes it easy."

Doris came back and she and Audrey chatted about the cake design. I hung out and rubbed Max's belly. Spoiled dog. When they finished, we said goodbye to Doris and left.

"I feel like after all that sugar, I need to walk around," Audrey said. "Do you mind?"

"Not at all."

We walked toward Lumberjack Park. A random summer storm had blown through earlier that morning and although most of the clouds were gone, it had cooled things off, making for a pleasant evening.

Out of nowhere, Audrey stopped in her tracks.

"What's wrong?" I asked.

She had the funniest look on her face. Her eyes widened and she pressed her lips together, like she was trying to keep herself from blurting something out. With a little squeak, she pointed.

Deeper in the park was a booth with a big banner on the front that read, Dog Adoptions.

"We have a dog."

"I know, but look."

To the right of the booth, a guy in a t-shirt that said Volunteer was playing with a dog that looked remarkably like Max. Medium size, long-ish fur in a mix of brown, black, and white. Big, bushy tail.

"What if that's Max's long-lost brother? Or sister?"

"Where did you get him?"

"Idaho."

"I kind of doubt they're related."

"Okay, fine, but can we go say hi?"

I shrugged. "Yeah."

We walked across the grass and she stopped a short distance away. Max looked like he might burst, he was so excited. The volunteer greeted her and when she asked if Max could say hi, assuring him he was friendly towards everyone —humans and dogs—he said sure.

"This is Maggie," he said.

"Oh my gosh, her name is Maggie," Audrey said.

I wasn't quite sure why she was gushing like that, but the

dogs liked each other from the first moment. Of course, Max liked everyone, and apparently his almost-twin did too. They jumped around, circling each other, clearly having fun.

"She's so sweet," Audrey said. "Where is she from?"

"We just got her from our partner organization in Idaho," the volunteer said. "She was wandering the streets and despite multiple attempts to find her owner, no one claimed her."

Audrey whipped around to look at me, her eyes huge. "Idaho," she whisper yelled. "She could be Max's sister."

I really didn't think this dog was Max's sister, but I had to admit, they looked similar. Maggie was a little smaller, but their coloring, face shape, and bushy tails were a lot alike.

As were their energy levels.

I watched for a few minutes while Audrey played with both dogs. And I already knew Maggie was coming home with us.

While Audrey was busy giving both dogs belly rubs, I moved closer to the volunteer. "That one's available for adoption?"

"She sure is. Are you interested?"

I nodded toward Audrey, who was rolling around on the grass with Max and Maggie, laughing. "We both know she's not going anywhere without that dog."

The volunteer smiled.

And that was how I went from living alone to sharing my space with a woman and two dogs.

But let's be real. There are a few extra bedrooms in our house. We have room for some kids, too.

Yeah, that's happening.

I was going to marry that bubbly, dog-loving girl. And she was going to have my babies. That was not the life I'd planned—not the life I'd convinced myself I wanted. I'd been all about solitude. Doing what I wanted, when I wanted.

Thankfully, a ray of sunshine had burst into my life. And nothing would ever be the same.

Audrey wasn't just my problem now. She was my everything. And she was going to be mine forever.

———

Bonus Epilogue

THE LIGHTS in the hospital room were dim. I peeked around the curtain. Audrey was fast asleep. Not that I blamed her. Neither of us had slept much in the last day or so.

Having a baby tended to do that.

I carefully shut the door behind me and set the car seat down, hoping I wouldn't wake her. She needed the rest. I was tired too, but she'd done all the hard work. I'd just been the guy on standby to get her ice chips, hold her hand, and tell her how amazing she was.

Because she really was. So freaking amazing.

She was curled up on her side with her lips parted and hands tucked beneath the pillow. I doubted she felt very sexy, but as far as I was concerned, she was as beautiful as ever. I gazed at her for a long moment, taking her in. Her messy hair, her flushed cheeks. I loved it all.

My gaze shifted to the tiny form in the bassinet next to her and I thought my heart might burst right out of my chest.

Our daughter, Abigail, slept peacefully. She was wrapped in a pink blanket and wore the little hat my mom had knit for her.

I couldn't get over how incredible she was. How perfect.

I'd already spent most of the morning just staring at her and I couldn't get enough.

I loved her so much.

Granted, I had no idea what I was doing. The reality of fatherhood had smacked me in the face when I'd looked at her squishy, pink face for the first time yesterday. I'd wanted to have kids with Audrey, no question about that. But that didn't mean I was prepared for the reality of being responsible for the life of such a tiny, innocent, beautiful baby.

Maybe there was no way to really be prepared, though. I seemed to remember Garrett saying something like that.

Abby scrunched her nose and pursed her lips. Was she waking up? I wasn't sure, but any excuse to hold her.

My hands seemed huge as I slid them beneath the little bundle and lifted her. I held her up and gazed at her face again. At her soft cheeks and tiny eyelashes. Her button nose. I had a feeling she was going to look like her mommy. I could already imagine her bright smile.

She squirmed, her face scrunching in discomfort.

"I'm sorry," I whispered. "Am I not holding you right?"

I gently laid her on my chest and held her against me. Instinctively, I swayed back and forth, softly patting her on the back as I moved. After a few minutes, she seemed to settle, so I lowered myself into the chair next to the bed.

Audrey stirred and her eyes slowly opened. "How is she?"

"Perfect."

Her smile grew. "She really is, isn't she? I can't believe she's ours."

The door opened and a nurse came around the curtain. She had short blond hair and wore blue scrubs. Her nametag said Jen.

"How's everything going?" she asked, her voice soft.

"We're fine," Audrey said. "Just tired."

"Of course you are," she said. "Everything looks great for

both mom and baby, so I have your discharge paperwork. Do you have your car seat?"

I nodded toward the side of the room where I'd left it. "Over there."

"Excellent. There's no rush, but when you're ready, go ahead and get her buckled in. We'll do a quick check and then you can be on your way home."

I glanced at Audrey. Her eyes were wide. I felt the same way. They were really going to let us leave with her?

Didn't they realize we had no idea what we were doing?

Jen left and we took our time getting ready to go. Audrey changed into her going home outfit—a loose t-shirt and the joggers she'd lived in for the first half of her pregnancy. We had a newborn outfit for Abby that was almost too big. She squirmed and made the cutest little noises while we changed her, but never quite woke up.

I didn't know what Audrey was worried about. She was already a natural with our daughter. She got her strapped into the car seat as if she'd done it a hundred times. When we were ready, the nurse came back and made sure we'd done it right, and then we were free to go.

The feeling that this was crazy—that they shouldn't be letting us leave with an actual baby—was hard to shake as we walked to Audrey's new SUV. We were leaving the relative calm and safety of the hospital and taking our tiny, fragile daughter out into the world for the first time.

A surge of protectiveness stole over me. No one was coming between me and my girls. Ever.

We got the car seat in place and Audrey sat in the back with her on the short drive home. When we got there, I parked next to Ledger's car. He'd been dog-sitting for us while we were in the hospital.

"I know Max and Maggie are good dogs, but we need to be super careful until they get used to her," Audrey said. "I don't know if either of them has ever been around a newborn."

I sent Ledger a quick text to put them in the backyard so we could go inside without any dog drama. "Don't worry. I won't let them slobber on her."

"Abby, we're home. This is where you're going to grow up. Isn't that exciting?"

I glanced at the house. Bringing my daughter here gave the place a whole new meaning. It wasn't just a house, it was our home. The place where we were going to raise our kids. We had years of birthday parties and Christmases, snowball fights and popsicles on hot summer days to look forward to.

My life was fucking awesome.

I got out and took the car seat out of the back. Abby was still sleeping and I wondered if we were going to pay for this later. Would she sleep all day and be up all night? Probably. But Audrey and I would get through it together.

"Did Ledger put the dogs out back?" Audrey asked as we walked up to the front door.

"Yeah. They'll be fine."

"I know they will. I'm just so nervous about everything. All she has to do is twitch a little and I jump."

I brushed her hair back from her face and tucked it behind her ear. "Don't worry. You're already the best mom. We've got this."

Her eyes misted with tears and she bit her lip. "I love you so much."

"I love you, too." I kissed the top of her head, then opened the door to bring our daughter home.

Ledger got up from the couch and slipped his phone in his back pocket. He wore an old Rolling Stones t-shirt with skinny jeans and I honestly wondered if he'd ever heard of the bands whose shirts he always wore. But the hardest thing with Ledger was fighting the urge to tell him to shave off his sorry excuse for a mustache and cut the damn mullet.

He was a good kid, though. He'd left the newspaper to come work for me—decided construction was his calling. He had almost no skills, but I appreciated his enthusiasm. At least he'd do a full day's work, which was surprising, considering his history of being a lazy-ass at the newspaper.

"Hey." He came closer to look at Abby. "Look at that."

"This is Abigail," Audrey said. "Or Abby."

"Hi, Abby," he said. "Wow, she's cute."

Hell yeah, she was cute. "Thanks."

I put the car seat down, unbuckled her, and scooped her up. Audrey and I stared at her for a long moment, pretty much forgetting that Ledger was even there.

Abby squirmed and grunted.

"Oh my gosh," Audrey said. "I think she just pooped. That was so cute."

"That's my cue to go," Ledger said. "Dogs were great. I can dogsit anytime, but diapers? Not so much."

"Thank you again," Audrey said. "We appreciate it."

"No problem. Bye, Abby. It will be cool to hang out with you when you're older."

Audrey laughed and took the baby. "I'll change her diaper and then we can bring the dogs inside."

I glanced out the back door while Audrey changed her. Poor Max and Maggie had their noses to the glass, their tails wagging. They didn't know why we hadn't let them inside yet.

"Give us a second," I said through the door. Not that they understood what I was saying, but it was habit at this point.

"Okay, I'm ready." Audrey had a freshly changed Abby cradled in her arms. "Go ahead and let them in."

I opened the door and they both tried to come in at the same time. Max almost got stuck but Maggie wiggled her way past him.

Both dogs beelined for Audrey. They circled her, sniffing, trying to see what she had in her arms. They'd been obsessed with Audrey when she was pregnant, constantly wanting to cuddle with her and laying their heads on her belly. Did they know that was where the baby had come from? Did they have any idea what a human baby was?

I stood close, ready to shoo them away if they got too excited. They were sweet dogs; I wasn't worried about them hurting Abby on purpose. But like Audrey had said, they'd never been around a newborn before. I didn't know if they'd understand.

"What do you think?" Audrey asked. "This is Abby. She's our baby."

Both dogs buzzed with excitement, their tails wagging like crazy. Max darted away, disappearing upstairs, leaving Maggie to sniff Abby's feet.

A moment later, he came back with his favorite orange ball in his mouth. I was about to tell him it wasn't time to play, but he didn't drop it at our feet, hoping we'd toss it for him. He kept it in his mouth, his eyes on Audrey, his tail still wagging.

"What do you want?" she asked. "My hands are full; I can't throw your ball."

Max kept looking at her expectantly, as if he wanted her to do something.

She leaned down a little. "Do you want to see the baby?"

He came closer and gently set the ball right on Abby.

"Oh my gosh, he's giving her his favorite toy," she said, her eyes filling with tears again. "Good boy, Max. Such a good boy."

Maggie seemed to get the idea. She ran into the kitchen and came back with another ball.

"Good girl, Maggie." Audrey leaned down so she could put the ball on Abby. "Good girl. That was so cute, I could die."

I crouched down so I could give both dogs some good scratches. "Good dogs."

"She's starting to wake up. I'll see if she's hungry. Then I'd love a shower."

"On it."

I helped get Audrey comfortable on the couch with her nursing pillow and brought her water and some snacks in case she got hungry. It took the dogs a few minutes to calm down, but eventually they settled on the couch next to her, content to be close to their mama and new baby.

When Audrey finished feeding Abby, I took her so Audrey could shower. She was out cold. We went upstairs and I settled on the bed with Abby on my chest. The dogs curled up nearby.

I drifted in and out of sleep until Audrey came out of the bathroom. She snuggled up next to me and my heart had never been so full.

I was surrounded by my favorite people—and the best dogs. My baby girl slept soundly on my chest and my wife's body molded against mine. I couldn't help but think about how I'd almost lost her. How I'd almost missed all this. And not just because a psychopath had tried to kill her. Because there had been a time when I'd been so closed off, I hadn't left any room for someone else.

Audrey's sunshine had broken through, her light shining through the cracks in my armor. I wasn't made to be alone. I was made for this—to be a husband and a father. To be their protector.

I couldn't imagine anything better.

———

Dear Reader

Dear reader,

If you're new to Tilikum, I hope you enjoyed your stay! And if you're making a return trip after the Bailey Brothers, I hope it was fun to be back.

Starting this book, I found myself in a bit of a conundrum. I'd always planned to write the Haven brothers as their own series after the Baileys, which meant I was contemplating these stories several years before it was time to begin writing. I had a loose outline that included the series order and basic ideas for each book.

But when it came time to start this book, none of it felt right anymore.

I know why. I lost my husband unexpectedly in 2021 and my life changed in every way imaginable. As I slowly and gently picked up the pieces of my life and heart, and began finding ways to move forward, there was a lot from "the before" that no longer felt relevant. That included my loose outline and ideas for the Havens.

However, I wasn't ready to give up. I'd set myself up to write this series and I knew there was a way to get excited about it. I just had to find it.

So I let go. I let go of my loose outline, the order of the books, the female main characters, the plot ideas, all of it. I looked at it with fresh eyes and spent a lot of time thinking about what I wanted to write.

The solution came in the title. I was thinking of ideas and already felt the nudge to lean into romantic suspense. I started playing around with words and, long story short, came up with this and several other title ideas.

I loved them and so did my team. I could picture them on book covers and they told me something about the direction I needed to go to jumpstart my brain again.

So I ran with it. Did I worry that existing readers would balk at the emphasis on romantic suspense? Oh yeah. Did I worry that new readers wouldn't take a chance on me? For sure. Was I afraid that I was straying too far from reader expectations? Definitely.

But did I do it anyway? Yep. Sometimes you just have to do it scared.

I also have to share with you how I came up with the identity of the stalker.

I have three kids who, at the time of this writing, are all in their teens. I was chatting with my oldest son about what I was working on and said I knew the heroine would have a stalker, but I wasn't sure who he was or why he was stalking her. He said something like, what if he's the brother she didn't know she had because her dad had an affair and he hates her because their dad rejected him? I thought hey, that's pretty good.

But the story doesn't end there. Later, I was talking with my middle son, and the subject came up. He suggested the EXACT SAME IDEA. His brother wasn't there and neither of them realized the other had suggested the unknown half-brother idea.

I figured that was a pretty good sign that I needed to run with it. So I did!

A big thank you to my boys for helping with the twists.

I loved writing this book and taking on the challenge of a suspense plot. I'm definitely in my small-town romantic suspense era and I hope you're enjoying the ride!

Love,

Claire

P.S. I don't know if you're ready for the next Haven book, my friends. This one was just a warm up...

Acknowledgments

Thank you so much to everyone who helped make this book happen!

To Nikki and Alex for not holding back when there were ISSUES. This book is so much better because of you.

To Lori for the exquisite cover.

To Eliza and Erma for cleaning up all the word (and comma) messes.

To my sons who each—separately—suggested the same idea for the identity and motive of the stalker. Good idea, boys! Thanks for helping me with the twists!

And to all my readers for taking a chance on the Haven brothers, even though they were once the rivals to our beloved Baileys.

Also by Claire Kingsley

For a full and up-to-date listing of Claire Kingsley books visit
www.clairekingsleybooks.com/books/

For comprehensive reading order, visit www.clairekingsleybooks.
com/reading-order/

————

The Haven Brothers

Small-town romantic suspense with CK's signature endearing
characters and heartwarming happily ever afters. Can be read as
stand-alones.

Obsession Falls (Josiah and Audrey)

Storms and Secrets

The rest of the Haven brothers will be getting their own happily ever
afters!

————

How the Grump Saved Christmas (Elias and Isabelle)

A stand-alone, small-town Christmas romance.

————

The Bailey Brothers

Steamy, small-town family series with a dash of suspense. Five
unruly brothers. Epic pranks. A quirky, feuding town. Big HEAs.
Best read in order.

Protecting You (Asher and Grace part 1)

Fighting for Us (Asher and Grace part 2)

Unraveling Him (Evan and Fiona)

Rushing In (Gavin and Skylar)

Chasing Her Fire (Logan and Cara)

Rewriting the Stars (Levi and Annika)

————

The Miles Family

Sexy, sweet, funny, and heartfelt family series with a dash of suspense. Messy family. Epic bromance. Super romantic. Best read in order.

Broken Miles (Roland and Zoe)

Forbidden Miles (Brynn and Chase)

Reckless Miles (Cooper and Amelia)

Hidden Miles (Leo and Hannah)

Gaining Miles: A Miles Family Novella (Ben and Shannon)

————

Dirty Martini Running Club

Sexy, fun, feel-good romantic comedies with huge… hearts. Can be read as stand-alones.

Everly Dalton's Dating Disasters (Prequel with Everly, Hazel, and Nora)

Faking Ms. Right (Everly and Shepherd)

Falling for My Enemy (Hazel and Corban)

Marrying Mr. Wrong (Sophie and Cox)

Flirting with Forever (Nora and Dex)

————

Bluewater Billionaires

Hot romantic comedies. Lady billionaire BFFs and the badass heroes who love them. Can be read as stand-alones.

The Mogul and the Muscle (Cameron and Jude)

The Price of Scandal, Wild Open Hearts, and Crazy for Loving You

More Bluewater Billionaire shared-world romantic comedies by Lucy
Score, Kathryn Nolan, and Pippa Grant

Bootleg Springs
by Claire Kingsley and Lucy Score

Hot and hilarious small-town romcom series with a dash of mystery
and suspense. Best read in order.

Whiskey Chaser (Scarlett and Devlin)

Sidecar Crush (Jameson and Leah Mae)

Moonshine Kiss (Bowie and Cassidy)

Bourbon Bliss (June and George)

Gin Fling (Jonah and Shelby)

Highball Rush (Gibson and I can't tell you)

Book Boyfriends

Hot romcoms that will make you laugh and make you swoon. Can
be read as stand-alones.

Book Boyfriend (Alex and Mia)

Cocky Roommate (Weston and Kendra)

Hot Single Dad (Caleb and Linnea)

Finding Ivy (William and Ivy)

A unique contemporary romance with a hint of mystery. Stand-alone.

His Heart (Sebastian and Brooke)

A poignant and emotionally intense story about grief, loss, and the transcendent power of love. Stand-alone.

The Always Series

Smoking hot, dirty talking bad boys with some angsty intensity. Can be read as stand-alones.

Always Have (Braxton and Kylie)

Always Will (Selene and Ronan)

Always Ever After (Braxton and Kylie)

The Jetty Beach Series

Sexy small-town romance series with swoony heroes, romantic HEAs, and lots of big feels. Can be read as stand-alones.

Behind His Eyes (Ryan and Nicole)

One Crazy Week (Melissa and Jackson)

Messy Perfect Love (Cody and Clover)

Operation Get Her Back (Hunter and Emma)

Weekend Fling (Finn and Juliet)

Good Girl Next Door (Lucas and Becca)

The Path to You (Gabriel and Sadie)

About the Author

Claire Kingsley is a #1 Amazon bestselling author of sexy, heartfelt contemporary romance and romantic comedies. She writes sassy, quirky heroines, swoony heroes who love their women hard, panty-melting sexytimes, romantic happily ever afters, and all the big feels.

She can't imagine life without coffee, her Kindle, and the sexy heroes who inhabit her imagination. She lives in the inland Pacific Northwest with her three kids.

www.clairekingsleybooks.com

Printed in Great Britain
by Amazon

38224609R00243